Praise for

A SPELL FOR CHANGE

"Tense, wonderfully atmospheric, and perfectly paced, *A Spell for Change* is an excellent blend of history, fantasy, and horror, with a dash of romance thrown in to sweeten the brew. Nicole Jarvis casts a spell with this novel just as surely as her characters do!"

ALYSSA PALOMBO, author of *The Spellbook of Katrina Van Tassel*

"Captures the dark heart of rural life at the turn of the century, when three outcasts forge unexpected alliances to challenge the dangerous forces haunting their small town in the shadow of the mountains. With writing so vivid you can taste the sweet tea and smell the cold minerality of underground caves, this is an essential read for anyone who has ever yearned to be more than their circumstances allow."

ALISA ALERING, author of *Smothermoss*

"*A Spell for Change* delivers on all the best aspects of a fantastical Southern Gothic, alive with magic as prickly, painful, and stubborn as the characters learning to wield it. Jarvis's characters are as vivid in their struggles as their joys: Nora Jo, a witchy bookish schoolmistress hiding her love for the girl next door; Kate, a preacher's granddaughter and a prophet; and Oliver, a prodigal son returned, forever ravaged by ghosts of war both physical and metaphysical. You won't be able to look away as lives and loves crash and tangle together in a struggle against powers of darkness as real as the trauma, prejudice, and hard living realities of rural mountain life."

GABRIELLA BUBA, author of *Saints of Storm and Sorrow* and *Daughters of Flood and Fury*

T0349419

Also by Nicole Jarvis
and available from Titan Books

THE LIGHTS OF PRAGUE
A PORTRAIT IN SHADOW

A SPELL FOR CHANGE

NICOLE JARVIS

TITAN BOOKS

A Spell for Change
Print edition ISBN: 9781835410943
E-book edition ISBN: 9781835412381

Published by Titan Books
A division of Titan Publishing Group Ltd
144 Southwark Street, London SE1 0UP
www.titanbooks.com

First edition: May 2025
10 9 8 7 6 5 4 3 2 1

A CIP catalogue record for this title is available from the British Library.

Typeset in Goudy Oldstyle 10.5/15.5pt

Printed and bound by CPI Group (UK) Ltd, Croydon CR0 4YY.

To my sister

1

NORA JO

April 14, 1920

Dawn crested cool and gray the day the witch from the mountains knocked on Nora Jo's door.

Heat would come with the sun, but mist still swirled through the schoolyard when Nora Jo peered from the window. Her small schoolhouse sat in the heart of Chatuga, near the town's main street; a small cluster of businesses before farms and cabins spread out like dandelion seeds in the wind. The building contained only a single room with rows of benches for the students. It was a bare, minimal space—there wasn't even a hearth, as the school shut down during the lean winter months. With the amount of snow that fell in this part of Tennessee, especially deeper in the mountains, people hid in their homes until spring. School had been back in session for only a month, and Nora Jo knew she only had weeks more before most of her students would be lost to summer planting.

Movement in the tree line caught her eye. She leaned closer to the window.

A stag stood at the edge of the grass. Its broad antlers blended with the branches behind it, and morning haze floated around its legs. It was a large creature; it must have been quite clever to avoid the hunters—human and animal—who would have feasted on it during the recent winter.

It stood frozen, ears flicking, tense, waiting. Nora Jo matched its stillness. Her breath fogged against the glass, as though bringing the mist inside. The moment felt suspended outside of time.

A large bird settled onto a branch over the creature's head, a black shadow in the morning light.

The stag startled. As it whirled and leapt back into the forest, its right antler slid off its head and crashed into the grass. Unbalanced, it disappeared into the woods.

Nora Jo jolted as well, pressing a hand to her chest. Her heart raced under her palm.

She laughed quietly at herself. So much for the majesty of nature. The deer had been spooked by its own shedding antlers. It would spend the next week trying to rub the other one off. She would take her students out into the grass later to pick up the abandoned antler—one of them would certainly want to take it home as a prize.

She shook her head and looked back out the window to mark the spot.

The bird, a large crow, was still on its branch, staring directly at her. She shivered and looked away. The stag had given her some of its unease.

Enough dallying. She circled the small schoolroom, making sure the benches were in place. The one in the corner would likely be empty today. The Evanses still hadn't been able to find the dollar-twenty needed to send their two boys to school that month. She had offered them a discounted rate to help them until they were back on their feet, but the Evanses were too proud to accept.

That, Nora Jo could understand. It was families like the Howards and Doyles, who had sneered that schooling was a waste of time and pulled their kids out this year, that made Nora Jo's stomach curdle.

Sighing, she pulled out her broom. It was long and jagged, the birch wood rubbed smooth near the top, with bristles of broom corn tied at the bottom. It fit in her grasp like the hand of an old friend, solid and familiar.

Starting at the back of the classroom, Nora Jo swept. She hummed a song to focus her thoughts as she moved, a tune she'd heard her ma sing a hundred times. Every day, the students brought with them their troubles from home, the twisting thoughts of youth, the petty romances and fights of their daily lives. That chaos built inside the schoolhouse the same as the dirt and dust from the road outside, carried in by a dozen small feet.

Her ma had told her that the song was a spell of protection, securing and cleansing. The tune reminded her of early mornings in the kitchen, before her dad and brother woke up. The room had been a sanctuary where her quiet ma would share stories of her own mother and grandmother, giving Nora Jo a glimpse at a secret legacy.

Her Granny Rhodes had been a midwife, using everything from herbs to animal guts to get babies safely out of their mothers. More than that, she had been renowned as the help one could turn to when the doctors had given up hope—or, as was often the case, had decided they were too busy to travel through the mountains to tend to a farmer's wife. Her gift had been shared in whispers; to talk about witches was to draw their attention, and even those who relied on their healing didn't trust them.

Her ma hadn't healed anyone but her own children. Though already twenty-six—nearly as old as her ma when she had passed—Nora Jo had healed no one at all. But she could keep her classroom clean and safe.

Her students began to arrive at eight thirty. The girls went to the east side of the room, and the boys sat on the west, settling themselves on the long benches. Many of them came from far outside the town center, walking miles from farms or the surrounding mountains to get to her classroom, but country children knew how to keep a schedule.

Teaching ages six to fifteen, Nora Jo structured her lessons to cover the full class. It was a delicate balance to keep her older students progressing without losing her youngest. In addition to reading and writing, Nora Jo taught basic arithmetic, geography, and history. Any child who worked on a farm learned young some of the math needed to manage their family's crops and livestock, and she could make the other subjects into storytelling—if she could tell it right, she could make them care.

After their dinner break at noon, the students ran outside. Nora Jo followed at a more sedate pace. "Slow down before you break your fool necks!" she called after them. The morning mist had dissipated, and the April sun brought lazy warmth.

A large patch of lawn bristled before the forest edge. The grass was plush, and several students took off their shoes to enjoy it. Outside of church and school, these children were accustomed to running barefoot during all seasons. Nora Jo glanced down at her own feet, bound in tightly laced boots. Part of her wished she could join them, but she had to maintain her dignity to keep the respect of her students and the rest of town.

Someone cleared their throat. Nora Jo looked up, a flush heating her cheeks. "Gloria!"

Gloria Daley's loose red curls were tucked under an embroidered kerchief, and her dress was a simple navy that suited her freckled skin. As always, her presence warmed Nora Jo more than the spring sun.

"Hi, Miss Nora Jo." Gloria held out a dish, lifting the white fabric that covered its contents. "I brought a snack for the kids."

Nora Jo breathed in the warm, sweet scent of cornmeal and molasses. "Tell me this ain't your famous rhubarb cornbread cake," she said, as if she couldn't have recognized it with her eyes closed. "Why, Gloria, you didn't have to do that for us."

"Those rhubarb stalks are the first real pleasure of spring. Teaching is such thankless work, and you do such a good job. I thought you should have a token of our appreciation. It's the least I could do. Take one."

Nora Jo plucked the corner square from the tray. A slice of dark pink rhubarb striped the top, soft under her teeth. Licking her fingers, Nora Jo pointed out, "Your brother graduated last year, Gloria. You don't need to bribe me now."

"Now that he's home on the farm all day, I appreciate your hard work even more. I don't know how you wrangled him. Besides," she added with a conspiratorial smile, "we don't want you to take your business somewhere else during apple season."

During the fall, Nora Jo hired Gloria's family to deliver a bag of apples once a week. It was a nice snack for the kids, and fall was a time of plenty. Nora Jo wanted them to remember those treats when the winter came.

"Kids, Miss Gloria made some cake for y'all! Come get some—and say thank you!" Nora Jo called, voice booming over the small green space.

Gloria laughed. "You have a voice like a hawk."

Nora Jo flushed again. "You learn how to speak up with a group like this." Like a swarm of ants, the students picked the pan clean in moments, taking their spoils back onto the grass. Each one thanked Gloria as they grabbed their squares of cornbread cake. "Little beasts," Nora Jo said affectionately, rubbing a boy's hair as he ducked past.

"You're good with them. They're lucky to have you." Gloria tilted her head, like she were noticing an unexpected bloom in her garden. "You know, your shawl makes your eyes look awfully green today."

Nora Jo clutched the fabric around her neck. "Thank you."

For a moment, they only looked at each other.

There was a shout as a tussle broke out between two of the students. Nora Jo gave Gloria an exasperated look. "It's like herding cats into a bath around here."

Gloria laughed. "I'll leave you to it."

"Thank you," Nora Jo said, and then turned to her students. "Michael! John Noah! What exactly do y'all think you're doing?"

By the time Nora Jo ushered everyone back inside for the rest of their lesson, every crumb of the cake was long gone. Aware that her students lost focus after dinner, Nora Jo pulled out a battered paperback from her desk. To learn spelling and memorization, she picked one book for the students to slowly work through together. She was taught to use the Bible, but she chose to use the fiction and poetry she ordered in from the Sears, Roebuck, and Co. catalog, saving her own coins for months for each precious new find. Since first exploring a used bookstore while training in Knoxville, she couldn't return to teaching from simple Bible verses.

Nora Jo cleared her throat and picked up where they'd left off. "The Scarecrow listened carefully, and said, 'I cannot understand why you should wish to leave this beautiful country and go back to the dry, gray place you call Kansas.' 'That is because you have no brains,' answered the girl. 'No matter how dreary and gray our homes are, we people of flesh and blood would rather live there than in any other country, be it ever so beautiful. There is no place like home...'"

Nora Jo had always loved that *The Wonderful Wizard of Oz*, which grew so fantastical, started with a child on a farm. So many books introduced worlds she couldn't imagine—not like the fictional yellow brick road, but true stories of big metropolitan cities to the north or castles across the ocean. They were alien and chaotic. Like Dorothy, Nora Jo knew her story would end the same way it began: in a small house in the town of her birth.

At the end of the day, after the students sprinted out of the small schoolroom, Nora Jo swept the room again and emptied the water bucket into the grass. She was gathering her bag when the front door opened.

"Hey there, Nora Jo." A man walked inside, tracking dust in on his boots. He was in his early thirties, tanned from years of work outside. A head of dark hair was hidden by a felt hat, and the brim's shadow masked the faint wrinkles etched into his forehead.

Nora Jo crossed her arms. "Beau," she said. "Have you forgotten how to knock?"

Her brother ignored that, clomping further into the classroom. "How're you doing?"

"Fine, just fine."

"You weren't at supper last night."

"I'm never at supper, Beau."

"You said you'd think about coming." He looked at the books on her desk, casually proprietary, though he'd only come to the classroom a handful of times since graduating. When they had been in school here together, he'd sat with his friends, ignoring the teacher and his sister.

"I thought about it." Briefly. Last week, when they had passed on the street, he had invited her for a family supper in his new house. It had been a short, stilted conversation. "It was a Tuesday. I had work to finish. I run a classroom here."

"Nora Jo, this job can't be that demanding. Not enough to stop you from coming for one meal."

"You know nothing about my work. Just because I don't stand at a forge all day doesn't mean this is easy."

Having taken over their dad's business as the local blacksmith, her brother saw his work as the backbone of the town. His steel was, to be fair, at the inception of every dollar made in Chatuga. The town relied on him for everything from wagon parts to the mill's machinery to horseshoes to farm tools. Still, she wished he'd be less of a pill about it.

"You have to have supper somewhere," he said. He rapped his knuckles on the desk and turned to her. "You can't pretend you don't know us forever."

"That's ridiculous. I don't pretend I don't know you."

"It's been almost a year since you've come over to my house. Not

since the funeral. I was surprised you even came to my wedding."
Beau had gotten married in the fall, just before the snows arrived.

"I wouldn't have missed your wedding." She leaned against the
desk. "Supper would have been terrible. We both know it, Beau.
Ruth certainly doesn't want me there. Do *you* even want me there?"

"Ruth likes you," he protested.

Nora Jo laughed. "Ruth has never liked me."

Beau's new bride was Nora Jo's age, and they'd known each
other since Ruth's family moved to town ten years earlier. Nora
Jo had been prickly and awkward in those days—maybe she still
was—but most of her stiffness had been an attempt to protect
herself from the mocking comments about her freckles and her
passion for learning. Those cruel comments had often been led, in
later years, by Ruth. At the wedding, she had come to Nora Jo with
a smile like a porcelain doll and welcomed her as a new sister. Nora
Jo had mimicked the smile, then left the wedding early. "It's not a
big deal, Beau. We don't have to like each other."

"We're family," Beau said.

"And what does that mean?"

He looked hurt and annoyed in equal measure. "It's only you
and me now. Ma's been gone a long time, and now Dad is too.
Don't we have to stick together?"

"You have your own wife, your own home, your own responsibilities. You'll have children soon." If Ruth wasn't pregnant
already. "I'm not interested in more lectures about how I'm wasting
my life. Be happy with your life and let me be happy with mine."

"With what?" He waved a hand around the classroom. "This
isn't a life, Nora Jo."

"There you go again. Teaching is everything I've worked for," she told him. "If you're done, I need to finish cleaning the classroom. You've tracked dirt across the whole floor."

He sighed. "I'm trying to be nice."

"You seem perfectly happy without me," she said. "I release you from your brotherly duty." She sighed. "Just leave, Beau."

"Someday, you'll regret being this way."

As he left, another clod of dirt fell from his boot, crumbling on the wood floor. He closed the door firmly, and the frame shuddered behind him.

Nora Jo walked along the stretch of farmland outside of town, detouring from her path home to greet the horses from the O'Malley farm that raced over to nicker at her. She pressed her face against the mare's warm nose, inhaling its musty scent. The apple and plum trees in all the orchards along the valley were bursting with white and pale pink blossoms. Dogwood winter was coming soon, when the petals would fall and coat the grass in a spring snowfall.

She tried to shake off the lingering tension from her conversation with Beau as she walked. He never failed to rile her, but the mild April weather and the long walk helped settle her before she finally entered her landlady's house.

It was empty. Of course. Wednesday already. Miss Ethel had a standing bridge game with some of the other ladies in town. Time seemed to slip past Nora Jo like a creek, murmuring and forgettable, but always moving.

When Nora Jo finally left her dad's house, it had been a miracle she'd landed with Miss Ethel. She had asked around quietly if anyone was looking for a boarder, but was turned down over and over. She was a young single woman striking out from her dad, one of the most influential men in town. Her dream of teaching had felt far away, and she was working in administration at the Chadwicks' gristmill.

But then someone sent her to Miss Ethel. The widow's spare room had sat empty for years before Nora Jo knocked on her door, but Miss Ethel welcomed her into her home. She'd even held the room while Nora Jo went to Middle Tennessee State Normal School for their two-year teaching program.

Nora Jo didn't pay enough in rent to justify getting meals as well, but Miss Ethel always insisted. She lifted a kerchief to find a plate of fried chicken and a bowl of green beans. Both were lukewarm now, but she was grateful nonetheless. Left to her own skill, she spent more time burning meals than eating them.

She bit into a chicken leg. Instead of the crisp, hot crunch she would have gotten earlier, the batter was cool and soft. Tomorrow she would need to cut her walk short and come home quicker—she missed the widow's fresh cooking.

There was a knock at the door.

Nora Jo frowned and put down her supper. There shouldn't have been anyone coming by, certainly not during Miss Ethel's regular bridge night.

The man at the door was a stranger. He was tall and lean as an oak tree in winter. Nora Jo was lanky for a woman, taller even than most men, but she had to look up at him. He wore a long black trench coat, and looked at her with bright blue eyes from under the broad rim of a wool hat. "Are you Miss Nora Jo Barker?"

"Yes, sir," she said, glancing beyond him to see if anyone else was on the road. It was empty. Nora Jo didn't appreciate unplanned guests. This wasn't her house, and she didn't enjoy the company of strangers.

And this man *was* strange. His clothes were worn and faded, but his jaw was clean-shaven, like a businessman from some big city.

"My name is Everett Harlow," he said, "and I'm in town looking for an apprentice."

"Ah, I see. What is it that you do, Mr. Harlow?" she asked. "I assume you've come to me because I'm the teacher around here?"

"That's right."

"If you tell me more about what kind of boy you're looking for, I should be able to help match you. I have a lot of bright students." It wasn't unusual for craftsmen to hire young apprentices from town, but they rarely asked Nora Jo's opinion. Most jobs outside one's own family in Chatuga were acquired through the friend of a friend. If this man didn't know anyone in town, perhaps he was a trapper. Some men stayed so deep in the mountains that everyone below forgot their names.

"You misunderstand me," Harlow said. "I'm here for you, Miss Nora Jo."

Nora Jo frowned. "What do you mean?"

"I'm looking for a smart person, an educated person. Someone who can learn quickly and absorb information like land after a drought. I believe that's you."

"Do you work at a school?" He didn't look like a teacher, or even a school administrator, but appearances could be deceiving.

He laughed, a gravely chuckle. "Not as such. I'm looking for an apprentice for my craft."

"And what is it that you do?"

"Well," the man said, those pale eyes intent on her face. "I'm a witch. Just like you."

2

KATE

Kate's fingers flew over the strings, and the bow sang in her hand. Music soared from the fiddle cradled in her arms, wrapping the room in sound as the setting sun through the window warmed it with light.

She didn't sing. She didn't have to. The fiddle eagerly met her direction and called out the fast, joyous tune.

"Girls! Supper is ready!"

The spell broke, and Kate's sisters scattered. Kate pulled the bow along the strings one last time, letting a note fade in the small room, then lifted her head. Carefully, she tucked the fiddle back into its beaten leather case. The case had taken endless damage over the years, first from her granddaddy, then her daddy, and now Kate herself, but the fiddle inside was polished to a warm glow, carefully tuned to perfection. When she closed the lid, the room felt dimmer around her. Playing her fiddle was the only time Kate truly lived in the moment, and she missed it immediately.

The smell from the kitchen finally hit her nose, and her stomach grumbled.

The rest of her sisters were gone, but the youngest, Mary Evelyn, was hesitating in front of a chair that had been knocked out of place during the mad sprint to the kitchen. Kate nudged it aside with her hip. "Stop leaving things in the walkway!" she shouted into the kitchen.

"Thanks," Mary Evelyn said, readjusting her weight on the crutch under her arm. Below her cotton shift, one small leg stretched barefoot to the floor. There was no second. When she needed it, she wore a wooden prosthetic, but it was too much effort for home. It chafed, and Mary Evelyn complained the tan color was all wrong—her skin was the darkest in the family, blue-black in the dim light. "They always forget."

"Just smack them next time," Kate advised, ushering Mary Evelyn through the door ahead of her. As the eldest daughter, recently eighteen, Kate felt like half a mother sometimes.

A handful of simple dishes were set out on the heavy wooden table—crowder peas and meat from the kettle over the fireplace, cornbread still bubbling in its cast-iron pan—and the smells were rich and mouth-watering. Chairs crammed close around the table. Mama and Daddy sat at one end with Uncle Christopher beside them. Willamae, Betty, and Eileen had already taken the best spots. Kate let Mary Evelyn take the last decent seat. The remaining chair creaked under her weight and left her of a height with Mary Evelyn, the table nearly up to her chest.

Mama grabbed their attention with a sharp cough, and Daddy led the table in a prayer. Kate closed her eyes and rested her elbows on the table, though the height made them splay uncomfortably.

Daddy and Uncle Christopher didn't have time to come home from the lumber mill for dinner, and breakfast was a sleepy affair, so supper was the family's biggest gathering. The meal was raucous—Kate had to snatch the last bit of white meat from under Betty's hand to place it on Mary Evelyn's plate instead. When Betty whined, Kate chided, "You already had a piece—don't think I didn't notice."

Mama and Daddy were having a quiet conversation with Uncle Christopher at the other end of the table, ignoring their bickering children with the skill only a parent could master. There was a tension among them that set Kate on edge.

Once everyone had finished eating, Mama looked down the table at the children. "Go on," she said. "Go play somewhere."

The kids left, only pausing long enough to drop their dishes in the wash bucket. Kate helped Mary Evelyn with hers and ushered her out of the door to the side yard. She watched her limp toward the other girls, then Kate shut the door behind her. She could hear the neighbor's dog howling. The hound was more silver than black these days, and his howl was gratingly croaky. The sound seemed to echo through the quiet room.

Once her sisters were out of earshot, she turned back to her parents and uncle. "What's going on?"

Mama sighed. "Kate, go keep your sisters busy. The adults are talking."

"I'm an adult," Kate pointed out. "I can help."

Daddy said, "Listen to your mama. This ain't your business."

Kate pointed at Uncle Christopher, whose expression spoiled her parents' poker faces. His brow was creased, and there was a dimple at the corner of his mouth like he'd swallowed a bitter secret. "Ain't it? Something's going on," she said. "I just want to help.

Just because I'm not married yet doesn't mean I'm not grown."

Mama and Daddy exchanged a glance. They could have entire conversations without moving an eyebrow.

Finally, Daddy waved her over. "Sit down if you insist, Georgia Kate." Everyone else called her Kate, but Daddy always used the full name he'd given her.

Kate sat. The divide between the kids' side and the adult side was invisible, but as firm as the state line. Standing, she was nearly as tall as Uncle Christopher, but all her height was in her legs. Sitting, she seemed nearly as short as Mama.

Uncle Christopher shrugged. "She's right, you know. She's a smart girl, and she needs to know this kind of thing."

Mama rolled her eyes, looking just like Gramma Rae. "Fine, Kate. If you insist on being in grown-up business, you can stay, but you best tell me if you get overheated."

Daddy folded his hands on the table. He looked older than she remembered, or maybe she just hadn't looked at him closely enough recently. The lines by his eyes and mouth had deepened like furrows during planting season. His shaved head hid how much of his hair was silver now. The long hours he worked in the lumber mill up on Mount Osborne nipped at his vitality, and coming home to care for five daughters didn't help. The bottom of the mountain had been stripped of the best wood for nearly thirty years, so the lumber teams were moving further and further up the mountain to search for the cherry, ash, and walnut that manufacturers needed.

"Georgia Kate," Daddy said solemnly, "we're moving."

She blinked at him. "What?"

"You heard him," Mama said briskly. "We're trying to figure out our plans."

"And you weren't going to *tell* me?" she asked. "Where are we going? Were you just going to pack up and hope I didn't notice?"

"They've been giving me fewer hours at the mill." Daddy sighed. "Every time I go in, they need me less and less. The new folks are getting all the jobs. They're pushing me out."

"The lumber mill can't be your only option. Surely there's something we can do. There's more work here."

"Only white folks can work in the gristmill," Mama said.

As though Kate would be fool enough to suggest Daddy apply to work for the Chadwicks. She opened her mouth to suggest the coal mines deeper in the mountains—then closed it again. She had seen what happened to the men who went underground. Nothing withered a man quicker inside and out than the mines.

Mama sighed. "There'll be more opportunities in the city."

"The city?" Kate repeated, horrified. "Which city?"

Uncle Christopher spoke up. "I have a friend in Nashville. There's an automobile factory opening in July that'll be looking for workers. My friend's apartment building always has some units for rent."

"Nashville?" Kate felt like a broken record, repeating unfathomable words. Nashville was far. By train, it would take eight hours. Would they even be able to afford tickets? She turned to Daddy. "You've always said Chatuga's our home."

"People move," Mama said, gentler than Kate had expected. "Things change, Kate. We've got to go with the times."

"But it's not fair. These people shouldn't be able to come into our town and push us out. This is our home too. What else can I do? I'll work more hours, find a new client to replace the Addisons." Kate had been doing odd jobs since she was ten and had realized she could make a dime by hauling water every day for their neighbors. The richer folk in town had water pumps inside their homes, but Kate's neighborhood, Tolbert-Vance, relied on the well. From there, she'd found a series of odd jobs: doing laundry, delivering vegetables, cleaning windows, and anything else that would bring in money.

But apparently it wasn't enough.

"I could help on the land, if that would be better," Kate said. One hand stayed on the table, but the other found its way into the pocket of her dress. Her thumb rubbed over the smooth surface of her wolf fang. She'd learned the hard way to avoid its sharp end, filed to a vicious point by her uncle, and instead rubbed the smooth edges. It was a familiar texture, but the comfort felt hollow. "We could finally get the cows we've been talking about."

"You need money to buy cows," Mama said.

"They pay for themselves. That's what everyone says."

"They pay for themselves once you have them," she retorted. "I'm busy enough with sewing and the garden, and I don't need more mouths to feed. We've made our decision. We're moving to Nashville."

"We can't give up. Chatuga is our home, the kids' home." Kate gestured toward the closed door, where her sisters naively played on.

"Georgia Kate Mayer," Mama snapped. Kate's jaw clicked closed, and she clenched her teeth. "Don't make this harder than it already is."

"It *should* be a hard decision," she pointed out. "You're uprooting us for a city that doesn't want us."

"Chatuga doesn't want us," Daddy said quietly. "We're not the only family who will have to leave before this is over. Times are changing. Chatuga is growing, and new white folks are taking the jobs. We've always known that when they have the choice, they won't pick us."

"It ain't fair," Kate snarled.

"No, it ain't," Daddy said.

"It's better than what happened to the Wagners," Mama said. "Sometimes it's better to choose to leave than to have that choice taken away."

The Wagners, like a few other families in Tolbert-Vance, had been driven out of the nearby town of Oak Springs back in 1915. Their white neighbors had decided they wanted their houses and jobs, so they beat a young boy nearly to death for stealing some corn. Then, in case that hadn't gotten the message through, they'd dynamited a few homes. The neighborhood knew they needed to leave before it got worse, and all moved out.

"We're making the best of a bad situation," Mama continued. "There are opportunities in Nashville. It's a better place for all of us."

"Daddy's been working for that mill his entire life. He's one of their best. They *owe* him."

Daddy shook his head. "Companies don't owe anyone anything. You can never trust them. They only look out for themselves, no matter how much time and energy and blood you've given them. Never forget that."

"They don't deserve all the time you've given them," Kate told him fiercely. "You're worth more than any ten of them combined."

"Thank you, Georgia Kate," he said. "But we have to be practical. That's what Mayers do. My daddy could have been killed when he snuck out of Georgia, but he ran because it was his best chance. He made his way here, took on the pulpit, and changed lives."

He'd died before she was born, but Kate had heard stories of her granddaddy a hundred times. Theodore Mayer had been born a slave. Even after he was freed at the end of the war, the landowners tried to trap him in debt. He'd barely been older than Kate when he fled Georgia, and had become a reverend at twenty-five. Folks still said he gave the best sermons anyone had ever heard.

"You said he loved Chatuga. He wanted us to stay here," Kate said.

"He wanted us *safe*. Now, we'll build our own lives somewhere new. We'll come out of this stronger."

"I…" Kate trailed off. A bitter, metallic scent filled her nose and mouth, harsh and choking. Her vision swam, shuddering as though she were on a train car. Pain lanced through her left temple, an invisible spike piercing her brain.

She gasped. "Mama, it's…"

Heavy clouds tumbled over the night sky, briefly allowing the crescent moon to peek down at the valley before it was covered again. The forest shoved its way onto the trail with branches ready to catch and drag any wayward scrap of clothing. In the woods beyond, cicadas thrummed and frogs croaked. Summer was heavy all around, acres of green perfuming the air.

Kate was walking through the forest outside Chatuga, led by the person in front of her.

The man was stocky, slightly shorter than her, and moved with the steady determination of a mountain lion. Muscle shifted under his cotton shirt. Her eyes moved from the broad shoulders in front of her down to their clasped hands. His fair skin was silver in the moonlight, her own blue beside it. He walked confidently over the loose shale, tugging her forward.

He glanced over his shoulder at her. His eyes were shadowed by a lock of hair, but his smile was bright as the sliver of moon overhead.

"It's okay, baby. Breathe."

Kate's eyes opened. She lurched upward, choking against the musky leather in her mouth. Steady hands pressed into her shoulders, forcing her to lie back down. It wasn't the cold wood of the kitchen floor beneath her back, but the familiar ridges of Daddy's legs. She relaxed, heaving a sigh.

Mama tugged the belt out of her mouth with a new set of teeth marks in it while Daddy ran a hand over her forehead. His palm was warm and light, draining away the last of the lingering pain in her temples.

"It was him again," Kate said.

"Him who, honey?" Mama asked.

Uncle Christopher was hovering by the table, face drawn and anxious. "Is she all right?" He still wasn't accustomed to her visions, even after so long.

"She'll be fine," Mama said.

Kate nodded and moved to get up. This time, Daddy helped her to her feet. The haze from the episode was already fading, and she could stand on her own. The room, lit by oil lamps, was bright compared to the dark night of her dream.

Why was that handsome white boy in so many of her visions? She could have traced the line of his shoulders, the twist of his lips, the fall of his hair, but she didn't know his name. He was hers in a way no one else was, a gift waiting in her future who held her hand and pressed his palms to her cheeks and laughed like sunlight. Her visions were rarely pleasant, and she dreaded the day most would come true. This man was an exception, and her curiosity burned like an ember in her chest.

She knew better than to tell her parents about him. They wouldn't understand the joy she felt, not when getting entangled with any white man created so much trouble.

"I'll get you some water," Daddy said, squeezing her shoulder.

"I knew we shouldn't have told her." Mama sighed, patting the front of Kate's dress to knock away nonexistent dust. "It agitated her."

"You can't keep secrets from me because of my episodes," Kate said. "I would notice if we got on a train to Nashville with all our bags."

"She's certainly feeling better," Uncle Christopher said wryly, though his skin was still ashen. Kate glared at him, and he held up his hands. "Just good to see your fighting spirit."

Mama hummed and shook her head. Daddy returned with a cup of water, which Kate drank gratefully. His hand hovered at her back to catch her again, but she grew steadier with every second.

"We don't need to talk about this all now," Daddy said, taking the cup when she finished. "We still have time to work something out here in Chatuga. We'll worry about the future when it comes."

Worrying about the future felt like all Kate was able to do. As she let Daddy lead her out to the yard where her sisters were playing with marbles, oblivious to the changes on the horizon, she wondered again about the man from her vision.

Kate's older cousins had all gotten married by eighteen and already had kids of their own. So far, Kate remained uncourted. Too many people knew of her fits—and her temper. She was too much hassle for men to show interest. But the man in her dreams looked at her with warm smiles and intimate eyes. It wouldn't be the same as her cousins, not with a white boy, but he would be *hers*.

How could that future come if they left Chatuga?

3

NORA JO

It was only polite to ask the stranger inside, though Nora Jo considered sending him away instead. She wasn't open about dabbling in witchcraft, keeping it as quiet as her ma had. It didn't seem right for it to be spoken of beyond her childhood home.

She moved her supper plates to the kitchen counter and set out a cast-iron skillet of cornbread. She poured them each some milk in the heavy silence and sat down across from Harlow. He observed her in silence, ignoring the food.

Finally, she prompted, "You think I'm a witch."

"I know you are."

"We've never met. How would you know something like that about me?"

No one had ever looked at Nora Jo and seen a witch before. Witches were old women who lived alone. The second cousin who could cure anything with the ingredients she found outside. The strange black cat that lurked outside a neighbor's barn and made the cows sick. The Cherokee man who could speak with his ancestors. Nora Jo, a quiet schoolteacher, drew no attention.

"I have my ways of detecting people with a connection to magic," Harlow said. "You leave a mark on the earth around you, more than the other people in this town. Mostly in small ways, from what I can sense, but the world still bends around you. It does for me too."

He lifted a hand—and the spoon on the table lifted with it, hovering like a cloud. The dull silver glinted in the candlelight, spinning gently over the scarred wooden table.

Nora Jo leaned back in her chair, startled.

That was magic unlike anything she'd seen before. Her ma's spells were mostly invisible. And more, her ma's magic was *uncertain*, understood only in the outcomes. The effects were subtle, if they worked at all. None of the herbs Nora Jo had desperately smashed together into healing tonics during her ma's illnesses had made a difference in the end. This levitation was undeniable.

"I can't do that," she said, mouth numb.

"Not yet. But I can feel your power."

"I'm nothing special, Mr. Harlow. I don't imagine you can feel anything about me." She chewed her bottom lip, then lifted a hand to show a ring on her pinky. The silver was polished to a shine despite its age. A marbled chunk of green agate sat in the middle. "Maybe you're feeling this?"

He examined it, idle. "Should I be?"

Nora Jo used her thumb to spin the ring. "My ma left it to me. She said it had the power to protect me."

"Filled with a mother's love, I'm sure," Harlow said, voice dry.

Nora Jo frowned. She had treasured the ring for years. It had once belonged to her grandmother and had been one of her ma's most prized possessions. "It is," she returned coolly.

"It's sweet, but trinkets ain't my specialty," he said, waving a hand. "You have potential. That's why I picked you. Teachers understand the need to seek out new information, new wisdom. Them who ain't looking to learn, won't. Them who understand there's still more to know will never *stop* learning. This type of magic takes effort, Miss Barker."

"Do you take apprentices often?" she asked.

"No. I haven't taken an apprentice in a very long time. I'm getting old though, and I want to make sure I've passed the craft down as it was passed to me."

He didn't look so old. If Nora Jo had to guess, she would have put him close to her pa's age when he'd died—barely fifty—but she was far better at estimating ages under fifteen. Harlow's skin was weathered from years outside, and his broad hat could have been hiding graying hair.

"I appreciate you coming to talk to me, but really, I'm happy here. Levitating spoons ain't quite the career change I'm looking for. It wouldn't pay better, I'm sure."

"It's more lucrative than you might think, Miss Nora Jo," Harlow said. "People don't admit it, but they respect the healing powers of a witch more than anyone but their own grandmother. The tinctures I sell are in high demand. I do important work. People turn to me when they're in need. But I don't just live off witchery. I'm a trapper. I find the best furs in Tennessee. Call it witchcraft, or call it knowing my land, but that brings me plenty of money. It's the type of work people yearn for all their lives."

"Where do you live? I haven't seen you around here before."

"I live on Old Blue."

Nora Jo looked up abruptly from her cornbread. "Old Blue?" She didn't know anyone who ventured up there. Chatuga was surrounded by the Blue Ridge Mountains. They loomed over the town and its farms. Plenty of men traveled up the mountains to work every day in the lumber mills, or to hunt.

In her youth, Nora Jo had trekked through the mountains with her brother, exploring the landscape. The mountains were part of everyone's blood here, even if they lived in the valleys.

But no one climbed Old Blue.

"That's supposed to be the most dangerous peak in Appalachia," she said. "I've heard there's a family of bears there with a taste for man flesh."

"If there are, I haven't seen them. It's a beautiful mountain." Harlow gave a short, reserved shrug. "Besides, witchery can bring protection too. There's safety in power. I would have no fear living anywhere. You could be the same."

She shook her head. "I can't leave Chatuga."

"Your family's here?"

"My job is here. I help people too. And my… friends are here." The widow Whitaker and Gloria were not her friends, precisely, but she had no better word. Miss Ethel gave her a place to rest, a place to make her own, and Gloria… Gloria was a glimmer of sunlight on the horizon at dawn. Not quite seen yet, but holding the promise of something life-giving.

"Luckily, I'm not asking you to move. I'll stay in town for a while, teach you what I know. You can still work at your job if you find the time. But, Miss Nora Jo? Everyone claims they want money," Harlow said, leaning forward, "but I know people like you. What you want, what you need, is *knowledge*. Folks who know things are more valuable than them who don't, and we all know it. You went into teaching because you care about the truth of things. There's an entire world you know nothing about. Your schools and your preacher and your family have worked together to keep you in the dark about the limits of this world. I can teach you things you've never dreamed of. It's the opportunity of a lifetime for one such as yourself."

Nora Jo watched him carefully. No one had seen her so clearly in a long while. People said she was difficult to read, but this man understood her better than her own brother. "Why offer? Why come down here and find me for this?"

"Why did you become a teacher? You had knowledge that needed to be shared—and someone worth teaching." His blue gaze was electric. "Ain't there things you want to change? People you want to help? When you know things beyond the limits of your society, you're not trapped within their rules anymore, Miss Nora Jo. I live as I want on the mountain. I make things no one else can make. I see things no one else can see. No one can control me. By offering this apprenticeship, I'm giving someone else the chance to follow in my footsteps."

Knowledge had always been Nora Jo's fuel. It sent her scurrying after her ma in the garden, helping pluck herbs to be ground into medicine. It kept her alert in school while the other students whispered to each other or stared out the single window. It kept her pursuing her career despite people telling her to stop. It drove her to educate the kids of the town.

A small smile tugged at the corner of Harlow's lips. He watched her with an intensity that suggested a sharp mind behind those bright eyes. "Take a chance, Miss Nora Jo," he suggested. "You don't know what it'll bring."

In Chatuga, Nora Jo felt like a man on top of a mountain trying to explain a vast landscape to those who had only ever seen the valley. But perhaps to someone like Harlow, Nora Jo was on a small hill, only thinking herself wise. The thought of becoming something beyond what this town wanted from her, to step into the unknown…

"You study the world," he pressed. "Don't you want to know what's out there?"

She looked around the small, empty kitchen. Outside, night had fallen like a curtain over Chatuga. She could hear frogs and crickets singing in the trees. Somewhere beyond the darkness, Old Blue lurked, unseen and unknown.

Folks were scared to even talk about Old Blue. What would people say if they found out she was training with a stranger from the mountain—and a witch, at that?

Nora Jo loved her town, her school, and her students. She was no Dorothy, ready to leave behind her small world for something new and fantastical. She had worked too long and too hard for her position in town.

Witchery may have been her ma's legacy, but she had lost it a long time ago.

Nora Jo turned back to him. "I do. But I stand by what I said. This is my life, Mr. Harlow. I don't need your aid."

He leaned back, sighing. "That's your choice to make." He rose, then hesitated. "I'm staying in town for the next week or so anyway. I don't make it down the mountain very much, so I need to take advantage of my time while I'm here. If you change your mind, I'm lodging with the Lyes on the south side of town."

"I appreciate that," Nora Jo said, "but I won't change my mind."

He tipped his hat and left. Nora Jo stared at the door as it closed behind him. Then, she took her glass of milk to the sink and rinsed it clean. She shook her head, scrubbing out the glass.

Soon, there was no trace there had been a visitor at all.

4

OLIVER

Oliver startled awake. The room was dark, and his body seemed far away. He felt like nothing but a ghost, suspended in time and haunted by swirling images he couldn't quite remember.

Where was he? The hospital? The long boat ride home? The trenches?

God, he could not still be in those damned trenches.

No. He was home. Wasn't he?

He rubbed a hand over his face, letting his eyes slide closed again, and then pressed it against his chest when his lungs seized suddenly. He coughed explosively. It was as violent as ever, like his organs wanted to smash their way from his body. Could the body have its own nightmares, memories it too couldn't shake? He fought through the moment until the cough eased.

He fought free from his tangled sheets and stood. His childhood bedroom was small and quaint, a ghost in its own way. His parents had finished building the house when Oliver was five, and the design still expected him to be smaller. A cedar chest of clothes he had outgrown sat against the wall. A thick quilt stitched by his grandmother hung over the end of the bed. Scuffs marked the walls from various boyhood misadventures. It all belonged to a version of Oliver that was no longer here.

He checked the grandfather clock sitting in the hallway. It once stood inside his room, but he'd pushed it into the hall his first night back home. He'd grown accustomed to steady noise while abroad, so the dead quiet of farm life combined with the single, unerring tick had nearly driven him mad.

It was late.

His hands still shook.

He'd learned early in his childhood how to sneak downstairs and out the back entrance of the house to avoid his parents' detection. At first, he had stolen away to explore forbidden pastures with his friends, laughing and goading each other into pulling a cow's tail or stealing a few eggs from a henhouse. When they finished school and his friends had either retreated to work on their farms or moved out of Chatuga for better jobs, Oliver used the quiet path to meet girls in haylofts. Flirting was fun, an innocent pastime that made him feel bold and alive.

Now, he had nowhere to go, no one to see. He just didn't want to be in the house any longer.

The night was brisk, the lingering chill from winter sweeping back in like a thief as soon as the sun was gone. He felt like the frozen mud of France still coated his skin, soaking into his bones.

He went to the fence a hundred paces from the back door that enclosed their four cows. They were sleeping, quiet and still. In the summer, the fields would flicker with the sporadic glow of fireflies.

The farm seemed dead without them, even though he knew everything was only asleep.

He leaned against a wooden post and pulled a bronze cigarette case from his pocket. His thumb swept over the monogram etched into the front: TSL. The top of the S swooped over the L like a tree sheltering it under its branches. The cigarettes inside rasped against each other as the container moved, but Oliver didn't open it. He inhaled, remembering the way the warm smoke curled down his lungs and drove away the cold.

He missed it. He missed so many things.

A loud, ragged caw startled him, and he looked up to see a portion of the night detach itself and swoop toward him. He lurched backward, shielding his face with his hands.

The cigarette case slipped from his grasp, pulled upward. He grabbed into the air after it, but the bird—and it was a bird, some dark, quick creature—was already flying away with the case in its claws.

"Bastard," he growled, and chased after it.

There was a full moon overhead, and the pastures were bathed in silver around him. The crow flew in wide circles, cawing in triumph over its prize. Oliver's lungs burned as he ran, his throat raw and aching. The strength he'd taken with him to Europe, as sturdy and reliable as his backpack, had been lost during his time away. Before the war, he could have run the length of Chatuga three times over. Now, he was short of breath within seconds.

He stumbled, foot catching in a dip in the field. He fell hard, his hands scraping against the grass and dirt. He bowed his head, fighting for air as his abused lungs begged for rest. He slammed his fist into the ground; even that motion felt weak. The crow would be long gone now, and the cigarette case with it.

He'd failed Tucker Lee again.

A caw made him lift his head. The crow had settled on a nearby fence post, just across the pasture. He couldn't identify the field—had he been running that long, or was it only his disorientation?—but there were only a few yards between him and the bird now. The bronze case glinted in the moonlight.

Oliver pushed himself to his feet, gritting his teeth and forcing his breathing under control. He crept toward the crow, heart thudding in his ears like explosions across a battlefield. If he could just...

The crow took flight again, the tip of one feathered wing grazing Oliver's outstretched fingertips. Cursing, wheezing, Oliver gave chase.

5

KATE

The moon was full again.

It felt nearer than usual, looming like an eye overhead. Thin wisps of lingering clouds drifted like cotton through the sky, painted pale blue and purple.

Could this be the night?

It wasn't the first time she'd wondered. She'd started getting visions of her man years ago. They were only fragments, wisps of a future without context. She'd grown obsessed, waiting to learn how they would meet. Somehow, this stranger would be woven into the fabric of her life. In an uncertain world, it was a promise of happier times to come.

A year ago, she'd finally had a vision that seemed like a glimpse of their first meeting. There had been wariness in the man's posture instead of their usual closeness. Most of her dreams showed him in orbit around her, but this was a strange encounter. A man, stumbling out of a dark wood into a clearing beside a burbling creek. He seemed lost, fumbling for something metallic in the dirt. And Kate would be waiting for him there. It would be the beginning of a connection that would last far longer.

A meeting on a night with a bright full moon.

She'd already spent five full moons in the past year by that creek, waiting for someone who never came. It had taken two days of wandering to find the exact spot. She'd followed Chestnut Creek as it flowed eastward and bled into the burbling streams that wove through Chatuga like a spiderweb. Finally, she'd found the distinct ovular clearing and massive fallen tree spanning the water.

The other full moons had been cloudy or snowy or rainy. None were the fated night.

For a moment, she thought to let tonight pass as well. She was already in bed, and would need to sneak past her entire family to get outside. If she rolled over and closed her eyes, she could fall asleep and see what next month brought. Her fate would come no matter what she did, after all.

But what would happen if she moved to Nashville?

After a few more minutes of listening to her sisters' steady breathing, Kate sat up. She removed her headscarf, pulled a wool dress over her nightgown, and shoved her feet into her boots without socks. Between Willamae's snoring and Mary Evelyn's nightmares, her sisters had all learned to sleep through nearly any noise. Her parents' room was silent as well, though she worried they would find her creeping through the dark house. She'd been switched only a few times as a child, but Mama would tan her hide now if she knew Kate's plan. As much as she reminded her parents that she was a grown woman who could have been married with a baby or two already if things were different, they had strict opinions about when she could and couldn't be out.

Her neighborhood, Tolbert-Vance, sat west of central Chatuga and tended to be quiet at night. Kate skirted the edge of town, staying on one of the paths that arched around the north of town like the outer edge of a wheel. She didn't need anyone spying her and gossiping about her activities. She didn't know as many people in the center of Chatuga, where only white folks lived, but she'd worked enough odd jobs for them that her reputation mattered. In a town this small, everyone knew everyone's business, especially if it was the kind they tried to keep secret.

After a while, the pastures and farms around the town gave way to the forests that packed the surrounding mountains. Within moments, Chatuga disappeared entirely.

The crackle of pine needles and leaves beneath her boots was loud as a brawl, and just as vicious. It took her a few minutes to realize it wasn't her nerves making her think so—the forest was dead quiet around her. Normally, the woods were filled with the song of insects and frogs, a pulsing, throbbing hum like a heartbeat. Tonight, it was as if Kate were the only creature alive in the forest. It was unnerving. What could have scared the woods into such absolute quiet, the silence of thousands of creatures holding their breath? Her footfalls slowed. She glanced over her shoulder. Perhaps she should turn around.

She shook her head, pressing onward. She would survive this night, and more besides. She'd seen it.

The silence of the forest was broken, faintly, then more loudly. The sound was a welcome respite from the overwhelming stillness. At first, it was a quiet murmuring, a conversation in the back room of a house during a wake. Then, the sound coalesced into the steady, familiar sound of Chestnut Creek. Water ran all through this land like blood through a body, rivulets twisting and flowing to power the countryside.

The clearing by the creek was empty, as always. The natural opening by the bend in the creek was a small oasis from the dark forest around it. The laurels nearby twisted among themselves, creating tangled shadows in the darkness. Across the creek, a weeping willow draped itself over the water, long branches brushing against the slow-moving surface. A fallen oak log stretched between the banks. It was a familiar scene.

Her pulse, which had climbed in anticipation as she approached, slowed again. There was no sign of the man from her visions. Tonight didn't seem to be the night either. Kate would be in Chatuga for at least one more month.

She sat on the log at the edge of the creek, lamenting her lost sleep as she examined her ankles under the moonlight. She'd needed to kick through a bush that had crept onto her path, and its thorns had pricked her bare legs. If there was blood, it was invisible in the dark. Behind her, the creek murmured its song.

She leaned her hands back on the bark, staring up through the branches of the surrounding trees. They created a frame over the clearing, giving her a perfect view of the full moon overhead. A thin cloud drifted across its surface, bisecting it like a knife wound.

This was the moment she had seen.

Kate looked west just before the crashing sounds began. Something—someone—was running through the forest, knocking aside branches and stumbling over roots. A ragged caw pierced the quiet just before a large crow swept into view.

It startled her. That, she hadn't seen coming.

The crow dropped something shiny onto the dirt of the

clearing and swooped over her head, barely missing her hair as she ducked.

The man followed a moment after, diving from the tree line onto the fallen object. On his knees, he examined the piece of metal, head bowed. His shoulders shuddered, his breathing labored. After a long moment, so silent the clearing seemed to echo with it, he put the object, some kind of small box, into his pocket and stood up.

He was short and stocky, hair slicked back off his forehead except for one lock that hung over his eyes. His fair skin was flushed from his run, dark color splotching his cheeks. He stilled when he spotted her.

Her vision of the moment ended there. Kate was left to find her own path.

"Hi," she said carefully, heart in her throat.

"Did you… see that crow? That… damn thief came out of nowhere," he said, panting and staring off into the darkness. His voice was deep and ragged, but familiar in a way that resonated through her. "I chased it for ages."

"What did it drop?" she asked. "I've been wondering." The man often stood with a hand in his pocket in her visions, the same pocket she'd seen him put the metal box into.

"Something of mine. Nasty critter," he said. "Sorry, miss. I didn't mean to interrupt you. I'll, uh, get out of your hair."

"I'm not taking up the whole clearing," Kate said quickly. "You could stay. Catch your breath."

"I'm fine," he said, rubbing at his chest. He stood straight, but his mouth hung open as he continued to quietly struggle to breathe. How far had he chased the crow? He looked fatigued.

"I'm Georgia Kate," she said, nervously bouncing a fist against her thigh. "Just Kate is fine."

"Do you always sit in the woods alone at night and introduce yourself to strangers?" he asked, striding over to the creek beside her. He knelt and splashed water on his face, slicking back his hair in the same motion.

"Not always," Kate said.

He stood up, shaking the water from his hands. The moonlight revealed that his right eye was divided into two colors. Half was the same simple brown as the other, but the second half was a lighter color.

And with that, Kate finally recognized him. He went from being the boy in her dreams to someone from this world. He had the same infamous eyes as his dad. Oliver Chadwick. This was Oliver Chadwick Jr., heir to the town's gristmill and the richest family in Chatuga.

"Well, I'll leave you to it," he said, patting his pocket again and turning toward the woods.

"Waiting for you," she blurted. He stilled, those familiar broad shoulders tense. "I was waiting for you. That's why I was here."

"How did you know I'd be here?" He glanced back at her. "Normally when I meet a girl in the woods, we plan it in advance." He raised his eyebrows. The words and smirk could have been flirtatious, but his tone was challenging.

"It's—it's not like that," Kate stuttered—though from her dreams, it might have been. The thought made her flush. How many girls had Oliver Chadwick Jr. met in this forest?

"So, what? Is that crow your pet or something?"

"No," Kate said. "That was a coincidence."

"One that you were here waiting for," Oliver said blandly.

"I said the crow ain't mine," Kate said, standing up. This wasn't the meeting she had anticipated. Where was the hand reaching toward hers? Where was the solid lean of his shoulder in a dark cave?

"Then how did you know I'd be here?"

Was there any way to explain this? There must be. He was supposed to be hers. "I saw it," she admitted. "I saw it a year ago."

"What are you on about? Look, I'm not impressed or interested," he said. "If you know what's good for you, you'll leave me be."

She hesitated. The utter stupidity of her actions was glaring. Here she was, alone in the woods, accosting the son of the richest white man in town. Had the glimpses in her visions all been some trick to lure her into a foolish decision? "I…"

He shook his head. "It's late, Georgia Kate. I don't have no time for this. Maybe a few years ago, this would have made me curious enough for… whatever it is you want, but you're barking up the wrong tree."

"I'm telling the truth."

What could she do? He had no cause to believe her. She had never told anyone outside her family, not after the reverend's reaction when she was young.

But she'd *seen* the look of tenderness in Oliver's eyes. It had to come someday. It *had* to. She couldn't change that, no matter what she told him tonight. Her visions had never failed to come true.

"You've never experienced something you couldn't explain?" she asked. "I don't understand it either. I never have. I knew you would be here tonight, and that I would be here to meet you. It's always been this way for me. I see what's to come. It comes. That's all."

"I don't know why you've chosen me, but I'm not interested," Oliver told her.

Fury flickered to life inside her, fueled by the tinder of disappointment and humiliation. "You're not special. All my dreams come true. I'm here because I'm here."

"Right," he said dryly.

"You're twisting it around. Tonight was destined to happen." A harsh laugh clawed its way from her throat. "I just expected it to go better."

"Sorry to disappoint. So, you're a witch?" He said the last word the same way he said everything else, as distant and unaffected as the moon overhead.

"No. I don't go looking for the visions. They come to me, whether I want them or not."

"I thought all girls peeled apples to see their future husband's name."

Kate's sisters loved festival games and midnight tricks to try to see their futures. It was a common pastime, especially during summer solstice. On that special night near the end of June, girls would drop apple peels into barrels and light candles in front of mirrors, looking for clues about their future husbands and children. Mama said that time grew blurry around the solstice, like a window misted over on a cool morning. If you squinted enough, you could make out the shapes of what was to come.

Kate wished that were true for her, that the future was lingering just out of view rather than regularly knocking its way into her mind and body.

"I see too much of the future already," she said. "I don't need to seek out more."

"But you came here."

She faltered. "Well. I had to. We met here. I can't change what's to come."

"Sure. You could have avoided this spot. You could have stayed in bed tonight. If it was some vision that told you to come here, you could have ignored it."

"The future isn't *optional*, Oliver Chadwick Jr. I can't avoid it. It's worse when you're not prepared. I've learned that the hard way." He hummed, skeptical, and she snapped, "You might be content to sit up in your fancy house and wait for things to happen to you, but the future is coming for all of us. I'd rather meet it at the front door than hide from it like you would."

He crossed his arms. "You think you know me."

"I'm starting to," Kate said. "And I'm regretting it."

For a beat, she worried she'd pushed too far, that she'd learn just how wrong her visions could be. He was right. She knew this man, but didn't know him at all. There were only visions and her own interpretations of those glimpses.

She'd always had a temper, but stalking down a man like this, shouting at him—those were things that could get someone into trouble.

"I didn't ask you to come here," he pointed out. Nothing she'd said seemed to have angered him. There was just a deep exhaustion to every line of his body, slumped shoulders and ragged breathing. "You can just leave."

"I will. But it won't help." She sighed and rubbed her palm across her forehead. "Why this?" she asked the night sky. "Why him?"

Nearly every vision she'd experienced during her episodes, all the things she'd bitten her tongue bleeding to be shown, had been a dark omen. Feeling pain only to foresee future pain. Her glimpses of Oliver had seemed different, soft and secret and welcoming. She should never have let hope warm her chest, never dreamed of a mystery lover destined to be hers. Her visions were a curse, not a gift.

"I hope you're not expecting me to answer that," he said. "I need to go home. You can go… do whatever it is you do. Harass the next fool who stumbles through here."

"Leave. I'm not stopping you," she said, voice thick as cotton in her throat.

He gave her a sardonic nod and turned toward the patch of woods he'd crashed through.

"You're going to get a cut near your eye before the next time we meet," Kate called after him. "Tell me then that I'm wrong."

He waved without looking back and stepped into the trees.

Kate crouched to yank a rock from the dirt and hurled it into the silver creek. The splash was cacophonous in the silent forest. There was a rustle of leaves overhead as a bird took flight.

She'd been waiting for *this*?

6

OLIVER

The general store smelled of flour, tobacco, and the sticky sweetness of hard candies. Oliver stared at the collection of baskets stacked on one shelf just above eye-level. He frowned, trying to tell if there was any real difference between them. Most were woven from straw, some painted or dyed to look more unique. Some weaves were tight as sycamore bark, some were loose, but all seemed functional.

He didn't know how long he'd been staring before there was a light giggle from behind him. "What are you looking at there, Oliver?"

He didn't turn around. "Why are there so many of these? A basket is just a basket, ain't it? Next we'll have a whole store of these, and its shop owner will tell me they're all special. It's just woven straw, Miss Lula May."

Lula May Mathis stepped up to stand beside him, staring at the shelf with him. "Well," she said. "That one has blue stripes."

"Why yes, it does," Oliver said dryly. He shrugged and plucked that one from the shelf. It was as good as the others.

His lungs ached from his unanticipated run last night and his walk to the store. When that damn bird had stolen Tucker Lee's cigarette case, Oliver hadn't stopped to think—he just ran. Now, his body was scolding him. The walk here was a solid twenty minutes on a good day. He rarely had good days anymore.

He moved along to the next aisle, finding a smaller selection of blade razors. Lula May followed, hovering like a fly over a rotting bowl of fruit. "Are you shopping for someone?"

Oliver nodded. "Our basket broke, so Ma sent me out to get a new one."

"Oh, she'll like that one," Lula May said, as though she were an authority on his mother. "While you're here, we just got our shipment of sugar in from Sieverville. It's almost jam season, so your ma will be needing it. You should buy some."

"I'll just come back when we need it," Oliver pointed out.

"I guess you could. Well, how about some candy?" she asked, hands folded over her apron. The Mathises had owned the local general store for twenty years, as long as Oliver had been alive. Lula May, a few years younger than him, had been helping her family with the shop since she was old enough to stand. She was sweet-tempered, but persistent. She stared at him the way every other girl in town seemed to—like a barn cat at a mouse.

At least she hadn't lured him into the woods to feed him mad stories. The girl from last night was like a stone caught rattling in his mind, strange and unsettling.

"What about some candy?" Oliver repeated, still staring at the razors. Why were there three brands? He would have sworn they used to only keep one of each thing here.

"Don't you want some for your ma?" Lula May asked. "Or for yourself? We have a great new cinnamon flavor that's just delicious."

"I don't have a sweet tooth," Oliver admitted. "Why did your pa put three different razors on sale?"

"People like having choices. That's how they're doing things in the city now. I thought you might like candy."

"Why?"

He grabbed the cheapest razor. If his pa had been there, he would have told him to go for the most expensive one. As the owner of the town's gristmill, Oliver Curtis Chadwick Sr. saw himself as something of a local lord. Oliver could find out if his pa could really tell the difference.

"Well," Lula May said. "You couldn't have gotten much sugar in Europe, what with the rations. I would have thought you'd come back with a big sweet tooth."

Oliver turned to her. "Sorry, Lula May," he said, flashing the bright smile he had perfected in his flirtatious youth, "I was too busy getting shot at by the Krauts to miss flavored sugar." He used the razor to give her a mock salute and went to pay her pa for his purchases.

It was late afternoon when Oliver walked back to the farm. The dirt road beneath his boots was familiar, the ground unchanged no matter who stepped upon it. The surface was malleable, the paths changed—roads becoming fields, and vice versa—but dig three feet deep and Tennessee would always be the same.

Not everything was so permanent.

He patted the bronze cigarette case in his pocket. Still safe, despite the scare last night.

The April sun was warm overhead, beating against the bare skin on the back of his neck. The sky was a scorching clear blue, relentless.

As he left town, tension ratcheted in his shoulders. After nearly a year back here, he should have been used to the walk, but he could never quite catch his breath on this stretch of road.

The farms surrounding Chatuga all led back to the center, with its general store, school, and gristmill. The roads were like the spokes of a wheel, and Chatuga was the center of everyone's lives. Oliver hadn't left town since he returned from the war.

He could have avoided the dirt road by cutting through the Wilkeses' pasture, but he wasn't sure he could outrun their temperamental bull, Duke, like he had in his youth. It would have been an ignoble way to die, gored in a Tennessee field by an angry herbivore, bleeding out beside a pile of manure. Instead, he continued on the dirt path as it led him past the old graveyard. The plot was attached to a rundown church, abandoned in favor of a bigger structure in the center of town when his grandpa, Herman Chadwick, founded the gristmill that had turned Chatuga from a loose gathering of farms into a real town.

The wooden building was decrepit, its windows boarded up like a coffin. It had stood empty for decades.

The graveyard… wasn't empty.

As Oliver walked past the rows of graves, he could feel eyes on him. The weight of the staring was like a blanket of burrs over his shoulders. He didn't want to look. He knew what he'd see, but if he refused to turn, he could pretend the feeling was only his imagination. He put a hand to his head, making sure his hat was firmly in place. It was an old superstition, one he no longer believed in, but he would not step near a graveyard with his head uncovered.

He should ignore them. But if he didn't look, he wouldn't know if something was following him home.

He tilted his head, glancing over at the graveyard.

The two usual figures were waiting for him.

A young woman paced in the eastern corner. She looked no older than Oliver. Her arms were wrapped tightly around her chest as she went between two small graves. Her skirts were coated in dark blood like a waterfall. Her expression was empty, but her eyes were locked on him.

He flinched and looked away.

On the other side of the graveyard, an old man knelt in front of a battered grave, clinging to the lichen-covered stone like it was a lifeline. The first time Oliver had seen him, he'd thought he was alive. There were no obvious signs of injury or illness, and it wasn't unusual for someone to mourn in a graveyard. It was only when he'd seen him in the same position and the same clothing the next day that he realized he was like the other one. He turned over his shoulder to meet Oliver's gaze.

Usually, ghosts were stuck in a pattern that never changed. In Chatuga, that meant mourners in the graveyard, slaves and farmers in the fields, natives hunting where there was once forest. They clung to the routines of life, though they were stained with their deaths. The dead were listless, walking the paths they'd walked in life and staring into nothingness.

That only changed when Oliver came near. Their eyes followed him. He wondered sometimes if that meant he was dead as well.

He ducked his head and hurried onward. Despite the heat, his sweat had chilled before he arrived back at the farm.

His ma was in the garden that sprawled from the left wall of the house like a fallen quilt. A broad hat covered her face from the sun; she tilted it to look up at him from where she knelt in the rich dirt, waving him over. He went, holding up the basket so she could see it as he approached. She brushed off her hands, showering the ground with dark earth.

The tulips and daffodils were freshly bloomed, bright and vivid after the gray of winter. Snow didn't fall as thickly here in the valley as it did on the mountains, but it was still a miserable season. The arrival of spring should have made Oliver happier. He'd thought it might. The disappointment was a dim stain on his mind.

"Thank you, Junior," she said. "How was town?"

"Fine." He took out the razor and handed her the empty basket, which she tucked under her arm. The blue of the straw matched her eyes, echoed again in the bright sky behind her. Oliver had inherited Pa's mixed eyes; the left was brown, the right split in two, half brown and half green. Oliver had always wished for a normal color.

"Did you see Lula May at the store?"

"Sure. She works there most days."

Ma turned to look over her flower beds. "Her ma said that Lula May had been looking forward to talking to you again. I was hoping you two might have the chance to chat."

Oliver sighed. "Ma. I've told you I'm not interested in any of the girls in town."

She leaned down to rearrange a clump of tulips, untwisting their stems and letting the heavy blooms bounce freely. "You haven't spent much time with anyone since you've been back," she said with studied casualness. "It might be nice if you gave some of them a chance. They ain't the girls you remember. People grow, Junior. They ain't kids anymore either."

He shook his head. "I'm just not good company," he said. "Do you really want some poor girl to suffer through living with me?

And don't pretend you just want me to chat with them. You're imagining me in a new house with your grandma's lace on the table and a bride in a green dress."

"Well, never in green. Marry in green, you'll be ashamed to be seen. Possibly a nice blue or yellow."

"Ma, I have nothing in common with those girls. They ain't seen what I've seen."

"People can live in Chatuga their whole lives and still grow into interesting people."

"That's not what I meant," Oliver muttered, running a hand through his hair. Now he was the one avoiding his mother's gaze. They didn't talk about it, this thing that loomed behind him with every step, the war that took him across the ocean one man and sent him back as another. "If you want me to move out, I don't need a wife to do it."

Ma turned to him, one hand pressing against her chest. "I'm not trying to kick you out. You know we can support you. I just want you to be happy."

Oliver snorted. "I don't know what that means."

She looked like he had slapped her. "Junior," she said, pity lying heavy over her words like spoiled butter.

He stepped back, hands up to ward off anything more. "I'm just bullshitting, Ma. I should go in. Put Pa's razor away."

"Okay, honey." She didn't even correct his language, which only made him feel more exposed.

He jogged up the steps of the porch like he was running from the Wilkeses' bull after all. He slammed the door behind him, tensing with regret even before it collided with the doorframe with an echoing crash. A beat later, something cracked nearby, and Oliver jumped. He whirled, crouching and reaching for his empty belt, but no one was there.

The portrait hanging by the entrance had fallen from its nail, clattering against the floor below. It was a grainy image of his own face just before he'd been deployed, puffed up and proud in his infantry uniform. The glass had cracked, covering his youthful face with lines like a branch of lightning.

7

NORA JO

It was a relief to have Saturday stretching before her. Nora Jo had been distracted the last few days thinking about the man who'd come to offer her an apprenticeship in witchery. She had told no one of the strange visit, but it weighed heavily on her mind.

"Good morning, Miss Ethel," Nora Jo said, coming into the kitchen and foraging for a smile. "How are you?"

"Shit, as usual." Miss Ethel waved her in. "Have a seat, Miss Nora Jo. I'll make you a plate."

"You don't have to do that," Nora Jo said, though she knew Miss Ethel would insist.

"Yes, I sure do. This is still my house."

Miss Ethel stumbled partway to the counter, catching herself against the lip. Nora Jo hovered close, hands outstretched in case her help was needed. Miss Ethel pulled herself to her feet and began putting together a ham biscuit as though nothing had happened.

"Are you all right, ma'am?"

"I certainly am," Miss Ethel said, carefully sawing through the hunk of ham. She moved slowly, her knife unsteady. When Nora Jo first moved in with Miss Ethel, she could have chopped perfect cubes with her eyes closed.

Nora Jo didn't move. "You're sure?"

"You worry too much, Miss Nora Jo. Sit down before I chase you over there."

Miss Ethel had been a widow for as long as Nora Jo had known her, living in her house to the north of town, always with a quick smile to spare for Nora Jo and Beau at church. Some people aged like trees—knobbly and bent, but still solid to the core. Old Mr. Cooper was nearing ninety, and still plowed his farm without hiring extra help. Miss Ethel had aged like a flower, growing thin and drooping. Inside, though, she was made of iron nails and tobacco.

Nora Jo sat and watched. Now that spring was here, Miss Ethel's joints should have stopped giving her such a hard time.

Fortunately, she didn't stumble again. She laid the ham onto a fluffy biscuit and sprinkled on a pinch of salt and pepper.

"Thank you," Nora Jo said when she put the plate down. "This looks great."

"I miss my fresh veggies," Miss Ethel said. "Nothing like a tomato with breakfast. I'll be right grateful when the garden blooms and we won't have to eat everything canned anymore."

Miss Ethel grew most of her own food; she was one of the best cooks in the county. She lived and breathed by the almanac and planned her entire year of gardening in advance.

She levered herself into her chair and tucked a bit of chewing tobacco into her bottom lip. "How have the children at school been?"

"Scoundrels," Nora Jo said affectionately. "But I always feel I'm in a race with planting season. I'll lose so many to the farms."

"Their families need them. You just do the best with them in the time you have with them, and trust you make a difference."

"The Howards and Doyles still haven't come back." Nora Jo picked at the crumbling edge of her biscuit. "How are those kids supposed to learn about the world outside Chatuga if they're stuck at home?"

"Well," Miss Ethel said, sighing. "Not everyone understands what you're doing. Don't take it too personally... and don't be surprised if they're not the last ones."

"What do you mean?"

"It's probably nothing," she said. "You know how people talk. Some people wouldn't accept change even if the Lord came down and personally carved them a new commandment." Miss Ethel reached for the pitcher in the center of the table, revealing a black-purple bruise on the papery skin of her forearm.

Nora Jo hissed in sympathy. "What happened there?"

"Nothing. I went to get a refill of water yesterday and slipped on the way back," she said. "Spilled the water everywhere. The bruise looks worse than it is."

"I could get another bucket in the mornings," Nora Jo said. Miss Ethel tapped her fingernails on the edge of Nora Jo's plate, so she dutifully picked up her biscuit sandwich to keep eating. "I could bring it back before work."

"Hush your mouth, Miss Nora Jo. You already do enough, and you pay rent."

"I can help," Nora Jo protested.

"You have your own job. You've got bigger things to worry about than running around doing my errands," Miss Ethel said.

"Teach those children. If I need to, I'll hire someone. I don't need to make you do more for me."

"If you're sure," Nora Jo said carefully.

"I am. Now eat up. You're too skinny, girl. People will think I don't feed you."

When Nora Jo left the house, late afternoon hung heavy on the air. Each day was growing warmer and longer, sliding toward summer like honey.

She had a book tucked under her arm, a recent delivery from the post. She was several chapters into the new title already, *Of One Blood* by Pauline Hopkins, and looked forward to losing herself again in the words. Like *The Wonderful Wizard of Oz*, the book swept the characters from reality into a fantastical world of danger and magic.

There were clouds on the horizon, heavy and purple. Her favorite spot in the meadow would be spotlit for the moment, but it would be a long, miserable trek home if the sky opened on her. Instead, she turned toward town. Her schoolhouse would be empty, and after so many years within its wooden walls, it felt like her true home.

As she walked by the central water pump, she stewed about Miss Ethel's growing unsteadiness. Nora Jo could bring home extra water, but Miss Ethel was alone most days either way. She kept up her garden despite her aging joints, and there were always dangers in the country. Anything could happen to her while Nora Jo was gone. She wanted to demand to know how to help, but she didn't want to be domineering. She wasn't Miss Ethel's daughter, and feared the day she'd overstep and lose the old widow's patience.

"Nora Jo!"

She turned, surprised.

Gloria jogged up beside her, her red curls bouncing and cheeks flushed. "I saw you going past, but you didn't hear me calling."

"Sorry, Gloria," Nora Jo said. "I was in my own thoughts." Gloria was in the same blue dress as earlier that week, but the handkerchief around her hair was new. It was blue with small embroidered red dots. "Are those strawberries?"

Gloria reached up and patted the fabric. "They are."

"It's lovely."

"Thank you. I wanted to try some new needlework," she said, cheeks still flushed. "Are you heading to the general store too? They just got in their new shipment."

"I—why yes," she said. "I am."

The Mathis General Store was the heart of Chatuga, the place where trade from the rest of the world flowed through like lifeblood. Most people in town relied on themselves, their farms, the mountains that surrounded them, and each other, but the lure of outside goods was unceasing. Some were more susceptible to the draw than others, saving their money to spend on white sugar and unnecessary machinery. Mostly, Nora Jo avoided it. Her teaching salary was limited, and her only indulgences were her books. Still, she let Gloria lead her inside.

Lula May Mathis sat at the counter, talking to Mrs. Hendricks, one of the town's biggest gossips. The four Hendricks children were in Nora Jo's class, all subdued and uninterested. Mrs. Hendricks glanced back at them when the door opened, but her conversation with Lula May didn't stutter.

"What are you picking up?" Nora Jo asked Gloria as they walked through the shelves. They were cramped with items ranging from sacks of flour to piles of envelopes, all clamoring for the eye.

Gloria pointed to the back wall, which was filled with glass jars of candies. "They were sold out last time I was in… Aha! They got them. Black Crows." She led Nora Jo to a jar of acorn-sized black balls. "I was hoping they'd order more."

"Candy?" Nora Jo asked. "I didn't know you liked it."

"Licorice drops. I spend so much time working on the farm, I get plumb tired of vegetables all the time. When I manage to save up the money, I can't resist coming here." Gloria picked up a small brown bag and poured in a scoop of the candy. "If I could eat these all the time, I would. Have you had them?"

Nora Jo shook her head. "They look like something my kids would fight over."

"They're great. You'll love it." Gloria plucked a black drop from the top of the bag and held it up. It smelled of sharp, dark spice, warm and cold at once, like a fireplace during winter.

She pressed the candy forward, bumping against Nora Jo's lips. She opened her mouth, and Gloria slipped the sweet inside. The licorice resisted against her teeth, but slowly and inexorably caved. The sugary taste was more cloying than she expected, as overwhelmingly powerful as the smile on Gloria's face. "Lord," Nora Jo said, surprised. The word was slow to emerge, caught where the black candy held her back teeth fast together.

Gloria laughed and leaned forward, nudging Nora Jo's shoulder with her own. The brush of their sleeves was like a burst of sunshine in the dim back corner of the shop.

A throat cleared, and they both turned. Mrs. Hendricks was at the front of the aisle, staring at them. Her lips were pursed, eyes narrowed.

Nora Jo raised her eyebrows. "We're about to pay for it, ma'am," she told her, pulling on the no-nonsense voice she used with her students.

Gloria stepped away from her, her smile gone. It was strange to see her face solemn. Most days, even if Gloria wasn't smiling, there was humor tucked at the corner of her lips, as though it were waiting in the wings to come out. Without it, she seemed smaller, a candle blown out. "We were." She held the bag tightly to her chest.

Nora Jo grabbed Gloria's free hand and tugged her toward the front of the store, giving Mrs. Hendricks a smile caustic enough to scrub rust. The woman stepped aside to let them past, still frowning. Nora Jo found a nickel in her pocket and dropped it on the counter after Lula May weighed their bag.

"Weren't you going to buy something?" Gloria asked faintly as they emerged back into the sunlight.

"The store was getting too crowded." She looked around the street. Gloria was pale and unsteady, but there was nowhere to sit nearby that wouldn't be in easy sight of Mrs. Hendricks when she came out. There had been something sour in her stare that had clearly struck Gloria like a copperhead bite. "I was going to go sit in the meadow. Do you want to come?"

"I should get home," Gloria said, pulling her hand from Nora Jo's and gesturing toward her farm. "Looks like a storm is coming."

"Are you sure?" Nora Jo asked.

"Yeah, Nora Jo. I'll see you around."

Gloria walked down Main Street, both hands now clasped around the candy held close to her chest. The taste of licorice lingered on Nora Jo's tongue, heavy as riverbank mud.

*

Nora Jo's room was dark, illuminated only by the orange circle spreading from the candle. Outside her open window, frogs and crickets called in a pulsing rhythm. The afternoon's storm had been raucous but brief, and the scent of wet grass still lingered on the air. The house was quiet and still; Miss Ethel went to bed not long after sundown.

She had been stiff again as she moved around the house that evening. Nora Jo had watched her carefully. She'd avoided Nora Jo's questions about her injury over supper, briskly changing the subject. Her sleeve stayed firmly over the bruise.

Nora Jo spent the evening thinking about her ma and half-remembered spellwork in the kitchen. Granny Rhodes had been revered as a healer, but her ma had struggled to make any significant cures. Nora Jo would never forget how she would stumble in the kitchen, ghost-pale and clutching her stomach, trying to brew another elixir, only to end up in the same position a few months later.

Magic had not saved her ma, but the witch from the mountains thought Nora Jo had power. There could be a bit of Granny Rhodes's gift in her.

Nora Jo carefully twisted a bundle of mint leaves into pieces. The scent was sharp and fresh, and the juices smeared her fingers. Shreds of green fell in a circle on top of her scarred wooden desk. The candle in the middle shocked her wrist with a breath of dangerous warmth as she passed too close.

Nora Jo inhaled the mint and candlewax, the combination she'd smelled a dozen times in her ma's kitchen. Had there been other ingredients? Her ma had often recited small poems or Bible verses as she worked. They lingered on the edge of Nora Jo's memory, but she couldn't recall any specifics.

When the wax pooled around the wick, she picked up the candle carefully. Like a mantra, she pictured Miss Ethel in a series of precise flashes. Her clever, wrinkled face. Her white ringlets. The silver chain of her cross necklace. The clack of her knitting needles. The taste of tomatoes that had been sitting on the windowsill, delicately sliced, seasoned with salt and pepper. A spare room made open to a lonely teacher.

She thought of shaking hands, a bucket falling to the dirt road, a knee jarring against the ground. She imagined strength and balance and purple skin fading pale again.

She breathed out, envisioning the scent of mint and beeswax carrying through the house toward Miss Ethel's room, lingering over her as she slept.

She tilted the candle, making the wax tremble, and then poured it onto the wood. In the puddle, she used the mint stem to draw a careful circle, keeping the image of a stronger Miss Ethel clear as daylight in her mind. It all felt familiar, the quiet ritual of her ma's kitchen closer to mind than she had known.

All that was left was to seal the spell. She righted the candle and inhaled again. Just before she could blow and finish it, a wind cut through the open window behind her. The gust swept away the candle's flame, leaving the dark wick behind.

The spell was ruined.

Nora Jo sighed. She set the candle against the wall and used a cloth to sweep the debris into the trash. The rag smeared the cooling wax, and she tossed it angrily onto the lip of the waste basket. With a nail, she dragged unrelenting lines through the wax, scrubbing it away.

What was she doing? No matter what some man from the mountains had said, she was no witch, not really. His words were a foolish promise, distracting her from her life. She was useless to her landlady. Miss Ethel insisted she was fine, and Nora Jo had nothing to offer her.

Steadily, she removed all traces of the failed spell from her room.

8

OLIVER

On the docks, spectral chains rattled on the wrists of Black men and women. A chorus of weeping rose and fell with the waves.

The victims of the Spanish flu, unmistakable with their blue skin and bright red nosebleeds, stared down from their windows along the grand streets leading to the Charleston train station.

Soldiers in bloodstained gray and blue lined the road outside the rattling train car, guns firing silently as they continued a war that for them would never end.

When Oliver woke, he pressed his eyes more tightly closed, willing away the lingering afterimages. For such a young country, the parade of death in America was never-ending.

When he opened his eyes, a shadowed figure loomed over him.

The wrinkled face staring down from only inches away was so contorted with emotion it was almost inhuman. Thinning black hair circled the man's balding head like an eclipse's corona—apart from his left temple, where the hair was caked flat with blood. With a soundless scream, he lurched toward Oliver.

Oliver shouted and jolted backward. His head collided hard with the solid oak headboard. He blinked, head throbbing and muscles tense.

He was alone in the room. It was still and quiet as any other night. Had there really been a ghost? Or was it only a lingering shadow from his nightmare?

The room was freezing. Nothing felt solid. Had he really seen anything?

Perhaps none of this was real.

The farmhouse was quiet, the walls of his bedroom muffling the sound of soft voices from the first floor and the dogs barking on neighboring farms. From the sound of quiet conversation downstairs, he thought it wasn't too long after sunset.

Outside, the branches of the oak and the night sky beyond were blurred by a layer of frost on the window.

Oliver stood up, wincing when his feet touched the cold hardwood. He put a hand against the window frame, peering through it. There was no frost on the grass outside. Winter hadn't mysteriously returned since he'd fallen asleep. But there was a smear on the window. Several smears.

Lines danced across the window, each leaving a dripping line of clean glass in its wake as the frost melted. The pattern was difficult to see.

He stepped back and tilted his head.

NOCT

There were more letters below, but they had melted too much for Oliver to read. Was the first letter of the second word an L, or an I?

Who had done this? And how? He was on the second story, and he'd broken the trellis outside his window climbing down to meet a girl when he was fifteen.

Frowning, he dashed a hand against the window, and flinched when his palm swiped through the letters, smearing them into nothing.

The words had been traced from inside the room.

9

KATE

"Hi there," Kate said, smiling brightly, her hands clasped in front of her newest dress. "I'm looking for work—"

The blonde woman on the other side of the door shook her head. "Sorry. No work here."

The door shut without fanfare. Kate slumped, closing her eyes for a defeated beat.

She'd spent the morning doing laundry for her existing clients. It took half a day—she had to haul the clothes in a sled out to the spring, where she boiled and beat them with a batting stick. After that, her back and arms were aching, but she left right away to search for work in town.

The specter of Nashville hovered over their house, though her parents hadn't mentioned the move again after her attack last week. It was there in the heavy glances they exchanged, the way Mama ran her fingers over the cabinets as if memorizing their shape. Daddy was around more often now as his hours were cut down further and further. Her sisters didn't seem concerned, delighting in the extra time with him.

Kate had spent most of her free time in the last week walking through the sprawling town, searching for work. She'd started in Tolbert-Vance, but many of the families in her neighborhood were in the same situation as the Mayers. At least there, she'd sometimes been given a glass of tea before the doors closed.

Main Street was for whites only, as were the church, school, and general store. Expanding her search out of Tolbert-Vance was a careful dance, following the sometime invisible, sometimes bold indications of where she was unwanted. When she reached the homes spread out with acres of farms and pastures between them, where the faces behind the threshold were pale and distant, the conversations were short. She was likely not the first to come through asking for work, and with the way the town was changing, she would surely not be the last.

She was giving the biggest house in town, the Chadwick estate, a wide berth. They collected the town's money like a dam, building it up behind their home's clean walls, but she couldn't work there. She hadn't seen Oliver Chadwick Jr. again since the uncomfortable night last week, in person or in her visions. They would meet again—it was inevitable—but she wouldn't seek him out. He'd made his opinion clear. She wouldn't let destiny make a fool of her.

It was the warmest day of the year so far, and sweat traced intimate lines down her back, clinging to the cotton of her dress. Her hair was bundled at the nape of her neck in a heavy bun, and her ear ached after being glanced by the hot comb before work that morning.

The next house was a long walk from the last. In Chatuga, the forest and farmland fought for ground, and she passed more woods than pastures as she trekked. This house was small and simple, its panels once painted white but faded to gray. A large garden sprawled alongside, still sparse apart from the bright leaves of rhubarb and chicory. The plants were lush, but so were the weeds sprawling across the dirt.

Kate considered moving on. If the owner of this house was unable to afford simple upkeep, they were unlikely to have the funds to hire Kate. There were many farms left to check, and it was sure to be another long walk to the next one.

As she hesitated, the angle of the sun and the trio of swallows swooping past overlaid with a memory in her mind, slotting into place like the chorus of a song. She had seen this moment before. Only this one moment, the flash of the house in front of her on this day, this instant.

For a breath, all was perfectly familiar. Then the beat passed. Her next steps were uncharted.

Kate walked up the path and knocked. A ragged voice called out for her to wait, and a few moments later the door opened. The woman who answered was as aged as her voice. White curls framed a face tanned and spotted from long years in the sun, and she wore a simple cotton dress and apron. She smiled in greeting, revealing a missing canine tooth. The dark space reminded Kate of Uncle Christopher, who was missing the same tooth on the other side. When she was younger, she'd imagined that the lucky wolf fang he'd gifted her was somehow tied to her uncle in spirit.

"Afternoon," the old woman said. "How can I help you?"

"Hi, ma'am. My name is Kate Mayer. I'm looking for work," Kate said, the speech rolling from her tongue like a boulder down a hill, familiar and quick. "I can do anything you need—laundry, gardening, errands—"

"Did Nora Jo send you? That girl worries too much."

"No, ma'am," Kate said delicately, worried it was the wrong answer.

"Hm. Why don't you come inside? I just finished putting together some sweet tea," the woman said, stepping aside. Her home was small but comfortable, cluttered with the trinkets of years past. Nearly every surface was covered in lace, like the fabric was a spreading mold. "I'm Miss Ethel. It's a pleasure to meet you."

There were flies buzzing by the kitchen window, droning lazily. Miss Ethel poured them both glasses of sweet tea. It was sweeter than what Kate's mama made, almost cloying, but it soothed her dry throat. "Drink up, drink up," Miss Ethel said. "You look exhausted. You been walking a long way?"

"I've tried just about every house from here to Tolbert-Vance," Kate admitted. "I'm just looking for some honest work, ma'am."

"That's some right dedication. Listen, I'm thinking it might be luck that you came by today. I've been just thinking of getting some help around here. The upkeep on the house got harder when my husband passed away, and that's been fifteen years now. My boarder works at the schoolhouse, so she can't be here all day."

Kate leaned forward, forgetting the sweet tea. "I can do whatever you need."

Miss Ethel hummed, tapping her fingernails against her glass. She looked at the back of her own hand. "I don't quite recall when I got old. It seemed to sneak right up on me." She shook her head. "Don't you dare tell anyone, but I'll admit to you that I have some trouble these days. Doing my laundry. Getting water. Pulling weeds. Life isn't easy for a withered old crone like me. My hands ache most of the time, and my knees seem determined to fall out of joint. I feel like a tree that's already been chopped in half and doesn't know it yet."

"I can help with all that," Kate assured her. "I already do the laundry for the Russells and Burtons." She flexed her hands, sore from that morning's work.

Kate took a sip of the sweet tea. A grain of sugar crunched beneath her teeth, sending a shock of sweetness through her mouth. The Mayers didn't spend their money on sugar. She always thought sorghum syrup was just as nice until she had a bite of real sugar and remembered the difference.

"I won't be able to pay much," Miss Ethel said briskly. "I could afford ten cents an hour. No more than two hours a day. You can tell me what you'll be able to do for that."

Kate smiled. "That'll be just fine. I'm looking forward to working for you."

It was nearing sunset by the time Kate went back home. After she negotiated her new job with Miss Ethel, she'd only been able to visit three more homes before she lost the light, and none could hire her. As the sun dipped in the sky, painting the clouds pink and orange, her single success felt hollow.

An extra dollar-forty a week, and that only if Miss Ethel needed her every day. It wasn't a lot of money, overall. It would have helped if Daddy still had his full-time job, but it wouldn't be enough to keep their family in Chatuga. What had she thought she could do? None of her work could replace a mill job.

But Kate needed work and Miss Ethel needed help. Surely, something was better than nothing.

Tolbert-Vance bathed in evening gold was a beautiful sight. Even the patched roofs and crooked doorways were perfect in this light, a home its residents worked endlessly to preserve. Chatuga had never wanted any of them. They were here anyway. Kate would make sure they could remain.

Her granddaddy had raised the Mayer house when he first moved to Chatuga. Since he died, Mama had carefully maintained the small patch of land inside their picket fence. Vegetable plants would grow in staggered rows as spring continued to roll in—more space for the sprawling vines like the squash and pumpkins, alongside tall trellises for the climbing plants. There was a dedicated patch for turnip greens, one of the first vegetables to grow after winter. Now the final frost was behind them, they would soon be eating fresh vegetables again. It was time too— they were nearing the end of their store of canned food. Bushes of blackberries lined the front of the house like thorny guardians. In the summer, when the land was bursting with life, only the narrow path of river rocks from the gate to the front porch was safe to walk on, at the risk of inviting Mama's wrath.

The only space not given over to the garden was the dead tree beside the fence. The wood was petrified, as sturdy as stone, and all the branches had been sawed short. An uncorked blue bottle was stuck on the end of each branch. The collection of beer and wine bottles had been saved over the years until the entire tree bristled with blue glass.

"And where have you been?" Eileen was in the front yard planting a line of seeds. She leaned back on her heels, dabbing at her forehead with the back of her wrist. She was shorter than Kate, her face and body round and sloping like the hills that led to the mountains. "You could have been helping me. Why I have to spend all day with Uncle Christopher's disgusting chickens and then still help with the garden, I'll never understand."

"Because if we just eat eggs and chicken all year you'll complain even more," Kate told her. The latch on the gate stuck as usual, and she leaned her weight into it to pop it open. Why were her parents having Eileen plant? Maybe there was still hope to avoid Nashville and be here for the harvest—or were they only hiding the truth from Eileen until it was more certain? Kate could hardly blame them; arguments with her sister were exhausting.

"You could just answer my question."

"I was looking for new work," Kate said. "The Addisons moved back to Kentucky."

Eileen huffed. "Why do you even bother asking around? Don't you just *know* where you're going to be working?"

"Hush," Kate snapped.

Two years younger than Kate and four years older than the twins, Eileen saw herself as Kate's equal. She had been around for Kate's early years, before she had learned to keep her foresight quiet. The dreams—and seizures—had been upsetting for them all. These days, Eileen didn't dare bring up Kate's visions in front of their parents, but she hadn't forgotten them.

"You know what's coming. You could see what your next job will be," Eileen said, though she kept her voice quiet. The weather was nice enough that some of their neighbors were sitting on their porches, sipping sweet tea and chatting with each other. "If I were like you, I'd waste a lot less time."

"That's not how it works," Kate told her. "You don't understand."
Eileen stuck out her tongue.

Kate rolled her eyes and went into the house. It was no cooler
inside than outside now that the sun was setting. Mama called her
into the kitchen to help prepare supper. She handed Kate a jar of
canned beets, ushering her to get to work. She didn't ask about the
job search, which only made the failures of the day weigh more
heavily on Kate's shoulders. They hadn't discouraged her from
trying to help, but her parents clearly didn't imagine she could
make a difference. Maybe they didn't even remember her plans.

Had they already given up? Would they even tell her, what with
Mama's fear of triggering another seizure?

As she diced the beets, knife snapping against the wooden
cutting board and dark juices coating her fingers, she wished that
Eileen had been right. Her visions were unpredictable, usually
bringing more mystery and anxiety than clarity. What would her
life be like if she could direct the visions, call them into being, and
truly learn what the future would hold?

What if?

That night, Kate stared at her bedroom ceiling, surrounded by
the snores and unconscious mutterings of her younger sisters. Her
thoughts had been swirling all evening. Mama was afraid of causing
Kate stress and inducing a vision. What if Kate really could have
one by design? If she could find a real trigger, she could finally,
finally, make the visions work *for* her, rather than controlling her.

The warm night air outside called to her, but she didn't want
to risk being in the woods if her plan worked. Sometimes, the

seizures left her unconscious for hours. Some people called her power 'dreaming true,' but it was no gentle sleep. She imagined herself torn apart by wolves alone in the dark. She would survive the night—she had to, if she was going to see Oliver again as her visions promised. Still, her glimpses of the future were achingly sparse, impenetrable. Her visions were always from her own eyes, flashes of experiences without context. She could lose an arm and not see it coming.

No, it was better to be cautious.

But how could she induce a vision? Over the years, Kate had learned only two things about them: they were unpredictable, and they came true. Most of the time, they arrived in her sleep. They were different than other dreams, full of scent and sensation. Sometimes, the worst times, they came while she was out of the house. She had once fallen while carrying a load of firewood outside of town and had nearly split her head open on a rock. There was still a scar along her hairline, a dark divot like a dried creek bed.

Had she seen anything that would tell her if her family would make the move to Nashville? The flashes were so brief, it was hard to tell. Was Oliver Chadwick Jr. proof she would remain in Chatuga? The visions of him could come true over the course of a single weekend, or Oliver could end up in Nashville as well. She rarely saw more than a year or two into the future. There had been no visions of an old man with two-toned eyes holding her hand on their front porch—nor of a life alone. Those far-off years were as invisible to her as to everyone else. Maybe fate was chiseled into place one bit at a time.

She slammed her fist against the ground beside her cot, scowling at the familiar wooden slats overhead. The only visions that ever seemed to bring her future self joy—her moments with Oliver—felt impossible now. Their meeting had been achingly disappointing. What if she'd misinterpreted the visions of them together, those glimpses of clasped hands and intimate conversation? So eager for attention she had misinterpreted their warnings.

Still, she was determined to pull one benefit from the episodes. If she could know her family's future, she could help. She needed to know whether to fight to stay in Chatuga or begin planning for a life in Nashville.

She closed her eyes and silently prayed. It was fumbling, halting. She was out of practice. The only voice of God she had ever known was her greatest enemy, and his baritone echoed in her mind. Reverend Castor had acted with His authority, and he had hurt her. Shouldn't God value prophets? The Scripture was full of them.

Surely He owed her something after that.

The ceiling overhead didn't change. No bushes caught fire, no voice spoke down from the heavens.

When she finally fell off the cliff into sleep, it was with no hope for success.

"Let me go," Eileen whispered. Her voice was hoarse and uneven.

Her words fell on deaf ears. Kate only stared down at her. She was lit by uneven light in the darkness, shadows deep as ravines.

Eileen whimpered. "Kate, please. I don't understand."

"Shut up."

Kate wrapped her hands around Eileen's thin throat and began to squeeze.

Eileen's eyes were wide and desperate. Her skin mottled as the blood and air halted in her throat. A vein pulsed against her skin.

Eileen thrashed, scratching Kate's chest with desperate claws. It should have hurt, should have drawn blood. But Kate could feel nothing. Not pain. Not the fragile warm flesh under her hands.

Nothing.

Kate sat up from her cot, breath heaving in her chest. Her sisters were sprawled around her, unbothered. Hands shaking, she crawled to Eileen's cot. At night, with their quiet breathing the only sound in the room, her sisters were mostly easily identifiable by their headscarves. Eileen's had once been bright blue, but was now faded like the sky before a rainstorm.

Kate leaned close in the dark. Eileen's long throat was unmarred. Her breathing was quiet and easy.

Resting her forehead against her knees, Kate listened to the soft sound.

10

NORA JO

At the end of the school day, Nora Jo's students rushed out into the sunshine. She hollered after Griffin Staley to come back for his abandoned slate, then swept the floor clean. Was there any true power to this old ritual? The stranger Everett Harlow had been sure there was power in Nora Jo, but her attempt to help Miss Ethel seemed laughable in hindsight. Nora Jo, a witch? She barely had a grip on her own life. If there was any legacy Nora Jo was supposed to carry on, it had been lost when her ma died.

There was a reason Miss Ethel had just hired some stranger to help her. She knew she couldn't rely on Nora Jo.

She couldn't imagine what Harlow had seen in her. Unless she was reading, when her own thoughts were subsumed by more interesting and meaningful words from another's hand, she was as bland as grits.

She set the broom aside and absently put her fingers to her lips. She had no magic inside her that could be stronger than the taste of licorice. Where was Gloria now? Working on her pa's farm, most likely.

Did she ever think of Nora Jo?

There was a knock on the open doorway. "Miss Nora Jo?"

She startled and turned. "Oh, hello, Mr. Neese." Johnny Neese was the mayor of Chatuga. He was a quiet man, awkward and slippery, but his pa had been the mayor before him, and his son would likely take his place when he retired.

It was unusual for Neese to come by personally. Education wasn't required by the state of Tennessee, and Neese looked at the school with indulgent skepticism.

"Can I help you?" she asked.

He nodded, eyes shifting around the classroom, but not stepping inside. "We need to talk, Miss Nora Jo."

"What's going on?"

"Well," Neese said, "it's time to discuss the future of this school."

She felt like a rabbit under the eye of a hawk, frozen, waiting to see if she was its prey. It was an uneasy and unusual feeling. As the town's teacher, she enjoyed some respect, and was the leader of her school. In this space, she should have been secure. "Go on."

"You've done a good job teaching these last five years," Neese said. "When you came back with that degree, it was clear you were the best person to teach while Mrs. Wilson took care of her family."

Mrs. Wilson had been Nora Jo's teacher. When her daughter passed during a difficult childbirth, she had retired to her family's farm to raise her grandchild.

"Thank you," Nora Jo said, cautious.

"However," Neese said, "it's time for Mrs. Wilson to come back."

She blinked. "What?"

"Her granddaughter is old enough to come to school while she teaches again," the mayor said. "With another mouth to feed and Joe's poor crop last year, they're looking for the extra funds."

Nora Jo folded her arms more tightly, as though she could hold her stomach in place. It felt like it had fallen to the floor. "But it's my job. She retired."

"I am sorry, but Mrs. Wilson was here first. The town still thinks of her as the teacher."

"It's been years. I'm the teacher now. I love teaching," she said, voice unsteady.

The mayor winced. "You're not, ah… Mrs. Wilson is a member of the *community*. A respected member of the church. She taught half this town. People still expect the lessons to be how she made them."

"I have the training for this job. I go to the conferences every summer. I'm qualified."

"Yes, I've heard about what you've been teaching. Dangerous ideas. You understand that our students shouldn't be in here learning about witchcraft."

Nora Jo flinched like she had been stabbed. "Witchcraft?"

Had someone discovered the little spells she did to protect the classroom? Had Harlow been seen visiting her that night?

Neese gestured to her desk where *The Wonderful Wizard of Oz* was splayed open. "When did schools stop teaching the Bible? That college of yours has some funny ideas."

"Mr. Neese, my curriculum is meant to help all my students. I plan it carefully. This is their chance to learn about the world outside the Bible."

"There is no world outside the Bible," Neese said, voice hard.

He sighed and lifted a hand to her shoulder, but she sidestepped it. "Your pa was worried when I first offered you this position. I told him then that you were the right choice until you had the chance to find a husband. It was never meant to be permanent."

"You never said that."

"I didn't think I needed to."

"My dad has nothing to do with this," Nora Jo said. "I'm a grown woman. I haven't lived my life by his whims in a long time, since well before he died."

"Regardless. You could take this time to settle down," he told her. "If after what happened with your grandmother—"

"Will people ever stop harping on about that?" Nora Jo asked. "It happened before I was even born. Grandma Gwen left Chatuga. I don't *want* to leave. I'm not like her. You're *making* me leave." Her voice broke on the last word.

"You don't have to leave Chatuga," Neese said. "We just want to make sure we have the best teacher for those kids."

"And that's not me," she said. "Because I'm young, and went to school for this, and brought in new ideas? You've got to see that you're being unreasonable."

"Our teacher needs to be a part of this town. You keep to yourself. You're twenty-six and unmarried. You've been living with Miss Ethel all this time instead of finding your own home."

"Miss Ethel hasn't asked me to leave," Nora Jo said, but uncertainty lanced through her. Surely Miss Ethel hadn't complained about her to the mayor?

Nora Jo wasn't a stranger to being betrayed by those close to her. Miss Ethel *had* just hired the new girl. There were always conditions to affection.

"I'm a good teacher," she said numbly. "These kids need me."

"They'll have Mrs. Wilson. I'm just trying to do what's best for everyone—including you. You deserve some time to find yourself. See what life has to offer beyond your books."

"Don't you dare pretend you're doing this for me." Her voice trembled. "All I've ever wanted is to teach. I worked my whole life for this."

"I'm sorry, Miss Nora Jo. Mrs. Wilson is ready to come back tomorrow," Neese said. "She'll take care of your students. We have to think of the moral upbringing of the town."

Nora Jo stared at him. She wanted to scream, wanted to beg, wanted him to say to her face just what everyone had been saying about her, but she swallowed her arguments like a bitter tonic. A knot of rage twisted in her chest, hot and burning, with nowhere to go but deeper inside.

It was a quiet afternoon, with a clear sky overhead. A crow sat on a branch overlooking the small courtyard in front of the school. Its dark eyes were like knives slicing into Nora Jo. Considering her life was being brushed away on a whim, the world around her looked so normal.

"You're making a mistake," she said. "*This* is why my granny left this town."

It was the wrong thing to say. Neese sighed as if she were a toddler throwing a tantrum. "Don't break your brother's heart by following in her footsteps," he warned. "There's more in this world for a woman than a classroom."

"There's more in this world for *me* than sitting under my family's thumb," she said.

Her words only seemed to harden Neese's resolve. "Family is all we have. We've made our decision, Miss Nora Jo. I hope you find your way."

"This was supposed to be my way." Nora Jo took a shaky breath. "What will you tell my students?"

"The truth," Neese said. "They'll go back to Bible study with Mrs. Wilson. Soon, they'll grow out of the classroom, just as you have. Seasons change, Miss Nora Jo. I hope to see you change with them. If not, I'm sure there will be other towns looking for teachers."

He left. Nora Jo looked at the big empty room, the rows of benches that would be filled with the small faces of her students tomorrow. She wouldn't be there to see them.

She went to her chair at the front of the room, curled over her knees, and cried.

When she pounded on the front door, Beau's wife Ruth answered. "Nora Jo?" she asked, surprised. She wore a red cotton dress with a white apron tied in place over it. It must be suppertime. Nora Jo had lost track of the passing hours. Ruth, closer to Nora Jo's age than her brother's, seemed like she was playing at maturity. They were both well into marrying age, but that life felt far away from Nora Jo.

She remembered, suddenly, what she'd thought the first day Ruth had come to school. It was rare for them to get new students. Mrs. Wilson told them they would have another classmate joining, and then Ruth Shore had walked in. Her hair fell in blonde ringlets around her shoulders, pulled back from her face by a blue bandana. She looked perfect, like some angel stepping into their small valley classroom. Blood rushed to Nora Jo's face, and a giddy energy sizzled like soda pop in her chest. She had no friends in the classroom. Perhaps this girl would change that.

That hope had quickly proven false. Ruth became close friends with the town's insular rich kids, Oliver Chadwick Jr. and the older Posoff boy. They never offered Nora Jo anything but laughing whispers. Nora Jo ignored Ruth's bullying and pretended she'd never imagined anything else.

"Where's Beau?" Nora Jo demanded. She had stayed in the schoolhouse for a long time, but she knew her face was still flushed and swollen.

"Ruthie, who—" Her brother came up behind Ruth, putting a hand on her shoulder. "Nora Jo? What are you doing here?"

"You," she said, pointing at him. "You did this."

"What are you talking about?"

"Don't pretend like you don't know," she snarled. "You never could stand to lose an argument. Couldn't you just let me be happy?"

"Ruth, go check on dinner," Beau said. Ruth looked between them, frowning, but went. Beautiful and obedient, the type of wife Beau wanted Nora Jo to become.

Beau stepped onto the porch, closing the door behind him. His house, small with graying edges from age, was tucked away from the road. Tall oaks cast long shadows, blocking the lowering sun. When his wife was gone, he said, "What are you talking about?"

"I was just let go, Beau," she snapped. "They took away my school. The mayor came by and spouted some horseshit about it being time for me to move on. Sound familiar?"

He shook his head. "I don't know what you're talking about."

"I'm not a fool. You never liked me working there, and you have dinner with the mayor all the time." As the town's blacksmith, Beau had inherited their father's broad influence. "If you said the right thing, you could get Neese to go along with it. But it was a mistake. They *need* me. I'm good at it. I know how smart the kids are. I know how much they have to fight to learn. The farms and mills are always calling them away."

What would happen without her there to push them or argue for them? How long would Carson Call's dad continue to make the trip down from the mountains with his son? She was in the middle of convincing Goldie Lee to pursue nursing instead of getting married next year; her future could still fall in any direction.

"This could be a sign," Beau suggested. "There's more to life than learning. For you and for them."

"This job was all I wanted."

"Nora Jo, I know Dad pushed you too hard to marry, but it's time to stop living to spite him. He's gone now, and you deserve happiness," Beau said, earnestness bright on his face. "Being married... It's swell. Maybe it's your time. Haven't you ever met someone who made you curious?"

She had. But that wouldn't redeem her in the town's eyes. "You're such a condescending ass."

He held up his hands. "Fine, sorry. What are you going to do now? How will you pay rent?"

"I... don't know." Nora Jo clutched at the fabric of her neckline, fighting for breath. What would she do? Miss Ethel was kind, but Nora Jo was her tenant, not her friend. Without rent, how long would she let Nora Jo stay?

"You could live here. If you need to."

"Oh, I'm sure you'd love that. You think this proves you right," she said. "You never thought I could do this. You never thought I could survive on my own."

He reached out, but his hand fell away without touching her. No matter Beau's dreams for a new version of their family, they had never had that soft comfort, the casual touch of skin, an understanding of the cycle of seasons in the other's head. Carefully, he asked, "Can you?"

She stared into his dark brown eyes. They had grown up in the same small house, but he was a stranger to her. "Go back inside with Ruth. Enjoy your dinner," Nora Jo said, shaking her head and turning away from him. "I'll find a way. I'll figure this out on my own."

He called her name, but she left without looking back.

Nora Jo couldn't face returning to Miss Ethel's house. Instead, she walked the streets of Chatuga, circling the roads that curled around the center of town like the rim of a wheel. The familiar dirt felt foreign beneath her shoes. She'd thought she had found her place here. But her plans had ended with the finality of a bullet. Such an abrupt, undignified ending to the dream of years.

What next? She could give up her career and ask the gristmill for her old job in administration. She could leave Chatuga behind, find another town looking to hire a teacher. Both options tasted sour.

Her feet ached. She wandered until sunset painted the sky orange and yellow, bright and explosive. She held onto her sharp fury at the mayor, her brother, and the entire town—because lurking below it, the rejection lapped against her heart like an ice-cold sea, waiting for her to fall headlong into its depths. Without the energy of anger to push her forward, she would drown in desolation. The unfairness of it all choked her.

The truth was that Nora Jo wanted Beau's life.

It was the life so many men had; quiet and alone with their wives. Their own land, their own space, their own passions, none of it dictated by the town. Tennessee was proud of its independence. But that independence only applied to men—and to white ones at that.

Nora Jo had been a fool to dream of building a life on her own terms here.

But perhaps there was still a way for her to forge her own path.

Wilbur and Torie Lye lived south of town along one of the central spokes out of Main Street. Nora Jo had only ever spoken to them in passing, but their names had been on everyone's lips two years ago. Their only son had been killed in France during the war. Now, they boarded the extra room to travelers.

Grief radiated off the house like a raincloud, washing the lane in gray. Nora Jo hesitated outside. If she wanted to defy Mayor Neese's assumptions, coming so late hadn't been a wise idea.

But she had nowhere else to go.

She knocked on the door. Wilbur answered. A straw hat covered his thinning hair, and he had ragged white whiskers on his chin.

"Evening, Mr. Lye. I'm looking for Mr. Harlow." She blinked, trying to recall how long it had been since Harlow had appeared at Miss Ethel's door. He'd said he would only stay in town for a week or two. "Is he still here?"

"He is," Wilbur said, cautious. He looked like he had forgotten how to smile. "I didn't know he knew anyone here. He keeps to himself."

"He's a new acquaintance."

"Well, come on in. You can wait in here while I go grab Everett from his room."

Inside, the house was subdued. The white paint was cracked on the doorways, peeling along the edges to reveal the wood beneath. A stuffed buck's head was mounted on the wall in the living room, glass eyes staring down.

Harlow stepped in from the back hallway. Wilbur hesitated, looking between them, then slipped past them into the kitchen. There was a window in the wall, so he could keep an eye on them while giving the semblance of privacy.

"Miss Nora Jo," Harlow said. "This is an unexpected pleasure."

"You're still here," she pointed out.

He tilted his head in acknowledgement. "I had hopes. You changed your mind?"

That was the question, wasn't it? She had come across town fueled by the need to act. Her agency had been snatched from her hands. She needed control, and no one else here would give it to her.

After her failed experiment trying to heal Miss Ethel, she'd put Harlow's offer from her mind. She had a career and a life in Chatuga; she'd had no need of an apprenticeship. The situation had changed, but did she truly want to be trained in witchcraft by this stranger? She too could end up living alone on inhospitable Old Blue, separated from the rest of Tennessee by miles of thick forest and superstition.

Tonight, that felt ideal.

"Is your offer still open?" Nora Jo asked. "I seem to have found myself in need of a new job."

11

OLIVER

Sweat slid down Oliver's face like the unwanted touch of a stranger. His hands, gone soft after months of rest, were already raw and sore from the brief work. The dirt was coarse from days without rain, and the tangled weeds were strong and covered in thorns. He jerked the mass of roots up, but they grasped the ground like the desperate fingers of a drowning man. He hacked at them with his ma's spade. Recently whetted, the blade sliced quickly through the mess. Finally pulling the roots free, he tossed them onto a pile nearby. Clumps of dirt rained onto the grass.

While his pa ran one of the two mills that kept Chatuga alive, his ma was in charge of the small farm attached to their land. It was unprofitable, but the flush of living plants gave her a purpose. While Oliver was away, his family had hired help from Tolbert-Vance to maintain it, but his pa let them go as soon as Oliver returned to American soil. He still believed that Oliver was helping with the vegetables and livestock. He wasn't home often enough to realize the burden of the entire farm had fallen onto his wife's shoulders. Ma, bless her heart, kept the fiction alive.

Age, however, was beginning to slow her down. When Oliver came home from the war, new lines creased her forehead like cracks in drought-stricken dirt, clawing beside her eyes and framing her mouth. She flexed her hands when she thought no one was watching, and often rubbed at her left hip.

When that morning she had sighed and cautiously said, "Junior, honey, will you help weed today?", Oliver hadn't been able to say no.

The weeds were more entrenched than he'd expected. Ma was falling behind with the upkeep. Small leaves and roots and thorns lurked under the shade of the spring vegetables, huddling near the dirt like conspirators.

The sun was merciless on the back of his neck. When he first stepped outside, it had been early, and a westerly breeze came to brush his hair from his eyes. Now, stooped beside the house, he could only feel the heat.

Oliver could push through. He would not be bested by weeds.

The cough, when it came, wracked his entire body, clawing from his throat like a living thing. He fought for breath, clutching his chest as though to push the air back inside.

There was a moment every time his lungs rebelled when Oliver wondered if it would be the final time. Before and after the spasms, he wished it would be. In the moment, as his body screamed for air, all he wanted was to live.

He collapsed forward onto the dirt, his face striking the spade with a sudden slash of pain. He pressed forward more firmly into the metal, focusing on the discomfort. His breath rattled like he was dying. It was a sound he'd heard too many times. He closed his eyes, remembering the way the noise faded into silence.

Tucker Lee's green eyes were bloodshot and watering as he wheezed his final breath. There was nothing Oliver could do.

Finally, finally, the shuddering subsided. He gasped for air, the warm rush burning his throat.

He sat up on his heels and spat over and over, clearing the mucus that clogged his mouth. He wiped the back of his hand over his lips. A bright spot of blood smeared his dirt-stained skin. He frowned, touching his lips with shaking fingers. Then he registered the pulse of pain on his face. He'd cut his cheek against the spade when he collapsed.

He went back inside, leaving the bloodstained spade on the upturned dirt.

Ma looked up from the kitchen counter. The emotion in her eyes was too much to bear. It was like her heart was breaking at the sight of him. He went upstairs without a word, turning his face away.

It took an hour for Oliver's hands to stop shaking. His throat remained so raw he might have been swallowing thistles instead of coughing. He could hear Ma moving downstairs. Would she finish the failed job for him? Surely she was as frustrated with Oliver's weakness as he was.

They had all thought he would be better by now. The doctors had been vague, too focused on the boys coming home missing limbs to worry about the boys with just a cough. By the end of the war, everyone had been exhausted.

Who had been luckier? Oliver, for surviving the mud and bullets and grenades and gas? Or Tucker Lee, for only coughing his way into death once?

With unsteady hands, he patted the bronze cigarette case in his pocket. Then, he slammed his fist into the nearest wall, denting the layer of paint over the wood. What self-pitying bullshit. Tucker Lee would have smacked him for that. He'd always shown his affection by gently abusing Oliver, whacking him upside the head or punching him in the arm. What would Tucker Lee say now, seeing Oliver defeated by his ma's garden?

What a fool Oliver was to wonder. He knew better than anyone that spirits were simply shades of the past, faded and strange. Tucker Lee would be as mindless as the rest, lost to Oliver in every way.

Only…

Could it have been a ghost who traced the message in the frost the other morning? That nightmare—that ghost—had tried to communicate with him. He didn't know what to trust, but it had looked so *real*. And the frost had come from inside his room.

Maybe some ghosts were capable of breaking away from the patterns of their lives to seek out the living.

Oliver looked at the window. He was pale in the reflection, other than the dark smear of blood on his cheek. The day was still bright and sunny outside. Against the clear blue sky, the smear of the message Oliver had wiped from the frost earlier that week was still visible, blurring the view behind it.

Was it possible to send messages to and from the other side?

Before the war, Oliver had never had much cause to think of death. There were the chickens they slaughtered, the elderly relatives they said farewell to during rote ceremonies, but death was a distant event, a tragedy that happened to others.

Oliver was one of two men from Chatuga to sign up for the

war—and the only one to come home. With the mountain folks' predisposition for isolation, the far-off war had no appeal. Oliver, though, had seen a chance at glory. When he'd realized that all the cold mud held was terror, the only thing that made it survivable was Tucker Lee Selecky.

Now he was gone, and Oliver was alone in a new hell. The endless death that haunted his mind dogged his footsteps as well, leaving nowhere safe. His body was tattered and threadbare.

Tucker Lee had been in his arms. One moment, the boy he'd known was there. The next, only a body remained. Tucker Lee had gone somewhere in that moment. Oliver had assumed that somewhere was far out of his reach, an unknowable shore.

But what if that distance could be crossed?

If he was going to be haunted for the rest of his days, he should at least be able to speak to Tucker Lee one last time. Apologize. Beg forgiveness. With that, maybe living would be worth it after all.

But how?

Oliver was as blind to the path forward as others were to the ghosts themselves. The glimpses he caught of the lingering spirits were a mystery. He didn't know why he saw them, or what caused those souls to remain. Were there others who could see them? If he asked around, his pa would quickly silence him. Having a layabout for a son was one thing. It was another to have a madman.

But he could talk to Tucker Lee again. And that thought, that thought alone, made something inside Oliver crack open like a new sprout and stretch toward the sky.

There was a chance. And that meant Oliver had to find a way.

Thoughtfully, he reached up to touch the cut on his face. The bleeding had stopped while he slept, but the trail it left was cold and tacky. A cut by his eye. Just where the girl in the woods had predicted.

No one else could see the ghosts or tell him how to talk to them. But he had met someone who knew the future. Perhaps that would be enough.

He could make this one thing right.

12

NORA JO

Rain pounded the forest around them. The storm raged and howled, desperate as a mourning mother. Nora Jo peeked out from under the overhang at the dark sky overhead, taking a breath of the damp, cool air. The leaves of the pawpaw trees in the grove outside rattled as they were pelted by the rain. "It's tornado season," she warned.

"There won't be one tonight," Harlow said. He was feeding a growing fire, tossing in logs that hadn't been dry when they collected them. Now, they crackled and popped in the orange flames, lighting with supernatural speed. Harlow used magic like breathing, changing the world around him to smooth his way. It was like nothing she had ever seen before.

After Nora Jo had agreed to become his apprentice, he had drawn her a map in smeared charcoal directing her to this spot in the woods. After a day of dodging Miss Ethel's pitying eyes—news of her job had spread fast—she'd snuck from the house once the old woman was asleep.

"How do you know?"

"Knowing the weather is one of the things I'll teach you," Harlow said. "The power in the air tonight ain't that flavor. It tastes like water and lightning, nothing else."

Nora Jo frowned, then opened her mouth and breathed in deeply. She could smell the storm, the scent of mud and wet leaves from the surrounding forest. Would she be able to taste electricity someday?

She had spent the day second-guessing her decision to learn from Harlow. Her ma had kept her witchcraft secret and small. What good could come of Nora Jo's new knowledge? But then she looked at the empty, purposeless days ahead of her without her career, and her resolve was renewed.

"Come," Harlow said. "The fire is nearly ready."

Nora Jo left the cool outside air and moved deeper into the overhang. The storm wind was faint here, blocked by the towering stone around them. The smoke from the blazing fire hung heavy in the air, thick as shadows.

"It will help to know where you're starting. What magic have you done with fire so far?"

She shook her head. "I've never used anything bigger than a candle," she said. "And even then—I don't know if any of it worked. My ma died when I was twelve. I never had time to learn more."

"Nothing?"

Nora Jo twisted her hands. "Small things. Cleansing rituals. Good luck charms. Anything more than that, I never learned, or it didn't work." She stared at the fire. "I tried. When my ma was dying, my pa and brother didn't know what to do. They left her to me. She'd lost another baby, and it made her really sick. We'd tried some spells she'd learned from my Granny Rhodes, who was a midwife, but the miscarriages kept happening. When she fell asleep and wouldn't wake up, I brewed a potion she'd taught me. I put it under her pillow. She'd told me that when the jar turned black, it would take the illness with it."

"But she didn't make it," Harlow deduced.

"No. My pa caught on and smashed it. Told me to stop playing like a child and to listen to the doctor. He told me I was going to kill her faster with my foolishness." Nora Jo looked up at the soot gathering on the stone ceiling overhead. "I'll never know if he was right, or if I could have saved her. She died that night."

"I'm right sorry to hear that," Harlow said.

"I want to learn," Nora Jo said. "I thought I'd lost my chance, but it's time. I want to know what you know."

Harlow nodded and gestured to the dancing flames. "Fire is a source of pure energy, heat given life. It carries secrets in its depths. It reflects the truth of things, both past and present. With enough training, you'll be able to read its language."

Nora Jo parsed that. "I can use the fire to see the future?"

There were many ways to try to glimpse the future—dropping apple peels in a barrel of water to see a future spouse's initial, looking to omens in farm animals for the gender of a new child— but they were wrong as often as they were right.

"Being able to see the future clearly is a rare and powerful gift," Harlow said. "For most of us, it's an intangible thing. The best you or I could do is glimpse parts of its shape. I'll teach you what to look for. You'll find symbols, the kinds of images that mean something to a generation. Flowers for love—or death. An apple for sin, or knowledge, or both." He shrugged when she gave him a look.

"They take interpretation. You have to keep your mind open to the possibilities."

"If nothing has a clear meaning, then no one can ever prove you wrong," Nora Jo pointed out. She'd like her future printed on a fire-seared paper, listing out what was to come. "In hindsight, I'm sure you could find all sorts of new meanings in the symbols to make them true."

"Surely so," Harlow said easily. "That doesn't mean the symbols weren't there."

Nora Jo hummed. She'd tried to explain symbolism to her students, but literature tended to be one of their more difficult subjects. Her students were smart, but they had been prepared from a young age to take over their families' farms. Idle speculation and metaphorical thinking were not encouraged. She sniffed the air. "Is there something extra in the fire?"

"Good nose," he said. "Sage leaves, for one. Pine needles. A few other things. You could see visions in any fire, but the herbs will encourage your mind to open." He picked up a long stick and nudged the base of the fire. A log fell out of place with a crash, and new life swelled in the heart of the flames. "Magic is as much about tradition as it is about spells. There's power in repetition. If your granny spat apple seeds into the fire, that's the method you'll have luck with. You'll believe it's going to work—you have generations of experience telling you that—so for you, it does."

Had Granny Rhodes ever tried to predict the future in a crackling fire? Nora Jo's legacy sat behind her, obscured by death and silence. She put a hand on her ring, wondering what her past held.

"What do you see in the fire, Nora Jo?"

The bright light was scalding compared to the utter darkness beyond the overhang. She must have looked a fool. She sighed. "Flames. Just flames."

"Did you ever stare at clouds when you were younger?" He stared at the smoke swirling toward the ceiling. "I used to watch the sky and imagine other worlds."

"Sometimes." When her ma had been alive and Nora Jo had still been frivolous.

"To see things, you have to loosen the elastic of your mind. There's no right answer. Just try." He glanced over at her, eyes dancing. "I swear that I won't place any bets based on what you say. I'm a gambling man, but I have my limits."

Nora Jo frowned at the fire. "Maybe this isn't part of my power."

"Your magic is still underformed. Unused. Without help, it'll stay dormant. Our goal is to help it emerge." From his belt, he pulled out a blade.

She started, jolting backward. How foolish had she been to agree to meet this man in the woods alone?

"Double-edged obsidian," he said, watching the dark blade reflect the firelight. "A black handle for ringing bells and pulling magic from blood. All witches need one—along with a white-handled one for cutting herbs. You'll need to learn how to use each. Some magic shouldn't touch." He flipped the blade and offered the hilt to her.

She didn't take it. "What's this for?"

"The power's in you. It's a root we're trying to dig up."

She stared at the knife. "I thought we'd just quote Scripture. Doesn't the Bible help ward off demons? Ain't they attracted to magic? My ma used to say that."

When her ma kneaded bread, she would murmur a line from John: "This is the bread that comes down from heaven, so that one may eat of it and not die." The Bible was the backbone of Chatuga. Read from the pulpit, whispered in the kitchen, proclaimed over fresh graves—taught now in Nora Jo's old classroom.

"Even the Devil can cite Scripture," Harlow said. "Like I said, power comes from belief. If the Bible speaks to you, if the tradition gives you faith in your magic, then that's what you need to quote. But if your strength comes from within, as I think yours does..." He waved the blade at her, hilt first. He knew her answer. "Slice your forearm. Sprinkle some blood into the flames. The energy has to come from somewhere."

"And it has to be my blood?" she asked tentatively.

"No." Harlow's voice had a sardonic edge. "But is there someone else's blood you'd rather use?"

Carefully, she took the blade from him. She held it over the pale, tender flesh of her arm.

"You've had worse cuts from splinters," he said. "Stop thinking. Let the magic use you. There are things that want to communicate with us, if we let them. This is what you'll have to learn."

Taking a deep breath, Nora Jo pressed down. The blade parted her skin easily. It was so sharp, she could have just brushed the knife against her arm and would still have made a cut. The slice went deeper than she'd hoped, and a line of blood welled to the surface.

"Flick it into the fire," Harlow prompted. "Don't waste it."

She shook her arm, and dark blood dripped into the flames.

"Focus. Let the future speak to you."

Brushing off her sickly unease, she focused on the fire. It seemed to have grown with the addition of her blood, roiling over the ground. "I see…" Nora Jo stared at the flames. Orange and yellow and black and white danced together, flickering and shifting. One of the logs beneath popped, and sparks sprayed out like stars. "Clasped hands."

"Good," Harlow murmured.

The flames shivered again. She watched them dance, letting her mind wander. "Bells ringing. No, they're not bells. It's lily-of-the-valley." Her ma had loved the small white flowers. Her eyes ached from staring at the bright heat, a quiet mirror to the throb in her arm. The smoke was becoming overwhelming, and she breathed shallowly so she wouldn't cough. The flames flickered again, caught in a draft from the storm outside. "Chains."

The smoke blew into her eyes, and she turned away, finally giving into the cough scratching her throat. She scrubbed at her eyes. Green and purple impressions from the fire echoed against the dark night.

When she straightened, she looked over at Harlow, who was watching her thoughtfully.

"Was that real?" she asked. "What did that mean?"

He had a hand on his clean-shaven chin, eyes narrowed. "Those symbols are all messages of bonding and cooperation. A life-changing meeting, and a deep union." He gave her a small smile. It eased the lines of his stern face. "Probably for our new partnership."

"That was… I didn't expect to see anything. But I did. It was there, waiting for me."

"Now that you've seen some of what's there, sit down and I'll tell you about the different images you may see and what they might mean." He clicked his tongue. "And give me your arm— you've cut yourself deep. I'll patch it up."

*

When the storm finally slowed, Nora Jo snuck back to Miss Ethel's house, careful to avoid the loose floorboards. It was still dark, though dawn was near. Her skin was sticky with the rain and sweat, the hair clinging to the back of her neck still smelling of smoke. A bandage was wrapped around her forearm to cover the thick, cool salve from Harlow.

She felt exhausted. And exhilarated.

Losing her position at the school had made the future nebulous and frightening. Control had been snatched from her hands, her plans crushed into dust.

But with Harlow's guidance, she would take back her fate.

13

KATE

"Why do you keep staring at me?"

Kate blinked and looked down at her half-eaten eggs, then back up at Eileen. "I wasn't," she lied. "Why would I look at you?"

Eileen raised her eyebrows, skeptical.

Since Kate's vision, she'd been stuck on its shocking images like a wheel in a rut. Every repeat of the memory carved the sight of Eileen's terrified face more deeply into her mind.

She'd hated her visions before, had seen terrible things, but nothing could compare to this. At least when she'd seen Mary Evelyn's accident on that horrible day years ago, it hadn't been her own hands.

What would drive such a horrible wedge between them? Had it already begun?

What could happen to make Kate kill her own sister?

"You've been acting weird," Eileen told her. She glanced down the table at Mama and Daddy, then said, "Maybe you ain't getting enough sleep?"

Had Eileen noticed Kate watching her at night? She always seemed sound asleep. Or worse—had she noticed Kate's nighttime journey to search for Oliver?

"Pass me the gravy." Mary Evelyn stretched her hand across the table.

"Please," Kate corrected, and handed over the gravy boat. The thick cream wobbled dangerously above the scarred wooden surface of the table, but it arrived at Mary Evelyn's plate without incident.

"And more sausage?" Mary Evelyn asked.

Kate met Eileen's eyes. They both looked at the final sausage patty sitting on the platter. Kate lunged forward and stabbed it with her fork, snatching it from Eileen's reach.

"She's eleven. She doesn't need two sausages," Eileen complained.

"She asked for it first," Kate said, putting it on Mary Evelyn's plate.

"You baby her."

Everyone at the table knew why Kate went easy on Mary Evelyn. Even sitting, Kate couldn't look at their youngest sister without seeing her missing leg.

Kate glowered at Eileen, stung. "Maybe I just like her better than you."

"Girls," Mama scolded, not looking away from her conversation with Daddy. Kate and Eileen murmured insincere apologies. Mary Evelyn ducked her head and ate her sausage.

During the spring and summer, these breakfasts happened in the hour just after dawn. Soft golden light swept through the window. The rich, salt-etched smell of eggs, gravy, and sausage was heavy in the air, along with the alluring scent of fresh biscuits. It was far more pleasant than winter, when breakfast was a hushed scene in the dark, everyone blinking slowly and searching for the energy to step into the snow. If it weren't for Mama waking before them all to get the fire going and breakfast sizzling, they might all sleep through their responsibilities.

Kate scraped up the last bright yellow remains of her egg yolk with her biscuit, and said, "I need to get moving. I have to get to Mrs. Riley's." She stood up and took her dishes to the sink. With Miss Ethel added to her work list, Kate was kept busy from morning to dusk.

Eileen began complaining about her own job, but since she worked with Uncle Christopher's chickens in exchange for their supply of eggs and meat, she didn't even have to deal with clients. Kate ignored her, dropped a kiss on her parents' cheeks, and walked out of the house.

By the time Kate left her three-hour morning shift with Mrs. Riley, her palms were dyed a deep indigo. Mrs. Riley made lace, tatting dollies and table runners along with collars and cuffs that could be sewn onto basic dresses. Her business, which was run mostly via tradesmen through Nashville, had grown bigger than she could manage on her own, so she hired Kate once or twice a week to help.

Mrs. Riley saved the worst jobs for Kate. That morning, she'd stripped the bark from the trio of dogwoods in the yard. Their delicate white flowers were just in bloom, heralding spring. While Mrs. Riley industriously tatted on the front porch, Kate stood over a hot fire in the corner of the Rileys' small kitchen boiling the bark. The strips of white slowly turned the water blue, making them look like bones floating in a lake.

Compared to Mrs. Riley's kitchen, the outside air was cool as she made her way back toward Tolbert-Vance for her next job. She was traveling on one of the northern roads, framed by a cornfield on one side and a cow pasture on the other. It was still muddy from last night's storm, splashing the hem of her dress. On Sundays, the dirt road was crowded with white folk heading to church, but it was empty today. At least there was a breeze. The dog days of summer were not far off, and everyone appreciated the lingering spring. The wind played with the hairs along Kate's forehead that had escaped her bun, lifting and teasing them.

"Georgia Kate!"

Kate looked up and blinked. For a moment, she was sure she'd fallen into another trance—nearly every time she'd seen Oliver Chadwick Jr.'s face, it had been during one of her episodes. But the sky was the same clear blue overhead, and the world was solid beneath her feet. The man himself was approaching her, hand raised.

"It's just Kate." She hid her stained hands behind her back. "How'd you find me?"

"I just came from Tolbert-Vance," Oliver said, gesturing vaguely. How many times had Oliver Chadwick Jr. been to Tolbert-Vance? Some white folks lived there—though not many—and others came through for business, but there was an invisible barrier between Kate's neighborhood and the rest of Chatuga. "I've been looking for you."

"Why? You made your opinion awfully clear."

He looked around, but the road was still empty. He stepped closer. "I need answers, and I think you're the only one who can give them to me." When she didn't respond, he said, "You were right." He pointed to his cheek, where a dark cut marred his skin, a crescent on his cheekbone.

"I'm not feeling very kindly to my visions at the moment."

Oliver shifted, and her vision of this moment clicked into place. He reached toward her, but let his hand fall down to his side. "I need you," he said. His mismatched eyes were bright under the clear sky, piercing through her.

The familiarity passed, leaving Kate stumbling in unknown territory again. That was one of the moments she'd held close to her chest on the long nights when she sat in the laurel grove, waiting for him. His hand, reaching toward her. His voice, gentle and urgent, as he begged for her.

Disappointment sat sour in her chest. This wasn't what she'd imagined.

"You're the only person I can ask." He glanced around again. "I can't talk about this here."

"You think the corn is listening?" she asked, gesturing to the short stalks rustling beside them.

He frowned. "What happened to your hands?"

Kate tucked them behind her back again. "You didn't believe me before. What changed?"

"It'll take time to explain. I'll tell you, but if anyone sees us together, there would be rumors all over town by tonight."

"I know," she said. "I hope you weren't shouting my name all over Tolbert-Vance."

"I'm not stupid. I was hoping to spot you from the street," he said, showing there was some lick of sense in his brain. "Let's meet in that clearing again tonight. The one where you found me."

"Fine," Kate said. "I have to get to work now. You can find your way back home. You should keep out of my neighborhood."

"Midnight," he said as she continued past him.

"Midnight," she murmured, not turning back to look at him.

14

OLIVER

The trek back from his search for Kate was difficult. He had to stop more than once, even needing to steady himself against a fence post at one point. His lungs rattled as he walked up the porch steps to his house, and he paused to cough, leaning against the railing. It was late afternoon, and the sun was golden over the fields around their farm. His horse, Magnolia, nickered at the fence, a familiar sound corrupted by the shudder of his coughs.

He had only ridden her once since he returned to Tennessee. He'd been grateful to bury his face in her familiar neck, but he couldn't stay seated on her back for long before having to jump off to catch his breath. She'd stayed still as he leaned against her, eyes watering. In the end, he'd returned her to the pasture on foot. One more of his old activities he had to leave behind.

Was he truly the same boy who had sprinted through this town and the surrounding mountains from dawn to dusk only a few years ago? He felt cored out. And he still had to find the energy to go back into the woods at midnight.

He napped fitfully for a few hours, seeing Tucker Lee's death again each time his mind began to drift. It was like a dent in the wheel of a bike, a sharp, jarring clunk that came back around with every pedal forward.

The more Oliver became unmoored from a standard sleep schedule, the more time at large seemed to slip away from him. The light outside his window was the only sign of how much of the day had passed—he woke in golden afternoons, gray mornings, blue evenings, and deep in black nights.

When he smelled the familiar signs of supper floating up from the kitchen, he was as exhausted as before he'd slept.

Supper at the Chadwick home was always quiet. Ma had always wanted more children, but Oliver was the only one to make it out of infanthood. Pa ate with the solemn determination of a gravedigger shoveling a new hole.

The food was good, though each bite threatened to stick in his sore throat. Ma had used freshly ground Chadwick flour to make chicken and dumplings, and their cows kept them in fresh milk to drink. There was a stocked wine cellar in the basement, but Pa refused to let anyone but important dinner guests touch it since the prohibition laws.

After dinner, Pa leaned back in his chair and complained about the rising prices of land around Chatuga. He was tall and flushed, capillaries running like the forks of a stream across his cheeks before disappearing under his beard. The redness worsened when he was frustrated, making his eyes, the same split colors as Oliver's, pink at the edges.

"You know, when my pa first came here, Chatuga was barely a blip on the map. Now, you can't spit without hitting someone trying to take a piece for himself. That's what the Chadwicks brought to this town. For all the gratitude we get for it."

Chatuga had first been settled back in 1819. Last year, there'd been a parade to celebrate the centennial. Oliver imagined fireworks over the fields, a row of officials marching through Main Street, schoolchildren cheering. It would have been a robust celebration. The town was full of men who hadn't shipped themselves overseas to be shot.

For its first few decades, Chatuga was a small settlement, just another stop in the foothills before the mountains. It wasn't until 1869, when Oliver's grandpa founded the Chadwick Mill, that the community truly settled in. Barely older than Oliver was now, Herman Chadwick set himself up to become one of the richest men in the region. Producing cornmeal for most of the small towns in traveling distance, the gristmill was the heart of a small empire. Most families had arrived in town then, the promise of money and work luring them from the fields and mountains to cluster around the mill.

Pa seemed to be waiting for a response. "Yes, sir," Oliver said. His throat twinged, threatening another coughing fit.

"It's about time for Chadwick Mill to grow. Continue my pa's legacy. You planning on coming back soon?"

Oliver swallowed with difficulty. Even weeding had made him faint. What would a full day in the mill do to him?

The gristmill sat alongside Chestnut Creek near the center of town. A sixteen-foot rust-red waterwheel sat against the north wall, churning steadily. The machinery and heavy wooden beams inside were as familiar as his house. He'd gone to the mill after school every day, learning the ins and outs of the business. When he first returned home, he'd tried to work there, but the powder in the air sent his lungs back weeks in their early recovery. The loud pounding of the mill was near the boom of mortar. He hadn't been back since.

"Your ma doesn't think you're ready yet, but I told her a man needs work for his mind and soul. Idle hands are the Devil's plaything. You're ready, ain't you, Junior?" He watched Oliver like the men in the trenches watched dud grenades.

Oliver had known it would only be a matter of time before Pa got tired of his mooching. "I sure am—"

As though in protest, the cough that had been lingering at the back of his throat erupted forward. He wheezed and hacked, eyes blinded by sudden tears. He put one hand on his chest to try to hold in the spasms and held up the other, asking for his pa to wait. There was silence from across the table.

Oliver choked on every breath, even as he fought to rein himself under control. There was that wet rattle in his lungs again, obscene and visceral.

Finally, finally, he took a shallow inhale that didn't end with another cough. He sipped air with cautious desperation, terrified of losing it again.

When he finally looked up at Pa, he found the older Oliver Chadwick staring at him with a stone-carved expression.

"I don't recall you being this damn theatrical before the war," he said.

Oliver winced. "Pa, it's not—"

"I get your message. We're done here."

"Pa," Oliver tried again, but his throat closed and stopped him from speaking more.

Pa shook his head and stood up. "Tell me when you're ready to earn your keep."

Oliver held his breath until he heard the back door shut, and then another cough burst out. Ma was still at the table, but he couldn't look at her. He scrambled for the front door and out onto the porch. Another fit wracked through his body as the night air hit the back of his throat. It would help clear his chest, but it *ached*.

The door creaked open behind him. A hand rested on his back, small and firm.

He finally coughed his last, spat over the side of the railing, and turned to his ma. She handed him a glass of water. The water was piped in from a nearby spring, thick with the minerals he associated with home. In France, the taste of the water had been as unfamiliar as the landscape.

"Are you all right?"

Was he? "Sure." He drank the water and stared back out over the dark fields.

Ma settled into place beside him, leaning her forearms against the rail. "You know how he is."

Oliver just shrugged.

Ma was quiet for a while. Finally, she cleared her throat. "Did you go back to the general store today?"

"No." Hopefully the question meant that no one had seen his meeting with Kate. Gossip traveled faster than rain in Chatuga.

"Hm. You really don't care for Lula May Mathis, do you?"

"Ma," he complained, surprised out of his angst. "Really?"

"What? She's a sweet girl, and she's plumb sweet on you."

Oliver bowed his head. The rail was more chipped than it had been before he left for the war. Had they been waiting for him to return and help repair it? They would keep waiting. "You're so excited to push me off on some woman?"

"Junior," Ma chided. She sighed. "You could settle down. Give your pa another Chadwick to take on the family business."

Since Oliver had just proven once again that he couldn't be relied on to run the mill. "If you're tired of taking care of me, tell me. I don't need your help."

She looked down at the glass in his hand, his fingers clenched around it. He felt the glass quiver, and loosened his hold before it could shatter.

"I can survive on my own," he said. "You just have to ask."

"I love that you're home. You know how badly I missed you. But you don't think you'd be happier out from under your pa's thumb? Somewhere quiet with a wife?" Ma asked quietly.

"You think there's a wife who'd be happy with *me?*" He rubbed a hand over his chest again and looked away. Oliver decided he couldn't stand to hear her lie. "I'll go clean up the plates. Thanks for the water, Ma."

The last time Oliver took the path through the woods, he was chasing the damned bird that had stolen his cigarette case. He had been blind with fear. Now, he could appreciate the way the trail had changed since his youthful days of sneaking this way. The heart of it was the same, beaten into the earth by animals and people alike, but some parts were different, forcing him to pick his way through more carefully. A tree had fallen, demanding a detour around the roots that towered into the air from its base, still entwined with clumps of dirt.

When he reached the clearing across from the weeping willow, Kate Mayer was standing in the center, looking up at the sky. "A storm is coming in," she said. The moon, when it ducked through the clouds, soaked her rich blue-black skin in pale light.

Now that he wasn't so focused on his footfalls, he could feel the crackle of energy in the air. A warm breeze blew in from the west, brushing away the familiar scents of Chatuga. "Did you... *see* it?"

She scoffed. "I don't need a vision to tell me that those clouds are about to break open on us. So, what is it you wanted to talk about?"

Her attitude was different than their first meeting. He'd thought her reluctance that morning had been because of their location, the risk of being seen. When she'd first waited for him in this spot, she had been eager, curious, engaged. Now, her arms were crossed tightly over her yellow cotton dress.

Perhaps he *could* have been nicer. He hadn't known then that he would need her help, or that he might ever believe her claims that she could see the future. He reached up to brush a finger against the scab on his cheek. "You saw what was going to happen to me."

"You thought I was lying."

"Wouldn't you?" he said. "I needed time to think about it. To believe it."

"But now you do?"

He gestured to his face. "Well, you were right."

"Normally when someone doesn't want to believe, they'll bend over backward to find other explanations." She didn't unfold her arms. "You're sure I didn't hire someone to shove you into whatever door you walked into?"

"I'm not here to fight with you," he said, exasperated. "You can't trust that I believe you? This is what you wanted. You sought me out in the first place."

"Forgive me for being confused," she said. "This is a big change of heart."

"I can see ghosts." The words fell into the clearing like a mortar shell.

He'd never told anyone before. Who would he have told? Pa would think he was crazy. Ma might too, or worse, be worried sick. His friends here—well, none of them had felt compelled to enlist. Oliver was a different man now.

"Huh," Kate said thoughtfully. "Not what I expected."

"Have you met anyone like me?"

"I have an aunt who's a witch, down in Atlanta. I can dream true. That's all I know. I'm not an expert on any of this. The older I get, the less I understand it. Everything's been… wrong, lately." She looked away. "Honestly, I hoped you wouldn't show up again. I've got some visions I'd rather not see come to pass. I'd rather be wrong, sometimes."

Thunder rumbled in the distance, and the hair on the back of Oliver's neck stood up. The leaves rustled overhead in a sudden gust of wind. "Look, if we talk here, we'll be rained out at any moment. I don't want to rush through this conversation," he said. "I know a place nearby where we'll stay dry."

She frowned. "Whose place? I didn't know anyone lived out here."

"No one's. It should be empty—you'll understand when you see." He hesitated. "I know you don't know me, and you already took a risk coming out to meet me. If you'd rather wait until we can—"

She shook her head. "Nah. Just making sure you're not going to get us lost."

"I know these woods," he assured her. "Follow me." He glanced up at the dark sky, then led her out of the clearing, heading west. Whether she wanted to help or whether he had just sparked her interest, he wasn't sure, but at least he would not be left without answers.

The trail hadn't been maintained since he'd last used it. The trees and bushes sprawled into the path, branches tugging at his clothes. The wind slowed again, creating an ominous stillness around them.

"I can't see," Kate complained.

He reached back to take her hand, leading her forward. "Don't worry. I remember the way."

She fell silently into step behind him. Her hand was long and calloused, warm in his palm. It was like cradling a chick, soft and rough, delicate and alive. He kicked at a tangle of thorns that wrapped around his boot, stomping them down before leading Kate over them. Her boots were not as sturdy as his.

As they approached their destination, the path underfoot changed from dirt and dried leaves to small pieces of shale. The land began to incline, a slight hill leading up in the distance.

He glanced over his shoulder at Kate, who looked up from their clasped hands to meet his gaze. He smiled at her reassuringly, but she only frowned in return, as though leading her out of an oncoming storm was a personal attack, and she was angry at him for being there at all.

He tripped on a root, stumbling slightly. He turned back to the path, but could feel her eyes on the back of his head.

The clouds opened moments before they reached their destination. The raindrops were as warm and heavy as tears. A bright flash of light heralded a booming thunder that rattled through the trees. Oliver pulled Kate down a slope, their feet slipping in the mud, then finally spotted the dark smear at the base of the hill stretching above them. At night, the open space beneath the large stack of rocks was nearly invisible.

"In *there?*" Kate demanded.

"Would you rather stay out here?" Oliver asked, already crouching to duck through the gap. Barely visible, a set of moldering wooden stairs disappeared down into darkness.

Kate groaned but followed.

The stairs were slick with rainwater, so Oliver held Kate's hand as they descended. They had to duck their heads to avoid the low ceiling that dripped spikes of stone like teeth. His lungs were rattling from the brief run, so he kept his other palm pressed firm against the cold, slimy wall. If they slipped and fell, no one would find them.

By the time they made it down to the first flat level underground, the patter of rain seemed far away. The air was colder already, like they'd left the world above entirely. The thunder, when it came, bounced off the cave walls and sloping ceiling until it seemed to have no start or end. The faint light from outside barely illuminated the space; there was only solid blackness ahead.

Oliver fumbled in the dark. It had been years since he'd come here. Would there still be…?

His fingers brushed against curved glass. He reached up to lift the lantern by its wire handle, struck a match, and lit the wick inside. An orange light washed over them, casting vivid shadows on Kate's face. He was still unfamiliar with its lines, and the new contrast made her seem timeless and unknowable.

"Where are we?" she asked, turning to look around. The light glinted off the stalactites hanging overhead, their sharp points glistening with drops of water.

"Come on. I'll show you."

15

KATE

Oliver's hand still held hers tightly as they ducked under low ceilings through a narrow tunnel. She would have protested, but the light from the lantern was the only thing illuminating the uneven ground. There were dark gaps around the edges where the stone was stacked, and she couldn't tell if the fall was ten inches or ten feet. The caves could have twisted for miles beneath them. Noise was strange this far underground, echoing with the sound of water both above and below. It smelled strongly of the earth—damp stone and minerals. The stone around them was oddly smooth, curved as though shaped by massive, gentle hands.

"My parents always say that only fools go crawling into caves," Kate said. She kept her voice hushed—it seemed wrong to be too loud down here, like she was interrupting something natural and sacred.

"Fair enough, but we're not the first folks down here. There's a better room to sit in nearby. I've been here before. We won't go too much further in, but the water from the rain will come down the steps back there." Oliver glanced back at her, like he had in the woods—and in her vision of the woods. "Don't worry—the water drains to somewhere below. We won't get flooded. They say there's a lake in here if you go down far enough," he said. "I ain't been that deep."

"You ain't?"

He laughed dryly. "You think I'm a fool, Kate?"

"I certainly wouldn't say so." Though she might think it. "You seem like an explorer."

Kate knew Oliver had fought in the war overseas. He'd been one of the few to enlist from the white side of Chatuga, which was unusual enough for the news to go through Kate's neighborhood. The idea of the son of the richest family in town taking a boat across the ocean to fight on foreign soil had been baffling. Was there not enough trouble in Chatuga to be getting by with? Most of the soldiers from Tolbert-Vance were drawn in by the promise of money, which everyone knew the Chadwicks didn't need. They had all shaken their heads at his recklessness.

"I used to be," he said, "but people get lost down here. Never come back out. I was an idiot, but I had my limits. After this next room, you have to start crawling to keep going. I had friends who tried to get further. There's no pattern to caves—you never know if the next turn is going to bring you to a palace or a dead end. They got pretty deep before they gave up. It got too narrow to even use their elbows to move. It was even harder to wriggle out backwards."

Kate imagined being lost in these twisting tunnels. It was cramped and intimidating even here, where she could stand. Being closed in by stone on all sides sounded horrifying. How long would it take for a lantern to burn down and leave someone in total blackness? "I knew there were caves around, but nothing like this," she said instead of considering the fate of the lost souls. "Who built the stairs?"

"I don't know. It's been passed around a bit. Moonshiners sometimes use it to hide their liquor. There used to be a cockfight every month in one of the side rooms. I don't know if it's still running."

He stopped and raised his lantern, illuminating a small, cozy space. The ceiling was higher than Kate had expected for something hidden inside the rocks. Neither of them had to duck to stand, and there was a decent stretch of flat ground. A strange pillar stood near the entrance, wider around than Kate was and stretching from floor to ceiling. In the lamplight, it was pale gray, smoother and slicker than any rock she knew.

"It doesn't look like anyone has been here in a while. They probably found a new hideout."

She snorted. "Somewhere less dangerous, if they're smart. And doesn't smell like damp."

"From my experience, smelling nice wasn't a priority."

Kate hummed. What business did the son of the town's richest man have down here? Cockfights were a cruel sport, not something she'd imagined the smiling man from her visions being involved in. He seemed to do nothing but disappoint her.

"We should be safe here until the storm passes," he continued. He sat down on the rock across from her, leaning over the lantern's dim gold light.

She hesitated, still standing. "There a place for that smoke to go that's not going to get us killed?" she asked, nodding at the lantern.

"The air in here goes outside. That's how they found it in the first place—a breeze where there shouldn't have been one. I told you, people have used this area before. We're good."

She shivered, still uneasy, but finally sat on a wide, flat rock. It was cool beneath her skirts. Down here, it might not have been the cusp of summer at all.

As though in disagreement with his reassurances, Oliver suddenly devolved into a loud coughing fit. It was a harsh, grating sound that seemed to pull from deep inside him. Kate started to stand and offer help, but he waved her away. When the worst of it subsided, he gasped for breath.

"We should get out of here," Kate said. "A little storm is better than choking."

"It's not the caves. It's been like this since the war," he said, voice raw as if a creature had clawed inside his throat. "There's something odd with my lungs. That's all." He took another ragged breath. "So, when did it start for you? The visions?"

She bit her lip. There was a wound in her from his reaction during their first meeting, something sluggishly bleeding that she didn't want to show him. "You really want to know?"

Every vision that came true took her a step closer to the vision of her hands around Eileen's neck. She should have left him in that cornfield. But in all her imaginings, she had never thought he might be like her—haunted by sights he couldn't control.

"I surely do," he said, and there was such anxious, unsteady hope on his face that she couldn't say no.

"It started when I was born, I reckon," she said, "My earliest memories are out of order. I remember seeing things, and then seeing them again. And I remember waking up from the visions. That part is always memorable."

"Waking up?"

"The future doesn't come easy," Kate said. "We ain't meant to see life out of order. I think that's why it feels so… violent." She looked down toward her hands, shadowed shapes in the dark. She felt disconnected from her body down here, as though not being able to see clearly meant she had floated free of its gravity. "My mind leaves for a while, and my body has trouble surviving. I come back, and my body returns to me. It's intense. It scares people."

"How do you control the visions? Make sure they don't come to you at the wrong moment?"

"I can't," she said.

"But you…"

"What?"

"You're here. You came into the woods alone that first night. You work."

"I, what, live?" She shrugged. "I spent most of my childhood at home. After one bad fall, I was terrified of waking up on the ground bleeding. My parents walked me to and from school, then kept me inside. But the visions didn't stop. Eventually, I realized I couldn't survive a life trapped inside. The visions would come, and the future would come after. I couldn't let it stop me from living."

"There *has* to be a way to take control," he said. "Your whole life, and you've never learned how? You've had this much longer than I have."

"You're new to this, so let me tell you—whatever forces have given us these abilities, they're not our friends. My visions give me nothing but misery, and it sounds like your spirits are the same."

"You came to the woods to meet me. You were *eager* for whatever fate was coming. Maybe my ghosts could bring something good too."

"I was wrong," Kate said. He frowned, and she sighed. "Don't take it personally. I stopped hiding from my future a long time ago.

I didn't think I could fight it. I tried and tried and failed every time. I decided I would be there, waiting, no matter what came. But I can't do that anymore. I don't want the future I've seen. I need to find a way to stop it."

"What did you try?"

"Everything. I don't get much in the visions. I don't know dates or times. If I try to avoid something, it happens anyway. This has been my whole life. I'm not a fool."

His voice, when he spoke again, was gentle, an outstretched hand in a dark wood. "I wasn't trying to call you a fool. Just curious. I'm new to all this. Tell me what you tried?"

She felt ridiculous to still be so soft for him. He would probably only disappoint her again. Maybe being here in these caves would lead her on the path that ended with the horrible fight with Eileen, and every breath she took was a breath closer to the future she couldn't bear.

Or… maybe together they could *end* this.

Kate took a fortifying breath. "I'd tried a few ways. Avoiding people I knew I'd see again. Hiding in my room for days. Turning away from anything that seemed familiar. Then, one day I saw something terrible: my youngest sister, Mary Evelyn, screaming on the ground. The leaves dark with blood. I didn't tell my parents. I felt like if I told them, it made it my fault. I'd already been accused of being possessed by a demon, of being some evil conduit. I decided I had to find a way to stop the vision from happening. I left her behind any time I went outside, even though she threw a fit. We'd always played together, but I put a stop to it. If she wasn't with me, she couldn't be hurt. I thought I could save her and beat the future. One day, I went out into the woods alone to explore.

I always liked wandering around the mountains.

"Mary Evelyn was feeling abandoned. She's the youngest, and always wanted to be a part of things. She snuck out to follow me. I was already across the creek when she caught up. I couldn't send her back on her own—she was only six. I thought I could just keep a close eye on her.

"We had a great time: climbing, exploring, playing pretend. The whole afternoon went by just fine. I thought I'd won. We stopped to pick some blackberries. I still remember how they tasted. It was too early in the year for them. They were so sour, but we were just excited to find them." Kate hesitated. Another rumble of thunder echoed down to them, dampened by the stone walls. It was strange, telling the story to this stranger who wasn't a stranger. With how much he had been present in her mind, it seemed he should already have known the ending. "There was a copperhead underneath the bush."

Oliver sucked in a breath.

"It bit Mary Evelyn. And there it was, just as I'd seen it. The blood, the screaming, the leaves. We were in the middle of the woods. She couldn't walk, and I wasn't much bigger than she was. We were on the wrong side of the creek." Kate had to stop talking for a moment. Finally, she said, "By the time I got her back home, they had to take most of her leg."

Oliver was pale in the light of the candle, the hollows under his eyes like a skull. He looked down at his hands. "I'm sorry."

"If I hadn't tried to stop my vision from happening, I could have *planned* it all better. I could have kept Mary Evelyn in the woods near our house. When she got bitten, I could have been ready, not stuck out there alone. We could have saved her leg. I decided then to meet my visions head-on. If I couldn't fight them, I could at least stop being blindsided." She shook her head. "But I shouldn't have given up, even after that. I need to learn how to stop them from coming true. Maybe it's me seeing the thing that makes it happen. I want them gone for good."

"You want to change the future," he said. "Is that possible?"

"Why not? Why should it be written in stone? I'm nobody—why should what I see come true? We can learn from each other. Tell me about your spirits," she continued, invigorated now. "Do you use a Ouija board?"

Her sisters had read an article about the talking boards and tried to recreate one by using chalk to sketch the alphabet on a flat piece of wood. Kate refused to play—she had enough trouble without inviting haints into her life—but she'd heard her sisters squealing in delighted terror. They had bored of the game quickly, and left the board to wash away in the rain so Mama would never find it.

"I can see them."

"Okay."

He waited. "That's not enough for you?"

"It's not especially unique." Uncle Christopher had regaled them with the story of his haint encounter down in Chattanooga at least four times. According to him, a frozen wind in a barn had tried to steal the air from his lungs until he warded it away. If he had ever been truly afraid of the spirit, that solemnity had disappeared over years of retelling. He delightedly used the story to scare Kate's sisters. "If we want to stop this, we need to understand it."

Oliver stood and paced. The swinging lantern in his hand cast dramatic, shifting shadows across the slick walls. Kate stayed seated, watching his silhouette. "I see ghosts. All the time. There ain't as many in Chatuga as there were in France, but they're here. Townsfolk. Natives."

"Do they speak to you?"

"I try not to get that close," he said, voice tight. He turned away from her, staring at the dark room beyond them. "They notice when I pay too much attention. They get upset."

She didn't like seeing him so uneasy. His face was a private treasure she had hoarded for years, and he was *here*. Even if he wasn't what she'd hoped, she didn't want his despair.

"Are they… aggressive?"

"I'm not scared of them," he said, immediately convincing her of the opposite. "Mostly, they don't try to interact with me. Mostly."

"What do they do?"

"If they notice me, they watch me. They seem confused. Lost. They're caught in loops, and I disrupt them. If I pay too much attention, they start coming toward me. Sometimes they're angry."

Kate shuddered. "I can't imagine seeing that all the time."

"Some days I stay home sunup to sundown. It's a new house with no ghosts," he admitted. "Though… There was something in my room the other day. It was… strange. It came from nowhere, and it flew at me—flew through me."

"Maybe you're not only seeing ghosts. They say demons don't have their own forms in our world. That's why we have the bottle tree in front of our house, to catch them if they fly close."

"I don't know about all that," he said, sitting down again. "The dead are just dead."

"Demons ain't dead; demons ain't from here. They're something evil. They put themselves into rats and black cats, and sometimes they try for humans."

Oliver frowned, rubbing his arms. "Would I know if I'd been possessed?"

"I don't think we're meant to fit two spirits. You would feel it. There are other signs—speaking tongues, strange strength… Not reacting right to pain." She swallowed. "But some people will take any excuse to cry demon."

"It seemed like a ghost. It shouldn't have been in my house, but it looked the same as the others. Bloody, I mean. I can usually see that part, how they died. Gunshots, disease…" He trailed off, face sallow. "Well, in any case, it seems similar to what you can do, doesn't it? We both see things humans ain't meant to. And if we can figure out why…"

"We can figure out how to stop it," Kate finished.

Oliver hesitated. "I want it gone. I wish I'd never started seeing them. But I've been thinking… What if I could summon someone?"

"Summon a ghost?" Kate exclaimed. "After everything you've said? You've got to be kidding."

"It'd be different. I'd have more control. And I could choose who to see."

She shook her head fiercely. "Trust me—you wouldn't have more control. I tried it once. I thought the same thing, but it was worse than ever." *Kate wrapped her hands around Eileen's thin throat and began to squeeze.* "These curses can't be used. We need to break them, not make them worse."

"And what then? The future and the ghosts will still be there, even if we can't see them."

"I don't know," Kate said. "But they won't have control of us anymore."

Maybe, finally, Kate would be free to change her future.

16

NORA JO

For the next two weeks, Nora Jo went deep into the forest every night to meet Harlow. The rain passed, leaving Chatuga greener than before. They stayed under the overhang with its fire pit some nights, but they spent most nights in the woods. Harlow showed her the secret magic in plants and animals that she had never looked at closely before.

The forest had the added benefit of secrecy. There were whispers in town about her unemployment. The mayor already thought Nora Jo didn't belong. Harlow was a middle-aged stranger from the mountains, already distrusted by the folks in Chatuga. Publicly associating with him would be a blow Nora Jo's unstable reputation couldn't survive.

Some of Harlow's teachings were familiar, echoing the tales of witchcraft she'd heard from her ma or around town. Others were journeys into new territory. There were endless false rumors about the craft, and witches kept their secrets close.

Every morning before she slept, she wrote notes from her lessons in the shorthand she'd learned at a teaching conference, creating a journal of spells and herbs only she could read. Harlow had endless information, and she was determined to learn it all. The shorthand let her take notes more quickly and secured them from Miss Ethel's accidental prying. The widow seemed willing to accept her new sleeping habits as a side-effect of her unemployment, but Nora Jo didn't want anyone to know about her nightly activities. Fortunately, most of her dresses covered the healing cuts on her arms.

When she woke in the early afternoon, she was faced with an endless stretch of free time. She could only draft so many letters a day seeking a school who might hire a new teacher. The first day after she'd been let go, she had offered to help around the house, but Miss Ethel told her that the new girl, Kate, was plenty, and ushered her outside. Perhaps Miss Ethel regretted that Nora Jo was no longer working to keep her out of the house all day. Or worse, Miss Ethel might realize how quickly Nora Jo's finances were set to dwindle and had already written her off. As a teacher, she'd been paid less than a thousand dollars a year, and most of her salary went back into school supplies.

To give Miss Ethel her space, Nora Jo began to wander the countryside on her own until suppertime.

One evening on her way to collect their water, Nora Jo passed the Barnetts' youngest, Rance Tyler, on the path. He nodded to her, but hurried along without saying hello. It was like a punch to the gut.

Nora Jo had taught all three of the Barnetts. How were they doing without her? Rance Tyler had been progressing well, but it was a task to stop his siblings from riling him into distraction. Mrs. Wilson had been soft even in Nora Jo's time, and now she was teaching again after nearly a decade of retirement. How could she be expected to keep the entire classroom in line?

Nora Jo had been guiding Rance Tyler for all five years of her teaching career, watching him grow from a clumsy six-year-old into a lanky teen. The classroom was filled with students she had watched grow up. She clung to her fury to drown out the ache in her heart at her newfound isolation. Their daily joys and struggles and triumphs had shaped her life for years. She *cared* about them, and that had been stolen from her.

Disheartened and sweat damp, she hauled the full water bucket back to the house, only to find someone in one of the rocking chairs on the front porch. His silhouette was distinct even from a distance—his shoulders were broad from his work at the forge, and he wore the same felt hat as ever. Unusually, Miss Ethel wasn't in her rocking chair. She would never normally have left a guest alone, no matter how uninvited, but she had been tired lately. And maybe she was fed up of dealing with Nora Jo's business.

Nora Jo briefly considered turning around and heading into the woods early. Instead, she climbed the steps and stood by the railing. "Beau."

"Nora Jo," her brother said, taking off his hat and nodding to her. "I thought you'd be home earlier. I've been waiting a while."

She shrugged and looked toward the door. Did he expect an apology? "I didn't know. Why are you here?"

"It's been two weeks since you lost your job. What are you planning to do?"

"People go longer unemployed." He didn't need to know about her daily visits to the post office, waiting fruitlessly for a response to one of her letters.

"Those people ain't my sister," Beau said. He twisted the hat in his hands. "You know that I'm trying to keep Dad's business going strong. The Barker legacy."

"You're the only blacksmith for miles. I promise, even my reputation won't be enough to damage your perfect life."

He stared up at the porch ceiling as though searching for patience. "I'm trying to offer you a job."

She stared at him. "What?"

"A job, Nora Jo," he huffed. "It's the Barker business; you're a Barker. I've got some new customers from over in Terryville. They're building a new lumber mill and need parts. You used to do administrative work for the Chadwick Mill. I could make a position for you. You could help... manage appointments. Or whatever you did there."

"*Make a position.*"

"Well, you won't accept my help any other way."

"I don't need it. If I wanted to do that work, I'd go back to the Chadwicks."

"It's my obligation as head of this family," he insisted. "Dad's gone. I'm the only one left for you."

"I get to decide that," Nora Jo said. "It's always about Dad, isn't it? You don't need to do things just to make him happy anymore, you know. He gave up on me a long time ago. He wouldn't blame you for doing the same."

"He didn't give up on you."

"Beau, you know he and I didn't get along. We never did."

"He was a good man, Nora Jo. He was trying his best. He just wasn't good at expressing himself."

"So it was my job to fix everything he broke? I was the child,

Beau. *He* was the parent. He never did anything but try to control me. There's a reason I left as soon as I could. I could never have been myself in his house."

He sighed, rapping scarred fingers on the arm of the rocking chair. "He worried about you. He was always afraid that Ma's death affected you too much."

Nora Jo gripped the wooden rail so tightly that her hands began to shake. She could feel the tension ricochet through her arm. "This has nothing to do with her."

"Ma always looked after you. Dad spent more time with me, and she spent more time with you. I think she drove you two apart more than she realized."

"You're blaming it on Ma? Dad was always scared Ma would leave him like *his* ma left. The town sure never let him forget. It made him afraid of women with their own minds. That's why he pretended Ma didn't have one."

Beau's nostrils flared, a sure sign of temper. "Well, maybe his ma is the one you really take after," he said, standing up from the rocking chair. "Abandoning your family to chase a silly dream."

"She was fighting for the life she wanted. Maybe it was for the best."

He held her gaze. "Grandma Gwen died alone in Chicago with no family, no friends, and no money. She wrote Grandpa a letter in the end, asking him for help. She needed money for food, for shelter. The winters get real cold up there. Did Dad ever tell you that? I bet he didn't. He wanted us to have a good opinion of his dad."

"Grandpa let her die?" Nora Jo asked, mouth numb.

Her brother stared out over the yard. "It's a hard world for a woman alone. If you change your mind about that job, let me know." He adjusted his hat and stepped down the porch stairs without saying goodbye. Nora Jo watched him stride down the path back toward the road, her heart small and cold in her chest.

"You all right?" Miss Ethel asked when Nora Jo walked into the house. She was sitting at the kitchen table—from that angle, she would have seen their conversation through the window.

She'd let Beau ambush Nora Jo, hadn't spoken in her defense. Nora Jo didn't know why she had expected otherwise.

"Just fine," Nora Jo said, and continued to her room.

That night, Harlow sent Nora Jo on her own into the forest with a strange mission. She was to pick a branch to keep as her dowsing rod.

"It'll be your conduit with nature," Harlow explained. "Of the earth, for the earth. The land has things to say—it's a matter of learning to listen. With enough awareness, you can use it to find underground springs or, more importantly, ley lines."

"Ley lines?"

"They're power centers within the earth, tracing across the planet. You'll find them gathered under places of influence where people have been drawn for centuries. An ancient ritual site becomes a temple becomes a church. There's a crossroads near here, in fact. Magic pulses throughout the world, feeding on the cycles of life and death until it finds its own paths. With the right focus, you can sense those paths."

"And I just pick any stick?"

He shrugged. "Use your senses. Good luck."

As teachers, they had different approaches: Nora Jo, with the mix of ages and skills in her classroom, had always made topics as simple as possible. Harlow preferred for Nora Jo to find her own way, stumbling in the dark. She thought he was testing her, perhaps ensuring he had made the right choice of apprentice.

She set off into the woods on her own, gritting her teeth. She had to prove that she was worth teaching. She'd stumble around the woods making a fool of herself all night if it meant freedom.

Her conversation with Beau had unsettled her, the story he'd told haunting her all evening. Her grandfather had left his runaway wife to die of cold and hunger up north. How long had it taken for her to fall to the point of asking her husband for help? One year? Five? In the end, she'd needed help, but found none.

Beau was right. The world was dangerous for a woman alone.

Nora Jo stared at the black woods ahead of her. She would never be that powerless. She didn't need to crawl back to Beau for his pity job.

She paused and examined the ground, squinting in the dark. There was a fallen branch half-hidden under fallen pine needles, the perfect size and shape for a makeshift walking stick. Perhaps that was what she was meant to look for? She leaned down and tugged hard, but the branch was stuck fast. Frowning, she bent her knees and pulled harder.

The branch came loose with a squelch, pulling along an enormous clump of mud and moss along with it. Her hand slipped and nudged away a layer of bark, revealing the slimy, mold-slick underbelly.

Just peachy.

She dropped the stick, flexing her hands but resisting the urge to wipe them on her dress. She didn't own enough dresses to soil one tonight.

She didn't want to wander so far that she couldn't find her way back to Harlow's overhang, but she'd taken this path enough in recent weeks to know that Chestnut Creek wove its way nearby. She headed in that direction—she could find the stick once she was clean. She crouched at the creek and scrubbed away the slime. The water was cool, the familiar murmuring helping to settle her nerves.

When she looked up, she saw an apple tree tucked near the bank. Its branches were heavy with white flowers, rustling in the late spring breeze. It was far from the cultivated orchards nearby—she imagined a child spitting a seed onto the bank years ago, creating this errant tree. Carefully, she found the straightest branch within reach and broke it off. A peeling piece of green-backed bark came with the young branch, twirling slightly.

For the first time that day, confidence settled over Nora Jo. This was it.

"There you go," Harlow said, nodding when she brought the long branch back to him. "Flowering trees make the most powerful dowsing rods if taken before they bear fruit. They're at their strongest point between being *of* the earth and beyond it." He handed the branch back to her, adding, "Good work."

In school, Nora Jo had always been eager to please. She'd nearly forgotten the pleasure of approval after years on the other side of the classroom.

"Tomorrow, I'll show you ways to use the dowsing rod, but you should practice on your own before we meet. Try walking around tomorrow and seeing what it tells you. The more time you spend with it, the more connected you'll be to what it's sending you," Harlow said. "You've spent so much of your life ignoring your instincts. You'll need to work to open your mind."

Nora Jo nodded—then hesitated. "You know… I need to find another job," she told him. "I've been looking for a school that might be hiring, but haven't gotten any responses. Once I find something, I won't be able to spend every day and night doing this."

"You're my apprentice. You shouldn't take another job." She bristled at his intrusion into her affairs, but he continued, "I was planning on paying you at the end of the first full month. If you need an advance, just say so."

"I—You don't have to pay me," she said. "I'm not a usual apprentice. I'm not *making* anything for you."

"I'm in Chatuga to train you. I'm not interested in wasting my time here because your attention is split."

"You have enough money to *pay* me to learn?"

"I have plenty enough to afford my rent in town and a stipend for you. Life in the mountains ain't expensive, and my skills are rewarded well."

"But I haven't—"

"Don't demur," Harlow advised her. "I have a vested interest in teaching you in a timely manner. I won't hear word of you not accepting payment. I wouldn't have an apprentice of mine left in the cold."

Nora Jo sighed, a weight lifting from her shoulders. He couldn't have known how much she needed to hear those words. "I wouldn't dream of it," she said. "Thank you, Mr. Harlow."

He nodded. "It took me a long time to find you. I'm not wasting your potential. A little payment's the least I can do."

17

KATE

Kate hid a yawn as she plucked another spiky weed from the garden. She was exhausted. The unseasonably warm May day made sweat prickle on her skin and frustration boil within her.

It had been nearly three weeks since Oliver Chadwick Jr. first invited her to meet in the woods. They'd met twice more since, including late into last night.

It was strange to have a secret from her family. Meeting a handsome boy in a dark place was a time-honored tradition for foolish girls across the world, but this was even more dangerous. To meet at all risked both their reputations, especially since they were discussing strange magic.

They should have kept their meetings brisk. To the point. The longer they spent together, the more likely they were to be caught. But talking to someone else with a sight that haunted them was a comraderie Kate had never dreamed of. There was so much to Oliver, so many pained and tangled roots—worse than any garden she worked on, to be sure. He was withdrawn, his smiles tired and self-deprecating. When she had imagined the handsome boy in her visions, she'd thought of someone soft, gentle, sweet. He was none of those things. After their first painful meeting, she should have given up on him. Still, she found herself at risk of being enchanted by the ways he breathed and spoke and moved. He wasn't what she had expected, and it made him all the more intriguing.

But she couldn't let her visions skew her mind and turn her into a fool. And every moment she didn't find a way to defy the future was a moment closer to the terrible vision of her hands around Eileen's throat.

She was spinning her wheels. She wasn't earning enough money, her visions were still far from her control, and she was slipping into complacency around Oliver Chadwick Jr. as though his rare smiles could cure the rest.

She tore up another weed and flung it onto the pile.

"Come on inside, Kate," Miss Ethel called, standing on the front porch. "It's damned hot out here."

Kate looked up from the garden. Under her attention, it had flourished in the last few weeks. Miss Ethel had given it solid bones, but wasn't able to maintain it. Now, strawberries burst bright red from healthy plants, dark green peppers peeked from heavy leaves, and the herbs were growing verdant and fragrant. "Thank you, ma'am, but I need to finish weeding."

All told, Kate worked for more than a dozen folks around Chatuga. Some were seasonal employers, or only brought her in on the occasional weekend, but others were regulars. She stopped by the Russells and Burtons every Monday to pick up their clothes for washing. She cleaned the Howards' house twice a month from floor to ceiling. In the beginning, her knuckles bled from the work, but they'd grown firm callouses over time.

Of all her clients, the widow Whitaker was quickly becoming her favorite.

"You can finish tomorrow," she said, waving a hand. "Come have some sweet tea."

Kate looked back down at the garden plot, then pushed herself to her feet. It was the warmest day of the year so far; leaving the relentless sun for the shade of Miss Ethel's kitchen was no chore. She knew from experience that Miss Ethel wouldn't take no for an answer, and wouldn't decide later that Kate's break had been a mistake. Kate had learned not to trust the folks paying her—they were too changeable when the time came to hand over the coins— but Miss Ethel was an exception.

Inside, Kate sipped the sweet tea and sighed. It had an interesting flavor—mint, she thought—and was refreshing in the heat. "Thank you, ma'am."

"We can't have you thirsting to death on my watch," Miss Ethel said, taking her glass back to the counter. She paused mid-step, shoulders hunching against an invisible blow. The glass fell. Time stilled as Miss Ethel's grip failed, but Kate's body was too slow. The glass cracked against the floor, amber tea spreading over the floor.

Kate ushered the shaking Miss Ethel into a chair, carefully picked up the broken pieces, and found a towel for the mess. Once it was clean, she sat across from the widow and put a hand on hers. She was frail as a bird. "Are you all right, Miss Ethel?" Kate pushed her glass across the table. "Here, you finish this."

"Don't you fuss over me," Miss Ethel said, but her voice was weak. When Kate frowned at her, she said, "I'm just growing old, Kate. There's nothing to be done."

"Is there someone to help you when I'm not here? Your Miss Nora Jo?" Kate still hadn't met Miss Ethel's elusive tenant. She was either sleeping in the back room or out of the house during Kate's working hours. Kate could almost have believed that Miss Ethel was seeing ghosts like Oliver if she hadn't smelled the smoke of recently lit candles coming from the closed room sometimes.

"Lord, that girl has been sneaking out of here every moment night and day since she got let go from her school," Miss Ethel said. "She's not ready to help anyone but herself. I need to give her her space."

"What will you do if next time, it's you that falls, not a glass of tea?" Kate asked. "You're here alone most of the day."

"I'll be fine," Miss Ethel said, waving a hand. "And the day I'm not—well, everyone's time comes to an end. There's nothing we can do to stop that."

"I don't like that kind of talk, ma'am."

"It's reality, honey. I used to say they'd have to drag me kicking and screaming into my grave, but that was decades ago. There's a reason we die. Time comes for everyone. Get that look off your face. I don't expect a child to understand. Listen, both you and Nora Jo have fates outside of this little town. I won't have you worrying about me."

Fate. The word had haunted Kate her whole life.

"What makes you so sure?" Kate asked.

"I've lived in Chatuga for most of my life, and alone since Robert died. It's a hard place. There's some kindness, to be sure, but country life has never been easy." She sighed. "It's hard to find a place that can love you back, but I have to think it's out there for you two."

"Do you want to leave?"

"Me? Oh no. I'm too old to move. This place is stuck with me until the end."

"Well, I have no plans to leave either," Kate said. Even if her parents were still thinking about Nashville, this was her home. "You're stuck with me too."

Miss Ethel smiled. "Then I'll be grateful for it."

Before she left, Kate rearranged the kitchen so that everything sat in easy reach, leaving the upper shelves bare and the lower ones crowded. Miss Ethel watched her with a tired indulgence, but didn't protest.

18

OLIVER

"This is a bad idea," Oliver said. He took shallow breaths through his mouth, eyes on the canopy overhead. The ceiling of leaves, lit dimly by the lantern in Kate's hand, nearly blocked out the sky entirely. Around them, frogs and cicadas called in an uneven, pulsing thrum, like the labored heaving of a vast animal. Kate was wandering ahead, illuminating the clearing, but he kept his eyes averted. He'd gotten a good enough glimpse of the tiny family graveyard when they first arrived.

Kate hoped to find a way to be rid of their uncanny visions, and he would be grateful if they succeeded. But if their investigations turned up a way that he could find Tucker Lee, apologize, and have one more moment with him—that had to come first. Then, only then, he would happily put aside this curse.

He might have argued against Kate's fear of inviting in their powers, but in the cave, it felt like they were the only people in the world. Sometimes, when her guard was down, Kate would look at him with wide eyes like he might be the answer to her prayers. How was a man supposed to think straight in the face of that?

Somehow, that had led him here. He was starting to think himself the worst fool of all.

"We can't go to the cemeteries in town. There are too many people there," Kate pointed out. Pine needles crunched as she walked, the lantern's light swaying across the leaves overhead. "My sisters and I stumbled across these one day when we were picking wild strawberries along the railroad tracks. Betty and Eileen ran away, but the rest of us dusted off the headstones to try to read them. Couldn't make out much. We thought it was some old family plot from before Chatuga was here."

"Kate," Oliver said.

"What?" Her footsteps stopped. She was breathy, eager. "Are they here?"

He took care not to look at the old woman standing hunched nearby. She was steadily sweeping a spectral broom over a lichen-crusted grave. "Just one."

"That's good." When he didn't react, she said, "Look, we can't find a way to stop our visions until we understand them. We can't hunt down the future, but we can find ghosts. If we want answers, we have to start here. Why us? Why you?"

"Bad luck," Oliver grumbled.

Kate ignored him. "Is there something you're meant to do? Something they want?"

"Most of them don't seem to know they're dead. They're walking the same paths they did before they died, or trying to patch the wound that killed them. When they notice me, they start to wake up. Sometimes they look scared. Sometimes angry."

"Is this one angry?" Kate asked carefully.

"If I look too closely, I'll find out the hard way," Oliver said. Fear was like a bird in his chest, a familiar companion. "She's stopped what she was doing. She's watching me. We don't know what a spirit will do if I confront it; I've never done that before. This is... wrong. Dangerous."

"Oliver," she said. "We won't beat anything if we're too scared to try."

A hand brushed against his, and he startled. But the touch was warm and gentle. Kate carefully took his hand between her own and rubbed circles against his skin. Had she touched him before? He'd held her hand to lead her to the cave that first night, but she had kept a careful distance between them since.

"Kate," he said, but there was nothing else to add.

"I'm going to put wildflowers by all the headstones like we talked about. Show them our respect. Then you can try to talk to her."

Oliver nodded and watched her walk around the small collection of graves. When she neared the final headstone where the ghost waited, he looked away.

"There, that's the last bouquet." Kate returned, standing reassuringly close to his side. "Are you ready? Where is it?"

"There's an old woman by the grave on the far right. I don't know how old. Seventy? Eighty?"

"Should I shine the lantern that way?"

"No," Oliver said. "Don't try to look at her. Besides, I don't need the light. Spirits are just... there. Whether it's light or dark. They're not part of this world. No matter what time of day it is, they look like I'm seeing someone at dusk. Close to night, when there's a slight blur unless you focus."

"You should say something to her."

He shouldn't. He should walk away.

But this was for Tucker Lee. And for this strange girl who had decided to trust him.

He swallowed thickly, then looked across the small graveyard. The old woman was staring back. She didn't have a clear cause of death—not the red marks of a pox victim, not the hemorrhage of blood from a fatal wound. She was achingly frail, her hands and face skeletal. The broom had vanished. "Ma'am?" he prompted quietly.

She stared, expression focused but unreadable. It was like she was trying to peer through him, to read something unintelligible written on his bones. Like the other ghosts he'd seen, there was a confused emptiness to her gaze.

"Ma'am, I'd just like to talk," he said. "Can you understand me? What's your name?"

Without breaking eye-contact, she pointed down at the headstone by her feet.

"May I?" Oliver asked, putting a hand on Kate's lantern. She relinquished her hold, and he slowly walked to the grave. The pine needles crunching under his feet were too loud in the quiet. The old woman stayed entirely still, watching him approach.

Suddenly, she barked, "Careful!"

Oliver froze, then glanced down. In his focus on the spirit, he had nearly stepped on one of the grave plots. "Sorry," he said, and carefully went around it.

The spirit's expression was even more intent, her eyes wide and wild. There was violence in her stillness. Oliver had seen a rabid dog once, before it had been put down. The ghost shared the baffled, hungry desperation.

"I didn't mean to," Oliver told her soothingly, looking just over her shoulder. Her gaze was too feral for comfort. "I'm sorry."

"So many," she said. Her voice was barely audible in the wind.

"So many what?" Oliver prompted, stopping just shy of her reach.

"There…" Her mouth kept moving, but no sound came out.

"Go on," he said. "I'm listening."

Her gaze met his. "So many of my babies here. Children. Grandchildren," she told him, voice hoarse.

"Oh," Oliver said. He hesitated. How could he comfort the dead? "I'm sorry," he said again.

"I buried all of them. None left."

"I'm sorry," Oliver said. He looked down at the grave. It was hard to read the lichen-coated name. He held the lantern closer, and then said, "I'm sorry, Miss Florence."

At the sound of her name, the old woman grew clearer, a grainy photograph come suddenly to life. She seemed nearly as present in the clearing as Kate. She frowned, intent as a hawk. "Why them and not me? Why them and not *you?*"

In a flash, she lashed out at him.

The blow connected. Three bright lines of pain sliced across Oliver's cheek. He staggered, reaching up toward his throbbing face.

"You're bleeding," Kate gasped.

"Kate, go," Oliver said, stumbling back. "Run."

The old woman followed. "Why?" She lunged forward. Oliver covered his face, but he felt a cold, eerie sensation on his other hand. The old woman was trying to pry the lantern from his grip, but she couldn't make contact. Her hand swiped through him; whatever burst of power she had used to scratch him was gone.

She shrieked.

"I don't want any trouble," Oliver gasped. "Please, Miss Florence."

Suddenly, Oliver felt cold fingers brush against his. He was so stunned that the lantern was knocked from his loose grip. It crashed to the forest floor, shattering. The oil and flame mixed, igniting the dried leaves and pine straw that covered the ground around the graves.

Oliver breathed an oath, stunned.

"Oliver!" Kate was suddenly beside him, grabbing his hat and throwing it down onto the fire.

It was enough to shock him into action. "Get back!" he said, then stomped on the fire and hat at once. The flames tried to lick his skin, but he ignored them. A fire could spell ruin for the whole town.

The ghost shoved at his chest, but her hands passed through him. He could feel her icy touch inside him, freezing his heart, but he was still breathing when she pulled back. He focused on the ground, grinding the flames back into nothing.

The clearing grew dark as the fire disappeared, only the silver moon overhead picking out the ancient headstones and the shape of his boot crushing the hat into the ground.

"You got it, it's out," Kate said. Her hands fell on his shoulders, and he stopped his frantic stomping.

He looked up reluctantly. The ghost still stood in front of him, the only thing in the clearing that didn't need the light to be seen. She was staring down at the ashes with a desolate expression.

"We're leaving," Oliver said, stumbling away.

"Of course," Kate agreed, though he hadn't been talking to her. She kept a hand on his shoulder, and they picked their way through the moonlit clearing. He let her lead—Oliver walked backward, keeping a terrified eye on Miss Florence. She didn't seem to notice them go, just watched the ground as if the snuffed flame had taken something from inside her, hollowing her out.

"Is it following us?" Kate asked quietly, helping Oliver around a fallen tree.

"No," he replied, voice barely a whisper. He held his breath, but it didn't draw Miss Florence's attention.

"Good, good," Kate said. "Come on, we're at the tree line. You need to turn around. It's too dark for me to guide you."

"What if—"

"Don't think about it," Kate said. "It's not following. We're getting out of its way, and we can do that faster if you help."

With a shuddering breath, Oliver tore his eyes from the spirit and looked at Kate. It was hard to see her expression without the lantern. The moon couldn't fight through the dense branches overhead. She seemed more a shadow than a person. The spirit they were leaving behind, grainy but bright despite the darkness, felt realer than anything else around him. He put a hand to his cheek, wincing when he brushed against one of the gashes. His fingers came away dark with blood.

"We gotta patch you up," Kate said, ushering him forward. She clung to his hand as she tugged him along. "Do you have anything on hand?"

"No," Oliver said numbly.

"Do spirits carry diseases? Could it fester?"

"I don't know."

"Right, of course not." Her voice was high and quick as a bird fluttering at the ceiling of a barn it couldn't escape. "Don't worry. Come on, we need to get back to town. We can figure things out from there. It's still not following?"

Oliver glanced back. There was nothing behind them. The trees covered the view into the clearing. Was Miss Florence still standing among the graves? Was something of her essence now stained with his blood? How had she *touched* him? "She's not following," he confirmed.

"Okay," Kate said. "That's good. Keep moving, Oliver. That's it."

He hadn't realized he'd stopped. He let her nudge him forward, following her voice and the fingers laced in his. Her hands were small and calloused, real in a way that grounded him amid the dark forest.

Finally, they stumbled out of the woods onto one of the dirt roads that stretched out from the center of Chatuga. Kate sat down heavily on the ground. Oliver didn't think twice before joining her. He hadn't coughed during their flight, but his lungs protested nonetheless. Each breath felt like it were being dragged through sandpaper, his chest shuddering with the strain. It was a deeper, darker pain than the bright cuts on his cheek.

"Lord," Kate said. "That was surely something."

"You can say that again," Oliver said hoarsely. He looked up at the stars. They were as cold and removed as ever.

They sat in silence for a long moment. There weren't more words in Oliver's brain to offer. The candle of his mind had been blown out, leaving only a lingering scent and the curl of smoke.

"I'm sorry," Kate choked finally. "I shouldn't have made you do that. You were right."

Oliver shrugged, and rasped, "I didn't know what would happen."

"You knew it wouldn't be good."

He hummed idly, still feeling oddly hollow. His body felt separate from his head. "I thought—It's just… The way they look at me sometimes. The ones like her. It's like they want me dead alongside them. Maybe they know something about me I don't. Like I'm also supposed to be dead and buried."

"There's nothing wrong with you," Kate said fiercely. "They're hurt, and they take it out on the only person who can see them. You're a target, not a problem."

"Maybe. We learned something, at least," Oliver mused, reaching for his cheek.

Kate grabbed his hand to stop him. He let her pull it down to rest between them. "Don't touch until we can clean it," she said. "What exactly did we learn?"

Oliver stared at the road. "That names have power."

It was later than usual when he finally got home. The grandfather clock pointed toward one in the morning. The house was dead quiet, and he took a handful of medical supplies from the kitchen without disturbing its peace.

In his room, he dabbed Rawleigh's Antiseptic Salve onto his cheek by the light of a candle. Brown rust edged the mirror they'd inherited from his grandma, but he could see himself clearly. Two of the cuts were shallow, just a scrape that would heal quickly, but the one closest to his chin was dark with blood. It stung as he cleaned it.

He tore a strip of clean linen from an old shirt and set it over the area. It was a sloppy job, nothing like what he had seen done in the military hospital in France, but the scent of blood and antiseptic still took him back. He waited to hear the groans of the dying, the screams of those in too much pain to survive, but there was only the thrum of frogs croaking outside.

He stared down at the tin of salve. *Heavily Medicated*, the label said. *For Man and Beast*.

Had Miss Florence been a woman or a beast—or neither? He hadn't known the old woman in life. She had died decades ago. Perhaps she had always been vicious, but somehow Oliver thought death had changed her. There had been a furious distance in her eyes, beyond human emotion. He had seen it in other ghosts too.

If he could get Tucker Lee to appear, would he be the same? In his memories, Oliver saw him as he'd been that first day at Camp Sevier, blond hair slicked back and green eyes creased with his cheerful smile. He couldn't imagine it.

"Tucker Lee," he murmured, staring at his own reflection in the mirror. Saying her name had made Miss Florence grow more solid. Maybe it would be enough to pull Tucker Lee back from wherever he was. But the room stayed quiet. "Tucker Lee?"

There was too much hope on his own face, too much fear. He turned away from the mirror and crossed to the window. He brushed his fingers across the linen on his cheek. If he was going to be stuck with this curse, surely he should get one gift from it.

Tucker Lee had been like the sun, indomitable. Some of the other boys at training camp found him overwhelming, but Oliver had stayed close, basking in his brightness. Oliver's friends in Chatuga were companions of necessity, other boys his age who needed someone to drink with. Tucker Lee had been Oliver's first true friend. He found Oliver's snide comments uproarious, and they pushed each other forward during the brutal physical training at Camp Sevier. When a rifle misfired in practice and killed a boy from Memphis, they got drunk together behind the barracks. In France, Oliver quipped in an undertone about their British tea rations to calm Tucker Lee during the endless chorus of artillery. Tucker Lee shared his cigarettes in the muddy trenches, leaning close as Oliver inhaled so he could cup his hand over the end, enjoying the heat and masking the light. Every time Oliver slipped, Tucker Lee was there to push him back to his feet.

Tucker Lee was the first person to make Oliver understand the idea of being connected to another human. He was a symbol to his parents; part of a legacy to the town; another fellow to get drunk with to his classmates. Around Tucker Lee, he was a person. His laughter felt more real, his ease deeper, his fears more grounded.

Surely there was a way. A bond like that couldn't just disappear in the mud of France.

"Tucker Lee, if you're out there," Oliver said, "I just want to talk. One more time. Tucker Lee Selecky. Come on."

The room stayed dark. He kept trying.

When dawn painted the horizon and there was still no sign, Oliver fell into his bed for another fitful sleep.

19

NORA JO

Afternoon shone brightly through Nora Jo's curtains when she woke. She transcribed her notes from her late night with Harlow in her worn journal, then dressed for the day. Yawning, she scratched at her sleeve and the bandages underneath. The cuts from her spells last night felt deeper than usual, and her forearm itched as they healed. At least teaching hadn't needed her actual blood—just her spirit.

When Nora Jo opened her bedroom door, she heard voices from the kitchen.

"… Everyone was heartbroken when her daughter Laurie May passed away. Having babies ain't easy business. She spent the last few years helping with the family, but the ladies at bridge are all glad to have her back. She taught most of their kids, and now she'll teach their grandkids."

They were talking about Mrs. Wilson. Nora Jo hesitated in the hallway.

"We had a teacher like that," another voice said. Young, female.

"Sometimes we'd also get a few months with some bright young teacher from Fisk University, out traveling to different towns."

"I thought that might be Nora Jo's path. Traveling and teaching," Miss Ethel said. "I saw her carrying out some letters, but don't think she's heard back."

She'd hoped no one had noticed her going to the post office. Even though Harlow was paying her now, it still stung that none of the other schools had written back. It was embarrassing that Miss Ethel knew, and worse that she was spreading the word around town.

Nora Jo let her footsteps slap the floor loudly as she approached, and she went toward the pantry without looking at the table.

"Oh, Nora Jo, you haven't met Kate yet," Miss Ethel said.

Hoping her cheeks weren't as flushed as they felt, Nora Jo turned. A young Black woman sat with Miss Ethel at the table, a glass of lemonade in her hand. Sweat dappled the edges of her faded blue dress. "Nice to meet you, Miss Nora Jo," Kate said, standing to curtsy. "Miss Ethel invited me in to take a quick break."

"Grab some dinner and sit down with us, Nora Jo. There's plenty on the counter," Miss Ethel said, patting the chair beside her.

"I'm not very hungry," Nora Jo said, taking a biscuit and wrapping it in a cloth. "I'll eat outside."

"Come on now, Nora Jo, you only just woke up. Surely you can take a bit of time for a real meal. Kate's been wanting to meet you."

Kate looked between Miss Ethel and Nora Jo, clearly uneasy. Who knew what else Miss Ethel had been telling her about Nora Jo?

"Not today." Nora Jo smiled stiffly. "Besides, I can see you two have a lot to talk about." Without waiting for their reaction, she nodded and left the house.

*

She went to her favorite spot in a field beyond the fences of town, listening to the creek burbling on its way to the forest. Her dowsing rod hung loose from her hand. She knew the path well, but she let the branch pick up the vibrations around her and connect her to the land. Violets, pansies, bluebells, and clusters of yellow tickseeds scattered the field around her. When she lay down, the long grass broken beneath her legs smelled sweet, and the rest waved around her like an ocean.

It should have been calming.

She dropped her head back into the grass, staring up at the sky. If that was the gossip in her own house, what were people saying about her across town? The folks at the post office had handled her letters to the other schools, and would know she had never gotten a response. The mayor might have told everyone his concerns about her; her decision to avoid everyone after losing her position only enforced the idea that she was strange and aloof. Were they all laughing at her?

Or worse, pitying her?

She pulled out her book and let the story slowly sweep her away. Soon, she wasn't in a meadow in Chatuga, only a short walk from Miss Ethel and her brother and Mayor Neese and her old students, with eyes on her back and unemployment nipping at her heels. She was sitting with Emily Dickinson, skipping through the flow of her words. None of her fears held her down.

Reading was the first magic she'd ever learned.

A crunch in the grass nearby made her flinch and turn. She blinked against the sun at the interloper, then smiled.

Gloria was approaching, a cotton scarf wrapped over her head and a straw basket by her side. Her fair skin had turned golden with the start of summer. Over the years, Nora Jo had lost her propensity to freckle apart from on the tip of her nose, but Gloria's face was scattered with them like pennies at the bottom of a well. As she grew older, Nora Jo had realized that there was nothing ugly about freckles, no matter what her classmates had said. In Gloria's freckles, Nora Jo saw constellations.

"What are you doing out here?" Nora Jo asked.

"I've seen you heading this way before," Gloria said, stopping close to her. Her boots were worn from long years of work, her dress frayed at the hem. "I was wondering where you've been going."

"The unemployed life is glamorous," Nora Jo drawled.

"Is this what you've been doing lately? Reading in the sunshine?"

"When it rains, I read inside."

Gloria laughed. "I was worried I would need to comfort you, but you seem happier than I am." She shuffled, tracing the line of her kerchief to be sure her curls were tucked neatly. "I finished my deliveries early today. Could I join you?"

"Please," Nora Jo said. There was only grass around them; still, Nora Jo closed her book and shuffled sideways. Gloria joined her in the impression she'd made, expanding the small bed of crushed grass. She sighed and leaned back on her hands, looking up at the sky and exposing her long neck.

"Your pa won't be looking for you?" Nora Jo asked.

"Not for a while," Gloria said, closing her eyes and basking like a lizard. One of her crossed legs was pressed against Nora Jo's outstretched calf. The fabric of their skirts pooled together against the grass. "I'll tell him Mrs. Shumate talked my ear off and I couldn't get away. It's happened before." She opened one eye and gave Nora Jo a sly grin.

Nora Jo's answering smile was brief, falling away as soon as Gloria's eye closed again. Gloria had to craft an alibi for spending an hour whiling away her time with Nora Jo by the creek, as though she were sneaking behind the church to drink moonshine or tumbling with a beau in a haystack. Was Nora Jo such a pariah?

They sat in silence for a long moment. Gloria seemed content to be off her feet, but Nora Jo felt the weight of the silence settling on her shoulders. Everything she could think to say seemed absurd, too heavy for the late spring afternoon. *Why are you here? Do you think I'm beautiful? Do you know I think you are? Do you dream of me?*

"How is the harvest looking this year?"

Gloria sighed. "That's all anyone seems to want to talk about. The sun, the rain, the soil, the yield."

"You do work on a farm," Nora Jo said, feeling a flush sweep over her cheeks.

"For now."

Nora Jo had only begun to truly notice Gloria after they both left the schoolroom they had shared for so many years. Gloria had been quiet, sitting with her friends, not talking to the lanky older girl who was so desperate for the teacher's approval.

After Nora Jo finished schooling, she saved money for a while by working in administration for the gristmill before finally going to Middle Tennessee State Normal School for their two-year teaching program. She'd taken the train to the college, located in a town called Murfreesboro south of Nashville. When she came back, degree in hand, just in time to take over the schoolroom from a grateful Mrs. Wilson, Chatuga had seemed just the same as when she'd left.

She realized, though, that she wasn't the only one who had grown over the years. Gloria had been in Mrs. Wilson's final graduating class, but her brother was one of Nora Jo's students. She came by when Teddy forgot his dinner, and then more often once Nora Jo began ordering apples from her family farm. Gloria—beautiful, friendly Gloria—always seemed happy to see her, and they began to chat whenever their paths crossed.

Nora Jo had never thought Gloria unhappy with her life. She hadn't shown any special interest in school or ever mentioned leaving Chatuga. Could Gloria also dream of power, of freedom?

"What do you want to do?" Nora Jo asked quietly.

Gloria shrugged. "I don't know. I suppose it will depend on what my husband does. I'd like to work inside. I've spent too much time on the farm."

"Oh." Nora Jo's heart clenched. "You have a beau?"

There were still some single men in town near their age, though none seemed good matches: Joe Wright, who had moved from Kentucky eight years ago and made no ripple in town; Oliver Chadwick Jr., with his silver spoon and spoiled childhood; Adam Underhill, whose first wife had died in childbirth at barely sixteen.

"No," Gloria said. "My pa has some ideas. He wants someone who can help expand the farm. I'm in no rush for him to choose."

"Do you... want to get married?"

Gloria ran her hands over the grass around them. She didn't look at Nora Jo.

"You don't have to," Nora Jo told her. "They tell you you have to, but you don't. Your life is yours to live. There are ways."

"You're braver than I am," Gloria said quietly.

"You could be brave." Their voices were barely louder than the creek murmuring nearby.

Gloria looked down. Nora Jo didn't like to see her so withdrawn. Her face was pale under her freckles, and her hands twisted in her lap.

"But you don't have to be brave today," Nora Jo said. "Just enjoy the afternoon off."

When Gloria gave her a relieved smile, it was brighter than the sun.

They chatted easily about their favorite parts of the oncoming summer, from splashing in the creek to picking blackberries from wild bushes. They laughed about the antics of the baby goats on Gloria's farm, who had been trying to teach the dogs to play by headbutting them gently. The tactic hadn't worked as well with Gloria's ornery mule, Old Charley. Nora Jo told her about Miss Ethel, recounting some of her funnier comments.

Everything seemed lighter under the spring sun, like everything in Nora Jo's life was an amusing story she'd saved just for Gloria.

Gloria plucked flowers from around them as they spoke, weaving them into a pair of crowns. She kept one of the violets for herself, and draped the other of aster on Nora Jo's head. The thin purple petals were soft against her forehead.

20

KATE

After the first week, the path to the underground caves had become familiar under Kate's boots. They didn't meet every night—she was worn down from working every day, and Oliver seemed exhausted from even the short walk to the woods. Instead, they met once a week at ten o'clock, just an hour after sunset, and tried to be home by midnight.

After their failed experiment in the local graveyard, it was a relief to be in the cave, far from that strange, empty clearing. Somehow, the cold stone here had become familiar and comforting.

"My sister has been driving me crazy," Kate commented as they settled into their usual spots.

"Which one?"

Kate had told Oliver all about her four sisters, and he had impressively remembered their names. He was an only child and seemed jealous of her family's dynamics.

"Eileen," Kate said. "She's been moodier than usual. And she keeps asking strange questions, but I can't tell if she's noticed me sneaking out, or if she's just trying to make me paranoid. She knows I've been talking to Mama and Daddy about something she's not allowed to know about, and it's making her furious."

"She's, what, fifteen? Sixteen?" When Kate nodded, he said, "That's the age where you really start to think you're an adult, even though you're not."

"Yeah, she's far too big for her britches," Kate said. "And the attitude isn't new. We used to call her Mean Eileen."

Oliver laughed. "So, what's the big secret? The one your parents are keeping from her?"

Kate sighed, picking up a stone and rolling it around her palm. "Daddy might be getting let go." It felt surreal to speak that possibility into this space, which felt so removed from her daily life. She had told Oliver secrets about her past she'd never told anyone else, but the future was scarier.

"Oh. I'm right sorry to hear that, Kate."

"We're still in the fight. He might be able to keep the job. But it's tough."

"Is that why you work so hard all the time?" He shook his head, huffing slightly. "You seem to do jobs for half the town."

She lifted her chin. "I work because that's what my family needs. I've been finding jobs since I was ten and helped Mama with her sewing before that. I haven't picked up my fiddle in weeks. Your family built this town, lured people in, and worked them to the bone for your coin. You wouldn't understand."

"You're right. I wouldn't understand," he agreed. "I've had it all laid out for me on a silver platter I'm too fucking weak to carry."

"We're a pair," she said, her ire deflating. "I want the world to listen to me. You want it to leave you alone. But it ignores me every day and it won't give you room to breathe."

He rubbed at his chest. "Now that's the Lord's truth. So, if you're all working to help your pa, why doesn't your sister know about it? She's old enough."

"Mama doesn't want to bring her into this until we have to. She'd throw a fit, and we have enough to worry about. We'll get it figured out soon and she'll never have to know it was even on the table."

Oliver whistled. "I used to wish I had siblings, but I have enough trouble dealing with just my parents. More family to dance around sounds exhausting."

"It's not all bad. There's something to be said for family you can argue with. It makes us all steadier."

"I can't picture that," he admitted. "I imagine most of the time, it's just more people to hide things from."

She shrugged. "Sometimes." Eileen could never know that Kate's secrets included a vision of her death. It was a fear she'd kept from Oliver as well, too raw and terrifying to expose. She shook her head, tossing the rock across the floor. It skidded against the slick ground until it clattered into the wall. "I've been trying to think of a new plan for our visions. Our, ah, little adventure in the graveyard wasn't the right approach. But there has to be a way around these powers. If only we could figure out why *us*."

"Maybe it's not such a deep mystery for me. I saw too much death, and now I can't escape it. It makes sense, if you think about it," Oliver said. "But what about you?"

"I don't know. The only magic in the whole family is a witch down in Atlanta, and she trained for years to learn her craft. I was born with this. She can't do half of what I do."

"Was your aunt at least able to help your parents understand what was happening to you? They must have known when you were young, right? If you were seeing the future and having those…"

"Fits," she finished for him. "Yeah, they knew, but it scared them. They told my aunt, but she didn't know how to help."

"Is there anyone else we can ask? Someone we trust, someone who will keep it secret. There might be some other witches in town. The preacher at my church is a bit of a bore, but we could—"

"No!" Kate snapped. "No preachers, Oliver."

He looked at her with those strange, enchanting eyes. He always heard more than she said. "Why?"

"People know I have fits, but we never tell anyone outside the family what I know. And for good reason. My parents warned me to keep it a secret. They were worried what people might do. I should have been more careful. They were right, more right than they even knew." She stared at the lantern, a chill dancing over her skin. "I accidentally gave myself away to a friend of mine. She told our reverend. He came to my parents, said that I was demon-ridden and needed help."

"He thought you were possessed?"

"I had frightening fits—I nearly bit through my tongue a few times—and I had unnatural knowledge. According to Reverend Castor, they were classic signs that a demon had its claws in me. I told you—demons don't fit easy into humans. There's too much of us and too much of them. It's a battle that can't be hidden from onlookers. He thought it was all a sign there was something *else* inside me." She huffed and wrapped her arms around her ribs. "It didn't seem to matter I didn't have the other signs. He saw what he wanted, and convinced my parents he was right. They stopped trusting me as soon as someone told them there was something wrong with me."

"What did he do?" Oliver asked.

"Took me away. Locked me in the church basement. He was worried I'd break loose, so he tied my hands to one of the support beams. It was covered in splinters. He started with shouting an exorcism. He always had the loudest voice; it scared me even before then. I just cried. He thought that meant it was working, but I kept having the fits."

"That bastard." Oliver sounded genuinely furious.

She had never told anyone this story before, and the validation was more warming than she had imagined. "He realized it wasn't enough," she said. "So he tried to starve it out of me. No food, barely any water. It was... It was a very hard time. In the end, my parents came to get me. It had been a week by then, and they couldn't wait any longer. They took one look at me and brought me home. I left terrified of him—and them. They had given me to that man for something I couldn't help. How was I supposed to trust them again? Then Mary Evelyn was born a few months later and they had someone new to worry about. We didn't talk about the reverend again."

"Mary Evelyn was born after? Wait, how old were you?"

"Seven."

"Lord, Kate."

"The reverend never fully believed I wasn't possessed. He was just looking for the chance to try again. I tried to forget my visions as soon as I saw them. I tried not to spend much time with people, staying in the house or exploring with my sisters. I started trying to stop them from coming true, but I told you how that ended.

After all that, I thought I just had to deal with it. Talking about the visions made people angry, and interfering seemed to make them worse. Even if there was a witch in front of me, I'd hesitate to ask for advice. We don't know who we can trust, and witchery is an unreliable art."

She dug into her pocket and pulled out her companion fang. He opened his palm for her. Her fingers grazed his skin, warm and soft. The fang was small in his hand, curved like a crescent moon and no bigger than one of his finger joints.

"This was supposed to protect me," she said as he examined it. "One winter, I had a fit while walking home. I ended up in the snow so long that when I came home, I needed to sit by the fire for ages to lose my chill. My Uncle Christopher gave me this. He said it would protect me from frostbite and other ills."

"And has it?" Oliver asked, twisting the tooth in his hand.

"I still have the visions. I haven't been foolish enough to test the frostbite part yet."

"But you still carry it." He rubbed the smooth bone and pressed his thumb down on the tip. "Ow," he said, pulling back quickly.

"Careful—it's fiercer than it ever was in the wolf's mouth. My uncle said sharpening it would help shape the wolf's energy into a protective force. Maybe it doesn't work at all, but it's a reminder that my family loves me. That's what most magic seems to be. Real powers like ours are rare," she said. "I was mad at my parents for so long after they let the reverend take me, but they've only ever wanted to help. They can't stop the visions. They've hurt me by trying. But in the end, the fact they *want* to help so badly is something I can hold onto. No one can keep anyone safe in this world. The wanting is all we have."

Oliver stared at the fang, his eyes shadowed. "If I told my parents what I see, they would send me to an asylum."

She frowned. The hurt in his face made her chest ache. "You don't know that."

"I do," he said. "My pa had a sister. No one knows about her. She was mad. They kept her locked away in their house until they started to worry that someone would find out about her. Grandpa Herman was growing the mill, so there was a lot of attention on the family. He sent her away."

"Do you think she might also have seen spirits?"

"I don't know. My pa never talks about her. He only told me to make sure I knew the truth—that the Chadwicks'll trim their own branches if it keeps the tree healthy. She didn't live long in the asylum. She just…wasted away."

"I'm sorry."

"I never met her."

"Not for that," Kate said. "I'm sorry you have no one you can trust with this. I can't imagine holding this secret alone has been easy."

"Well," he said, a slight flush staining his cheeks. "I'm not alone now." A smile flashed over his face, quick and sharp as lightning. He handed her back her fang, pulling back before their fingers could brush again.

"You're not," she agreed.

Kate was home by midnight, according to the old standing clock in the kitchen. The house was dead quiet, and each step toward her bedroom rang like a thunderclap. She made it to her bed and stretched out without incident. Around her, her sisters slept peacefully.

For once, Eileen wasn't snoring, only resting quietly on the bed beside her.

Kate stared up at the ceiling, resisting the smile that tugged at her lips. Despite the heaviness of the conversation, she felt lighter after meeting with Oliver.

Perhaps her dreams of a soft future with him hadn't been entirely misinterpreted. She brushed her fingers over the fang tucked safely in her pocket, and let sleep take her over.

Dark liquid pooled at her feet. It was like a puddle, but not at all. Water was fluid and easy. This was viscous and slow.

Drops had sprayed on the surrounding leaves, leaving them with black freckles.

The scent was heavy in the air, metallic and cloying, overpowering the green summer breeze.

She followed the pool of blood to its center.

A pair of large bare feet rested limply against the forest floor.

21

OLIVER

Oliver woke slowly. The wisps of the dream were already slipping away, but for once it hadn't been a nightmare. He could only remember the feeling—soft joy—and the spread of Kate's smile. He pressed his head into his pillow, trying to sink back into the warmth, but he couldn't find it again. Despite his layers of blankets, his room was freezing.

When he'd returned from the cave last night, exhaustion from the journey and difficult conversations had sent him to sleep right away, but he felt more rested than he had in a long time. Unburdening secrets together was like dropping an anchor in a churning sea, finding an unexpected tether to stability.

If he ever met that Reverend Castor, they'd find out just how much more blood Oliver was willing to spill.

Oliver sighed and opened his eyes. Early morning sunlight washed his childhood bedroom in robin's egg blue.

Thin scratches covered his wallpaper. In places, they gouged deep enough to uncover the wood below, leaving a strip of paper to curl weakly toward the floor. In a rough circle as wide as a hay bale, the scratches created uneven rows of spindly words.

Oliver scrambled upright, and the icy cold of the room slapped his bare skin.

NOCT

ULTIO

AMANS

LEGATUS

NOCT

NOCT

N O C T

The letters were nonsense, but etched with a manic sharpness that sent horrified chills through Oliver.

The rocking chair creaked.

A man sat in it, his eyes locked on Oliver. He was tall and slender, uncomfortably folded into the chair that was more suited to Ma's slight frame. Blood painted his left temple. At first, he looked as solid as the room around him, but every few seconds he would flicker like a lightning storm. His expression was intense, unrelenting, and desperate in some existential way that Oliver could hardly bear to witness.

One of his fingers traced a pattern onto the arm beneath it. An N was engraved deep into the wood beneath his nail, but he had lost the corporeality that had let him carve it—now, his finger went through the wood with every stroke.

"Who are you?" Oliver demanded, fisting his hands into the sheets. "What do you want?"

Fury. Despair. Frustration. The ghost pointed a long finger at the carvings in the wall and flickered again, more violently now. His mouth moved, but no sound came out.

Oliver swallowed hard. "How are you here? Tell me how I can summon one of you."

The spirit's anger intensified like a wildfire through dry leaves. He slashed his hand through the air, an unmistakable denial. He stood up and marched toward Oliver's bed, but left wisps of himself as he moved. He dissipated like morning mist, gone before his grasping hand could reach Oliver.

But not before Oliver recognized his eyes.

Pa was packing his bag when Oliver rushed down the stairs. Oliver wore a canvas coat over his pajamas and woolen socks without shoes. His hair fell in his face without his pomade, but it was almost time for Pa to leave for the mill.

"Junior?" Pa looked him up and down, frowning.

Shock still flooded through Oliver's body like a river after a storm. "Pa, tell me—how did Grandpa Herman die?"

Pa looked like he had come home to find a vagrant on his doorstep. "This is what you came thundering downstairs like this for?" he asked. "What's gotten into you?"

Oliver took a short breath and tried to sound calm. "I just want to know."

With a sigh, Pa closed his bag and put it over his shoulder. "Heart attack."

"Oh."

"He went out for a hike somewhere in the mountains. He always liked the woods. It took a while for anyone to find him. But I knew he had gone on. A man like that doesn't up and leave his mill. Or his family. You were only two or three, at the time. His only grandchild." He cleared his throat. "They said it would have been quick. He passed out when it happened."

"And he hit his head?" Oliver asked, brushing his fingers over his own left temple. It explained the blood.

Pa's eyes widened. It took Oliver a moment to realize it was fear on his face—he'd never seen that expression before. "What the hell are you talking about?"

"N-nothing." Oliver stumbled over the word. "Nothing. I had just heard it somewhere."

Pa huffed, making his pale mustache tremble. "Don't go spreading that nonsense anywhere else, you hear?" He jabbed a finger at Oliver's face. "We don't need people talking about you any more than they already do."

Oliver swallowed. "Yes, sir."

"Now go get dressed. Being a layabout is no excuse for looking like one." With one last unreadable look, Pa left the house, slamming the door behind him.

It took a long time for Oliver's hands to stop shaking.

22

NORA JO

"I can't wait for okra season," Miss Ethel said, waving a piece of pickled beet on the end of her fork. "I'm tired of this."

Nora Jo nodded, suppressing a yawn. The long nights were exhausting her, though she slept for much of the day. "Not too long now, right? Thank you for making dinner."

"We just finished planting the okra, so in a few months we'll be in business. I have more time to cook now that I have Kate to help in the garden," Miss Ethel said. "She'll be by later this afternoon. Maybe you can finally sit down and have a chat with her."

What was it about this new girl that so endeared her to Miss Ethel, when she had refused Nora Jo's help?

"I'm going out after I eat," Nora Jo said, "but I'll be sure to say hello one day."

"You've been going out a lot."

Nora Jo hesitated with her fork halfway to her mouth. "The weather's been nice, and I don't have nowhere else to be."

Miss Ethel hummed, skeptical.

"I'll have your rent for you on time," Nora Jo said. Harlow's pay was more generous than she had expected—fifty dollars a month. It was nearly as much as she would have made if she'd kept her teaching job, and none had to go back into the school.

"Don't be a fool. You can't pay me."

"I have savings, I promise. I'm still staying in your home, and now you have your new girl as well." Perhaps this was the reason Miss Ethel had turned to Kate—Nora Jo was already threatening to become a burden.

"You don't tell me what I can afford," Miss Ethel told her. "I can manage it, no matter what your brother thinks."

"You've talked to Beau?"

"I didn't have to," she said. "He's never liked you staying here. Your dad was worse. He used to ask me every Sunday when I'd let you fail on your own."

"I'm sorry. Beau…"

"Look, I've lived in this town my whole life. I knew your granddaddy in his time. He was the same type. Your brother is the least offensive of the lot, to be honest."

"Miss Ethel… Did you know my grandma? The one who left?"

"Gwen Ellsworth Barker," Miss Ethel mused. "I sure did."

"Do you know what happened to her after she left Chatuga?"

"I can't say I do." She took a breath, as though speaking so much had wearied her. "After she left, it was like she was a ghost. The Barkers never talked about her again."

"Everyone else in town did," Nora Jo said, tearing off a piece of biscuit and letting it fall to her plate.

"People will gnaw on a piece of gossip until it's nothing but mush. Gwen leaving was a blow to your grandpa. A lot of people had been waiting to see that happen. People don't always think of what children will hear. I'm sure it left its scars on your pa. He lost his ma, and was stuck being raised by your grandpa. There wasn't much softness in Dusty Barker."

"So, do you think she was right to leave? To try to follow her own heart?"

Miss Ethel set down her fork and looked at Nora Jo with sharp eyes. "I can't say I think that. She made a promise before God, and she broke it, leaving your pa on his own. But there's not much a person won't do when they feel it's their survival on the line. I don't know what life was like inside that house. But she ran, and left other people to suffer in her stead." When Nora Jo nodded, staring down at her plate, Miss Ethel added, "Being born into a family isn't making a vow. You're still deciding your future. Until you've sworn yourself to one life and written off any others, you're beholden only to yourself. No matter what they say, we get to *decide* who we love in this world."

Nora Jo took a sip of tea, fighting to control her expression. Miss Ethel couldn't possibly know how closely that hit Nora Jo's heart.

Miss Ethel paused, her eyes snagging on Nora Jo's bare wrist. She had rolled up her sleeves for dinner, aware of how easily grease could spread and how little she could afford new clothing. She had tanned over the last few weeks spending her afternoons outside— and a scab from her work with Harlow the night before peeked out from the fabric.

"You've been having a rough time lately," Miss Ethel said slowly.

"People have it worse," Nora Jo said cautiously.

"I'm sure you're feeling right dejected."

"Well. Yes, ma'am," Nora Jo said.

"When we're angry, we look for easy answers."

"Ma'am?"

"Miss Nora Jo," Miss Ethel said briskly. "Your hair smells like sage and woodsmoke, and now you've been slicing yourself up. You're taking the quick route."

"I don't know what you mean," Nora Jo spluttered.

"There's a right way and a wrong way to do things, you know."

"There's nothing for you to worry about."

"I make it my business to worry. There are omens in the air these days in Chatuga, to eyes looking for them. There's power budding in this town, as sure as the spring. And that kind of power is a beacon to dark forces."

"Dark forces," Nora Jo repeated uneasily.

"There are great and terrible things in this world, and fools like you don't know what you're stepping into. Are you looking to have a demon ride you?"

"I don't think we have to worry about that in Chatuga," Nora Jo said.

"Don't mock what you don't understand. You're having enough trouble keeping afloat. No need to make it worse."

Nora Jo gritted her teeth. So everyone kept telling her. Everyone thought they could control her, push her in the direction they wanted. She had thought she'd at least have peace in her own home. Miss Ethel's home. She should have known better than to think there was anywhere she would be accepted.

The old woman shook her head, staring at Nora Jo with disappointment. "Look, I know you don't have a ma to tell you these things anymore, but—"

She couldn't sit there and listen to Miss Ethel try to take her ma's place. Ma, who had been a witch herself and had died before she could pass on her knowledge to Nora Jo. She would be *proud* of Nora Jo, and yet close-minded biddies like Miss Ethel had the gall to put words in her mouth.

"I'm done with dinner," Nora Jo said shortly, standing up. "I'll leave the rent by the front door as usual when it's time. Have a nice day, Miss Ethel."

As she walked away, she heard Miss Ethel sigh.

That night, Harlow led Nora Jo deep into an unfamiliar part of the woods. She hadn't realized how comfortable their usual path had become until she saw new landmarks all around.

The forests surrounding Chatuga were vast, sprawling freely until they crawled up the nearby mountains. Nora Jo normally met Harlow due north of town, but tonight they walked west. The pine needles and dried leaves beneath her feet began to mix with flat pieces of shale. Large rocks jutted from the earth around them like teeth in a giant's jaw. They reached a vast boulder that towered overhead, its face flat as if it had been sheared from the edge of a mountain.

"Over here," Harlow said, and led her to a narrow crack along the forest floor. Without hesitating, he crouched and slid feetfirst into the hole.

Swallowing nervously, Nora Jo followed. It was a tight squeeze, and her breasts and stomach scraped against the rough rock. She lost all sense of up or down for an instant, fear turning gravity on its head. There was only stone.

Then, one of Harlow's small flame lights appeared beside her. Her face was mere inches from the rock, but the light meant she wasn't alone. She took a loud, shaky breath. Her torso was compressed, but her arms could stretch out to her sides. She used her hands to push herself further forward, following Harlow.

Suddenly, her legs emerged, dangling in chill, damp air. Still, she pushed harder, desperate to leave the tight rock pinch. As her chest slid free, her boot finally landed on a ledge below.

She fell the rest of the way, then stood up in a cavern lit by a scattering of floating flames. They cast eerie shadows against the stone, catching on crevasses and stalagmites to create abysses and mountains.

"This is…" Nora Jo spun in a circle, looking around. "Lord."

"There's more," Harlow said, waving for her to follow him into a small tunnel.

She walked carefully, mindful of the slick, uneven ground beneath her boots. The only sound in the tight space was her steps. The world above seemed to have disappeared. The ceiling closed over them like two cupped hands, narrowing quickly until the stone pressed together.

Finally, they climbed down a pile of rocks, and Harlow held out his hand to stop Nora Jo from moving further. He sent his flames out beyond them, flying into the vast empty space ahead. After the squeeze of the tunnel, it felt like stepping into nothingness. Her eyes adjusted, and she realized they were standing at the edge of a dark underground lake.

The chamber was vast. The shore, if it could be called that, was a ledge no wider than ten feet that led toward the lake below. The water was still as the grave, and oddly clear. In the firelight, the flat water reflected the jagged cave ceiling overhead like a polished mirror.

"What is this place?" she asked. She had heard of something like this under the caves of Chatuga. "Why does the lake look like that?"

"The water has been sitting there for longer than this town has existed. Still water in places like this tends to pick up some unusual characteristics."

"How did you know this was here?"

"I'm sure I'm not the first person to uncover it," Harlow said. "There are traces of humans here, though they're a few years old. I found it because this lake sits at the crossroads of two ley lines that run through Chatuga. It's a powerful spot."

"You said the ley lines draw people to them. Why is this abandoned?"

"These places of power come and go. There are still so many unexplored areas in America, even here in the east. There have probably been times of gathering here—the natives first, and then anyone looking for a place to hide—before it was lost again. There are easier hiding places, and ones less likely to result in a cave-in."

Nora Jo blanched. "Could that happen? How far underground are we?"

"You're sure you want to know?" Harlow asked, raising his eyebrows. When she winced, he said, "Don't worry—this cave isn't close to a collapse. Anyways, not everyone is sensitive to places of power, and not many want to crawl into the dark, even if they can feel a pull. I can sense that there are animals down here— small ones, spiders and crickets and salamanders. They've probably never been out of the caves, nor their parents or grandparents or great-grandparents. I've seen caves like this before. A cricket feels the pull and hops in. After a few millennia, they lose their eyes and their color. They're mute and blind because they don't remember the other world. There's no sunlight here, no predators—only the steady pulse of the magic." He looked over the dark lake. "Here, at the right time, with the right knowledge, magic would have no limits. Can you feel it?"

With the flames dancing around them, reflecting off the flat water and sharp edges of the cave, Nora Jo could believe there was power in this space. She closed her eyes, seeking it out. The cave was cool and damp, and sounds echoed strangely around her. Despite that, she felt nothing. "I… don't. Not really."

"Your sensitivity's been muted by years of neglect. A bit like the cave crickets. You'll see the difference in your magic here. Summon a flame for me."

It was one of Harlow's favorite spells, but the magic had always eluded her no matter how hard she tried. Nora Jo held out her hand. Harlow was right—her power tasted different. It was stronger and louder, hovering in her spine instead of deep in her belly. She pulled at it, but it refused to come out.

"Let me have your knife," she suggested. That helped ease the way, pulling her magic to the surface.

"Not tonight. You need to do this on your own."

She gritted her teeth, focusing on her palm.

Nothing happened.

Who could conjure flame from nothing but air and desire? She wasn't strong enough for this.

One by one, each of Harlow's floating flames snuffed out, crashing the cave into a blackness more impenetrable than blindness.

"Mr. Harlow," she said, her heart suddenly pounding.

She couldn't feel her magic. What she felt was… darkness. More than the lack of light. There was *evil* in this cave. She was suddenly certain of it.

An animal fear clawed at her. She shouldn't be here. Something was watching her, licking its chops and tensing to rend her to pieces.

"Focus, Nora Jo," Harlow said.

"I can't," she said, voice thin. "Please…"

"You *can*," he insisted. "There's power inside you. I know it. You want light? Find it."

She scrambled inside herself. There was an infinite web of complexity in her body and mind, tangled and sticky and beyond comprehension. Lodged inside, somewhere, was her magic. She needed to find it, needed to bring light into this cave.

The sound of her own breathing was ragged in the quiet, echoing darkness.

The magic wasn't hidden inside her.

The magic… *was* her.

There was no part of her that wasn't touched by the power. She didn't need to plead with some god to unleash it. It was right there, in her thoughts and lungs and fingers. Her salvation was only a breath away.

Flame blossomed in her shaking hand.

The cave was normal around them. There was no great evil looming over her shoulder. She pressed a hand to her fluttering heart and tried to calm it as she looked around.

It had been nothing but a child's fear of the dark.

Still, the terror and the intensity of the cave had unlocked something inside her. These lessons were not going to create some new strength. She finally understood what Harlow meant. They were *unearthing* what had always been there.

"Very good," Harlow said.

He set her to work repeating the spell. After the first time, the magic flowed as easily as a stream. By the end, her brow was sweaty from igniting and snuffing a fire in her hand over and over, but she was flushed with victory.

This was what she had hoped to find with Harlow. Power. Potential. Maybe Miss Ethel was wrong that it came with too high a price.

Nora Jo frowned down at her palms. "My landlady made some… comments today about witchery."

His expression darkened. "You think she knows about us?"

"Not exactly," she said. "She thinks *I* might be practicing. She didn't mention you. But she said that magic could bring attention. She warned me about 'terrible things.' Demons." Nora Jo forced a laugh, but it fell hollow in the vast cave. "Earlier, I thought I felt something. Something watching. I think it was probably just in my head, but…"

"She's right," Harlow said, making Nora Jo's breath catch. "Some things are drawn to powerful magic. Demons among them."

"Demons? Truly?" Nora Jo felt she had been warned about demons every day of her life. If a screech owl calls at night, a demon is near. If the apple tree rots, a demon's passed by. If every omen that was said to herald a demon truly did, the town would be overrun. But Harlow was no preacher or paranoid granny, and his expression was grave.

"Have you noticed," he asked, "that I ward our training ground each night?" Nora Jo had not. "Magic—especially the magic of

more than one witch—calls to the demons untethered in this
world. It shines to them like a lighthouse."

"Have you seen them? The demons?"

"One came to me on a dark night when I was a young witch.
He called himself Amans. He was clever, but weak. With no body
to ground him, he was just a flame in the night. Dangerous, bright,
powerful, but insubstantial. My power had drawn his attention—I
was self-taught, and didn't know to protect myself. I ward us so we
can't be found by others like him."

"And it truly was a demon?"

"That's the word we use. They're not of this world," Harlow said.
"Like I said, they don't have their own shape here. They can try to
slip inside a human, but it's a tight fit. But magical bodies—there's
more room inside to spread out. The more power a human has
developed, the more likely it is they will make a good host. That's
why they're drawn to magic, as your landlady said." He shook his
head. "I'm more concerned about her. People don't treat witches
kindly. I've been run out of more than one town."

"She's been kind to me for a long time. She's never done me
wrong."

"I'd keep my distance if I were you. You have to be careful about
who you trust with this part of yourself."

"I will," she assured him.

"Good. And don't worry about demons. You should be safe for the
moment. You're still growing, and I protect you when you're with me."

"That's all I can do? Hope you're nearby?" Nora Jo asked. "There
must be some kind of magic to protect me from them. You were able
to find me, and Miss Ethel saw through me easily enough. Surely a
demon could as well."

He tapped his chin. "You make a right fair point. I don't want to lose my apprentice." He gave her a small smile; it made him look younger. He twisted his hand. When the motion finished, a small flannel pouch sat in his palm. In the glow of the floating fires around them, she could see a red string tying it closed. "I had planned to teach you to make one of these yourself, but this will do you for now."

He handed it to her. It was light in her hand. She rattled it, but the fabric wrapping muffled whatever was within. When she reached toward the string, he stopped her.

"If you look inside, it will break the spell. This is a jack—it will bring you luck, and protect you from harm. It's filled with stones and feathers—vulture for safety from death, crow for agility, and others. I can teach you its secrets later. Keep it on you at all times, sprinkle a few drops of running water on it every new moon to keep it active. Whiskey works better, but that's harder to get hold of these days. It will protect you when I'm not around. You only have to trust it—and yourself."

"Thank you," she said. She tucked the jack into her pocket. Compared to its power, it was no wonder Harlow had laughed at her grandmother's ring. Harlow's magic had rules and structure. A bauble to comfort a lonely child was nothing compared to that.

"You still look uneasy," Harlow said. "What if I show you that there's not as much to fear as you think? People are scared of all sorts of things they don't understand—demons included."

The next night, they met in the cave again.

Nora Jo had hardly been able to focus all day. She'd spent most of it regretting bringing up the question at all. A *demon*. Surely

Harlow wouldn't truly show her one, wouldn't put her face to face with the terror of humanity. He seemed calm, making her feel like one of the superstitious townsfolk he disdained.

Nora Jo's pulse hammered in her throat while Harlow set up his supplies on the lake's rocky shore. He was vague about the exact items, only giving her a censorious look when she asked what they were. She was seated across from him on the uneven stones, ordered to be still and quiet no matter what happened.

He started to speak words she couldn't understand. The cool damp of the cave seemed oppressive, and the exit far away.

Dread curled down Nora Jo's spine when Harlow bent to light a candle. The flame was small and peaceful and utterly terrifying.

"Legatus," he said.

The fire blossomed and turned a bright, rich red.

"Legatus," Harlow said again. "I bid you to listen to me. Answer my questions. Do you hear me?"

Nora Jo held her breath.

The voice, when it came, was cold and alien and indescribable. She couldn't have said if it was man or woman, adult or child. It seemed beyond that, made of something *else*, as different from Nora Jo as the flame was from her flesh. "Yes."

Nora Jo looked frantically at Harlow, but he was unconcerned. "Why are you here?" he asked.

"You told me to come here," the flame said.

Harlow nodded. "And why do you look this way?"

"I have no body. This plane only rewards the corporeal." There was fury in its voice. Nora Jo didn't know how she could tell. The emotion seemed to spill out, wider than the boundaries of that small flame.

"Tell us what you can do in this form."

"Listen. Watch. Perform like a foolish monkey for your whim."

"Can you hurt me?"

"I could, if you made a mistake," the demon said.

"But which of us is more powerful?"

The flame only flickered.

"I bade you to answer," Harlow said firmly.

"You," the demon hissed. "For now."

Harlow leaned forward and blew out the candle.

Nora Jo jumped, startled, but the flame simply disappeared. Smoke curled up from the wick, lazy and pale.

"Spiteful critter," he said.

"Where did it go?" she asked, following the trail of smoke as it faded against the cavern's high, dark ceiling.

"It's likely still near," Harlow said. "Stewing in its powerlessness. People fear what they don't understand, but they ain't in danger. Those concerns are for animals, which a demon would burn through quickly, or for children and old folks too weak to fight back."

"There's so much I don't know," Nora Jo said. It was astonishing and overwhelming. Her heavy, choking fear had gone, leaving a sense of wonder.

"Keep to your training, and you'll learn," Harlow said. "It's dangerous for powerful people to be ignorant. But you have me, and you have yourself. Someday, you'll have to trust in that."

23

OLIVER

The candle flickered on the windowsill, its reflection dancing on the glass pane.

Tonight wasn't one of his scheduled meetings with Kate, but Oliver's body refused to rest nonetheless. He had slept in hazy patches for a few hours, but his nightmares seemed to last days. He'd given up near six in the morning. The sun would be up soon, and the sheets were beginning to feel like shackles.

He sat in the worn rocking chair, watching the candle flicker. He rubbed over the N that the ghost of Grandpa Herman had carved into the wood.

One of his first memories was in this same chair, climbing onto his ma's lap after his pa had scolded him for breaking a plate. He had been young, but he could remember the steady rhythm and his ma's comforting whispers. The chair had stayed in his room even after the crib had been replaced with a bed, the floor beneath it worn raw over the years.

Soon, the sky outside would grow light.

Another image appeared in the black window beside the candle. The man standing behind the rocking chair was as defined as Oliver in the reflection. The blood on his temple was like a smear of darkness in the blurred window.

Oliver sat very still. His heart thudded, remembering the snarling face standing over him while he slept, Miss Florence's claws in his skin, Grandpa Herman's nails slicing apart his wallpaper. Tonight, Grandpa Herman was still, watching him with the intensity of a photograph.

Did Grandpa Herman know they were related? Would there be any connection between them, or was it only cruel chance?

"Hello," Oliver said cautiously, not turning from the window.

The spirit flickered again. It appeared directly behind the chair. Could Oliver feel the iciness of its presence, or was the chill from fear? Oliver met his own eyes in the window, wide in a pale face.

Kate would be disappointed if Oliver let this chance slip by. Oliver would be disappointed too. He wanted answers about his curse. If he wanted to talk to Tucker Lee again, he had to resist his fear.

Oliver cleared his throat. "It's me. I'm Oliver. Junior. I want to understand why you're here."

As always, Oliver's attention seemed to make the ghost clearer, more present. His grandpa stared at his reflection, and then down to the back of his head. He felt the gaze like frost against his nape.

"You haven't always haunted this house. You came to find me. Please. Tell me how. What makes you different?"

A deep voice came as though from across a field, drifting on the wind to Oliver's ear. "Noct…"

Oliver gestured to the wall. After the last incident, he had dragged the grandfather clock back in from the hallway to try to cover the writing carved into the wallpaper. "Right. I don't know what that means. What are you trying to say?"

The ghost looked furious and frustrated, pulsing just behind Oliver's shoulder. He seemed to barely cling to the room, flickering like a storm and lit by flashes of anger.

"You've been communicating with me. If I know what brought you here, then I can learn how to do it. Grandpa Herman," Oliver said. The candle's flame flickered. "You have to give me something else."

"Run," Grandpa Herman said. The voice now seemed to be in Oliver's ear. "Run or die."

Oliver flinched back, putting a hand to his cheek. The mark from Miss Florence had mostly healed, but the gashes had been unsettlingly long-lived. "Why?"

But the ghost was already gone.

Oliver stayed by the candle, trying to control his trembling. The room behind him was empty again, but he kept his eyes on the window just in case.

Run *where*? The danger could have been in the room, the house, or the whole state of Tennessee. Even more concerning, Oliver didn't know if it was a threat or a warning. Grandpa Herman hadn't hurt him yet, but from the ragged scratches on his walls he could.

Oliver rubbed his tired eyes, but sleep seemed miles away.

Grandpa Herman hadn't lived or died in Oliver's house, and he hadn't haunted it when Oliver first returned from Europe.

He wasn't stuck there. Something else had drawn him there—a purpose. *Noct*. What did it take to pull a spirit from its usual place? It had to be important. There had to be a reason.

Could ghosts be given a reason?

Oliver snuck from the house. It was strange to ignore the path to the caves, turning instead toward the barn.

Magnolia perked her ears and nickered when he slipped through the doors.

"Rest, girl," he murmured, rubbing her nose as he walked by. "I'm not going anywhere."

He climbed the ladder into the loft. The hay bales smelled musty and sweet, and the loose straw crunched under his boots. He sat on a bale by the small window, overlooking the farm. In the dark, the only light came from the moon overhead and the candles in the Wilkeses' home down the road.

Carefully, he put the bronze cigarette case on the windowsill. It was a quiet night, apart from the shuffling horses downstairs and the ever-present crickets and frogs in the fields around him.

How was he supposed to do this? Every ghost he had ever encountered had come to him. Grandpa Herman was the only one who seemed in control of his movements without Oliver's attention—the others drifted aimlessly, shackled to the paths of their lives until Oliver pulled their attention away. Oliver was in a dark wood with no map.

Would Tucker Lee's ghost be at his home in Raleigh? In that trench in France? Maybe he hadn't left a spirit behind at all. If he had, surely he would have found a way to Oliver by now.

He wished Kate were there. She was an invigorating presence, always gesturing as she spoke in a way that made shadows dance on the stone walls. Talking to Kate was the closest he had felt to his friendship with Tucker Lee since coming back to America.

And in the light of the kerosene lamp, she was strikingly beautiful.

Though, of course, she wouldn't help him with this attempt. Kate would be furious if she knew he was trying to expand his powers instead of finding a way to get rid of them.

He tried to clear his mind, tracing the shape of the cigarette case with his eyes every time his thoughts tried to wander. In the dark, it looked small and dull. His thumb had begun to wear down the engraving on the front—the filigree of the monogrammed TSL was fading.

Oliver remembered Tucker Lee flicking the lid open and tapping out a cigarette with short, deft fingers. Leaning into Oliver's shoulder at Camp Sevier, trading half his egg salad sandwich for Oliver's pimento cheese. Blond hair falling over his green eyes in the early morning before he slicked it back. Laughing when one of the British soldiers mocked their accents. Leaning back in his chair to cheer on the dancers in a club, both of them high with the excitement of sneaking off and watching metropolitan ladies. Draping his warm arm over Oliver's shoulders after too much to drink, the smell of sweat and alcohol thick in the air.

The cigarette case was unmoved on the sill. Oliver scrubbed a hand over his face. "Tucker Lee," he said, voice croaking. It felt cacophonously loud in the silent barn. "Are you there? I need to see you."

He remained achingly alone.

"Come on, man, now's the time you decide to be quiet?" he asked the air. Was Tucker Lee's spirit avoiding him? The boy he'd known had been incapable of holding a grudge, softening an hour after their arguments and striking up a conversation as though nothing had happened.

But perhaps Oliver had finally done the unforgiveable.

Oliver reached out to pick up the case from the windowsill. It was warm in his palm. There was still no sign of any spectral movement, no chill in the air.

Had Tucker Lee truly cared about the cigarette case? Tucker Lee had used the case and shared its contents with his friends, but he had never fucking cradled it to his chest.

All its meaning came from *Oliver's* memories.

Oliver was still where he had started—alone.

He clenched his fist around the cigarette case, lifting it to throw it out the window. At the last moment, he pulled the case close to his chest and let his head hang. He squeezed his eyes shut. The case had no heat, no heartbeat, but he would imagine for just a moment it had some of the life his friend had lost. He held it closer.

Oliver had failed Tucker Lee once again.

24

KATE

Kate's hands held the evidence of her years of work, recording her past like a book. Dyed blue and yellow from brewing colors for Mrs. Riley, dried out from scrubbing laundry for Miss Ethel and the Russells and Burtons, scarred on her right thumb from Mr. Swift's barbed wire fence, calloused at the tips from gardening and playing the fiddle. Tonight, as she went back to Tolbert-Vance for dinner, they were red and sore from the lye she'd used to scrub the News' floors.

No matter what her future held, she had her means to survive with her. Still, she would have appreciated a bit less sting.

She flexed her hands, then pushed open the door. Her parents often had guests over, so the deep voice in the kitchen didn't alarm her until she saw Willamae and Betty lurking in the hallway, clearly trying to eavesdrop.

"Who's in there?" Kate asked, making them both jump. "Where's Mary Evelyn?"

"In our room. She's afraid of getting caught," Betty said, voice hushed. "She's always been scared of the reverend."

Kate's breath stuttered. The reverend? She leaned over their heads to press her own ear to the door. She had to bend awkwardly over their forms—they had grown this year—and the tuft of Willamae's bun brushed her chin.

"… see why I should permit this. The whole affair has happened behind my back."

The familiar voice made Kate's knees lock. She gritted her teeth, willing her heart to slow. That man had no more power over her. He didn't.

"We didn't know either," Daddy pointed out. Where Reverend Wells David Castor was a cloud of bluster, always swelling as he spoke, Daddy was as calm as a lake.

Had they found out about Oliver? Sneaking into a cave at night to talk to a white boy about magic would warrant this sort of private meeting. Her parents would be upset, but the reverend would skip straight to handing out torches and pitchforks.

"I don't appreciate you acting as though this is a tragedy," Mama said. Kate was well-accustomed to her tone, which said her temper was pounding at the door. "Eileen is a good girl. You should feel blessed."

Eileen? Kate didn't wait any longer. Ignoring the hissed protests of her sisters, she pushed open the door and went into the kitchen. She and Eileen might clash like bulls in a field, but she wouldn't leave her to face the reverend on her own.

"I know you know how to knock," Mama groused.

The reverend sat next to their parents at the adult end of the table. Eileen and a boy sat close together at the other. Kate had seen him in the front pew every Sunday morning she could remember; he was the reverend's son, Josiah Castor.

"What's going on?" Kate demanded.

"I see you're no less wicked than you've ever been," Reverend Castor told Kate. "The adults are speaking."

"Reverend Castor was just leaving," Mama said.

"You know, I've been seeing signs of a demon in Chatuga," the reverend commented. His tone was offhand, contemplative, but his eyes locked on Kate. "Strange birds lurking around, black dogs howling, cows and pigs only birthing twins. The omens are all there. Have been for months. Maybe the Devil had a hand in this."

"Oh, hush your mouth, Reverend," Mama said. "There'll be none of that. We've proven there's no demon here. We need to talk to Eileen about whether *we* think this is the best idea for her. Marriage is a big step. We'll talk again tomorrow with more level heads all around."

The reverend had been watching Kate with cold, venomous eyes, but he shook his head at Mama's words and stood up. His chair scraped against the floor. "Fine. Josiah, with me." He tipped his hat to Mama, slighting both Kate and Eileen, and ushered his son out the side door.

As soon as the door closed, Kate turned to Eileen. "Tell me you're not thinking about marrying that boy."

"Georgia Kate," Daddy chided.

"We're in love," Eileen said, chin lifted stubbornly. Her body was still tilted toward the empty chair beside her, as if Josiah were still there.

"The reverend's son? You want to make Reverend Castor part

of our family?" Kate asked. "You don't want him to have control over you, Eileen. Trust me."

"The question here is whether Eileen is ready for marriage, not about her intended's family," Daddy said.

"It should be. That man is a snake. We should be stomping on him, not welcoming him into our kitchen," Kate said.

"Your granddaddy held that pulpit before Reverend Castor," Mama said. "He'd roll in his grave to even hear this conversation. Reverend Castor may not be our favorite person, but he deserves respect for his position."

"I'm not going to decide my life based on your feelings," Eileen told Kate coolly.

Feelings. How dare she act as though Kate were irrational? The rage that always lurked so close to the surface inside her boiled. Wildly, Kate thought perhaps her vision was right. She could strangle her sister. "You shouldn't trust that man. You don't know what he did to me."

"Kate, he was trying to help you," Mama said. "We all were."

"When people get glimpses of the future in the Bible, they're blessed by God," Kate snarled. "When I got them, the reverend tried to pray the demon out of me. When that didn't work, he tried to starve it out. Do you know what it was like?"

"You kept getting hurt. We didn't know what else to do," Mama said. "You would fall and twist around and come to talking about visions. We were worried it would kill you. He promised he would help."

"I don't blame you," Kate said. She had, for a long time. The reverend's methods hadn't worked, and they had taken her from him before he could try a worse tactic, but that didn't stop the nightmares. "You asked him to help, and he hurt me. I can't forgive him that. I blame *him*. I don't want him near our family."

"Josiah ain't his dad," Eileen said, but her face was ashen. She'd only been five when Kate was taken by the reverend, and had been sheltered from the bitter reality. Could she remember when Kate had come back, weak and terrified? When she flinched at every touch? When they had all cried as, despite everything, the visions kept coming?

"There's poison in that whole family. That man is the one possessed, not me," Kate said. "I wouldn't be surprised if *he* were demon-ridden."

"Reverend Castor is just a man," Mama said. "Men make mistakes."

"This isn't about the reverend or Kate," Eileen interrupted. "It's about me making my own decisions."

"I won't see you married at sixteen years old," Mama said. "You're too young."

"All our cousins got married then or younger!"

"And their babies nearly split them in two," Mama said. "Both of you, go to your room. I'll call when supper's ready. It'll be late because of our unexpected guests."

Kate and Eileen silently jostled each other down the hallway to their room. Eileen jabbed a sharp elbow into her stomach, and Kate shoved her against the wall. A painting wobbled—they both froze, watching as it settled back into place. Rolling her eyes, Kate let Eileen move ahead of her.

Kate was eighteen. She worked a dozen jobs and had dealt with some of the worst of life. Somehow, around her sisters, she became a child again. She was sure that when she and Eileen were in their eighties, they would still needle each other into tantrums. Ignoring Eileen, she went to her cot and sat down, staring at the wall. She heard Eileen settle in behind her. Their younger sisters were elsewhere—they'd probably scattered when the voices had risen in the kitchen.

"You don't even know that boy," Kate commented after a while. "I've never seen you spending time with him."

"You're not the only one who sneaks out at night."

Kate rolled over and stared at her sister. When had Eileen had time to sneak out? Kate was only gone for three hours at a time at most. Then again, there was a long time between when Kate snuck back into bed and the eventual dawn that woke her.

Kate was trying to find a way to stop her visions, to prevent a future in which she would try to murder her sister. What was Eileen doing? Flirting with the son of that bastard. What charms could Josiah Castor possibly hold?

"I won't tell if you won't," Eileen added. She had her arms folded tightly over her chest, and her jaw was set defiantly.

"Fine."

After supper, Daddy found Kate on the porch. She was leaning her elbows against the rail, watching lightning bugs flicker in the garden. One landed on the bottle tree, and its light echoed through the blue glass. She rubbed her hands up and down her arms, though it was a warm night.

Some days, she could forget about the cold, dark room under the church. About the way her stomach had clawed like a beast inside her. How her mouth had been dry as cotton. The reverend stomping down the stairs to shout Bible verses at her. How the seizures had come anyway, and she had woken up alone, half-slumped on the splintered pole.

"Hey, Georgia Kate," Daddy said. He wrapped an arm around her shoulders. She still fit easily against him. If she had been lost, blindfolded in a crowd, she was sure she could have found him by smell alone. The fresh-cut lumber he handled every day had seeped into him, a wild green scent that sharpened the warmth of his skin.

Kate hummed in response.

"I hate that man too," Daddy confided. Kate glanced up at him, surprised. "Your mama can't admit when she's wrong. She can't stand to think that we caused you pain. But I can't forget how you looked when you first came back to us. You were scared. Scared of us. We were trying to help you, but we could have lost you forever."

"Then why did you do it? Why hand me over to him?"

"Because if he had been right about a demon inside you, it would have been even worse. He was trained by your granddaddy, you know. I trusted his judgement."

Kate snorted.

Her daddy nodded out to the bottle tree near the fence. "You know why we have that, don't you? My daddy warned me about demons. They scared him more than anything else in the world. They could be here, around us, and we wouldn't know. Even with your dreams, you wouldn't see them coming—they know more about that sort of power than any of us. They won't be seen unless they want to be seen. They float around on the wind like drowning beasts in a creek, desperate to grab onto the first living thing they can find, especially ones too weak to fight back. That's why we have the bottle tree, and the horseshoe over the doors." He stared at the blue glass. "My daddy told me once that he'd seen a group of poor souls who had been possessed."

Kate had never heard this story. "Really?"

"It was a few years before I was born. Back in seventy-six. There are signs of demon activity, to those who know how to look. He tracked one of them into the mountains. He found four of them capering around a bonfire. They were new to their bodies, twitching and jumping like puppets."

"Lord," Kate murmured.

"He did his research beforehand, learned a bit about them. Demons have their own names—dozens, really. They're older than time. A witch warned him about these monsters and told him what to expect." The breeze rustled the leaves in the garden, and Kate shivered. "He wouldn't tell me their names, said that names have power on their own. But he wanted me to know what was out there."

"What happened?"

"He exorcised them. One demon got away with its host. One person died in the process. I could never tell which part haunted him worse."

"So there's only the one left?"

"No," he said. "Exorcism is just temporary. There's no destroying demons. It sends them far from here, holding them at bay for a while. My daddy only talked to me about it once, and it gave me nightmares for years." He shook his head. "When the reverend suggested that's what had happened to you, I was almost relieved. Possession, at least, has a cure. I thought we could save you. We were desperate."

"I know, but… what he did left a mark on me. I don't know if I'll ever forget it."

"I know. I'll never forgive myself for making your childhood even worse. You already suffered so much, and our foolishness could have killed you. I have to live with that."

"I'm sorry." The words were the only ones that came to her, though she couldn't have said what she was sorry for. She leaned further into him, letting him take her weight.

Together, they watched the sky darken, and the lightning bugs appear and disappear.

25

NORA JO

Nora Jo lay in the field, a book resting open near her hip. She left it there to stare overhead. The early June sun was low, but heat still hung heavy like a blanket in the air.

The evening was so clear she could turn her head and see the peak of Old Blue in the distance. How much longer would Harlow stay to train her? It had been more than a month, and though Harlow seemed content in the back room of the Lyes' house, he had never expressed a desire to live in Chatuga.

Working as a teacher, she'd missed the thrill of learning new information herself, of expanding her horizons. The world was so much larger than she ever dreamed, and she was learning how to reshape it. She never wanted to stop.

Something small and vicious bit Nora Jo's hand. She winced and slapped it away. She'd grown accustomed to Harlow quieting the woods around him—without his presence, the mosquitos were happily feasting on Nora Jo's blood.

When the sun set, Nora Jo waved a hand to ignite the small oil lantern she had brought with her—fire was easy for her now—and picked up her book. She could have made the flames float around to illuminate the text, but she was hoping for company who would certainly notice such obvious magic.

She was rereading one of her old favorites, *Aurora Leigh*. The book had become a constant companion since she'd lost her job. After training with Harlow, lost world novels like *Of One Blood* had lost some of their glow. Why read books about the magic that slept in your backyard?

When the setting sun was only the barest hint of blue at the horizon, Gloria came carefully picking her way through the field, and flopped onto the grass beside Nora Jo.

"Long day?" Nora Jo asked.

"We planted from dawn to dusk," Gloria said. "I wanted to get away earlier, but it's that season. The dog days of summer are getting too close."

"I'm sure you're exhausted. You didn't have to come."

"I won't stay long," Gloria said, closing her eyes.

"You might fall asleep here." Nora Jo's voice was heavy with affection.

"Maybe," Gloria said. "I'd rather be here than at home."

It made something wild roll in Nora Jo's chest. "Why?"

Gloria opened one eye and looked up at her. "I like spending time with you, Nora Jo. Do I need another reason?" She frowned. "I'm not bothering you, am I? I know you come out here to be alone."

"No, no," Nora Jo said. "You're always welcome wherever I am."

"And why is that?" Gloria challenged. When Nora Jo hesitated, she said, "Well, then, there's no reason I can't feel the same way. Can't two people just enjoy each other's company?"

"Of course."

"I think you're the only person in this town who actually notices me." Gloria closed her eyes again. "Not just as another girl who might make a decent mother to kids that don't exist yet. Not just as my pa's daughter who delivers their food. You look at me like you see me. And when I look back, I see someone different than the other people here."

"Different?" Nora Jo repeated, her heart in her throat.

"You're so damn smart, Nora Jo. Thoughtful. You've been places."

"Only as far as Murfreesboro," Nora Jo muttered. She was grateful for the darkness and Gloria's closed eyes. Her face felt hot.

"You went alone to learn," Gloria said. "You've never let anyone tell you how to live."

"I've always had something to prove. I've never felt like I could belong." She swallowed. "You make me forget that."

Gloria smiled, her lips curving like the crescent moon overhead. "Read to me, Nora Jo," she suggested. "Start from wherever you were."

"You'll be lost. I can start at the beginning."

"I just like your voice," Gloria said.

How could she say no to that? Nora Jo picked up her abandoned book.

"But I could not hide my quickening inner life from those at watch," she read. Her voice wavered for a moment, feeling strange and loud in the quiet field, but she picked back up her usual rhythm as the text pulled her in. "They saw a light at a window now and then, they had not set there. Who had set it there?"

"You were right," Gloria said idly, eyes still closed. "I'm already lost."

"Sorry," Nora Jo said, closing the book.

"No, keep going. I just want to listen."

Nora Jo found her page again and read, "My father's sister started when she caught my soul agaze in my eyes. She could not say I had no business with a sort of soul, but plainly she objected, —and demurred, that souls were dangerous things to carry straight through all the spilt saltpetre of the world."

She read until she realized that Gloria had fallen asleep in the grass.

Nora Jo set the book aside and stared up at the night sky overhead, imagining a life alone with Gloria's bright smile. Perhaps Harlow would leave his house on top of Old Blue to her someday, and Nora Jo could use her witchcraft to provide them a quiet, simple life. Gloria could build a garden in the back with only the vegetables she wanted to grow, instead of selling them. When they grew as old and gray as Miss Ethel, Nora Jo could find her own apprentice to teach. Maybe a whole class.

Soon, she would have to wake Gloria and send her home, but they had a few more moments of peace. Nora Jo leaned back and counted the stars.

"You're daydreaming."

Nora Jo blinked. Harlow was standing in front of her, arms crossed. They were in a small clearing in the woods by the creek, just a few miles upriver from where Nora Jo had spent her afternoon.

After she woke the sleepy Gloria and ushered her back home, she'd quickly eaten the supper Miss Ethel had set out for her, then snuck out again. Harlow waited for her in the forest beyond Miss

Ethel's house. It had been difficult to follow his dark coat through the wood to the night's training spot. He hadn't conjured flames to light their path tonight—unlike Nora Jo, he had no trouble walking without tripping in the dark, and sometimes forgot her limitations.

"Sorry," she said. She still felt flushed and warm from the evening with Gloria.

"Don't waste my time," Harlow warned, voice harder than usual. He was in a strange mood this evening, distracted and irritated. "I chose you because I believed you wanted to learn."

"I do," Nora Jo assured him.

"You're not paying attention."

"I'm sorry. I'm just distracted. I was out late with a friend, but I got here in time, didn't I?"

Harlow frowned. "What friend?"

His tone was gruff, dampening the warmth in her chest. "A girl from town. She works on her family's farm. We've been spending some time together lately."

"Hm. This is a new friend?"

"Not quite," Nora Jo said. "Her brother was in my class. Now that I'm not working, we have more time to meet. She's… nice." The word was too weak. Speaking about her felt clumsy—nothing could express the strength of Gloria's glow.

"You should be careful who you trust, Nora Jo."

"What? Why?"

"You're growing more powerful by the day, and you'd be more so if you dedicated yourself to the craft. There are people who would take advantage of that. Be wary of their motivations. You don't know how to protect yourself."

"She's not like that."

"There's a lot you don't know. There are those who are drawn to power. They'll use you for it. You'd be lucky to leave with your life."

Nora Jo's joyous cloud had fully dissipated. When had Gloria first approached her directly? She'd been bringing treats to the school since before Teddy graduated, but had she ever stopped Nora Jo on the street until Harlow had come to town?

Surely there couldn't be a hidden motive in the beautiful girl who had shared her candy and smiled so sweetly?

Nora Jo felt hot and itchy, her soft ease from earlier churning like venom in her stomach. He was wrong. He had to be.

No one would just let Nora Jo be happy.

She swallowed. "She won't interfere with what we're doing."

"She already has. I need your focus," Harlow said. "Maybe you should stop seeing her."

"No!" Nora Jo said, the word tripping from her mouth reflexively.

He stared at her, eyes only a glint in the night. There was a rustle nearby, and his black coat spun. Nora Jo blinked, trying to track the movement in the darkness. He had launched himself toward the ground, faster than she would have expected for a man of his size.

When he stood up again, he was composed. He held a bundle of fur aloft in one hand. Nora Jo stepped closer and saw a small brown rabbit cowering in his grasp, its ears tucked and legs dangling.

"Fine. Prove you were paying attention. You weren't interested in my lecture, so perhaps a practical lesson is in order," he said, holding the rabbit up by the scruff. "Rabbits' feet are one of the luckiest charms a witch can make. They can protect the wearer from evil spirits, and are less limited than a corncob over the door.

Only the left hind paw, of course. Each rabbit only has one lucky foot. Hold this." He thrust the rabbit toward her.

Nora Jo took the rabbit cautiously. Its fur was soft beneath her fingers, its pulse beating so rapidly she could feel it thrum through her own body. It didn't try to twist away, only hung frozen from her hand. "I..." She hesitated. Like every child in Chatuga, she had grown up with the slaughter of animals. There'd been a small farm attached to her parents' home, and she had helped butcher rabbits, deer, and chickens over the years. Seeing Harlow dive into the underbrush like a wolf to snatch the rabbit from its home, however, made her sympathize with the soft, fluttery thing in her hand. It had only been living its life when change swooped down upon it. "It has to be a rabbit?"

"There's nothing more powerful than an innocent life cut short," Harlow said. "But we're not taking this one's foot tonight. The charm only works if the foot is dipped into moonshine poured into a tree stump in a graveyard—we would need to walk halfway across town with that one. At some point, we'll make that charm too, but not tonight. Tonight is for more interesting magic."

He gestured for her to follow him. She stepped carefully through the dark woods, matching his footsteps as closely as she could. The moon was barely a sliver overhead, covered by the broad clouds rolling past. The clear sky of the afternoon had given way to a night that threatened to storm.

There was a small pond in the forest, visible only in the absence of undergrowth. It seemed like a fallen patch of starless night sky, shadowed by a thick canopy of trees. When Harlow summoned a burst of fire into the clearing, Nora Jo blinked against the glow. The orange flame illuminated the small pond, which was flat and still as a mirror. He tipped a small white candle from his pocket into the flame to light it.

Nora Jo realized that the rabbit was the first animal she had seen in the woods since she had begun her nighttime ventures with Harlow. The forest was always quieter around them than when she was alone, as if it were holding its breath as they passed through. In the far distance, she could hear the thrum of unseen frogs and insects. If there were any animals in the pond, they were hidden or asleep, leaving the surface unmolested.

"Most spells need creeks, streams—something quick and displaced, easily directed, thrumming with energy. But we're not using the water. This magic works best in a dark room with a mirror, but neither of our hosts would approve and we're far from my cabin."

Harlow hadn't invited her up to Old Blue for their training even after Nora Jo lost her job. She thought, perhaps, he was leaving an easy out—for her and for him. The sensation of being tested hadn't lessened. Was he regretting choosing her as his apprentice? She wished she hadn't allowed herself to be so obviously distracted by Gloria at the start of the lesson. "Sit here," Harlow said.

Nora Jo knelt beside him at the edge of the pond where the dry leaves gave way to mud, keeping careful hold of the rabbit. Her boots slipped before she tucked them closer to her knees. The candle's glow lit their faces, casting them in harsh shadows on the surface of the pond.

"First, look at the rabbit."

Still concerned the night was going to end with having to chop the poor rabbit's foot off, Nora Jo held the creature aloft and examined it. Its wide black eyes glinted like buttons in the candlelight. Its ears were pressed against its skull, brushing the hand that gripped its scruff, but it didn't try to kick free from her grasp.

"Feel its heartbeat. So much quicker than yours. See its body, the way it holds its life in a different vessel than yours. It's smaller than you in every sense. Its brain is the size of a walnut, tucked in a small, fragile skull. But you're the same. You breathe the same air. The blood in your veins looks the same when it's spilled. You touch the same earth."

The rabbit twitched in her hand.

"Give me your other arm."

Without looking away from the rabbit, she held out her left arm. She knew what the request meant. Over the past weeks, she had spilled a fair amount of blood in pursuit of her quest. Instead of rolling up her sleeve to reach her forearm as usual, Harlow pricked one of her fingers with the knife. She winced, but kept her eyes focused. She would prove she was worth teaching.

"Brush the blood over its forehead," Harlow instructed. "Create a bond."

Carefully, Nora Jo dragged the wound over the rabbit's head. Even with the sting in the pad of her finger, she could feel the soft fur and quivering ears. The blood was difficult to see in the small light.

"Breathe slowly. Focus on the candle's reflection in the water. Imagine seeing through the rabbit's eyes. What the world looks like to the creature. Put yourself in its mind."

The mirrored candle flickered in the evening breeze. The light seemed to float in the water, part of a portal to somewhere strange and unfamiliar.

The dark circle of the pond was like the eye of the rabbit, black and unfathomable.

Nora Jo could tip forward and disappear into it.

Something massive was gripping her neck, holding her in the air. She kicked out, searching for the ground, but she was suspended in nothingness. She kicked again, and was slowly lowered down. She froze in terror before her feet touched the ground, and she bounded away from the monsters who had trapped her. Old leaves crunched under her feet. The night smelled wild around her.

She stopped a few feet away, staring at the two enormous shapes crouched by the pond. One, a slender figure with long hair, sat perfectly still. She seemed part of the landscape, a tree or boulder stuck in the mud. Unmoving, unalive.

The other, a large man, was staring back at her.

She knew him. Harlow.

And the woman beside him was Nora Jo.

She blinked, and then gasped as if she'd been drowning in the pond. She was in her own body again, back across the clearing. She scrambled on her hands and knees to turn and look at the last spot where the rabbit had crouched. She could see nothing in the darkness.

She gaped up at Harlow, pressing a hand to her chest. Her heartbeat, though rapid with confused alarm, felt deadly slow after the flutter it had been moments before. She felt too large, her body clumsy and imbalanced.

"Was that real?" she panted.

"Everything is connected," Harlow said. "Witchcraft, at its core, is about harnessing those connections. Sharing a body takes understanding your host, and the willpower to maintain the hold. When you stopped accepting your place in the rabbit's mind, you lost your grip on the connection. With time, you'll be able to hop around all night."

"You could have warned me," she said, rubbing at the back of her neck. She could feel the ghost of her own grip.

"Magic works best when you allow it to happen without examining it too closely," Harlow told her. "Would you have believed me if I told you that you could look through the eyes of a rabbit?" He raised his eyebrows, and she flushed. Harlow had gotten to know her well over their time training together. Her skepticism had been a regular sticking point. "Better to let you experience it for yourself than try to explain it."

"And I could do that with any animal?"

"Anything that lives and breathes," Harlow confirmed.

"That's astounding."

"We'll keep to small land animals for now. More can go wrong if you're swimming in a pond or flying overhead when you're startled back into your body." He nodded toward the last place Nora Jo—the rabbit—had been. "This can be dangerous."

Now that her eyes had adjusted, Nora Jo could see a small, still form huddled in the grass. "Did I kill it?" she whispered.

"It likely died from shock. With a weak animal body and your untrained mind, there are many risks. In time, you will find the form that suits you best, and dip in and out of its eyes with ease."

She frowned at the small animal she had briefly shared her life with. "'Animal body.' Could someone do this to a human?"

"Humans are far more complex than a rabbit. There's the will to contend with, which is a powerful thing. An intelligent mind can fight back. It would take a miracle for anyone to catch hold of someone like you and keep you."

Nora Jo nodded, rubbing at the back of her neck where she'd felt her own grip on the rabbit's body.

"There is so much more magic than you've understood yet, Nora Jo. This ain't the time for distractions. You have the power," Harlow said. "Your imagination holds you back. If you can break free of what you believe the world should look like, you'll find many surprises in what it truly is."

26

OLIVER

There was enough perfume in the church to overpower a mortician's garden.

Oliver mouthed his way through the opening hymns, trying not to breathe too deeply. Summer had arrived to sit on Chatuga, and the ladies seemed determined to bathe in perfume to hide any sweat. Pa was stoic beside him, seemingly unfazed by the heat or smell. Across the aisle, on the ladies' side of the church, Ma waved a fan in front of her face, swirling and spreading the floral cloud. They had another two hours to go, and it felt like time was crawling.

Were all churches this suffocating? Kate would be attending church in Tolbert-Vance right now, learning the same lessons in parallel across town. Did her church have the same hymns, or their own?

Before he had gotten to know Kate, he had always thought of Tolbert-Vance as secondary, like a reflection in a pond. If it weren't for Kate, he might never have looked beyond the people he knew.

She was fierce and clever. Her stories about her family made him wish their friendship weren't a secret. He wanted to exchange knowing glances with her at Eileen's tantrums, feel the warmth of her daddy's smile, meet the youngest sister she spoke about with such aching fondness. He wanted to know her life. There was still so much for him to learn.

Instead, he was trapped here, lungs burning, unable to breathe without fear of losing his careful control.

When everyone shuffled to sit down and hear the sermon, Oliver could stand it no longer.

"Excuse me," he muttered, slipping past his pa into the space by the wall and hurrying toward the door. It was better than needing to take the central aisle, but he could still feel eyes on him. People in Chatuga were always looking for a new source of gossip. Near the back, he saw the pale blue skirts of Lula May Mathis, who had roped him into conversation before the service started. She'd asked him to note the skirt, as it was part of an exclusive collection the general store was considering carrying. She'd twisted her hips to flash her ankle, as though the sight of it alone would put him on one knee for her. Oliver smiled at the floor as he passed by, though it felt like a skull's grimace, and didn't look up.

He burst outside, lungs heaving, and nearly collided with an elderly man in fur trappings. The thick furs made him seem bulkier than possible, more bear than man.

In Oliver's surprise, he caught the old man's eye. He wasn't alive. The ghost scowled at him, his mouth moving as though he were shouting. Oliver couldn't hear anything. The ghost lurched forward, and Oliver stumbled backward, shoulder slamming against the doorframe.

"You all right?"

He glanced down to find a woman—not a ghost this time, thank the Lord—sitting in the grass and leaning against the church wall beside the ladies' entrance. He looked back up, but the ghost had gone.

He wheezed for a moment, searching for the breath that had been startled out of him. In the fresh air, away from the perfume smog, his lungs were able to find a rhythm. The coughing fit that had been threatening since the moment he stepped inside faded, though it wasn't gone. It would be back soon.

The young woman on the ground was delicate as a blade of grass. Her brown hair was plaited, draping from under a straw bonnet. When she tilted her head to look up at him, the sun hit her face, and he recognized her.

"I'm fine, Miss Nora Jo."

The schoolteacher hummed. She had never taught him—he'd graduated while she was still training—but they'd been students together and she had worked a few years at his pa's mill. From what he remembered of her, it was no wonder she had become a teacher. She always had her nose in a book, seemed allergic to fun, and could make you feel two inches tall with a single word. His friends had complained that she was worse than Mrs. Wilson, even before she'd graduated. Ruth Shore had always said that the worst thing about Beau Barker was his sister.

He folded his arms, praying his lungs would cooperate. "What are you doing out here?" he asked, glancing down the empty street.

"Miss Ethel got me this far," Nora Jo said. That was right—she lived with one of the old ladies on the edge of town. "It's too nice a day to sit inside. I can hear the singing here, and with the way Reverend Hill shouts, I'll hear him too. I'm sure that counts."

"I don't rightly know," Oliver admitted.

"So why did you come out? The reverend has never been concise enough for it to be over already."

He shrugged, staring out at the street again. His throat was raw—he wondered if his voice sounded hoarse. What would Nora Jo think if she heard him coughing? If he had a fit where the whole church could hear? Oliver Chadwick Jr. taken out by some ladies' perfume. What a joke. Pa might truly send him off to an asylum if he made such a public scene.

"I was trying to avoid Miss Lula May," he said. "I can hardly get a moment's peace in the same room as her."

"Oh, you poor thing," Nora Jo said, plucking a piece of grass and rubbing it between her fingers. "To have girls throwing themselves at you every day. No wonder you had to run out like demons were chasing you."

"You're not inside either," he pointed out. He hesitated, then sat down on the grass beside her. In school, they had never shared more than a passing word, but she could provide a conversation and an excuse if someone asked why he didn't go right back in for the rest of the sermon.

"I've lost some of my tolerance for crowds," Nora Jo said.

"I reckon I have too." How long until Pa started checking for his return? Then again, maybe he wouldn't mind the break. He hadn't spoken more than a few words to Oliver since their conversation about Grandpa Herman the other morning. He tapped his knee. "Say—you read."

Nora Jo shrugged. "More than most."

"Do you know what 'noct' means? N-O-C-T."

"Hm." For the first time, Nora Jo seemed like she was engaged in the conversation. She mused quietly like she were savoring a hard candy. "That would have something to do with night, though I haven't heard it by itself. Maybe you're thinking of 'nocturnal.'"

"Maybe." Grandpa Herman had written his gibberish on the wall enough times that he should have been able to write out the longer word, but it could have broken somewhere in his memory.

"It sounds like they're almost done in there," Nora Jo said, as a hymn drifted from the building. "Lula May will be missing you. You'll break her heart hiding here."

"She doesn't even know me."

"She doesn't need to," Nora Jo said idly. "A Mathis-Chadwick alliance would own half this town. The Mathises have probably made it Lula May's homework to be your betrothed by solstice."

"Always the teacher," Oliver said, snorting. "Don't you ever get tired of it?"

Nora Jo's languid expression hardened, and Oliver remembered the gossip Ma had mentioned over dinner a few weeks ago. Nora Jo had been let go. There was some hint of bad blood; his pa had grumbled that Nora Jo always had thought herself better than the rest of the town.

"What's it like having everything you could ever want thrown into your lap?" she demanded, standing up and dusting off her skirts. "You laugh at girls like Lula May, but you should pity them for being stuck relying on *you* to give them a way to leave their parents' house."

"I never asked for it."

"No," Nora Jo said. "You've never had to ask for anything. Good day, Mr. Chadwick."

He watched her leave, rubbing his chest absently. The argument had aggravated his lungs again, and he took shallow, open-mouthed gulps to keep from succumbing to a cough.

Oliver napped for most of the afternoon. He'd gone back into the sermon after his encounter with Nora Jo Barker, and the assault of the perfume on his lungs had left him weak and shaky.

When he woke, it was dark outside. He lit a candle and sat in front of the window. Sleep had left him in a haze, and he couldn't find the energy to be surprised when Grandpa Herman appeared behind him.

"You're back," Oliver said. Since the first attempted conversation, he'd only seen the spirit in brief glances. He would flicker into the room at odd times, but wash away again before Oliver's next breath.

"Noct," Grandpa Herman said. His voice crackled like an untuned radio, coming from a great distance.

Oliver rubbed his face. He was so *tired*. "Want to give more vague warnings? I don't know what you want. I don't even know what you're saying."

The spirit responded, but the words disappeared before they could reach Oliver.

"Grandpa Herman. That does it, right? Names help. Herman Chadwick," Oliver said.

"Foolish child," the ghost spat. His face and voice grew clearer, though his phrases came in patches. "Bait on a line."

"I don't know what you mean," Oliver pointed out, unable to muster more of a reaction. His lungs protested even this much talking after their stress at church.

"Run. Leave," the spirit said. "The Chadwick line can't end here."

"Is Pa why you're here?"

"You're weaker than I was. You'll never be able to fight."

Oliver rubbed his aching forehead. "Well, you sure sound like Pa."

Grandpa Herman flickered. When he reappeared, his face was stormy. "You're weak and you've always been weak. Don't let the monsters get what they want. You—"

The window in front of Oliver rattled as something slammed into the glass, visible only as a dark blur in the night. From the sound, soft flesh colliding with a solid surface, Oliver suspected an owl had flown into the glass.

The chair creaked beneath him, rocking with the force of his alarm.

Fighting for breath, he turned around, but the room behind him was empty.

27

KATE

More and more, Kate caught herself smiling over her chores. She was going to see Oliver again tonight. They would try to learn more about their powers, but she was more excited to hear about his day, to sit in their quiet cave and talk again. Her work went by faster with thoughts of Oliver on her mind, and she was still thinking of him when she went home to help Mama prepare supper. Her sisters were still outside, enjoying the early summer warmth and lengthening days.

"What has you in such a good mood?"

Kate looked up from the potato she was peeling. The sudden silence made her realize she'd been humming. "Nothing, Mama."

Mama shrugged as she knocked the logs in the stove on the other side of the kitchen. Sweat dampened both their foreheads from the fire burning there. "I'm not complaining. You should play fiddle for us once we're done with supper. Everyone will enjoy that. I thought you'd have a chip on your shoulder about Eileen and the reverend's boy for the rest of your life."

Her good mood soured. "I keep thinking you're going to put your foot down and stop this," she said, going back to her potato. The mottled brown peels fell into the sink.

"As much as I hate it, your sister is near a grown woman," Mama said. "She's convinced me she's thought this through, as much as any sixteen-year-old can."

"But the Castors?" Kate asked. "She'll be flattened by the reverend and his witch of a wife in weeks."

"You know as well as I do that Eileen is no pushover. You've both got enough fire in your hearts to burn yourselves."

"We get it from you," Kate pointed out.

Mama sent her a quelling look and continued, "She's not the youngest person to marry in Chatuga, though I rightly think she'll struggle to be a wife and a mother—especially with her family so far away. I don't like to leave her here."

Kate imagined standing with Oliver while the train took her family away. It didn't seem so bad to stay behind if it was with the right person. She pushed his warm mismatched eyes from her thoughts—even if he were interested, it was illegal for them to marry.

"We might not need to go to Nashville," Kate said. "I've been working more."

"There are more people there. More jobs. You won't be scrounging so much for work. I've seen how you work your tail off," Mama said. "You know, I always thought you would be the first to plan on moving out of here. You used to talk about playing that fiddle at the Ryman Auditorium when you were this high." She put her hand down by her hip.

"I forgot about that." For years, Uncle Christopher had told her stories about the beautiful music he'd heard at Nashville's enormous concert hall. Kate practiced her fingers raw imagining herself on that stage.

"Chatuga hasn't always been kind to you," Mama said. "You'd turn a new page in Nashville."

Kate sighed. "I don't think they give concerts to girls who might have a fit mid-song."

"Maybe getting out of Chatuga will stop those too."

Kate wanted to tell her that she was searching for a solution, but she couldn't explain her nights with Oliver. Mama might approve of her goal, but not of her company.

Oliver's ghosts had first appeared in France, though he'd skirted past the details with the air of someone jumping over a bear trap. If his power had a start, it must have an end. Did Kate's have either?

"When did they start?" she asked. "The episodes? Do you remember... what happened to me?" Her memories of her childhood were hazy. Before she'd known what her visions meant, time had seemed incomprehensibly layered. She would see someone fall, or fight, or drop a dish. When she referenced the event, her parents would exchange an amused glance. Then, when the events unerringly occurred later on, the glances became alarmed.

Mama's jaw was tense as she stared into the fire. "You've always been this way," she said. "Even as a little babe, you would twist and cry. It broke my heart."

"Oh," Kate said, looking back down at the brown and white potato peels layered like maggots in dirt.

There was a wounded noise from her mother, like someone had struck her. "And it's my fault."

Kate turned to find a sight she hadn't seen since they'd gotten word of her granny's death: tears in Mama's eyes. She sniffed and looked at the ceiling, avoiding Kate's gaze. "I knew something was wrong before you were born, but everyone said I was being a paranoid first-time mother. I was so scared you'd been hurt inside me, but the midwife Claire said everything seemed fine. The birth was a long one. A day and a night. By the end, I was just praying for you to get out. And then you did. And you didn't make a sound.

"I was scared out of my mind. You weren't breathing. You were bloody and still. Claire looked at me with these big sad eyes. And I knew you were dead."

Kate put her hand to her chest, feeling her thudding heartbeat through her dress.

"I begged her to try to save you. I cried on the bed while she walked you up and down the room, rubbing a herbal tincture into your little chest and praying. I still remember how the stuff smelled over all the grime of the birth. Like a forest in winter. Finally, she brought you over to me. You were so still. It was like you weren't real." She dashed a knuckle under her eyes. "I asked you to wake up and… you did. You coughed and wheezed and wailed like a wolf. Claire was laughing when she took you back to clean you up. I kept crying. I didn't think it would last." She shook her head, arms crossed tightly over her chest. "I think it broke something in you. Separated you from the rest of us in your first moments."

Kate tried to sort through the thoughts spinning through her mind. Could her stillbirth truly be the cause of her visions? If she had touched death, why was it life that haunted her, rather than the ghosts that trailed Oliver? Or had breaking back into the world of the living given her a stronger hold on what life would bring her? "You never told me."

"You were just a baby. It was *my* heartbreak. You can't know what it was like. My first try being a mother, and I somehow hurt my new baby girl. Every time you cried, I was sure I'd caused it. I couldn't talk about it. Not even to your daddy."

Mama hadn't been much older than Eileen was now. Was this why she was so concerned about Eileen's early engagement?

Babies often died. It was the way of things. They were too frail, too gentle. There had been many a woman in town with a swollen belly who emerged at the end with empty arms. She imagined her mother screaming at the midwife to save Kate's small life. And she'd gotten a child with unnatural knowledge who seemed eager to dash her own brains out on the rocks every time she walked outside. She had never been able to stop fearing for Kate's life.

"I don't know if that's why you're the way you are," Mama admitted, "but I can't help but blame myself. I loved you so much. From the first kick, I only ever wanted to give you an easier life than I'd had. I was so scared I wasn't a good enough mother to you."

Kate swallowed. "You always have been."

After supper, as Kate played the fiddle for her family, Mama watched her with a hand pressed to her chest.

28

NORA JO

The air tasted of fresh water, green grass, and a sour spark of tension. "It's going to rain," Nora Jo commented.

"It's a clear sky, Nora Jo," Gloria said idly, staring overhead. June was well underway, bringing the sweltering heat of summer with it. The sky was a searing blue, stretching endlessly above the trees and distant mountains.

"We'll see," Nora Jo allowed. She couldn't read the weather as accurately as Harlow could, but he had trained her to sense the shifts in the air, the sound of the birds, and the energy swirling around them.

Usually, Gloria could only sneak out after dusk, but she was on delivery duty today and had asked Nora Jo to meet with her for a stolen hour just after noon. May and June were the busiest months for planting, and Gloria needed to spend most days at the farm.

Despite Harlow's warnings, Nora Jo hadn't given up a moment of the time Gloria could make for her. She could hardly stand to go into town anymore, constantly aware of the hypocritical and close-minded eyes on her. Stepping into church was beyond her, and after her spat with Oliver Chadwick Jr., she hadn't wasted any time even lurking on its steps. Miss Ethel looked at her with disappointment, no matter how carefully Nora Jo hid the cuts on her arms. Gloria was the only joy of Nora Jo's days; she wouldn't sacrifice her. Harlow was wrong. She could have both.

Nora Jo stretched her arms over her head, feeling the grasses bend beneath her. Her skin felt hot and her muscles loose, the world slowing down under the fierce gaze of the sun. "Sorry, go on. You were telling me about your adventures in candy-making."

"My failures," Gloria corrected, laughing. "You should have seen my pa's face when he came into the kitchen. It's too warm for the mint to set, I think, even at night. Instead, I had a ball of goop. It covered just about every surface in the room from where I'd tried to get it back onto the table. My hands felt like I'd been playing in the creek bed. In the dark, I must have looked like a demon dripping some evil goo from the beyond, hair half-done and wild-eyed."

"What did he say?"

"Not much. Just told me he wasn't buying more sugar and to get out to the field if I was so wide awake," she said, sighing. "You know my pa."

Nora Jo hummed. She had only met Mr. Daley a few times, but understood his nature from Gloria's stories.

"The farm is doing well—real well—but he's sure it won't last. He could have enough money to last a decade and he'd still be out before dawn every day working the land. He wants to find another income. Plus, he's worried about me. All my cousins are already married. He can't keep taking care of me."

Nora Jo hated when Gloria brought up marriage. "You never did say why you were up so early," Nora Jo said. "You must have been up near midnight to do all that before he even woke up."

"Well," Gloria said, sitting up. Nora Jo levered up to mimic her. "I couldn't sleep. You know how sometimes the future just looks... Well, it looks long and hard. My pa is so tired. Everyone in this town seems so tired. I'm afraid that will be me. I can already feel it, some days. So, I thought I'd try to make something sweet. But it didn't work."

The idea of Gloria, soft Gloria, worn down by a lifetime of labor and lean meals made Nora Jo's stomach twist. Farm work was taxing on the body, and motherhood was even worse.

Nora Jo reached forward and put her hand over Gloria's to comfort her. They both stilled at the first touch. The air between them was more charged than the oncoming storm.

"Oh, don't touch my hands," Gloria said, but she didn't move them. "I was picking carrots and onions all morning. I must smell a fright."

"I don't think so," Nora Jo said. She looked up at Gloria, and carefully lifted and kissed the back of her hand. It smelled of the farm, of dirt and life, but Nora Jo focused on the feel of her warm, freckled skin.

Gloria's eyes widened and her breath hitched, but she still didn't pull away. Her gaze was locked on Nora Jo's face. On her lips.

Carefully, Nora Jo leaned closer. She stopped a breath away. Their noses were nearly touching. Gloria's familiar face was distorted this close, moving from the seen to the felt. Nora Jo's heart pounded; she couldn't cross the final distance between them.

Who was she to touch Gloria Daley?

Then, Gloria surged forward and kissed her. The press of her lips was fierce, nearly painful. Her hands fisted in Nora Jo's dress. Nora Jo leaned forward. Neither of them quite knew how to move their lips, but Nora Jo could read the message being passed between them anyway. There was desperation threaded in every tilt of the head, every slick press of mouths.

Nora Jo rested a hand on Gloria's face, warm from the sun, and pulled back. She leaned forward to kiss her again, more gently. She wanted to trace the shape of Gloria's pink mouth, the divot of her upper lip, the plumpness of the lower. Gloria shivered as Nora Jo slid her hand down her shoulder and cupped it gently. The bone beneath was sharp and hard as a rock buried beneath dirt.

When she pulled away again, they were both panting. Gloria was red and gold as a sunset. Nora Jo marveled in the closeness of that flushed body. They had been experiencing the same moment, the same sensations. The same magic. Nora Jo had never felt a connection like this.

Why, then, did Gloria seem on the verge of tears? There was a sheen in her eyes as she stared at Nora Jo.

Nora Jo reached out to press her hand against that freckled cheek, no longer sure of her welcome. "What's wrong?"

"Nothing," Gloria said. "I just… I wish we could have this."

"We do."

Gloria shook her head, finally looking away. "You know we can't," she said, rubbing at the back of her neck. "This—this ain't what folks do."

"It can be what *we* do," Nora Jo said. "If we both want to. Don't you… want to?"

Gloria's mind was unknowable. Did she not feel the fire licking between them? To Nora Jo, it was the pull of bees to flowers, birds to the sky, deer to water.

"I've wanted to for years," Gloria whispered. "Even though I knew I shouldn't. I thought it would go away once you weren't such a mystery. But it's worse now. You're not a mystery. You're a girl, a living, breathing girl, no matter how poised and clever you are. And you look back when I look at you." She darted a guilty glance at Nora Jo's face. "I shouldn't have kept coming to see you."

"Why not?"

"Nora Jo," Gloria said, and it was the first time Nora Jo had heard the other girl sound annoyed. "You know why. You know it's unnatural. *We're* unnatural."

The words gnawed in Nora Jo's stomach, roiling in acid and tearing at her flesh. "Who decides what's natural?" she asked, voice rising. It seemed to echo in the still field. "Who says those people can control us? We don't got to live by their rules. They don't even follow them. How many men are raising babies that ain't their own? Everyone knows Mrs. Riley has been carrying on with Mr. Waites for years now. How many girls are sent away to hide babies outside of wedlock? Who can say what *we're* doing is wrong?"

Gloria shook her head, arms wrapped tight around her stomach. "I kissed a few boys during school, you know. You were older and so focused on your work. I don't think you ever saw us younger kids. We played games and laughed about it. Kissing was what everyone did to feel grown, like stealing sips of moonshine.

"But all I wanted was to kiss my best friend, Barbara. I was thirteen, and she was the first real friend I'd ever had. We could tell each other anything. I hadn't realized that I was always wearing a mask until I could take my smile off around her. I didn't have to be happy around her." She looked away. "I kissed her one night when we were playing in the woods. I thought she liked it too. It was… fun. Exciting. She giggled when it happened. I remember thinking I could taste her laughter. I thought… I don't know what I thought. I didn't know she'd tattled on me to her parents until I got home from school the next day and my pa whipped me raw."

"She was a fool," Nora Jo said. "That doesn't make it wrong."

"Barbara never talked to me again. The only good thing was that she was so embarrassed, she never told another soul. Both our parents wanted to keep it hidden. The kids at school thought she and I had had some secret fight. I guess we did. I never would have done it again, but… You treat me like I'm special. And the way you look at me—I feel like I really *am* special."

"You are special, Gloria. You're the loveliest girl I've ever met," Nora Jo said. Her voice sounded low and raw. "Why should Beau get to marry the girl he loves, but not me?"

"That's just the way it is."

"It shouldn't be. No one has to know but us. It's none of their business what we do together."

"What are we supposed to do?" Gloria asked. "You don't have a job. How much longer can you live with Miss Ethel before she needs a new tenant who can pay for that room? We're stuck here, Nora Jo."

"But you like me too," Nora Jo insisted. "You *feel* this."

"I do," Gloria said, voice unsteady. "But I shouldn't. We shouldn't."

"I never wanted you to feel like this was something bad." Nausea made the world sickly yellow around Nora Jo. "I wanted to spend time with you. I wanted you to want to spend time with me. I wanted you to want me. This whole time, you thought something's wrong with me?"

"No, no." Gloria reached toward her, but pulled her hand back to hide it in her lap. "You read to me, even when I don't understand what you're reading. You let me drag you around and bother you when you're trying to have your own time. You're the only person in this town who doesn't think I'm a little fool. But no one will let us do this."

"We'll keep it a secret," Nora Jo insisted. "No one has to know. You deserve to be happy. I… I deserve to be happy. They've already taken too much from us. They can't take this." She gestured to the quiet field around them.

"You've never cared what people thought of you," Gloria said. "I've always liked that about you. Everything I do is for other people."

"Their opinions don't matter. This is about us, you and me. We only need each other. We'll know, and that's what matters. Here, you can take this…" She twisted her mother's agate ring off her pinky and held it out.

"Nora Jo, you've worn that ring for as long as I've known you," Gloria said, taking it and sliding it back onto Nora Jo's finger. "That's not as subtle as you think. Everyone would know."

Nora Jo slumped.

"But thank you." Carefully, Gloria reached out and laced their fingers together. "You always seem to know how to live your life. I want that. I want… you."

"I'll find a way for us to be together," Nora Jo said. What else was she training with Harlow for? He lived on Old Blue alone. No one would question the eccentricities of a witch as powerful as Harlow, as powerful as Nora Jo would become. She didn't need Chatuga's rules—she could forge her own path.

Did she dare show Gloria some of the spells she was learning? She'd said she didn't think Nora Jo was a monster. Would seeing her magic, the bloody lines she'd need to draw on her own skin, change her mind? She remembered her dad's reaction to any sign of her ma's abilities. Even her most benign spells, like sweeping away the day's troubles, had to be hidden.

Nora Jo swallowed. One step at a time. "I'll prove that we don't need anyone else. I promise."

Gloria smiled and twisted so she could lean her head against Nora Jo's shoulder. Her hair smelled of crushed grass, lilacs, and sweat. "Be with me now, Nora Jo. The future isn't here yet."

They stayed curled together in the field until their hour passed and Gloria had to run home.

"Show me."

Nora Jo took a deep breath. The patch of grass was lit by a trio of candles stuck in the mud by the creek, illuminating the stack of rocks piled in front of her. The small flames bent as she spread her attention out, seeing the whole scene at once. The forest was silent around them, free from the constant thrumming that normally ricocheted through Tennessee nights. All Nora Jo had to do was let her mind unlatch from the anchors of expectation.

She lifted a hand. A stone lifted with it.

It spun slowly in the night air, its dark surface smooth.

Slowly, she raised her other hand, stretching her awareness to the larger stone at the edge of the pile. It wobbled, and Nora Jo forced herself not to hold her breath. The two stones orbited in front of her, swirling together until she finally let them drift back to the ground.

A ferocious smile tore across her face like lightning.

Harlow nodded to her. "You're doing well. You've grown even stronger than I expected."

She *felt* strong. Her kiss with Gloria that afternoon had given her a new energy, more than any spell had ever done.

The storm she'd predicted had swept through at dusk, heralded by a sickly green sky and quickening wind until the sky opened, leaving the ground soggy beneath her skirts. No matter. Miss Ethel had hired her new girl to help with chores, but Nora Jo did her own laundry to hide the stains that came from her daily wandering and nightly training.

"If you'd told me three months ago that I would be moving things with my mind," Nora Jo said, shaking her head and climbing to her feet. Harlow had taught her things she had never dreamed of: finding ley lines, walking in an animal's skin, moving the world around her, reading omens in flames and the natural world, summoning fire. Her notebook was filled with crammed notes in her private shorthand, detailing wonders that would not have been out of place in Oz.

"The power was inside you. It just needed to be released," Harlow said. "You've been dedicated to learning. It's why I chose you."

Gloria was afraid to fight against the world's expectations.

Nora Jo could become strong enough to fight for them both. With Harlow as her teacher, the future was limitless. Wasn't it?

"Not everyone takes kindly to witches," she said. "Has anyone ever tried to stop you?"

"Of course they have. Being a witch means you'll be ignored for the good you do, and blamed for any bad luck that happens in your county," Harlow said. "But it also means you have the power to protect yourself."

Nora Jo nodded, pleased. "And you can teach me? Not just the jack you gave me, but real magic, real ways to protect myself if someone comes for me?" She kept the jack in her pocket, a ward against harm, but it was flimsy in the face of Gloria's fears.

Harlow raised his eyebrows. "You can't think of any ways to use what I've already taught you? You're supposed to be a clever girl."

Nora Jo bristled. "What, should I throw rocks at them?"

"I don't appreciate your tone. Think about the powers you have. You could share eyes with a snake to strike them down. Call a storm down to drown them. See the omens and prevent them from ever making it to your doorstep. Witchery is useless without the will and imagination to see a new world." His black trench coat blended with the shadows of the clearing until only his face was visible. His eyes were bottomless in the night. "You want me to teach you ways to hurt your enemies? I could. I'll show you how to wither their womb or dry their seed so there will never be another in their line. You could curse them to bleed from every pore. Or, if you'd like, we can carve wax dolls in their shape. You can drive needles into their skin or melt them over a fire, and be rid of them for good. Humans are fragile. It's not too difficult to destroy them. Is that what you're asking to learn?"

"No!" Nora Jo's voice was a gunshot in the still, quiet clearing. "I don't want that."

Harlow hummed. "You ask for help, but you're afraid of your own power."

"I'm not," Nora Jo insisted. Why was he saying such horrible things? Did he want her to repent asking to learn harmful magic? "I just want to know how to protect myself. I don't need to be cruel."

"Of course not," Harlow said dryly.

"It's not just me I'm worried about," Nora Jo said. "I need to protect the people I love."

"Ah," Harlow said. The cold frustration swept out of him, leaving him mild again. "You're in love. Of course."

"Of course?"

"We all do rash things for love."

"You've been in love?"

"I have." He sat down by the creek, and she joined him, though her dress would protest more time in the mud. "I used to play the fiddle. No one could ever resist a man playing the fiddle. It took some time—love is never easy, is it?—but when we joined together, it felt like we could move mountains together. It was like being on top of the world."

It was strange to imagine the stoic hunter in a field of flowers, holding hands with a beautiful girl and dreaming of the future. "What happened?"

"The end of the story isn't done yet," he said. "It never is, is it? Not until death. And even then…" He shrugged. "The point is, trust me to teach you what you need to know."

She plucked a stalk of grass and twisted it between her fingers. "This town is against me. They have been from the start."

"You need to focus on the work. I have a plan. By the time your apprenticeship is done, you'll have the power you need and more. I won't rest until then." Nora Jo nodded, and he held out a hand to help her to her feet. "Come on. The night's young yet, and there's more to learn."

She followed him into the night, the flames floating alongside them.

Let the town tell her she couldn't live on her own, couldn't make her own path, couldn't love who she wanted. She would show them power they couldn't imagine.

29

KATE

In the beginning, Kate and Oliver had hidden in the caves as shelter from the storm, but it was obvious that their meetings had to remain secret. If they were caught, there would be no marriage negotiation like for Eileen and Josiah. Kate had heard of compromised girls being given fifty, even a hundred dollars to keep quiet and raise their bastard children. The girls and their children became pariahs, even if everyone knew the father was striding down Main Street without a care.

Conversations that had seemed romantic in her dreams were often innocuous in context, simple words rather than the perfect shells of happiness she'd gathered in her pockets. Still, Oliver had a way of watching her with those mismatched eyes that made Kate feel like the only person in the world.

She understood why a girl might make an unwise decision.

"The bull chased us all the way to the fence," Oliver was saying, laughter brightening his voice. She watched his hands dance in the lamplight. "I've never run so fast in my life."

Kate had told him Mama's story about her stillbirth, and he'd told her about recognizing the ghost of his grandfather, but after a while the conversation drifted to their childhoods. They rarely stayed on their mission the whole night. Conversation flowed too easily between them.

"What did you think would happen?" she asked, shaking her head and snorting.

Oliver shrugged. "We didn't think that far. Boys ain't known for their foresight."

Kate leaned back on her palms, legs stretched on the cool rock beneath her. "Your poor mama. It's a miracle you're still alive."

He stared at the lamp, smile fading. "Maybe that's why I see what I see," he said. "Because I'm supposed to be one of them. One of the dead."

When they first began to meet, Oliver had used dry humor to cover his bitterness, like adding maple syrup to medicinal castor oil. As they spent more time together, he had sloughed off some of the forced wit, giving her a glimpse behind his mask.

"That's not true," Kate said. "You've been in my dreams. This was meant to be your future. Besides, I died the day I was born. If anyone isn't supposed to have made it here, it's me."

"Hm. Then maybe all the death around me just soaked into my skin," Oliver said. "It was a different kind of death over in Europe. You were an innocent, Kate. I'm not."

Compared to the stories of Tennessee's own Sergeant York on the radio, Oliver's scarce references to the war seemed horrific. It wasn't a place of heroes. After weeks of talking to him in the caves, Kate saw it for what it truly was—tragic. The Great War had taken a boy, promised him glory, and chewed him up.

"It makes sense, if you think about it," Oliver continued. "I was poisoned by thousands of pointless deaths. You must have some bright future ahead of you for it to have already seeped into your mind. You're filled with the glow of potential." His tone was sarcastic, self-aware in its grandeur, but his eyes were intent on her face, as if there were truly a light on her skin.

"You're more than what you've seen."

Could Kate say the same for herself, when her own hands would choke Eileen one day? Mama talked about the Ryman Auditorium, but the only future promised to Kate was horror.

She stood up, holding out a hand to him. Though short, he was heavier than her, but he let her help him to his feet. "Come on."

"Where are we going?" he asked, voice hollow as a grave.

"The past and future ain't here tonight," Kate said, leaning to pick up the lantern. "We've never left this room."

"The rock is slick, and the tunnels are a maze," Oliver said. "Have pity on my ma. She thinks I've grown past recklessness."

"I can see the future, remember?" Kate said. "We make it out of here tonight. Trust me."

As they explored the warren of caves, grasping onto each other to save themselves from slipping and then laughingly stepping apart, Kate was filled with a sense of adventure. Let the visions wait. There was a world for them to explore together.

"You're sure you didn't miss a vision of us lying at the bottom of these caves?" Oliver asked dryly, but he followed her into the next area.

Kate was grateful for the dark. She didn't want him to see her expression. Of all her visions of Oliver, there had been one moment she had been sure predicted a love story worth waiting for. Despite the violence of receiving the vision—she'd woken from it on a road outside of Chatuga, an armful of firewood strewn in the dirt around her—she had kept the image close.

Oliver's face, only a breath away. Darkness around them. Warm hands against her cheeks, holding her in place. A thumb stroking over her cheekbone. Her name on his tongue. Maybe they *would* lie together in these caves.

She wanted the vision to happen, and she was terrified it might. The intimacy would be a gift, yet it would bring her another step closer to the horrible moment she would try to kill Eileen. How could her future hold both? How could any life contain so much good and so much bad?

"Pretty sure," she said. "Come on. Let's try this way."

They continued down into the caves. Each new turn seemed to unlock another endless branch. It was enchanting and mysterious, so far removed from her daily life.

"Do you hear that?" she asked, pausing. She kept her hands braced on the slime-covered walls. They were walking down a narrow, steeply declining tunnel.

Oliver stopped behind her, his heat pressing against her back. "Hear what?" His breath brushed her ear. She shivered.

"I don't know. Something." It sounded like the scrape of something against the stone. Were there any creatures down here?

The noise echoed, bouncing around the cave. She turned one way, then the other, but was always sure the noise was coming from the other direction. "I'm sure it's..." She turned, chasing the sound, and found herself eye-to-eye with Oliver. On the incline, they were the same height.

His eyes were dark in the lamp's light. She wanted to lean

closer, search out the subtle green and brown threaded through his irises.

"Kate," he murmured.

She knew this moment, this angle. She had just been thinking of this vision. Perhaps something in the air had already started to feel familiar to her. He would stare into her eyes, say *I'm glad we're here together* in that quiet, amused voice.

She wanted it, wanted his attention, but for every prophecy she allowed to happen, she was one step closer to trying to kill Eileen. She had to fight for her sister. She *could* be more than what she'd seen. She hadn't protected Mary Evelyn, but she could still save Eileen. She could break the flow of the future. She knew its steps like a dance. She could fall out of line.

Oliver brushed a thumb over her cheekbone, curious and gentle. "What's wrong?"

"Nothing," she snapped, breaking the quiet like a slap. "Let's go."

She turned to continue down the path, but her foot slid on the damp stone. She lost her footing, arms pinwheeling. Oliver caught her around the waist before she could hit the floor. They danced for a moment, unbalanced, before he turned her and settled her upright again. Back in the same position as before.

"Careful," he said as they steadied.

"Damn it," she swore.

He sighed with relief and cupped her face, tugging her closer to rest their foreheads together. "That was close, Kate." With a sigh, he rubbed his thumb across her cheekbone. "I'm glad we're here together. Otherwise, I think I'd be at the bottom of the tunnel."

And so the future had arrived, stumbling forward without her consent. Was there no escape?

Oliver was still smiling at her, oblivious. She put her hands on his chest and shoved him.

She regretted it immediately. With his hands still on her face, when he lost his balance, she did as well.

They skidded in a heap of limbs down the slick stone. The lamp shattered against the floor, dropping them into darkness. The world seemed to have no up or down as they slid into nothingness. Kate scrambled for purchase until she was suddenly pushed against the wall by a solid weight. The world stilled.

Once her mind settled, she realized Oliver had managed to grab onto the wall and use it to stop their momentum. She panted in the cradle of his arms. She had ended up pressed face-first to the wall, with Oliver curled behind her. Other than her racing heart and a sting on her arm from scraping the rock, she was stunned to find no pain in her body.

Oliver was wheezing quietly, the noise hollow and fast in the unfettered blackness.

"I'm sorry, I'm sorry. Are you all right?" she asked.

He started to speak, then fell into a coughing fit. She'd heard him cough before—he seemed unable to walk more than a half mile without his lungs protesting—but this was like his body was tearing itself apart. She stayed as still as she could, worried a wrong move would send them tumbling down the tunnel again.

Slowly, she twisted one hand to clasp it over the arm at her waist, gripping him tightly.

When the coughing finally subsided, he inhaled shakily and pressed his forehead against her back. She felt his warm breath through the thin fabric of her summer dress. Even midway through June, the caves were cool around them.

"You all right?" she asked again quietly.

"Fine."

"You don't sound fine," she said, rubbing a thumb over his forearm.

"You know how my lungs are." He adjusted his grip. She tensed, but the movement didn't start them sliding again. "Want to explain why you tried to kill us?"

"I…" Her excuses felt childish in the darkness; a toddler rejecting the realities of the world. How much longer did she have before she would turn into the person who would try to kill her own sister? This unquenchable anger might be the beginning. She could have hurt them both.

But not killed.

Even when she was fighting against the pull of the future, she found comfort in the assurance she would see Oliver in sunlight again. There was more to come for them.

"I'd seen that conversation," she said. "I've been trying to change the future, and that was my chance. I thought I could stop it."

"And did you?"

"No."

He sighed. "I know you don't want your visions, and you have good reason. Life has not been kind to you and your family. But they brought us together. We may never have spoken if you hadn't been waiting for me after that damn crow tried to rob me. Fate was good that night. I'm grateful for it. There's not much in my life that feels right. This does."

Carefully, she twisted in his arms. The stone scraped her legs, but she managed to turn so she was facing his voice. She reached out a hand to find him. Her fingers met the soft bump of his nose.

She dragged them down to his lips, chapped and full, then down to press against his chest.

"Even if it leads to something bad some day?" she asked.

"Even then." She could feel the thrum of his voice in his chest. The sound seemed to be getting even closer. "There are lots of sad times in this world, Kate. I won't regret the good ones."

His lips brushed against her cheek. He pressed a soft kiss there, then found his way to her mouth. It no longer mattered that they were surrounded by darkness, scraped and bruised. All she could feel was the heat of his lips on hers, his warm tongue. It was tentative, gentle, a hand outstretched in offer.

She pressed into him.

It was nothing like the giggling pecks she'd exchanged with boys in her younger years, curious to try what the adults all were doing. It was deep and intimate, sending flames licking down her throat and into her stomach.

Slowly, they pulled back. Kate grinned. "Why did you stop?" It was like running in an open field, diving into a lake, hiking through the mountain and coming across a clear view of the valley. There were endless miles ahead to be explored.

He laughed, a huff against her cheek. "There are better places for this," he pointed out. "And no reason to rush."

"So you say," she grumbled. She could think of nothing more appealing than falling into this new discovery.

"Come on up, Kate." Her name on his tongue felt like another caress. "We need to find our way out of here. I don't know how far we got from our usual cave before we fell, and the lantern is lost."

"Don't worry," Kate said as they leaned against each other to find their feet. "We'll make it. I can promise that."

*

It took them time to journey back through the caves, relying on Oliver's dwindling supply of matches to determine up from down. By the time they reached the exit, the night was growing late. They kissed again at the mouth of the cave, knowing they couldn't stay out longer. Eileen had already noticed Kate's adventures; a word to their parents would ruin their secret meetings.

Oliver's expression was warm and affectionate as they parted ways. Kate and Oliver were both angry people, too hurt by the world for gentleness. The softness between them felt all the more special for it, something they had carved for themselves and kept safe in their cave.

Kate smiled to herself as she walked through the familiar woods just outside Tolbert-Vance.

She put a hand against her lips. They were no longer swollen, but she thought she could still taste Oliver on her tongue. Her home was waiting for her. It might all change soon, if they had to make the move to Nashville. But she was changing too.

Maybe she'd pick up her fiddle in the morning. Her heart itched to play.

A branch snapped up ahead, and she realized the forest had fallen dead quiet around her. Her steps slowed as she peered forward into the woods. A massive, shaggy shape lumbered into view. She froze. Broad shoulders and hips rolled under dark fur. A broad face swung toward her. Dark eyes met hers.

The bear was large, twice the height of the biggest dogs in town and round as a barrel. Its mouth glinted wetly, its dark fur matted around fangs far longer than the one she carried in her pocket. It met her gaze for a terrifying moment. Its eyes were cold with raw pitilessness.

Then, it huffed through its mouth and continued into the forest.

She held herself still as stone in the quiet, her heart fluttering in terror. Each crunch of the bear's paws against the dried leaves and pine needles beyond was like a whip crack. Any moment, it could turn back toward her. Even once the footsteps faded, she stayed frozen for a long moment, terrified of its return.

Finally, she stepped forward. She watched the ground, careful not to break any errant sticks. She stopped when her boot found the edge of a viscous puddle.

Suddenly, she recognized this moment.

Dark liquid pooled on the forest floor at her feet. She smelled the same hot, sticky scent she knew from days they slaughtered their livestock. Blood had a weight to it. There were claw marks in the dirt, deep raking lines like the beginning of a garden.

She already knew what she would see next, but she couldn't stop herself from following the blood pool. The bare feet were horribly vulnerable left naked. A faded cotton nightshirt brushed against hairy calves.

The nightshirt had been white once. Now, its edges were smudged gray with wear, and the center of the fabric was only gaping darkness. The man's chest might have not existed at all if not for that wet gleam. His blood was black and shining in the moonlight.

She tore her gaze from the torn chest to the face. After a stunned moment, she recognized the heavy brow and wide lips.

It was Reverend Castor.

30

OLIVER

A noise startled Oliver from his sleep. He jerked awake, expecting his grandpa back to give him another warning, but it was only a rap at the door. "Come on down, Junior," Ma called. "It's time."

He stared at the ceiling. Decoration Day. His first since returning to the States last September. In June, everyone in Chatuga gathered in the main graveyard to decorate the graves old and new with flowers while the choir sang hymns. Before the war, Oliver had been dragged along with the other local young men to clear the brush and trim the grass to prepare for the celebration.

He'd always thought it was a boring holiday. Those in the graves couldn't appreciate the gesture, and the flowers would wither by the end of the week. Other than the choir, which practiced for weeks to prepare, no one seemed to enjoy it.

Now, the prospect filled him with dread. How would the ghosts react to the loud group of mourning locals? The abandoned church plot near his house was bad enough—he'd never had the courage to go to the active graveyard on the other side of town. Would the ghosts notice Oliver among the crowd?

Even in such a small town, there was too much death. How many of Chatuga's small graveyards would it take to inter every man who fell in the muddy fields of France?

If you killed every man, woman, and child in all of Tennessee ten times over, you might finally have a stack of bodies to match the war.

Oliver yawned and got up. He shouldn't have stayed out so late with Kate, but he couldn't regret getting the chance to kiss her. At least she was one right thing in his life.

He allowed himself a smile as he got dressed and wandered downstairs with mussed hair, following the smell of brewing coffee and sizzling bacon. Even Pa would be off work today. Ma must have decided to make one of the traditional breakfasts she saved for holidays. It was easier since they'd bought their first mechanical icebox last year. Before, the family had used the spring that ran between their farm and the Wilkeses' to cool their milk and butter, trekking over to the cool water to gather their stored dairy.

Oliver walked into the kitchen and then stopped as though he had slammed into a wall.

"There you are, Junior," Ma said. "I told you he was probably still sleeping," she added to their guest.

Sally Lou goddamn Walters smiled up at him. The last time he had seen her, her hair had been disheveled in grief, her beautiful face swollen and splotchy from tears shed in private. Today, her blonde hair was pulled tight under her bonnet, and she wore her Sunday best. She was even prettier than the photograph Oliver had seen a dozen times clutched in Tucker Lee's palm.

"Sally," he said, voice hoarse. "What are you doing here?"

"Junior," Ma admonished.

Pa frowned at him. "Is that any way to greet a guest?"

"I wanted to see you," Sally said. She twisted the ring on her finger. Her engagement ring. "I thought you would come to Raleigh." Decoration Day was celebrated at different points in the summer for different towns, based on their local schedules. Raleigh's celebration had been two weeks earlier. "You didn't answer my letters."

Oliver had burned each one after reading it. "They must have gotten lost."

"Why don't you two go out to the porch while I finish making breakfast?" Ma suggested, smile wide and brittle. "I'm sure you have lots to talk about."

Oliver found himself shoved onto the porch, a mug of coffee in his hands. Sally had tried to decline a drink, but ended up with a glass of sweet tea anyway. She shook her head as the door closed. "Your ma is a sweetheart. She seemed to think you'd be happy to see me."

Oliver didn't answer.

"I've been thinking about you a lot lately," Sally pressed. "I spent Decoration Day with the Seleckys. It was the first time I'd seen them in a long while."

Oliver had first met Sally and the Seleckys when they visited to bid Tucker Lee farewell after training camp. His own parents had been unable to make the trip—Oliver's private belief was that Ma was too distressed at the idea of seeing Oliver in his uniform—so Tucker Lee had dragged him along to meet his family and fiancée. They were given one weekend in Charleston before they shipped out for Calais. The Seleckys and Sally welcomed Oliver immediately. They were kind and outgoing, though it was strange to see Tucker Lee with the people who had mattered to him before Camp Sevier. They didn't know the version of Tucker Lee that Oliver knew, and he would never know who Tucker Lee was to them.

Most young lovers married before being separated by the war, but Tucker Lee had given Sally a carefully selected engagement ring and told her to wait for him to come back. "I don't want to rush it," he'd told Oliver in their bunk. "She deserves for it to be about more than fear."

She was still wearing the ring. But she would never become a Selecky.

"Are they…" What could Oliver ask? They couldn't be doing well, no more than he was.

"As good as they can be," Sally said, guessing his question. "I was glad to see them. But they don't remember Tucker Lee the way he was. You're the only one who knew him at the end. He wrote about you all the time."

Oliver snorted, staring out over the fields. Tucker Lee had gotten stacks of letters from home, but his responses had always been brief and nearly illegible. Oliver, with only dwindling correspondence from his ma, had resented him sometimes.

He wished he could go back in time and shake sense into himself, to not waste any of their time on petty jealousy.

"I'm surprised you could read his handwriting. I always told him you'd need a decoder."

"I got by."

How long had she pored over each short letter?

Oliver gripped his mug tightly. "He talked about you too. You know he loved you."

She rubbed a thumb over her ring. The gold gleamed in the morning light. It was simple, thin and fragile. Tucker Lee had spent most of his savings on it. He'd been sure the army money would make up for the splurge by the time they got married. He had been prouder of that ring than anything else in his life.

"I decided he'd want us to stay in touch," Sally said. "You couldn't come for his Decoration Day, but I could come to yours."

"I don't have no one buried here," Oliver said. "No one like him."

"Still," she said. "These days are hard on anyone who's lost someone. You'd have been thinking about him anyway. That's what happens on days like this. Everyone talks about death, and you think about your own losses. It doesn't matter where his grave is. You were his best friend. If anyone understands how much I miss him, it's you." She hesitated. "Ain't it?"

"Of course," Oliver snapped, turning to look back over the porch railing. "I'm always thinking about him."

It hurt deep in his chest to talk out loud about the only ghost he wished would haunt his steps.

Seeing Sally's solemn face made Oliver feel suddenly like the worst kind of traitor. When had he stopped fighting to talk to Tucker Lee? Kate was supposed to help, not distract him. He'd spent so long last night wandering the caves with her, holding her hand and watching her quick, clever mouth, yet he was no closer to summoning Tucker Lee.

He and Tucker Lee were supposed to always be each other's most important person.

"Me too," Sally said, touching his elbow. "Come on. Let's eat breakfast, and then we'll go to the graveyard with your family. We don't have to talk about him anymore, I swear. It's just… Tucker Lee wouldn't want either of us to be alone."

She was pale and red-eyed, her smile painted into place with doll-like perfection. Oliver fought a pang of anger. He didn't want her there. He didn't want to be confronted with another reason Tucker Lee should have lived instead of Oliver. He didn't want her understanding smiles. He would not be able to hide away from the painful Decoration Day ceremony with her and Ma pushing him toward the graveyard.

But she wasn't really there to comfort him. He knew that. She was there because she'd been unable to stay in Raleigh for another day alone. She saw a kindred spirit in Oliver and had sought him out. If Oliver did manage to summon Tucker Lee, he would disappear out of spite if he learned Oliver had abandoned Sally.

"No, I reckon he wouldn't," Oliver agreed, taking her arm and leading her back inside.

In stories, ghosts usually appeared when the hero was alone at night. There was something about loneliness and fear that set the atmosphere to lure spirits forward.

Watching the spirits roaming around the gathered mourners for Decoration Day in the late afternoon sunshine, Oliver knew it was a lie.

Alone, a stray sound or the unexpected brush of a cool hand was worth concern. In a crowd, it was expected. There were people all around, stuffed in their Sunday clothes and fanning themselves in the summer heat. Most had come straight from church that morning and were still talking to each other. They couldn't see that within the milling group were half as many ghosts.

He was sure there were more ghosts than there should have been, even with the crowd complicating his view. Were the spirits summoned by the ceremony? The attention from their families? Or was it *his* presence luring them in?

Oliver watched the spirit of an elderly woman in a tattered nightgown reach for a young boy. He must have been eighty years her junior, but the same arched nose protruded from his small face. The boy turned to look when her hands passed through his shoulders. He frowned, staring past the old woman, but relaxed when he saw one of the choirgirls passing nearby. He returned to his parents. The old woman's shoulders slumped. Suddenly, she twisted violently to look at Oliver. He quickly turned back to Sally to avoid her gaze.

Everyone in Chatuga was within the low gates of the graveyard, placing flowers on plots, polishing headstones, listening as the choir began to sing their hymns, and unknowingly walking through spirits.

Not quite everyone though—Tolbert-Vance had its own church, its own graveyard. Was Kate cleaning graves on her side of town, or did they celebrate on another day?

Suddenly, he wished he were at her side rather than with his parents and Sally. It had been hell to say goodbye last night. The most interesting part of him, the only part he hadn't left behind in France, was Kate.

"Who do you have here?"

At first, Oliver thought Sally had heard his thoughts, but she was gesturing to the headstones. Ma was carrying an armful of fresh flowers from her gardens, bright purple and yellow against her dark dress. "My ma's parents, my pa's parents, and his sister."

There were fewer spirits wandering the graveyard than headstones—no more than one for every five plots—and so far, Oliver hadn't seen Grandpa Herman or any of his other dead relatives. It was a relief; he didn't want to imagine confronting his grandpa's spirit in the middle of this crowd.

As he watched his parents, he suddenly glimpsed a uniform the color of river mud nearby. His mind and body froze.

He knew that uniform. He'd worn its twin.

Had Sally's presence drawn Tucker Lee to them?

Not daring to breathe, he looked up to the soldier's face.

It wasn't Tucker Lee. Wilbur and Torie Lye were standing by one of the newer headstones. They were both whey-faced, holding each other up. They looked even frailer than they had when Oliver first came home, right after the news of their son Noah's death. Oliver wasn't the only one unable to recover from the war.

Noah was watching them, his expression devastated. The front of his uniform was riddled with dark blood, holes pocking the fabric and flesh below. He was blurred like a dream, but Oliver could picture every stitch of that uniform.

Noah had been several years older than Oliver, twenty-four when he enlisted, but as the only two men from Chatuga going to Europe, there had been a quiet solidarity between them. Noah ended up stationed further south than Oliver. He'd been killed a year before the ceasefire. News of his death had reached Oliver months after it happened, traveling first to Chatuga, then through a tear-stained letter from Ma back to France.

Noah snapped his head to look at Oliver.

"I think the lilies should go to your ma's parents," Sally said.

"Sure," Oliver replied, unable to turn from the man in the bloody uniform. How many men had he seen die that same way? Their bodies shook with the impact of the bullets, like a tree in a storm. Had Noah been sent forward into the no-man's-land between the trenches? Or had he stood at the wrong moment, revealing himself to the enemy?

Had anyone been there to hold him while he died, or had he fallen alone in the mud?

Noah's expression grew furious as Oliver held his gaze. The ghost advanced toward him. He wasn't bound by the laws of nature—he passed through headstones and mourners alike at a speed too quick to follow, moving like wind across the graveyard.

Oliver took a startled step back.

"Help," Noah rasped, reaching toward him.

"Leave me alone," Oliver said, forcing himself to stand still. He couldn't run from a ghost, not in front of the entire town. He shouldn't have allowed himself to stare. Attention only made the dead stronger. Coming today had been foolish.

Instead of taking Kate's advice and trying to free himself of this burden, he'd spent his time deepening death's grip on his mind. But if it *had* been Tucker Lee in that familiar uniform—

"Oliver?"

"Help," Noah pressed. "Save them." The man's blood-soaked spirit was right before him. There was no scent beyond the flowers and people pressed around them, but Oliver knew the smell of that lifeblood. It would be coppery and bitter, would feel hot and slick against his hands.

"I'm sorry," Oliver breathed.

The ghost lunged forward, his hands passing through Oliver's chest. Iciness gripped his heart like a vice, his breath rushing from him in a winded groan. Noah shouted with fury as he pulled back and reached again, clawed hands stretching for Oliver's throat. "You have to stop it!" Noah shouted.

"Oliver!" Sally was suddenly between them. One of Noah's hands reached straight through her head, emerging through her eyes. She frowned, shuddering slightly. "Are you okay?"

Thwarted, Noah screamed again, then flickered out of sight like a broken movie reel.

Oliver gasped for air. Sally's hands fluttered over his shoulders as though looking for a puzzle piece to slot back into place. She leaned forward, catching his eyes. She didn't say anything for a moment. Then she declared, "We're leaving."

Dazed, he followed as she dragged him toward the graveyard gate. He stumbled over the grass and clustered townsfolk, but she didn't let him fall.

His parents were talking quietly with the Daleys while their two children—a daughter near his age, Gloria, and their younger son, Teddy—rearranged a bundle of flowers on a grave marked with their last name.

"Mr. and Mrs. Chadwick," Sally said. "Oliver is going to take me home. I'm feeling plumb faint." She leaned into him, supporting his weight while making it seem the reverse. "I'm sure y'all understand how hard this is for me, and it's just so hot. I didn't want Oliver to leave the celebration early, but he insisted."

They responded. Oliver couldn't listen though, focusing instead on not looking at any of the ghosts around them. They seemed to have pulled closer to him during the altercation with Noah.

Something was lurking just behind his ma's shoulder. He got the impression of dark eyes and a misshapen skull before he focused his gaze firmly on the ground.

On the walk back from the graveyard, Oliver fell into a vicious coughing fit. The terror had finally loosened its hold on him, and his lungs protested the rush of relief. He bent double on the side of the road, fighting for breath. If he could have found the words, he would have sent Sally back to the graveyard. Instead, he wheezed as she stood beside him, quietly waiting for it to pass.

"I still talk to my friends whose husbands did make it back," Sally commented when they began walking again. "They say there are scars no one can see. Their husbands can barely talk to them about it, but there's no hiding the changes." She sighed. "I shouldn't have made you go today."

"It wasn't that." Oliver rubbed a hand over his chest. Between the lingering chill from Noah's spectral hands and the cough, his lungs felt shredded.

They walked in silence up the path toward his house. "What was it?" she asked finally. When he didn't answer, she said, "Talk to me. Please."

"I'm not him," Oliver snapped, turning to her. "And you're not him. We're not friends, Sally. You don't need to do this."

Her face, flushed from the afternoon heat, reddened further. "Oliver Chadwick Jr.," she scolded. "You don't get to tell me we're not friends. You can't scare me away. I told you why I'm here. I'm not leaving you." She stepped closer. "Talk to me. Tell me what happened back there."

Other than Kate, no one looked at Oliver like he could be their tether in a storm. He could barely keep himself afloat.

But he couldn't let her down. Not Tucker Lee's girl.

"You'll think I'm mad," he told her.

She laughed. "The *world* is mad, Oliver. Try me."

"A ghost attacked me. In the graveyard. That's why I had to leave." He shook his head, shoving his hands in his pockets. "I told you how it would sound."

"A ghost?" she repeated, expression difficult to read.

"Didn't you feel it? It had its hands in you," Oliver said. He winced at the memory, shoulders hunching forward as if he could protect his chest from another attack. "I thought it was going to hurt someone."

Frowning, Sally raised a hand to her nose. "I thought I felt… Was that really a ghost?"

"Come inside. I'll try to explain." He glanced at the ring on her finger. "And if you believe me," he said slowly, "I have an idea. I need to think, but tonight… There's something I want to try."

31

KATE

It felt like a tasteless joke for Kate to sit through Reverend Castor's funeral. She might have skipped it entirely—maybe spat on his grave once the mourners had cleared—but Mama had asked her to come to support Eileen.

The reverend had left one last horror for her in his passing. The memory of his torn body would not leave her, nor the way it had shattered her sense of security. She'd spent countless nights in the woods over the last few weeks. It could have been her—or Oliver—under those claws.

Kate sat beside Eileen on the pew as the funeral went on, leaning into her arm despite the heat in the church. Eileen didn't seem to notice. She spent the entire ceremony staring at Josiah, who was holding himself together with visible difficulty. He was still so young, but with his mama wailing on his arm, he kept his face clear.

It was well known that the louder the mourning, the more loved a person had been on this earth. Kate and her family sat tight-lipped, but there was enough weeping in the church to flood the town.

After the elderly preacher from the town over spoke about Reverend Castor like he was God's gift to Tolbert-Vance, there were hymns and more wailing and long-winded speeches about Reverend Castor's grace and wisdom. The mourners stared at the closed casket like someone wonderous were inside.

Kate had barely made it through without laughing. Or screaming.

She was one of the few who knew what horrors that casket contained. He was holy to everyone here, but she knew better. He had tortured a young girl to rid her of a demon she didn't have, ignoring her hungry cries and chattering teeth for days. And in the end, he hadn't been protected by God. He was just a foolish mortal man who had been ripped apart by a bear.

Good riddance.

After the service, they followed the pallbearers to the small graveyard alongside the church. They'd decided to combine the funeral with Decoration Day, as the entire congregation would already be gathered. Someone had arrived ahead to prepare the graveyard, cleaning the old headstones and plots for vines and bramble, and setting out baskets of fresh flowers for people to use.

Kate rested a lily on the graves of her grandparents, lingering over her daddy's father. What would he have said about the man who'd replaced him as reverend? Had he truly been any better, or was the love of a son clouding Daddy's memory? Few men could take the power of the pulpit and not misuse it.

Kate's life would have been so very different with a preacher man who truly cared for her. Would her granddaddy have worked with her to solve her curse, or would he have been as close-minded as Reverend Castor?

Everyone gathered in small clusters around the graveyard, paying their respects to the reverend and their ancestors. The choir organized themselves by the gate and began singing a hymn. The song, mournful and haunting, echoed over the graveyard.

Oliver would have seen ghosts if he'd been there. He might even have seen Kate's granddaddy. He could have, in his own way, a stronger link to her long-dead relative than Kate ever had.

"Hell of a thing, isn't it?" commented Dicie, Uncle Christopher's youngest daughter. She was Kate's age, already married with two children. The children hovered beside her husband, a lanky man who worked with Daddy in the lumber mill, as he decorated a headstone. Dicie was wearing traditional black, a veil draped like netting over her short hair.

Uncle Christopher was over at their house more often than not, but his kids rarely came by. Kate never sought them out either—her older cousins had always treated Kate like a pariah, giggling at family functions when they talked about her within earshot. She was happy to avoid them when she could.

Weddings and funerals brought the community together like nothing else, shoving everyone together whether they wanted to be or not. Another thing to thank Reverend Castor for.

"It is," Kate agreed. She wondered if she could slip on home while everyone was distracted. Surely she'd paid her respects to the old bastard long enough.

"I was talking to Trudy—his daughter, the one that got married last year—this morning, and she could barely keep ahold of herself. She and I have always been friends, you know. But what she told me… Something like that, in the middle of Chatuga. It's a hell of a thing," she repeated.

Kate hummed in agreement.

"I mean, honestly," she pressed. "Is it true that *you* found him?"

Kate sighed. "Yes."

Dicie whistled. "I bet that was horrible. A bear attack, right here. Trudy could barely talk about it." She waited, but Kate didn't respond. These games were why Kate had never chased after her cousins' approval. "I'm sure you thought it was weird that he was out in the woods so late at night like that. Say… Why were *you* out there?"

"I assumed the bear got him earlier in the evening," Kate said, ignoring the prying question. She had already given her excuse to Daddy and the other men in town—she hated to use her visions to her advantage, but a tremulous mention of needing to walk off an episode had made them look away.

"No, he went out well after dark. Trudy's mama said the reverend came tearing downstairs, muttering something about a voice calling to him, and then ran off. She called for him—he was still in his bedclothes, without even his shoes—but he didn't come back. The next thing they heard was about you finding the body."

"I didn't know the preacher was mad. It explains a lot," Kate said.

Dicie leaned forward, eyebrows raised. "I never said he was mad."

"Why else would he run off like that?"

"Maybe something really *was* calling him," Dicie said. It was clear she was delighted to be sharing such a fascinatingly tragic story. "Apparently, he's done nothing but talk about demons for the past few months. Maybe one finally got him."

He had mentioned seeing signs in their kitchen. Kate had dismissed it as the ramblings of a bitter old man. "He was always talking about demons," she said coolly.

"Trudy said it had been worse than usual. He'd gotten right paranoid lately."

Kate shrugged. "He was fixated. Nothing more."

"Is it true he wasn't wearing his cross?"

Vividly, Kate remembered the empty hole of his chest. There had been no glint of gold. "I... He wasn't. How did you know?" Had the bear gotten a mouthful of it along with everything else?

"It was on the ground by his front door," Dicie said. "He threw it off when he went running. So strange. He never took it off, you know. Even in his sleep. That was how his wife knew something was wrong."

"Not when he took off running into the woods in the middle of the night in the first place?" Kate asked, raising an eyebrow.

Dicie shrugged. "Just telling you what I heard. He never took that cross off. You said yourself it wasn't there. So what happened?"

Could it truly have been a demon? She should have felt vindicated that he might have been killed by the very thing he'd accused her of being. He'd been looking at the wrong person and paid the price. But if it were true... Daddy said demons were the only thing his daddy ever feared. If there *was* one in Chatuga, why had it killed the reverend?

And what would it do next?

Pop. Pop. Pop.

The green bean snapped crisply under Kate's fingers. She broke off the stem and the butt, pulled the string free, then cracked it in half. The ends and string she tossed in a scrap bucket, while the two pieces went in a bowl between their rocking chairs.

Kate, Eileen, and Mary Evelyn sat in a circle on the porch, plucking green beans from a silver pail to peel and snap. When they'd gotten home from the funeral, Mama had instructed them to change out of their church clothes and set them to work on supper. The twins were helping Mama in the kitchen with the chicken and potatoes, though Betty tended to take out large chunks with the peeling knife. The green beans were from their garden, and the potatoes were from a patch they maintained deeper in the woods. Any unclaimed land around town could be used for growing, and potatoes sprawled enough underground to interrupt their other crops.

There were piles of food at the wake, but Kate had only picked at it. She wasn't sure if Mama had noticed, or if she just wanted to keep them all busy by preparing supper.

The porch was near silent as they worked. No one felt much like talking, so the only sounds were the snap and shush of the beans. Beyond the porch, Tolbert-Vance was subdued as well. A gray fog seemed to hang over the neighborhood.

Kate's mind was far away as she methodically prepared the beans. Her mind was stuck on the gossip Dicie had shared at the reverend's funeral.

The demons Daddy had described were lost and desperate, searching for the first thing they could cling to. She had heard of them taking over cats and rats and birds, cursing people's livestock and crops. Had one been trying to take over the reverend's body before he'd been attacked by the bear? Or had the demon *been* the bear? The look in its eye had been strange. But surely, if that had been the case, the beast wouldn't have walked away from her so easily.

Mary Evelyn bent to pick up more green beans. Kate lightly batted her hand away and grabbed some for her. She dropped them in Mary Evelyn's lap, the pale beans nestled in the drape of her cotton dress.

"She's not missing a hand," Eileen snapped.

"Excuse you?" Kate blinked at Eileen.

Eileen snapped the bean in her hands and threw it into the pail. "You heard me."

Mary Evelyn stared at her lap. Kate glared at Eileen. "That was uncalled for."

"So, are you happy now?" Eileen demanded. "Did you get what you wanted? I keep waiting for you to go grab that fiddle of yours and play a jig. Don't hold back on *my* account."

"You mean the reverend? I didn't do this," Kate said.

"No, but you wouldn't have said anything if you knew it was going to happen. You found the body. You're trying to tell me you didn't know you would?"

Kate glanced at Mary Evelyn.

"You think Mary Evelyn doesn't know about you?" Eileen asked with a harsh laugh. "You think we don't talk about you?"

Did they?

"What is your problem?" Kate snapped. "You're being a real pill right now." She tried to rein in her temper. It was difficult to look at Eileen without remembering the vision of throttling the life from her. Surely there wasn't so much anger in Kate's body, even if Eileen attacked her first.

"You were at the funeral. You're here now. You could have seen any of this. I know you see things. You knew when the Butlers were going to move to Florida."

"You remember that?"

It was the vision that had thrown Kate into Reverend Castor's path. She'd seen a vision of Mama telling her they had moved away, and spent the night crying about her best friend, Regina Abigail, leaving without saying goodbye. She'd been confused when she saw the Butlers at church the next day, and ran to Regina. Mr. Butler hadn't yet told his daughter he'd found a job in Jacksonville, and had been furious with Kate for spilling the secret. Kate's protests convinced the Butlers to alert the reverend.

"I can't control my dreams, Eileen. I would have told you if I'd known."

"It just doesn't make sense."

"It doesn't. But it doesn't usually. I'm not an almanac."

"But you—"

"I saw blood. That's it," Kate said, leaning forward. "I didn't know who it would be. I didn't know he'd be dead. But if I had, I would have been happy. You should be glad too. Your life will be better with him gone. You wouldn't want him as your father-in-law, Eileen, I swear it. You should have wanted him gone too."

"Of course I wanted him gone," Eileen snapped. "He hated the idea of us getting married. He was never going to support us. I wished he'd get out of the way. Without him around, Josiah should be jumping to marry me."

"Then—"

"Josiah called off the engagement this morning," Eileen said, tears welling in her eyes.

"Oh."

"So go ahead. Laugh all you want. You've gotten what you wanted."

"I'm not going to laugh. I don't like seeing you hurt, Eileen," Kate said. "I never thought it was a good idea for you to marry into that family. Maybe you're better off—"

"Don't you dare," Eileen said, wiping at her eyes. "Just because you're a bitter hag."

Kate shook her head and let that slide. "Did he say why?"

"He wants to be a preacher like his daddy, but doesn't have the schooling or money," she said. Reverends didn't accept payment for their preaching, and needed to support themselves with a job during the week. "He's going to finish training with his uncle in South Carolina. He's leaving tomorrow."

"So soon?"

Eileen nodded. "He can't stand being in that house after what happened to his daddy. Hell, he may never come back to Chatuga."

"Can you blame him?" Kate asked.

"But *I'm* here. I thought I'd be enough." Eileen stared down at her lap of unpeeled green beans, then shoved them into the bucket. "You two finish this. I need to take a walk."

"Don't go too far," Kate said. "The woods are dangerous right now."

"So I've heard," Eileen said, and swept off the porch.

Kate sat in silence for a long moment, watching the slow rock of Eileen's abandoned chair. Finally, she looked over at Mary Evelyn. "Sorry you had to hear all that."

"I'm old enough to hear arguments. And I *can* pick things up myself," Mary Evelyn said quietly.

"I know. That doesn't mean I won't help you when I can." Kate rubbed the back of her neck. She was sweating, though it was near seven in the evening. The solstice was soon. After that, the nights would finally start coming earlier. At this point of the summer, the light seemed to last forever. "And I meant all that talk about my... episodes. You didn't need to hear about that."

"Eileen was right," Mary Evelyn said. "It's not like I don't know about them."

"We never talk about it," Kate said carefully.

"Mama and Daddy told us not to," Mary Evelyn said. "But I'd have figured something out. I'm eleven, not five. You look at my leg like you cut it off yourself."

"Mary Evelyn," Kate said. "I'm sorry. It was my fault."

"You told me not to follow you, but I did anyway. You were so upset. You've always been so upset about it," Mary Evelyn said. She picked at her fingernails. "It was like I lost a leg and a sister at the same time."

"That's not it," Kate said. "Mary Evelyn, I was trying to keep you safe. That was the only reason I tried to stop you from coming out with me. I knew what was going to happen and I couldn't stop it. I dreamed about it. I knew. And it still happened."

"Then it happened," Mary Evelyn said. "What could you have done? You were barely older than I am."

"I don't know," Kate said. "I've never known."

"Stop taking it out on both of us."

Kate shook her head. "I've tried not to treat you any different."

"Well, you do. I—I don't like being the sister you look at when you're mad at yourself," Mary Evelyn said, choking on a sob.

"Oh, sweetheart," Kate said. She tossed the last of her pile of beans into the bucket and stood up so she could grab Mary Evelyn in a hug. The girl was stiff in her arms before leaning into her, crying into her shoulder. Her hot tears pressed through Kate's dress. Her emotion wracked her little frame like a tornado. "I'm sorry. I'm sorry."

Kate held her sister until her crying tapered off, stroking her hair and murmuring quiet apologies.

32

NORA JO

Many evenings, supper in the Whitaker house was a quiet affair. Miss Ethel had been quiet and watchful since confronting her about witchcraft, and Nora Jo always had other things on her mind. She could eat an entire meal and only notice when her plate was clean. The flavors usually disappeared under the memory of woodsmoke and still forest nights and free-floating fire. Tonight, it was the thought of Gloria.

Nora Jo had felt electric since their kiss, sizzling hot. She was sure that only Gloria's touch could calm the riot under her skin again.

Nora Jo had waited in the field the last two days, turning her head at each rustle in the grass, but Gloria hadn't appeared. Anxiety quickened her heart, but she reminded herself there was no cause for concern. Gloria was still working on her pa's farm. She was rarely able to slip away several days in a row. With her fear of being discovered, it was no surprise she hadn't made an exception this week. It was probably wise—they had each other now. There was no need to rush and stumble.

"The fish sure are tasty," Miss Ethel said.

"Thank you for frying them up." Nora Jo had caught two catfish before she'd come home that evening. She could have slipped into their minds and flung their bodies up on the shore, but there was something horrifying about that level of control—and of sharing something's head before she killed it. Instead, she'd sat by the riverbank and levitated them out of the water when they got close enough for her power to reach.

"So, you were fishing instead of coming to Decoration Day?" Miss Ethel added.

"Oh, was that today?"

Miss Ethel was silent. Nora Jo looked up from her plate. Where she had grown tanned over the past two months, Miss Ethel seemed paler than ever. Kate did the gardening, so Miss Ethel was spending more and more time inside the house. Purple ropes of veins twisted over her hands, as clear as if her skin were a pond, her age spots the shadows of leaves on the surface. If she pulled down her collar, Nora Jo felt she could have seen straight through to her lungs.

"I reminded you last night," Miss Ethel said. Nora Jo couldn't remember them talking over dinner. She had still been thinking about Gloria. "I'm sure your absence was noticed."

Nora Jo couldn't contain a laugh. "By who?"

"The dead, if no one else. You have kin in that graveyard," Miss Ethel chided. "It's an important ceremony. A chance to remember them who are gone."

"It's a performance for the living," Nora Jo said, her tone clipped.

"Your parents are buried there, Miss Nora Jo."

"I don't need a special day to remember my own parents. I think about them all the time."

Miss Ethel hummed skeptically, shaking her head.

Nora Jo gritted her teeth. "I'm sure my absence was *appreciated*. Everyone in this town would rather pretend I don't exist. I'm doing everyone a favor."

"That's not true. There are people who would invite you in, but you've been hiding away from all of us for months. It seems you don't want to live here at all."

She set down her fork. "People only want me here if I can conform to their ideas of what life should look like," she said. "Including you."

"You're not living a life at all. You've been missing church, missing meals. Hiding in the woods all day, spending all night Lord knows where, messing with things you don't understand," Miss Ethel said. "I tried to give you your space, but it's too much."

"I had a perfectly nice life planned here, but Mayor Neese took that from me. He was the one who decided I don't fit in. I'm trying to find another future."

"Do I think you should have lost your job? Of course not. But it doesn't look to me like you're trying to find a future. It looks like you're hiding from the present. People lose their jobs all the time. It's time for you to move on. Stop these games and come back."

"I don't want to move on," Nora Jo confessed. "I don't want to play by their rules."

"They're the only rules we've got."

"Only if we let them be." Nora Jo stood up. "I'm not hungry."

Miss Ethel stayed seated. She had also barely eaten. "I'm just worried about you, Miss Nora Jo. About what you'll do on your own."

Nora Jo took a deep breath. "Are you going to kick me out?"

"No, honey," Miss Ethel said sadly. "I'm not."

Nora Jo nodded stiffly, and retreated to her bedroom. She held Harlow's protective jack in her hand, rubbing a thumb over the rough flannel. Her stomach twisted; she didn't know if it was from hunger or anxiety. The solstice was this week, so light still spilled through her bedroom window like it was mid-afternoon instead of seven in the evening. She had hours until she met Harlow for their nightly lesson, but the tension marching under her skin like ants pushed her to move.

Did Miss Ethel know the extent of what she did at night? Did she know about Harlow?

What would be worse for Nora Jo's reputation—rumors of an affair with the mysterious visitor from the mountains? Assumptions that she was drinking moonshine with young men?

Or the truth?

She was learning witchery. She had kissed a girl. She knew what the world did to those who didn't fit in, whether it was the witch trials in old Salem or the modern lynchings of any Black person who stepped out of line. Those who fit society got peacekeeping, the status quo. Those outside were punished with swift, brutal violence. Even if they spared Nora Jo for being young, white, and female, she could still be driven from Chatuga—alone.

This was why Gloria was afraid of their town, of the world.

And why it was up to Nora Jo to defy them.

33

OLIVER

It wasn't difficult to sneak out after dark.

Oliver's ma insisted that Sally stay for at least the night, if not the week. The train back to Raleigh was a full day's trip, and the inn she had stayed in the night before was ten miles up the road near the station. It had been reckless of her to come to Chatuga without knowing her welcome, but that had been Tucker Lee's style too. He assumed he was invited wherever he went, and was usually right. Together, they would have been unstoppable.

Sally was staying on the ground floor in the room beside his parents, but she made it out of the silent house without alerting them. She wore a shawl wrapped over her nightgown, her blonde hair loose over her shoulders.

"Keep quiet," Oliver said, leading her toward the barn. "My ma will have a cow if she catches us."

"This would be an awfully complicated ploy to get me alone," Sally teased.

Oliver snorted. "If I were trying to compromise you, we wouldn't need this ritual. Tucker Lee would kick my a—behind, no matter what stood in his way."

It felt strange to talk about him so freely with someone else, someone who had known him just as well. Oliver usually kept Tucker Lee close to his chest like a locket. "Then again, if my ma thought I was seducing you, she'd throw us a wedding herself. She won't hush about setting me up with a wife."

"That's likely why she's encouraging me to stay. She'll be disappointed," Sally said. "But I'm sure there's some pretty girl in town who'll catch your eye eventually."

He was supposed to meet Kate later tonight. They usually waited longer between meetings, but after their kiss, neither of them wanted to waste time apart.

It was dark. Sally couldn't have seen his reaction, but she still said, "Or maybe one already has?"

"Come on," Oliver said, opening the barn door. "We're going up to the loft."

Sally hummed and followed him. Magnolia snorted in greeting. He gave her a quick pat before climbing the ladder.

Some of the hay bales had been moved out, preparing for the new harvest. He led Sally to an empty patch of floor and sat down on the dirty wood. A stray stalk of hay crunched under his thigh. Carefully, he lit a candle, keeping it below sight of the window. It flickered, illuminating the dark, dingy space. A luna moth fluttered, a pale flash in the night.

The last time he'd sat here, he'd failed to find a link to Tucker Lee. The cigarette case was still in his pocket, as it had been since he had returned, but he'd stopped hoping it would be his answer.

Tonight was different. He could feel it in his blood, a frantic thrumming that hummed like lightning.

Oliver held out his hand. Sally carefully tugged off her ring and set it onto his palm. There was a pale line around her finger where it had sat for the last three years. "Tucker Lee told me how long he saved for this," he said. "He wanted you to have the best he could afford. He wanted you to be proud of him."

"I was," Sally said. "So very much."

He set the ring on the ground by the candle, where it caught the dancing glow of the flame.

"Now what?"

"I've learned that names have power for spirits, giving them more power, more... solidity. I tried that, but it wasn't enough. But I also think that spirits can defy the usual rules if they have a purpose. I think I need to have something that mattered to him, something that connected him to this world. Right now, I have two things. This—and you. I think this will work."

"How can you be sure he's a ghost at all?" she asked. "What if he's in heaven?"

Heaven. Some of the clergy on the battlefield would talk about heaven, but it had seemed absurd in the setting. Who could leave the battlefield and find peace?

With the flame flickering in the darkness before them, he was reminded that there was a third option. Surely that wouldn't have been the fate for Tucker Lee Selecky, the best man Oliver had ever met.

"I don't know for sure," Oliver admitted. "Maybe that's why I haven't been able to find him." If Tucker Lee was at peace, what right did Oliver have to dredge up the pain of earth for him again? It could be that spirits in heaven couldn't come back to earth, or that Oliver would accidentally drag him back down, taking away his paradise. "We don't have to try."

They were silent for a long moment, both watching the ring. "No," she said finally. "I want to."

"Do you really believe me that this could work?"

"I don't know. But we have to try, don't we? We deserve to say goodbye. If he's somewhere out there, I want to see him."

Oliver nodded and stared down at the ring. The loft felt achingly still. He could feel Sally breathing beside him. What would she do if this failed? He shouldn't have given her hope. But if it did work, it was right that she was there. Oliver had a claim to the last years of Tucker Lee's life, but Sally had had his heart since they were children. This was what Tucker Lee would have wanted. Sally was his world.

He imagined his friend watching them sitting together in a hayloft, both staring at the ring like it held the answers to the universe. Maybe he would have laughed at them. Maybe he would just have been glad they were there together. He'd always talked about wanting the three of them to be friends.

"Tucker Lee. We're waiting for you."

The barn was quiet.

Oliver's breath hitched on a desperate gasp. He watched the ring until his eyes burned and blurred. "Tucker Lee, come find us."

She's here, he thought as loudly as he could. *We're here for you.*

A pair of boots stood beyond the candle. They were blurred, nearly invisible in the shadows. Oliver followed the uniformed legs up, up, to the pale face of Tucker Lee Selecky.

In the dark loft, the burst capillaries in his eyes and the blood on his face were an odd stain, blurring what should have been familiar features. His blond hair was unrecognizably dirty. But he was here. It had worked.

"Oliver?" Sally whispered. She followed his gaze, but looked past Tucker Lee toward the barn wall.

"Tucker Lee," Oliver breathed. At the sound of his name, Tucker Lee grew clearer. He had been a short man, but looming over them he seemed impossibly large. How could Sally not see him?

He had seen the blue faces of flu victims, the gunshots in Noah's chest, the blood on Grandpa Herman's forehead, but he'd still imagined that he would find Tucker Lee with the slick hair and bright smile of their first day at Camp Sevier. Seeing him bloodied like this, trapped forever as he'd died, gutted Oliver.

They were both trapped in the moment of Tucker Lee's death, and always would be.

Tucker Lee's voice seemed to come from a far-off distance, though his spirit was close enough to touch. "Where... What's going on?" He patted his chest, tugging at his jacket like it was suffocating him.

"Tucker Lee, it's us," Oliver said. "We wanted to see you."

The ghost looked between them with bloodied eyes that shouldn't have been able to see. The green of his irises was stark against the red. "Oliver. Sally?"

"I'm so sorry, Tucker Lee," Oliver blurted. "I'm so sorry."

"Why is she here, Oliver?" Tucker Lee asked, plaintive. Friendship forged in a warzone was different from those built at home. For the first eighteen years of his life, Oliver had only seen a friend cry once, when he broke his arm falling from a poplar tree. But he knew what Tucker Lee sounded like on the verge of tears. It was the same tremor Oliver had heard countless times in the dark nights, listening to distant shells and gunfire. "She shouldn't be here."

Oliver glanced at Sally, who didn't seem to have heard. She was looking between Oliver and the space around them, searching for something. Had Oliver been wrong to think Tucker Lee would want to see her? Had there been some secret fight between them even Oliver had never learned?

"Is he here?" Sally demanded. "Did he say something?"

"Why not?" Oliver asked Tucker Lee.

Tucker Lee looked around anxiously, stuttering like a broken film reel. "Danger."

"This isn't France, Tucker Lee. We're not there." Had they pulled Tucker Lee's ghost from one of the abandoned trenches? How many men were still trudging through spectral mud in France?

Tucker Lee shook his head with the quick insistence of a child, more erratic than he had been in life. "It's this place... The darkness. It's near. It's not safe here." He paused, staring out the window. "It wants you. Oliver, please, you were supposed to be safe."

"What darkness?" Oliver asked. "What are you talking about, Tucker Lee?" He had imagined this conversation a hundred times. Despair, anger, accusations, even forgiveness—he had thought he was prepared for anything Tucker Lee might say. He had never imagined *fear*. Tucker Lee looked out at the dark night as though it held every Kraut they'd ever faced and more.

"You were both supposed to be safe. Isn't that why... Isn't that why I did it all?" Tucker Lee patted his face, his throat. Could he feel the blood? "Leave. Save Sally."

"Save her from *what*?"

Sally's voice grew shrill. "Wait, what is he saying?"

"I can feel it. It's in the air." He spoke slowly, blinking like every word took a mountain of effort to find. "There's something evil in this place. It's watching. It *hurts*."

A chill ran over Oliver's back. He remembered Grandpa Herman's strange warnings about monsters.

"You're shining bright, Oliver. I could see it, feel it, from far away. You brought me here. I found you in the river. It can too."

"The river? What evil, what darkness?"

"I don't know. I don't know. I needed you to be safe, I—"

There was a loud skittering noise. Sally shrieked. A black rat slammed into the candle, sending it rolling onto the floor. The pest scurried into the shadows as the flame licked the surrounding dry hay. With a fierce crackle, fire began to spread.

Tucker Lee disappeared in a blink, like he had never been there at all.

While Oliver sat frozen, Sally leapt into action. She flung the shawl from her shoulder onto the flames and stamped them out with her boots. She stood, panting, on top of her ruined scarf and stared down at Oliver. "What just happened? What was wrong? Was that Tucker Lee?"

"It… I…" Oliver shook his head, fighting to find the words in his dry throat.

There was a slam as the front door to the house opened. Oliver clamored to his feet and looked out the window. His parents were on the front porch, Ma wielding a lantern and his pa holding a rifle. "Who's out there?" Pa shouted, staring at the dark yard.

"Geez," Oliver muttered. "Pa, it's me! Me and Sally." Alone. In the hayloft. At night.

At least the barn hadn't burned down. If it had, his pa might have shot him anyway.

"We heard a shout," Ma called, tucked slightly behind her husband. "Are you two okay?"

Was he okay? That was a question he couldn't answer. He had finally summoned Tucker Lee, and it had only left him more lost. Tucker Lee had been terrified, and horrified with Oliver for bringing Sally into it—whatever *it* was.

Could it be the same monster Grandpa Herman had tried to warn him about? *Noct.*

What could scare dead men?

Beside him, Sally's breath hitched. Silent sobs wracked her shoulders.

"Oh, Sally," he said, reaching for her. She leaned into his chest, pressing her face against his shirt as if it would hide her tears.

"That was the most terrified I've ever been, Oliver Chadwick," she said, voice muffled. "What evil? Save me from what? Is Tucker Lee okay? What were you *talking* about?"

"I don't know," Oliver said. "I'm putting you on tomorrow's train back to Raleigh."

"You can't send me away. There's something wrong with Tucker Lee. Isn't there?" she asked, pulling back to look up at him. In the dark, with clouds masking the moon outside, her face was impossible to read.

"Kids?" Ma called.

"I think… I think it's something wrong with *me*," Oliver said. "Can you go talk to my parents? I need to go."

"Go *where*?"

"There's only one person I know who might have answers," Oliver said. "I need to talk to her."

Sally laughed wetly. "You're going to make me explain this to your parents on my own? Your pa is terrifying. I thought you were supposed to keep me safe."

He pressed a brusque kiss to the top of her head. "I will. I swear."

34

KATE

Kate watched the flame flicker in the lantern. It cast dancing shadows on the cave walls.

Oliver was late, but she barely noticed the time passing. Between the chaos of the reverend's funeral, the rumors of demons haunting him, and the arguments with her sisters, she welcomed a few minutes in the dark to think.

Could there really have been a voice speaking to the reverend inside his own home, luring him out to his death? If so, why him? He was a reverend—perhaps demons had a special hatred for men of the cloth. It could have targeted him for that.

Or maybe... someone had put the reverend in the demon's path. Eileen had been sneaking out at night too, hadn't she? She had been so *angry* lately. Kate might not be the only Mayer with a touch of magic to her.

Perhaps there would be a reason for Kate's hands on her sister's neck.

Kate picked up a stone and chucked it at the wall. What was *wrong* with her? Eileen had lost her engagement. It was no wonder she had lashed out at Kate. It didn't give Kate the right to assume the worst of her sister.

If there was a demon around, it had probably been drawn to the reverend's vile air, and that was that.

Kate had enough problems of her own without worrying about demons.

Finally, clattering footsteps hurried toward her. The echoing of labored breathing confirmed it was Oliver before he stumbled into view. He was pale, alight with nervous energy. "You're still here," he said, putting a hand to his chest. "I wasn't sure you would be."

At the beginning of their acquaintance, Kate might have left if Oliver had been so late. The thought hadn't occurred to her tonight. She couldn't have gone home without knowing if he was okay. She would not be able to sleep for imagining him choking in some field, unable to stand up. He never talked about his breathing issues, but she heard the wet, pained nature of his coughs. Sometimes, it sounded like his lungs had fallen free from their mooring, and he was breathing through a gory mess.

"Are you okay?" she asked.

He sat down across from her and told her about his strange day—stranger even than hers. Oliver rambled frantically about his eventful Decoration Day, the successful summoning, and the ghost's warning about watchful evil and encroaching darkness.

"It seems like nonsense when I say it out loud, but they're all so scared." He sighed and reached forward to take her hands. She pulled them out of his reach. "What?"

"It's exactly what I told you from the beginning. That our

abilities ain't nothing but trouble," Kate said. "Oliver, we're trying to get rid of these curses. When did you decide to *summon* a ghost?"

Oliver hesitated. "I've been trying. This was the first time it worked."

"The first time it..." She ran a hand over her face. "You said the ghosts in that graveyard scared you, but secretly you've been trying to summon one? And then coming here at night to nod along with me and say that you want to get rid of your sight as much as I do?" She huffed. "I told you, this magic can only lead to pain. And if you had waited one more goddamn day, I could have told you what your friend was warning you about."

"What?"

Quickly, she told him about finding the reverend's body and Dicie's theory. "If there's something in town hunting us, it has to be this demon, right? I must only have gotten away thanks to luck. I think it lured the reverend right into the path of that bear."

"But why him?"

"He was a threat. He knew how to exorcise demons, as I remember too damn well." She wrapped her arms around her stomach. "Why is it *here*?"

"My friend said I was glowing. Like a beacon," Oliver said. "Maybe this is what he meant. I'm bringing the demons here, somehow."

"Like a beacon," she repeated. "You said you've been trying to summon him. You've been lighting yourself up all this time. Lord, Oliver, you saw what happened just talking to the woman in the graveyard. Why invite some ghost closer?"

"He's not just *some ghost*. He's different."

"Who knows what you might have unleashed with all of this? The reverend might be dead because of you. *We* might be next."

"I didn't know," Oliver protested. "I didn't mean to hurt anyone."

Kate shook her head. "Why is this boy so special? What was worth messing with ghosts? What was worth lying to me all this time?"

"His name was Tucker Lee Selecky," Oliver said quietly. "We were in France together."

That was how Oliver always talked about the war. France. Abroad. Vague references that seemed as distant as the stars to Kate, who had never left the South. Usually, he stopped there. Tonight, though, he kept talking.

"I thought war was going to be an adventure. I've always been in my pa's shadow, and my grandpa's. I thought the war would make me different. Respectable. Grown-up. I had always wanted to prove myself, and the reels said that Europe was the place to do it. I met Tucker Lee at Camp Sevier. 30th Infantry Division. A bunch of ignorant Southern boys about to be tossed into the British Second Army. We had no clue what we were doing, but me and Tucker Lee were thick as thieves right away.

"I've never had a friend like that before, Kate. We understood each other. The two of us, we saw the worst parts of the world and were there for each other through it. He was... He was something special. Kept me going, just to get the chance to have the next day with him. I thought I was going to die there. You can't know what it was like, and I'm glad you don't, Kate, I really am. It was... Well."

He shook his head and stared down at the cave floor. "In September 1918, something went wrong. Everything was always going wrong, but this was worse. There was a call for us to put on our masks. A Green Cross shell was shot into our trench. We were all scrambling. We'd done it so often, and it was terrifying every time.

"I can still remember the sound Tucker Lee made. There was a hole in my mask. I'd pulled it out of my bag without looking—we all learned to put them on in our sleep. The hose was barely hanging on. Must have gotten clipped by shrapnel at some point that day. It was busted. I hadn't noticed, and it was too late."

Kate could hardly imagine it. Two boys staring at each other in a muddy trench, one marked for death by a horrible mistake.

"I dropped it and tried to get a handkerchief out of my pack, anything to cover up with. And that's when Tucker Lee shoved his mask onto my face." Kate gasped, but Oliver kept talking. "He pressed the mask down so hard my nose ached, and held the back of my head so I couldn't push him off. He was a strong bastard. I could see it then, the pale green gas pooling in the trench. Around our boots." Oliver shuddered. "Well. It was horrible. He was dead in minutes. Tucker Lee was my best friend. There were rumors the war would end soon. He was so close to going home. And he was gone.

"I didn't give myself another thought, but I started developing symptoms a few days later. I'd gotten too close. I ended up in the hospital. The war ended while I was lying there, coughing and thinking about Tucker Lee.

"By the time they let me out of the hospital, people were preparing to get shipped home. It was chaos. We'd been brought over in waves for months, and now everyone was desperate to get back to the States all at once. It wasn't hard for me to slip away. I went AWOL for a few months, drinking every bottle of liquor left in France. My throat couldn't hurt any worse, even if I was throwing up, and I wanted some time off from my brain. The first ghost I saw, I was sure I'd started hallucinating. Thought I was one of the crazies who ended up on the streets. I wasn't the only soldier who got too lost to get on the first boats. And the civilians had it just as bad. There were a lot of folks drowning in booze." His fingers twitched, like he was reaching for one of the liquor bottles.

"When someone finally dragged me onto a ship, I thought I'd leave the ghosts behind. Then I landed in Charleston, and they were everywhere. Real haunted, them Charleston ports. Anyway. That's why I've been trying to summon him. I needed to talk to him. I needed to know if Tucker Lee regretted what he did."

"He chose to save you," Kate said quietly.

"That was before he coughed up his lifeblood in a muddy trench with only my rotten self for company," Oliver said. "Tucker Lee should still be here. Not me. Sally shouldn't be alone. And what he said to me tonight… I'm not sure he's happy with his choice."

"I don't care. I'm glad you're here," Kate told him.

"You shouldn't be."

They were sitting down on the ground, eyes locked over the kerosene lamp. They always sat across from each other, keeping a respectable distance. It was too far. Kate stood up and joined him on his slab of rock. She felt the heat of him as surely as she had the summer night outside, despite the layer of cloth between their skin.

He was still pale, looking at her with wide eyes. "If it was your demon Tucker Lee was talking about, it's enough to scare a ghost. Have you had any visions that could explain what's happening? What could be so bad it scares the dead?"

"I haven't seen anything to warn me about this, but my daddy says demons can hide themselves from visions. My visions of you are the only ones in my life that are never a warning. There's only ever… us."

"I wasn't sure there'd still be a you and me after what I did," Oliver said softly.

"You're an idiot for summoning Tucker Lee, and a worse idiot for not telling me what you were trying," Kate said, then reached out to touch his arm. "But you're stuck with me. I don't care what's out there. I won't let it hurt you, and I won't let it come between us."

Oliver cupped her face in his hands. He brushed a warm thumb over her cheek. "Kate," he murmured.

She'd seen this moment before. For once, the reality of it was precisely how she'd imagined. He stared at her like a dying man seeing his last sunrise, her name golden on his lips.

So she did exactly what she had imagined doing next when she had turned this jewel of a moment over and over again in her mind. She kissed him.

Their first kiss while exploring the tunnels had seemed secret and dreamlike, stolen from a world that would stop them. The dark had been impenetrable around them. This kiss was slick and solid and real. In the light of the lantern and Oliver's story, it was a precious thing they owned together.

He was reserved at first, but she coaxed him forward, into her. He met her, then pressed her down onto the cool slab of rock. She stretched beneath him, gasping when his lips drifted to her neck.

His hands ran from her waist up until they cupped her ribs. She felt small beneath him, a flower he was coaxing to bloom. "Please," she said, not sure what she was asking for, but asking nonetheless.

When they shed their clothing, she lay down on a pile of her dress and his shirt. The cloth smelled of them both, like he was echoing around her. As they moved together, the clothing slipped. The rock was cool and slick in thrilling patches beneath her back.

It was clumsy and beautiful. She laughed when his hand slipped against the rock and he landed heavily on her torso. Her teeth chattered under his touch, as though her body was misinterpreting the gooseflesh across her skin as a reaction to the cool caves. He soothed her with a hand on her cheek. His mismatched eyes were shadowed in the dim light, but his affection was clear. Compared to the lines of his face when they'd met—sharp, exhausted, suspicious—he could have been a new man.

She felt different too—alive in her body and in the present like she never had been before.

35

NORA JO

Harlow was tense during their training. He kept glancing up toward the nearly full moon overhead. "Focus, Nora Jo," he snapped when she lost her hold on a levitating boulder and it hit the earth with a thud.

"I'm trying," she said through gritted teeth. She had paced her room for hours after her conversation with Miss Ethel. She could hear the old woman shuffling around all evening, first in the kitchen, then in her bedroom. Miss Ethel had still sounded restless when Nora Jo finally slipped out of the house. Would she knock on Nora Jo's door in the night to see if she was still there? Would there be a punishment for sneaking out again? Nora Jo might finally be kicked out.

Harlow only frowned. "What's wrong with you?"

"I'm *trying*," she repeated, her tone waspish, defensive. She waved at the pair of floating fires circling their clearing, summoned and maintained by her focus. "I've learned so much since we started. I just need more time."

"You're distracted."

"I'm concentrating as much as I can." The fires flickered, pulsing larger and then dwindling until she reached out with her mind to steady them. It was fortunate they were practicing fire tonight rather than animal possession—over the last months, Nora Jo had gone from controlling the rabbit to taking over a fish to dancing through a variety of bugs. Not all of them died—but not all had lived. With her current unsteadiness, she might have torn some poor mouse's mind apart.

"Power comes from belief," Harlow said. "I've told you before. Whether it's faith in a higher being, faith in the land, faith in yourself—it requires conviction. You're lacking that tonight."

"What is there to have faith in?" she demanded. "Who am I? Why am I special? Why should I trust that I can do this?"

"You don't believe you have enough power?"

"I don't know." The well inside her was fickle. Her magic was a dream, and she was trying to remember it in the light of morning. Sometimes, it came strong and vivid, undeniable. Other times, it was so faint that it seemed on the verge of disappearing.

He glanced up at the moon again. "I'll prove that you do. The day after tomorrow is the summer solstice. It's the most powerful night of the year for those like you and me."

"I've heard that. Even Chatuga has a celebration for the solstice. I didn't think it really meant anything."

"It's the shortest night of the year. The balance of the seasons. There's power in change. Even those without a touch of magic can sense that. Can't you feel the energy in the air?"

She took a deep breath. There was, now that she was looking outside herself, a tension similar to an oncoming storm around her.

"I have a plan," he said. "We'll meet at the underground lake, midnight, the night after next. Between the solstice and the ley lines in the cave, there will be a perfect confluence. Trust me, Nora Jo—you'll be more powerful than you can imagine. We'll work magic together that will prove your strength. You won't doubt after that."

He worked her to the bone, running her through spell after spell, until the night grew old and dawn threatened to crest.

By the time she trekked home, her eyes were exhausted, her arm coated in salve over a long line of wounds. They had needed more of her blood than usual to focus her power. Harlow had seemed satisfied by the end, but she still felt empty, haunted by what she didn't yet have. On the solstice she would find the outer reach of her power, he'd said. Would it be enough?

As she approached Miss Ethel's house, she heard a cow lowing from a nearby farm. It was a strange sound in the predawn dark, sending an uneasy shiver up her spine. Harlow had been teaching her omens. What was it he'd said about cows making noise after midnight? *Animals feel death more easily than we do.*

The predawn was warm and quiet. The creak of the empty rocking chairs and the breeze dancing through the summer leaves were the only noises. Still, an ominous feeling swelled in her gut.

Nora Jo hesitated, fingering the jack in her pocket. What had she been training for if not the unexpected?

She went inside. The house was silent.

Carefully, she made her way through the familiar halls. It smelled, as it always did, of frying oil, cold ash, and Lysol. There were no unexpected shadows, no tingling in the air to warn of magic.

The uneasy feeling refused to dissipate.

She went to the back of the house. Her room was as she'd left it, her coded notes still tucked in the vanity drawer.

Wondering if her training had made her paranoid, she went back out. She paused by Miss Ethel's door, waiting for the sound of her breathing. It was usually slightly labored when she slept, audible even from a distance.

There was nothing.

"Miss Ethel?" she called quietly, prodding the door. It swung open.

The room was gray in the dawn light. There was a dark shadow in Miss Ethel's bed. The old widow lay peacefully under the covers, face slack and still.

"Miss Ethel?"

There was no response.

Once, when Nora Jo was a child, she had woken up from a vicious nightmare. The plot faded like the tide as soon as her eyes opened, but her heart still pounded in her chest. She'd crept into her parents' bedroom and waited anxiously at her ma's side of the bed, hoping she'd sense her presence and wake up.

She felt like that little kid again. This time, she knew there was no comfort to be found.

36

OLIVER

The only good news was that his parents waited until Sally had been safely driven to the station and put on the next train to North Carolina before they sat him down in the living room to yell at him.

The space was overly formal, decorated with embroidered chairs that scraped against Oliver's hands as he tried to find a comfortable position. It was well into the afternoon, but Oliver was hiding yawns. His sleep in the caves had been sporadic, despite the warm body in his arms.

"I know Sally told you that nothing happened between us," he said before his parents could speak.

They were sitting on the couch facing him. Ma had her hand on Pa's shoulder. Oliver wasn't sure if she was comforting him or holding him back. "She did say that," Pa said, voice like iron. "But we're not damn fools, Oliver."

"Sir—"

"You put her reputation at risk by meeting her after dark. You disappeared for the rest of the night Lord only knows where and didn't come home until dawn. You've refused to lift a hand to help around the house since you've been back. You won't come to the mill. You certainly haven't looked for another job."

Ma's lips were pressed tight together, but she didn't interrupt.

"That's not…" Oliver couldn't find the words.

"We've given you time, but you're a man now, Oliver. You can't stay here forever. It's clear you have no interest in following the rules under this roof."

Oliver clenched his jaw. Ma knew about his coughs, his erratic sleep. She had been gentle with him since he'd returned, covering for his deficiencies. They had both been sure that, with time, he would be normal again. He tried and failed to imagine explaining his mysterious ailments to his pa without being kicked out of the house. "What are you suggesting?"

"I've been talking to the Daleys," his pa said. "Their farm runs right by the spot in the creek I've been eyeing to set up a second mill. It's time for the business to expand."

"You want me to run a new mill?" He hadn't realized Pa still trusted him so much.

"No," Pa said. "You're gonna marry their daughter."

"Marry their daughter?" Oliver was nearly speechless. "She and I have barely spoken in our lives."

His pa shrugged. "That doesn't matter. You're a good match."

"When did this happen? Why didn't you talk to me?"

"You've not been around for conversation. When you're not sleeping, you're off somewhere wandering. Wilkes told me he's seen you coming in and out of the house at all hours."

"I'm an adult."

"Then act like one," Pa snapped. "You can't sit in my house forever. I can't trust you with the company. This is what you can do for the family."

"You just want a new heir. I'm not enough for you."

"If you paid a lick of attention to the mill, you'd know we ain't bringing in what we used to. The Mathises were interested in working with me, but we don't need someone else's product to move. We need more of our own, and fast."

"And you're miserable here," Ma said. "I've told you, you need a wife. It will make your life better. I promise."

"But I don't even know Gloria Daley."

Pa raised his eyebrows. "You have someone else in mind? A reason you were out so late?"

He did. Of course he did. He had spent last night with Kate in his arms, and never wanted to go another day without her.

The Daleys' daughter was sweet as pie. Where was the fire, the spark?

He had a responsibility to Kate. She wasn't some girl for a quick roll. She was the only person left who really knew him. She was the best part of his wretched life.

But Pa was staring at him like he was a disappointing crop. He was a step away from tossing Oliver on the garbage heap and looking for a new son. What would he do if he learned that it wasn't Sally he was sneaking around with in the night, but Kate? The gristmill only hired white folks. If Oliver suggested he was planning to marry a Black girl from Tolbert-Vance, Pa would throw him out without thinking twice. Worse, he'd likely find a way to make sure Kate was no longer in the picture.

Oliver wasn't a fool. It wasn't uncommon for white men to sleep with Black women, but there would be no marriage, and any children from the match were to be ignored. It was illegal for them to be together—punishable for them to even live in the same house, and impossible to ask for an official marriage certificate. There could be prison or worse for them both if they were discovered, but Kate would bear the brunt.

A flickering shadow walked behind his parents' couch: Grandpa Herman. He moaned piteously, the sound low and haunting.

Oliver stayed still and kept his eyes on his parents. After Noah's attack the day before, he feared drawing the angry spirit's attention. "I…"

Ma sat up like a fox in a field. "Do you? Have someone else?"

"No," Oliver said. "No. Of course not."

"Then it's settled," Pa said. "I'll tell the Daleys."

37

NORA JO

It took all morning to settle the funeral arrangements. A body normally rested for three days before being buried, but Tennessee summers were hot.

The bell at the church tolled eighty-three times when the news reached them, one for every year Miss Ethel lived. It took several minutes. Nora Jo stared out the window, waiting to see if they would lose count. They didn't.

The pastor had left as soon as everything was complete. He had been fond of Miss Ethel, had known her his whole life, but he was a brusque man. He took care of business and had nothing additional to say to Nora Jo. He had seemed to look through her.

Nora Jo sat in the empty kitchen. Miss Ethel had been sitting in the chair across from her only last night. She'd looked worn, had been growing weaker for months. There was pain in her eyes, fear, when she spoke about Decoration Day. Miss Ethel had been afraid of being forgotten.

And Nora Jo had stormed away.

How had Nora Jo not seen the truth? With Harlow, she learned how to read fire, float objects, share minds with animals, detect changes in the weather. How had she not foreseen this? What else was the world trying to say to her that she couldn't understand?

She stood up and went to gather the ingredients for dinner. She hadn't slept or eaten breakfast, and her hands wouldn't stop shaking. If she kept moving, perhaps it would feel normal.

Somewhere in the kitchen, a fly buzzed.

She went to the stove in the corner. Food. She needed fire. Where did Miss Ethel keep the flint? No matter—Nora Jo had other means.

Her arm was still healing from last night's training, so instead of finding a knife, she plucked a firm tomato from the windowsill. At her nudge, it withered in her palm, rotting into mush, and the flames licked to life.

Miss Ethel had been so proud of those tomatoes.

Why had Nora Jo not stepped out into the garden and found a flower to drain instead? Miss Ethel would be disappointed that the tomato hadn't been appreciated.

Would have been disappointed.

Nora Jo waved the fire back into nothingness and took a tin of dried jerky from the cabinet instead.

As she chewed the seasoned venison, she stared out of the side window at the forest. The breeze of the morning had fallen away, and there seemed to be no movement anywhere in the world.

The day was bleeding into a sweltering afternoon. The air was sticky. Nora Jo sat on the front porch, a warm glass of sweet tea forgotten in her hand. The tea was from a pitcher Miss Ethel had left in the kitchen. It smelled sickly sweet—Miss Ethel had spent more of her money on sugar for her tea than on any other grocery.

"Miss Nora Jo?"

A young man stood at the foot of the stairs—Teddy Daley, Gloria's younger brother. Nora Jo had been his teacher until he graduated last year. She'd hoped to have more time before the flood of callers arrived to pay their respects.

And if any of the Daleys were to come, she'd hoped it would be Gloria.

"Teddy," she greeted. "What can I do for you?"

"I'm sorry about Miss Ethel," he said. "She was a good lady."

"Thank you, Teddy."

He scuffed his shoe into the dirt. He was near eighteen and working on his pa's farm every day, but he still had the rawboned lankiness of youth. "I'm here with a note from my sister," he said, waving a slip of paper in the air. "She paid me a nickel to give it to you."

"Is she all right?"

"Seemed fine to me," he said with a shrug.

Nora Jo unwrapped it eagerly.

Nora Jo —

I just heard about Miss Ethel. Please know that we're praying for you.

I have my own news to share. I am to be married this autumn. My dad arranged the match.

I can't make our meeting today.

—G

"I... Let me just write her back," Nora Jo said. Was her voice trembling? "Hold on for one second. I'll give you another nickel."

He shrugged, and she dashed into the house. Running a shaking hand through her hair, Nora Jo flipped over the paper and wrote a new note, begging Gloria to meet her in the field one more time. It was delicate work to be subtle enough to send with Teddy, and she had to start over three times. The ink over the scratched-out words threatened to bleed through the other side.

If Gloria's dad had learned about them and was marrying her off to stop their involvement, asking her to meet again would only cause more damage. Why else would Gloria warn her she would not come to the field—and send her brother today instead of coming herself? Still, Nora Jo had to try.

After she gave Teddy the note and his pay, she gathered her supplies and trekked toward the field. Sweat clung to the back of her dress and glued her hair against her neck. It would take time for Gloria to get the note, and more to make her excuses and come to the field, but Nora Jo couldn't sit in that empty house for another moment.

Engaged.

She paced through the long grasses, unable to sit down. Her nerves threatened to burst free from her skin. She was clutching a book to her chest, fingers clawing the cloth cover.

Gloria wouldn't come. Nora Jo would never be alone with her again. She would marry whoever her dad had found and live the life she'd dreaded while Nora Jo watched. All alone.

Everything Nora Jo had done was for nothing.

Then, finally, she saw a slight figure on the horizon, stepping from the trees into the meadow. Nora Jo walked to meet her, stumbling over the long grass. Gloria looked the same as ever, golden and freckled in the summer sun.

They stopped in front of each other.

"You came," Nora Jo whispered.

Gloria nodded, but didn't speak.

"Does your dad know about us?" The words tumbled from Nora Jo's mouth. "Are you okay?"

"He doesn't know about us. I don't think. He didn't say anything. He's been hoping for this for a while. I'm to marry Oliver Chadwick Jr."

"Him? He was a brat in school, and he hasn't changed," Nora Jo snapped. "You have nothing in common."

"That doesn't matter. Going into business with the Chadwicks will give us the money to save the farm."

"They can't make you do this. Your dad doesn't own you," Nora Jo said. "We'll run away. We can leave tonight."

"I can't run away, Nora Jo. Where would I go?"

"Anywhere."

Gloria shook her head. "I'm not like you. I wouldn't know the first thing about how to live on my own. I've never even left home. Women *die* on their own. A husband will keep me safe."

Nora Jo thought of Beau's story about their grandmother. *It's a hard world for a woman alone.* "It wouldn't be like that. You'd have me."

"Nora Jo," Gloria said, holding up a hand. "Stop this. Stop pretending like this was ever a possibility. We both knew it had to end."

"Don't say that."

"It's true. It's too late. I just wanted to see you one more time. I didn't think I could, but I had to say goodbye. Especially after I heard about Miss Ethel. I'm sorry, Nora Jo. For everything."

"But—"

"Don't make this harder than it has to be."

Nora Jo fumbled to open the book in her hands. "You once said you liked to hear me read," she said, flipping through the thin pages to the one creased on the top corner. "And I couldn't find my own words. Please, let me. This is from a poet named Alice Dunbar-Nelson."

Gloria sighed. "Okay, Nora Jo. Go ahead."

She stared down at the black text and took a deep breath. It felt shaking. "Aye, with you love the red and gold goes from my life, and leaves it cold and dull and bare."

She looked up from the book when her voice caught, meeting Gloria's eyes for a long moment. They were bright with tears.

Nora Jo cleared her throat and continued to read, "I murmur not, dear love, I only say again farewell. God bless the day on which we met, and bless you too, my love, and be with you…" Her voice cracked along its edges like glass under the crushing pressure of an unfeeling boot. "And be with you in sorrow or in happiness, nor let you e'er me forget."

Nora Jo looked up, imploring Gloria to understand. She had to understand.

Gloria reached out and put her hands over Nora Jo's, closing the book gently. She smiled, though it seemed to pain her. "Goodbye, Nora Jo. I wish you… everything."

And then she left.

Nora Jo waited until she was out of sight before the sobs tore free from her throat. It was like a tornado ripping her apart from the inside.

She sank to her knees in the field, clutching the book of poetry tightly.

38

KATE

The sun was low by the time Kate got home from work. Bright zinnias bobbed along the gate, their orange and pink blooms as large as Kate's palms. With the summer solstice tomorrow, the days were the longest they would be all year. Dawn came early and sunset seemed like it might never come at all.

Her body ached pleasantly, reminding her she hadn't slept in her own bed. Kate and Oliver had stayed wrapped in each other's arms until early in the morning. They had dozed, limbs overlapping, then moved together again when they woke. It was even better the second time, less unfamiliar and without the bite of newness between her legs.

When they'd first met in the clearing, Kate had been heartbroken to learn Oliver had used the space to meet his lovers, but now she was grateful for his expertise. Just like he had first led her down into the secret caves, he was leading her into a new, hidden world between them.

Under the gentle adventure in his touch, the frightening revelations at the reverend's funeral seemed like a dream.

Supper was a simple stew, too warm for the season. Mary Evelyn sat beside Kate and smiled at her. Eileen raised her eyebrows at Kate, her expression communicating a dissertation of meaning. She must have noticed her absence overnight. She didn't say anything though, just sat down in her usual seat. Kate could feel the broken shards of their argument lurking between them.

At the head of the table, her parents were quiet and withdrawn. Finally, Mama cleared her throat. "Girls," she said. Her tone was the same she'd used to tell Kate that they needed to amputate Mary Evelyn's leg. There was a level of calm that came from having already reached despair and passed through it to the other side. Had the demon attacked someone else while Kate was away working?

She glanced over at her sisters, but no one seemed to anticipate what Mama would say.

Mama hesitated, then sighed. "We're moving to Nashville next week."

"What?" Kate exclaimed, the stew turning to rocks in her gut. "You said we had time to figure it out!"

"You knew about this, Kate?" Eileen demanded. "Of course you did. When was this decided?"

"Hush," Mama said. "This isn't the time for that."

"What changed?" Kate insisted.

"Daddy was let go from the mill. This morning. They let go of a whole slew of people at once. Sent them back out the door."

Daddy was silent, staring ahead.

"We knew this might be coming," Mama continued. "We have a plan. There's a factory in Nashville looking for workers, but the window won't be open forever. We have to move where the work is."

"All our friends are here," Willamae said.

"And Uncle Christopher," Betty added.

"I have to wait for Josiah," Eileen whispered. "What if he comes back for me?"

"We don't have no choice," Mama said. "We need to be settled somewhere before winter. This is the best time this could have happened. We'll have time to find a new home in Nashville. There are opportunities there for all of you that you'd never have here. Schooling. Jobs. It's a city built for fiddlers like you, Kate."

Surely Kate would know by now if she were on the verge of moving to a new city. She'd told Oliver that she hadn't seen any sign they'd get lost in the caves, but how many more moments did she *know* they'd have together? She couldn't think of any she hadn't already experienced. All the visions she'd treasured had come to pass, culminating in last night.

She stared down at the kitchen table, rattled by the realization.

Did she have any more visions waiting *at all*? Her mind was blank as she tried to find the future. She had duplicate memories littering her mind like reflections in a creek. Were there any left to come that she hadn't already experienced? She wracked her mind, but she could only remember one image that hadn't yet occurred: her hands around Eileen's neck, strangling the life from her.

With her focus on Oliver and Eileen, she hadn't noticed the dwindling hourglass of dreams stored in her mind.

This was what she had always wanted: a life without visions. Now, she felt adrift at sea. She couldn't guess what the future held.

"I'm an adult," she said, tasting the words on her tongue. "I could stay here."

Mama stared at her, expression schooled into impassivity. "You could. I suppose that's a decision you'll have to make."

39

OLIVER

That night, Oliver sat outside the cave entrance. It was the hottest day of the year so far, and the air seemed to press down on his shoulders. Tucker Lee's cigarette case sat in the dirt in front of him. He had instinctively pulled it out, but the faded monogram held no comfort for him anymore.

"Oliver," Kate said, jogging up to meet him. She looked preoccupied, but as lovely as ever. He would never get over the slope of her nose, the ridge of her lip. She stopped a step from him, frown deepening as she drew into the circle of the lantern's light. "What's wrong?"

"Are you okay?" he asked, standing. Her face was drawn and ashen.

"I asked you first. You don't usually wait out here. You look like you've… I'd say 'seen a ghost,' but, well." She looked around the tree line as though the source of his stress would be visible. Grandpa Herman had, in fact, followed him to the woods. The spirit was moaning still, quiet, and flickering in and out of his periphery. "Is it the demon? Has it found you?"

Oliver shook his head. "No, not that. Last night my parents found out about my sneaking out. They were... not happy."

"What does that mean?"

"They've decided it's a sign I can't be trusted to make my own decisions."

She huffed. "You're a grown man. Who you spend your time with is none of their business." She took his hand and squeezed it.

"Try telling my pa that. It's not just about the nights. They don't trust me in any way. He wanted a son to carry on the family legacy. They're tired of me being... broken."

"Oliver," she began, but he held up a hand before she could defend him.

"They're right. I am. I'm no use to them. I can't work, Kate. I can't weed without passing out. I can't ride my horse. I can't walk into the gristmill without coughing up my lungs. Grandpa Herman built that mill, and my pa wanted me to take it over. He can't rely on me now."

"There's more to you than all that. You've weathered a lot worse than some disapproval. We've just found out there are demons in these woods—this is nothing in comparison. You've never cared so much what they might think before. You know yourself, Oliver. It'll blow over. I swear. We can do this together."

"They don't trust me to take care of our family's legacy," Oliver insisted. "I'm useless."

"Oliver," Kate snapped. She was blazing with protectiveness. He didn't deserve her. "So what, are they disowning you? For being injured in the war? Jesus Christ, your pa is a piece of work."

"They're not disowning me, but they've made a decision." He tried for a deep breath, but it caught in his throat like a burr. "Kate, they're making me get married."

Kate grew very, very still. "What?"

"They need more land, and they want a new Chadwick to pass the business down to. My job is to get that for them."

"And you… agreed to this?"

"What could I say?"

She dropped his hand. "You could have said no."

"Didn't you hear me? They're right. I can't work, not anywhere in Chatuga. I sleep most days. I need my family so I don't end up begging on the street. I argued, I swear I did. But once my pa has his mind made up, there's nothing anyone can say to change it. You don't want my pa to be your enemy."

"So, how long did you argue? One minute? Two? And then you came out here to tell me you had no other choice."

"I don't, Kate."

"It's supposed to be you and me against the world. After last night… We have something together. Or do I mean nothing to you?"

"You mean everything to me. You, you made me realize I'm still alive. But what we're doing out here, it's *dangerous*. We're hiding from everyone, being stalked by demons, fighting at every turn. I can't risk you. They're right—I don't have anything to offer anyone. You deserve more."

"You see dead people and I see the future. We were never going to be normal. I don't care what the rest of the world thinks. We could find a way. People do it—they stay discreet, they keep their private lives private. Instead, you're marrying the first white girl to come along."

He sighed with more air than he'd thought his battered lungs could hold. "I don't want this any more than you do, Kate."

"*I* would have argued."

"It would have been a waste of time," Oliver said.

The slap surprised him. Pain bloomed like fire across his cheek, and the sound echoed through the forest.

They were still for a moment, staring at each other. Kate's eyes were shadowed in the darkness.

"You didn't even think to fight for us. After everything you've struggled for, you didn't think this was worth the effort." She shook her head. "Did you know, I was coming here tonight to ask… No. It doesn't matter anymore. I'm moving to Nashville, Oliver. Next week. You won't have to worry about seeing me around town while you're taking your new little wife on nice *slow* walks."

"Nashville? Did your daddy lose his job? I thought you were trying—"

"That's none of your business anymore."

"Kate, I—"

"You're getting *married*. This between us is over."

"I'm doing what's best for both of us. You have to understand that."

She jabbed a finger at him. "You don't get to tell me how to feel about this. You get to shut up."

Oliver bit his tongue on his response.

She searched his face and found him lacking. "Last night shouldn't have happened. I never should have trusted you."

Last night. He swallowed. "Kate. What if you're with child?"

"You didn't think of that before you got engaged?" she snapped.

"I can at least give you some money. Whether or not there's a child, it could help you."

She closed her eyes and took a deep breath. "I don't want your money. If there *is* a baby, I'll take care of them without you—just like I will everything else." Shaking her head, she turned on her heel and stalked back into the woods. She didn't glance back once.

Oliver stood frozen. He could still run after her, but there was nothing to say. It was a cold, empty ending to what they had created between them.

Beside him, Grandpa Herman moaned again.

"Is that why you showed up today?" Oliver snapped. "To get a good seat for the fireworks?"

Grandpa Herman watched him with mournful eyes. When he whispered, "Monster," that time, Oliver knew who he was talking about.

There was no monster in these woods except Oliver.

40

NORA JO

N ora Jo had left the book of poetry in the field yesterday. She didn't need it anymore.

What would she do now? And why bother?

All she had wanted was to find a way for them to live together on their own terms, but Gloria had given up. She'd never wanted Nora Jo, not with enough fire to fight for her.

Perhaps Gloria had never loved her at all. It was a lark for a lonely girl, and Nora Jo, in her desperation, had flung herself forward to be the fool. Every person in this godforsaken town scorned Nora Jo, but she'd thought Gloria was different. She was likely off laughing with Oliver Chadwick Jr. about the silly teacher who had fallen in love with her.

Nora Jo sat at the kitchen table, still as a doll. Miss Ethel was dead. Gloria was gone. There was no one left to care what Nora Jo did.

A knock cracked through the house.

Nora Jo's hand was on the jack in her pocket before she heard an unfamiliar voice. "Miss Ethel?"

Nora Jo opened the door and found Kate on the front porch. There was a tired slump to her shoulders before she straightened to look at Nora Jo. "Good morning." Kate rocked on her heels and then glanced past Nora Jo into the house. "Excuse me. Is Miss Ethel home?"

"Oh. Can you… come back later?" Nora Jo asked. She leaned heavily against the doorframe. She needed only two words—*she's dead*—but they were too large to fit in her mouth. She couldn't be the one to pull someone else into this strange surreality. Wasn't this the point of the bells, to tell the town who had died? Maybe the tolling couldn't be heard out in Tolbert-Vance.

"I'm just trying to do my job, ma'am. I need to know where she wants me for the day, and I need to talk to her."

"She's…" Nora Jo swallowed. Those two words were too short, too harsh. "She passed away."

"What? Good Lord."

Nora Jo sighed. "I'm sorry. I can't pay you anymore. I don't—I don't even know all of what you were helping her with."

"You don't need to pay me," Kate said, still stunned. "I'm leaving town soon. I wanted to say goodbye. Now I…"

There was a long stretch of silence.

"Look," Nora Jo said. "There's some lemonade. Why don't you come sit for a bit?"

At the kitchen table, Nora Jo rubbed her palms together and looked away while Kate sipped the lemonade. The house was so quiet. She tried to remember Miss Ethel's stories about Kate, but they were spider silk in her mind.

She wasn't sure why she'd invited the girl in—only that Kate had looked as lost there on the front porch as Nora Jo felt. "I'm not very good company today," she admitted.

"I'm not looking for entertainment," Kate said. "I sure am sorry for your loss. Miss Ethel was a good woman."

"I wondered sometimes if she really needed a boarder, or if she was just being kind." Nora Jo stared at her hands. "I never asked. Guess I'll never know now."

"Lord," Kate exclaimed. Those words seemed to rouse her from her subdued shock. "I knew she was sick, dying-sick, but I didn't... I thought I'd..." She put a hand to her head as though it pained her. "I can't believe she's gone. I'll really miss her."

"You knew she was this sick?" Nora Jo asked. "How?"

"She told me," Kate said. She met Nora Jo's gaze and there was unexpected fire in her eyes. "I only worked here for a couple of months, and she told me. That woman needed someone to talk to. I listened."

Nora Jo felt numb. "What was wrong with her?"

"People grow old, Miss Nora Jo. There's a point where it's just a matter of when. A hollow tree waiting on the last storm that will send it crashing over. She knew it was coming. She's been waiting. There was hardly a day when she didn't have some sort of fall. She made peace with it." Kate shrugged. "She said she'd had a long life. She was losing the things that mattered."

"Why didn't she tell me?"

"She thought you had enough to deal with already, with the job and your... distractions. She was scared for you."

"Oh." *I'm just worried about you, Miss Nora Jo. What you'll do on your own.*

Kate stared down at her glass. "She always liked me. She used to invite me in after I worked so we could talk."

"I didn't know you were so close."

"You wouldn't, would you?" Kate snapped. "Ma'am."

"What does that mean?"

Kate looked away, swallowed. "You weren't around much."

"I—" Nora Jo didn't know how to react. The world was blurred like watercolor, but this stranger was as sharp as cut glass. "I was just her boarder." She'd once thought there had been more than that, but since she'd been let go, Nora Jo had done everything she could to avoid the house. Miss Ethel hadn't wanted her around. Had she?

That night, Miss Ethel had tried to bridge the gap between them. Nora Jo had scorned her.

"You said yourself she never needed the money that bad," Kate said. Her voice trembled. "Do you know what a gift that woman was? She loved you. She spoke about you like you were family. She was a lonely old lady who only had a few people to look out for her." Kate shook her head. "She'd been getting sicker for a long time. Either you weren't looking, or you didn't care."

"Don't say I didn't care. I've known her far longer than you. I knew something was wrong, but nothing like this. Nothing... nothing that could kill her."

"You could have asked her how you could help, instead of skulking around behind her back. Then you could have actually done something."

"I did ask. She always told me to go out and leave her be," Nora Jo said quietly. "I'm not good at pushing."

"Nor much at talking neither. She left you the house, and you still did nothing for her."

"She... left me the house?" Nora Jo repeated, stunned.

"Who else? She said she wrote you in for it ages ago. Now you get what you really wanted—this place, without her poking into your business. Now you can be happy."

"You don't know me," Nora Jo said coldly.

"Did she die alone?" Kate looked toward the hall like Miss Ethel might walk in and tell the story herself. "Was anyone here? I assume you weren't. I should have stayed last night. If I hadn't..."

She had been alone. Why? Miss Ethel had known Nora Jo was leaving most nights after dark, had surely heard her sneak out again. Death was already knocking on her door, but she hadn't called out for Nora Jo's help.

Had Miss Ethel not trusted her? Or simply not wanted her around for the end?

"Get out of here," Nora Jo snarled. "Now."

For a moment, she thought the girl would not leave. Then, she stood abruptly. "Ma'am." She said the word like it was a hunting knife she could throw at Nora Jo's chest.

Nora Jo followed her to the porch and slammed the door. She leaned against it, staring up at the ceiling.

Kate had been right, when Nora Jo finally checked.

In the will by her bedside, Miss Ethel's slender handwriting declared that the house belonged to Nora Jo. It was an astonishing kindness, but it changed nothing, apart from making her chest ache. Nora Jo wouldn't have money to keep herself fed once Harlow ended their training. The garden could keep her in vegetables for the next few months, but that wasn't enough to live on. Besides, Miss Ethel's home was too close to the center of Chatuga. This town didn't want her here, and she couldn't stand to see Gloria walking by with her husband. Perhaps she could sell the house and use the money to buy a cabin near Harlow on Old Blue.

The rocking chair creaked beneath Nora Jo as she stared over Miss Ethel's yard. The sun was warm and golden in the late afternoon. The longest day of the year—it had certainly felt that way so far. Since she'd found Miss Ethel's body, her life had stopped making sense.

Kate was right to scorn her. Nora Jo had given everything for a chance with Gloria, and now it was gone.

How long would it matter? If Gloria told her fiancé what they had done together, Nora Jo might be run out of more than just her schoolhouse. The only person in town more powerful than the mayor was Mr. Chadwick.

And, maybe, Harlow.

A sparrow flitted and landed on the porch rail, pecking at a smattering of biscuit crumbs. Miss Ethel must have had her final breakfast on the porch.

How long would it take until every footprint Miss Ethel had left behind was erased?

Nora Jo watched the sparrow carefully. Birds were like the stuttering pictures she'd seen in a cramped cinema while studying in Murfreesboro, their heads moving so quickly she couldn't see the transitions. She closed her eyes, exhaling slowly. The wind rustled through the trees bordering Miss Ethel's yard. The shift of the bird's feathers was nearly imperceptible, but Nora Jo had been training for months. She opened her eyes and lunged forward in the same moment, capturing the bird between two cupped palms.

It fluttered with alarm, the small wings beating furiously against her unmoving hands.

She carried the bird back to her room, ignoring the scrape of beak and talons. She and Harlow used a still pond rather than a mirror, but any reflective surface would work. She propped open her window with one hand, and spoke a word to light her candle. The bird stopped struggling at some point, sitting so still in her hand it could have been dead—if not for the tremble of its heartbeat against her palm.

Lifting her chin, she stared into the mirror, and fell into herself.

She hadn't been to the Daleys' farm often, and the roads of Chatuga looked different from above. What looked like a wheel from the ground was more twisted than she'd known, wobbling even on flat ground and dodging copses of trees. From above, those obstacles were laughable. She had never moved so fast and unimpeded, not as rabbit or fish or firefly. The wind caught under her wings and sent her soaring forward. The sky beckoned her onward.

The Daleys' farm was pressed against the creek, which was swollen from the recent storms. The small house was flanked by a field and orchard, the small building overwhelmed by the vastness of nature around it. A mule brayed nearby, dogs barking in return. The scents of green and growing things were on the air. Bugs hummed in every direction, tempting her eye. Her stomach begged her to follow them, but she had another purpose.

The house was in poor repair, its white paint gray with age. Splinters of wood poked through the coating like broken bones. The windows were all flung open, begging for a breeze. On the longest day of the year, the heat was unbearable for those trapped on the ground.

One window led to a small kitchen. Another showed an empty bedroom with crisply made sheets over an ancient iron-frame bed.

A third was guarded by neatly sewn curtains that hung limply. She fluttered onto the windowsill, landing lightly on the warped wood. There was a gap in the curtains, just enough for a beady eye to peer through.

Stretched across a narrow mattress, one leg draped against the floor, was Gloria. One hand clutched something brown to her chest; the other was pressed to her mouth to muffle shuddering sobs.

Nora Jo leaned closer, talons clinging to the windowsill.

The token Gloria held onto so tightly was a wreath of flowers, once purple, but aged to a crumbling brown.

The crying was nearly silent, but it wracked Gloria's body like a tempest. Nora Jo longed to comfort her, but her arms were far across town. She had only the bird's small, silent body and its slender wings.

And that feathered body was now trying to escape her grasp.

It hadn't been difficult to fall into the bird. Nora Jo had practiced the technique on rabbits and frogs and insects, training her mind to let go of her own body and slide into another. As always, there was a slight moment of resistance, no more substantial than the fragile membrane of a bubble. After that, the path to controlling the body was clear and simple.

The bird's mind had settled under her control with the same resignation as its body, but it suddenly began to thrash under Nora Jo's hold.

It was a strange sensation. Nora Jo had become so accustomed to animals' minds being suppressed or obliterated when she slid into place that the struggle felt unnatural. With no prompting, the bird began trying to regain control of its wings. Nora Jo could feel the muscles flexing. Her body wanted to fly away.

No. She needed to stay and keep watch over Gloria for another moment.

She snapped her wings tightly against her body, and looked inward. There was no language in the bird's mind, only a blind panic. Carefully, like blowing out a candle, Nora Jo snuffed its resistance.

The mind, so small and fragile, bowed under her will.

Teeth speared her torso. Sharp pain rent through the bird's body.

She glimpsed an orange paw land on the windowsill in front of her, and then Nora Jo opened her eyes.

She pressed a hand to her chest, gasping for air. She was in her bedroom again. The pain had been strange—it was a deadly blow, but the sensation had been like a dream. Still, the bird's residual terror—now explained—lingered. Her hands shook violently. How had the bird's mind known it was being stalked when Nora Jo herself had not?

Gloria had spoken of their barn cat having kittens recently. Nora Jo should have been more careful.

It was unsettling that she could force a bird to betray its body's instincts. In her focus on Gloria, she had ignored its warnings and left it to be killed.

Shaking her head, she stood up. There were more important worries now. She'd been wrong. Gloria wasn't dismissive, as she had feared. Across town, the love of her life was as heartbroken as she was. And what could Nora Jo do but watch and mourn?

It was no wonder that Gloria didn't believe that Nora Jo could keep them safe and together. The world argued against Nora Jo's promises at every turn.

Perhaps the world was right.

41

KATE

It was a miracle Kate got any more work done that day. She stared blankly at the dye vats in Mrs. Riley's kitchen. The steam and heavy scents were smothering.

Oliver was getting married.

Miss Ethel was dead.

The Mayers were moving to Nashville.

Every solid wall Kate had built her life on had fallen apart in one vicious day, leaving her crouched amid the ruins. She'd seen the aftermath of a tornado once when it touched down along the south end of Chatuga, leaving a straight line of devastation through an otherwise unscathed world. Her parents had taken them down to see its path, a warning that nature couldn't be trusted. Trees were toppled like dominos, houses reduced to rubble.

Kate had wondered back then what the families would do next. How did you rebuild after seeing how easily it could all fall apart?

Learning about Miss Ethel's death was devastating, and she'd topped it off by being a loudmouthed fool. Kate must have lost her mind to yell at a strange white woman like that. Would Nora Jo retaliate? According to Miss Ethel, she was difficult to predict at the best of times.

Kate had been honest—she hated that Miss Ethel had died alone while her tenant drank or gambled or did whatever she did secretly at night. But someone so unreliable couldn't be trusted for empathy or self-reflection. Hopefully she would forget the incident in the mess of everything else.

At least in Nashville, Kate would be far from Nora Jo, Oliver, Oliver's *wife*, and the demon, or whatever it was that had killed the reverend. She and her fiddle could forget everything she was leaving behind in Chatuga.

Sweat dripped down her skin in rivulets as she walked home that evening. The hottest days were still to come, but the heat felt more draining each year. It was the summer solstice; the sun clung to the sky with sticky fingers despite the late hour. The families in the fields would work until the last of the light drained, then join in the local festivities. Kate had no interest in celebrating.

The house was quiet. Kate glanced into the kitchen, but her family was nowhere to be seen.

"Mrs. Moning offered to let them look through Natalie's old clothes."

Kate jumped and turned, finding Eileen tucked on the couch, darning a sock. There was a pile of jumbled cloth on either side of her.

"Natalie has outgrown them all, and the girls wanted new dresses for Nashville. Mama offered to resize anything they like," Eileen continued. "Mama and Daddy are trying to keep them excited about the move. Just watch—Willamae will come back with two lace bonnets."

"Oh," Kate said, hesitating by the kitchen door. She hadn't spoken with Eileen often since their argument after Reverend Castor's funeral. There was a new tension between them, both from the spoken and the unspoken, and Eileen had been avoiding the house.

"Mama told me you're coming too," Eileen said. "I wasn't sure you would. I wouldn't, if I could find a way to stay."

Kate finally moved into the living room and sat on the far end of the couch from Eileen. The house was stifling, and the sweat from her walk lingered on her skin like dew. "You'd stay alone?"

"Josiah is already in South Carolina for his training. If I'm not here waiting for him when he comes home, I'll never have a chance."

"I'm sorry."

"No, you're not. You never knew Josiah. You judged him because of his pa, but he's dead now and Josiah is gone. He never had a chance to prove y'all wrong. People can be different from their parents."

"They can," she agreed.

"Do you know if he's coming back? Can you see it? I need to know if he's gone for good."

"I don't know," Kate admitted.

"Do you even ever have visions of me?" Eileen asked. "It's always Kate, Kate, Kate."

"I do," Kate whispered.

"Then why don't you know if I'm going to have my fiancé back? This parish was supposed to be his once his daddy died. We're supposed to be happy here. Tell me if that's true."

Kate sighed and rubbed her forehead. "Is that the only reason you're talking to me again?"

Eileen huffed, but didn't dispute it.

"Look, I don't understand either," Kate said. "My visions have been strange lately. It's like they're... ending. I only have one left that hasn't happened, I think. And it's..." The worst one. The one about Eileen.

"Only one? What does *that* mean?"

"I don't know," Kate said. She looked at her younger sister, at the dark circles under her eyes and the slump to her shoulders. She couldn't let that last vision come true. "You know I love you, don't you?"

"What's going on with you?" Eileen asked, looking uneasy.

"I know we argue," Kate persisted. "We don't see the world in the same way. But you're my sister. I'd do anything for you. You know that, don't you?"

"I know you'd do anything for Mary Evelyn," Eileen sneered.

Kate faltered. "Mary Evelyn... She lost her leg because of me. I thought I had to protect her. You were always strong. You didn't need help from me. Besides, I know you—you know how to speak up when you need something."

"Everyone always thinks I'm fine on my own," Eileen said. "No one ever worries about me. They only notice me when I complain. You have your fits, the twins are their own handful, and Mary Evelyn is the baby who lost her leg. If I stayed quiet, I'd have disappeared entirely."

"That's not..."

"No one ever even asked why I wanted to marry Josiah. You were all so focused on me being sixteen and him being the reverend's son that you never even asked if I love him. I do. He's the only person who saw me for me, not just as another Mayer. I would have been a good preacher's wife, Kate. I would have. I could make a difference. But now I'm stuck moving to Nashville with everyone like I'm still a kid."

Kate looked at her sister. They had slept only feet apart for the last sixteen years, and yet there was so much unknown between them. Eileen was her little sister. Kate had always assumed she understood her. But at some point, Eileen had changed.

Finally, she said, "I'm sorry."

"I don't want to move to Nashville," Eileen said, and her voice quavered.

"Me neither," Kate said. They sat in silence for a moment, each with their own thoughts. "But maybe… maybe we can leave behind everything from Chatuga and build something. Like Granddaddy did here." Leave Oliver behind, leave her remaining vision behind. Let it all go.

"I don't want to leave my life behind," Eileen said, sounding miserable.

"Here," Kate added suddenly, reaching into her pocket. She pulled out her wolf fang. "Uncle Christopher gave this to me to protect me. I want you to have it."

"You love this thing," Eileen said, cautiously taking it from her palm. She rubbed a thumb over the well-worn bone, carefully avoiding the sharp point.

"I love you more. I know we've had our misunderstandings, but everything I've done, it's been for this family. It's been for you. I…" She shook her head. The world was spinning around her, and her pulse was racing.

"You can't just fix everything with a gift," Eileen said quietly.

"Eileen, I—"

She put a hand out to steady herself, clutching the loose pile of fabric at her side. Kate blinked hard, fighting the swell of darkness, but it washed over her in a crash.

There was a naked body crumpled on the ground.

Kate crouched on her knees, body screaming in agony that seemed too sharp to be real, but she only had eyes for the man in front of her.

Oliver's skin was stained black and red with burns from head to toe. His mismatched eyes were coated in a sheen of tears.

Blood pulsed from a wound in his chest. The gash was jagged, dark, and terrifying.

"Kate," he rasped. His breath shuddered. "I tried. I'm sorry."

He stared past her, and she followed his gaze. A dark lake stretched endlessly in front of them. A cavern stretched overhead, the dark stalactites stabbing down toward them. One pale form interrupted the darkness. A naked white woman lay nearby, sprawled face down on the ground, unmoving.

"I'm sorry for..." Oliver's voice trailed off. He coughed, and blood flecked his lips.

"Kate? Kate!"

A slender hand cupped her face, patting her cheeks and stroking her skin.

Kate blinked. She had fallen sideways onto the pile of socks. The banality of the room around her was as jarring as the cave had been. Everything was too quiet. "Eileen," she croaked.

"What was it?" Eileen asked. "What did you see?"

42

NORA JO

Nora Jo hurried across town, her human feet feeling large and slow after her wings. The early evening painted stripes of orange and red across the horizon overhead. She walked so quickly she nearly stumbled into a jog several times. There were people passing down the central streets of town, and all looked at her as she passed. She avoided their eyes. Did they know about Miss Ethel? Or about Gloria? Or was the sight of Nora Jo itself simply unusual after more than two months of isolation?

Finally reaching her destination, she raced up the pathway and rapped hard on the front door.

It opened to reveal Mr. Lye, who blinked at her. He was paler than the last time she'd seen him, the night she came to ask for Harlow's tutelage. Dark circles were stamped under his eyes, and his shoulders hunched as if pressed down by an invisible hand. "Miss Nora Jo?"

"I need to talk to Mr. Harlow. Is he home?"

Mr. Lye's face grew even paler, as if his blood had been replaced with sour milk, slogging through his body. "Mr.... Mr. Harlow? Miss Nora Jo, I—"

"I'm here," Harlow said. Both Nora Jo and Mr. Lye jumped, turning to where he had emerged from the hallway. He'd left off his usual trench coat, but his hat was in his hand. He ignored Mr. Lye completely, focusing on Nora Jo. "What's wrong?"

Nora Jo hesitated. Harlow nodded. "I'll be back," he told Mr. Lye, putting on his hat and stepping out onto the porch with her. He closed the door between them, cutting off Mr. Lye's wan gaze. "This way," he said, and strode around the yard toward the back.

Nora Jo glanced at the street, making sure no busybodies were spying, before following. The small yard was fenced in by dense oak trees, which loomed dark against the sunset.

After her first visit to the Lyes, Nora Jo had never returned. She always met Harlow deep in the woods, sparing them both from prying eyes. It was strange to see where he lived. It was so mundane compared to the mysteries of their work. He'd stayed in Chatuga away from his home in the mountains for months now to train her.

And what had it brought either of them?

"Go on," Harlow prompted, folding his arms. His hat shadowed his face, but his blue eyes were intent, scanning her like he was reading crackling flames. Despite his focus, his shoulders were relaxed. He didn't once look back toward the house to make sure they were not being watched.

Now that she was here, she felt foolish. What could he do? What could she do?

She'd spent the past couple of months certain that his witchery would solve all her problems, but it had only distracted her from the people who needed her.

"I shouldn't have come. There's nothing you can do."

"Tell me."

She shook her head. "I'm sorry. I… I quit. I can't do this anymore."

He frowned. "What are you talking about?"

"My landlady just died, no one wants me to stay in this town, and now—" She broke off, looking away. Her breath stuttered in her throat, but she refused to cry. "It's all pointless. I've been wasting your time with all this, and nothing's gotten better. I should never have asked you to train me."

"Pointless? You're stronger than you've ever been," Harlow said. "You could barely touch your magic before we met."

"I know," she said. "But what does it matter? I can't do anything. I can't fix any of this."

"Magic can't raise the dead," he warned. "No one can. You could speak to a spirit, at most, but there's no permanence in that. I'm sorry to say your landlady is gone. But you can't stop your training. Not now. Not today. We're too close."

"I don't expect to be the Lord. I can't bring back Miss Ethel. But I didn't even know she was dying. I wasn't there. I couldn't even… Look, it's not just about Miss Ethel. There's so much." She hugged her arms around her stomach. "I can't even fix my own life."

"Perhaps you can. Your power is still being shaped—you can't see the full potential yet. Tell me what's happening," Harlow suggested. "There's something you're not saying."

"I can't," Nora Jo said, voice shattered.

"You can."

"You don't understand. I *can't*," she said, glancing back at the house. There was a movement in the back window. Mr. Lye was watching them. He disappeared when he caught Nora Jo's eye. At this distance, he wouldn't be able to hear, but it was still too close for comfort. Her relationship with Gloria had only ever lived in that field. Bringing it into town was a risk.

No wonder Gloria had been too afraid to reject the proposal from the Chadwicks. Nora Jo could do nothing to help either of them.

Harlow folded his arms. "I understand more than anyone else in this town. Tell me."

"You might hate me for it," she whispered.

"The other people here would hate you. They're small-minded. They hate everything they don't understand. No sense of curiosity. No sense of larger things. Humans," he said, sighing, "are weak."

"Fine. I'm—I'm in love with someone who is engaged to be married to someone else."

"Ah," he said. "That is difficult."

"I know," she said, fighting back a sting in her eyes.

He tapped his finger to his lips. "Magic can excite lust, but it can't create love. Love needs to be able to change and grow. If lust is all you want, we can make that happen. Or even marriage. There are ways to bind someone. But if you want love that isn't there…"

"She *does* love me," Nora Jo snarled. Then, she froze. She held herself as still as the rabbit she had first overtaken.

The summer evening was quiet around them. As always, the forest remained silent whenever Harlow was nearby. The frogs that would have begun croaking around the rest of Chatuga were hidden.

"Ah," Harlow said. He was always difficult to read, and the dramatic shadow from his hat hid his expression.

"She does," Nora Jo said quietly, feeling like she was diving over the edge of a cliff. "And I love her."

He nodded thoughtfully. He hadn't recoiled yet, but she tensed to flee. "But she agreed to marry this other person."

"She's afraid," Nora Jo said. "It's like you said. People hate what they don't understand."

Harlow hummed, nodding more. She hadn't dreamed of someone reacting like this, taking her words as a fact to consider rather than a delusion.

"What we have is real. And we deserve a chance," she continued. "But we need to avoid suspicion. They already dismissed me for teaching secular books. By training with you, I'm making myself more of an outcast."

"There's still magic you don't know," Harlow said. "That's what tonight is for. I told you—this is the most powerful night of the year."

"What could we do to fix *this*?"

"I have a plan. Everything will be better by dawn."

"It would be better to just give up now. Stop wasting your time."

"You have to come tonight," Harlow said fiercely. "I won't let you stop. Not now. You'll see. Tomorrow will be a new world."

A tear finally spilled from Nora Jo's hot eyes. "I don't know if I can believe that anymore."

"You've got to trust me. Come to the lake at midnight like we planned. Promise me." He was firm, implacable. There was no doubt in his expression, no hesitation. He had taken her confession and would not turn away from her. She wasn't alone.

"Okay," she said. "Okay. I'll be there."

Harlow stepped past her toward the house's back door, and then paused. He looked over his shoulder. "Don't tell anyone else," he warned, voice like iron. "Not about tonight, and not about this girl."

"I know."

He nodded, and was gone.

She stood in the backyard, trying to control the emotions leaping in her chest like clamoring hounds. It had been a heart-wrenching week, but perhaps things were not doomed to be out of her control. They could do this. Miss Ethel was gone, but that meant there was nothing left to hold Nora Jo back from changing her life.

Neither Harlow nor the Lyes appeared in the windows again.

43

OLIVER

Oliver spent the day aimlessly wandering the farm with nothing but the memories of Tucker Lee's fear and Kate's scorn to keep him company. That, and the ghost at his heels. Grandpa Herman was following him, vanishing for minutes at a time before reappearing once again. His mouth was moving, but as long as Oliver ignored him, he sounded like a radio between channels. Some syllables slipped through, but he was incomprehensible. He couldn't talk to another ghost, not after Tucker Lee. Grandpa Herman should go back to where he belonged and leave Oliver alone.

The summer air filled his lungs, making him strain to find each breath. During the noon heat, he slipped into the barn to sleep by Magnolia's stall, close enough to smell her, and then woke in a daze to continue wandering through the evening.

He felt like a spirit reliving the steps of its past over and over.

He should have learned after watching that first fool blow out his brains at Camp Sevier that growing attached to people would only lead to pain. Death could be a lightning strike on a cloudless day, unexpected and devastating. Instead, he had tied his soul to Tucker Lee Selecky with a strength he hadn't known was possible. When Tucker Lee died, choking and suffering, he had come back to Chatuga with his heart hardened.

And then a beautiful girl found him in the woods, telling him about fate and the future. She'd made him believe there *was* a future, not just a past.

But he had hurt her.

Oliver couldn't seem to do anything but hurt the people he cared about. He wouldn't make a good husband, not for Gloria Daley *or* Kate.

He felt unsettled. He wanted to crawl out of his own skin.

After the things he'd seen, what hold did Pa have over him? If Oliver was the man he wanted to be, he couldn't let his parents dictate his life.

He knelt to grab a handful of water from the creek and splashed his face. Then, he left the farm.

Despite living in town all his life, Oliver had only ventured into Tolbert-Vance a handful of times. That neighborhood was a separate world, out of sight and mind. He had rarely thought about anyone else, much less those he had never met. The residents weren't allowed to work at his pa's mill, and they kept to themselves. Perhaps one had led to the other.

When Kate's daddy had been about to lose his job with the lumber mill, they had all known he wouldn't find a place at the Chadwick Mill. That had been the law set firm by Grandpa Herman, and Pa upheld it. The Chadwicks would rather see families like the Mayers leave town than hire one Black man.

It was a miracle Kate bothered to talk to him at all. She should have known at first glance that he would bring her nothing but suffering. He could give her nothing but trouble.

Still, he found himself standing in front of the Mayers' small house on the dirt road. The garden was well-loved, lit in flashes of blue from the bottle tree. He hesitated. He'd already gotten some curious looks from the neighbors as he'd passed through, and they'd grown more curious once he'd asked for directions. By coming here, he risked them being discovered. It wasn't his reputation at risk from their relationship; Kate would suffer far more if it came to light. He could ruin Kate's life. He could ruin her entire family.

But she had been the one to shout at him for being a coward. She wanted him to fight for her. Now he would. He took a breath and knocked.

The girl who answered the door was close to Kate's age, with lighter skin and broad apple cheekbones. She wore a faded red dress and a matching bandana over her hair. Her eyes widened when she saw him, and she glanced at the street beyond as though expecting more people.

"Hi," he said, smiling. It felt crooked on his face. He'd once wielded smiles like blades to get his way, but after holding a rifle in his hands, it seemed an empty weapon.

"You're Oliver Chadwick Jr.," she said, stunned. His distinct eyes gave him away to anyone in town.

"That I am," he said. "I'm looking for Kate."

"Our Kate?" she repeated, blinking. She recovered herself quickly, and there was more caution in her stance. "Might I ask why?"

He glanced over his shoulder. How many people were watching this conversation? He had hoped Kate would be the one to answer the door. "I need to talk to her."

"Sorry, sir. She's not here."

"Where is she?"

"Maybe I can help with whatever it is you need." The girl's face was neutral, but Oliver could tell he was losing her. There was a fierceness to her, an iron edge to the tilt of her chin. She couldn't send him away, but she wasn't planning to help him.

"You're Eileen," he said. "Ain't you?"

She startled. "I am. How did you…?"

"Kate's a friend of mine. I need to talk to her."

Eileen looked him up and down, a frown burying itself in the lines of her young face. "A 'friend.' That little hypocrite," she huffed. "After giving me so much grief about Josiah…"

"Please," Oliver said. "Where is she?"

"I don't know," she said. "She left in a hurry half an hour ago. Tore out of here like the dickens. She didn't say where she was going."

"Did she… Did she have an episode before she left?"

Eileen's eyes grew ever wider. She tilted her head, looking at Oliver anew. "She did," Eileen said carefully. "I don't know what she saw. Only that it scared her."

Oliver bit back a curse. Kate would have his head if he swore in front of her little sister, no matter that Eileen was already sixteen. What had Kate seen? Where had she gone?

"If she comes back, please tell her I was looking for her. Tell her… Tell her that I'm sorry."

"What did you do?" Eileen demanded.

"I'm going to fix it," Oliver promised. "I swear."

Eileen gave him a cold look.

"Tell her to meet me at our cave in the woods, she'll—"

"No. I'm not your messenger. If she wants to talk to you, she'll find you," Eileen said. She glanced over his shoulder again at the street beyond. "You should go before my parents get home. Kate won't thank you for making a fuss."

"You'll at least tell her you saw me?"

"Have a good night, sir."

Oliver stared out his window, watching as the dusk turned to darkness. The moon drifted up over the horizon, illuminating the farm in a silver glow. The shortest night of the year was upon them, but it seemed to stretch out endlessly before him.

He had limped through town for the rest of the evening trying to find Kate, but she was nowhere to be seen.

She'd been right. He *was* a coward. After everything he'd gone through, he had thought nothing could scare him again, but he had seen a difficult path ahead and turned away. She was right to be furious with him. Even Eileen had seen that. He just needed a chance to make it up to her.

He couldn't marry a stranger. He loved Kate too much to let her go. He only wished he had been bolder before he'd broken her heart.

But he could still fix this.

A candle flickered on the sill, a hazy figure pacing behind him. Grandpa Herman's mixed eyes tried to catch his attention in the mirror, but Oliver kept his gaze distant. He would not give the ghost a grip on the world tonight. He didn't need another lecture.

"… save her…" the ghost said.

Oliver froze. Slowly, his eyes dragged over to meet Grandpa Herman's in the glass.

His gaze was intense. Mournful. Furious. The emotions distorted his face like a mask. "Run," he said, the attention letting his voice filter through more clearly. "You can't save her."

"Kate? What do you know?" Oliver asked. "Where is she?"

The ghost shook his head. "Danger. Monsters. Demons. You…" His form flickered. His voice was lost for a moment. "… them. Leave."

Oliver's pulse thudded in his chest. His lungs seized, but he forced his cough down. "No more riddles. *Herman Chadwick*, tell me what's happening."

"They'll *eat* you," the ghost snarled. His image grew larger in the window. He was very close to the back of Oliver's chair. He pointed a gnarled finger at the wall where he had carved the strange words over and over. "Just like they tried to eat me. And this time they'll win."

A caw from the night beyond the window broke his attention. He looked away from the reflection and found a crow sitting on the sill outside. It was staring at him, its jet-black eye glinting in the candlelight. It cawed again.

"Run…" the ghost cried, but his voice was as faded as a conversation in another room now that Oliver's attention had moved on.

Oliver stared at the crow, frowning. It was unusual behavior for a bird, to say the least. Even stranger, crows were rarely active at night. The last time he had seen one behave so oddly had been… the night he met Kate.

Hadn't the crow led him directly to her? It had taken Tucker Lee's cigarette case, drawing him to the clearing where she waited for him.

Danger. Monsters. Even if that was what waited on the other end, Oliver couldn't leave Kate to face it alone.

He stood up, making the rocking chair clatter. "Do you know where she is?" he asked the crow.

The bird hopped up and down, eye still fixed on him.

"Wait for me," Oliver said, jumping to his feet and racing down the stairs. When he stepped outside, the crow swooped past him and flew toward the forest. In the night, it was only a suggestion of moonlight on black wings.

Oliver followed.

44

NORA JO

That night, Nora Jo summoned a small flame to hover at her side and light her way, then stepped into the woods.

Over her months of training, Nora Jo had learned to use her applewood dowsing rod to track the lines of magic around Chatuga. The rod had dried since she first carved it from its tree, but it held the echo of new life. It was attuned to the land from which it had grown, fed by the blood and bones of her ancestors who had become the soil. She kept a loose hold of her thoughts, letting the rod lead her through the underbrush toward the lake. So far off the beaten path, the magic would guide her to the entrance more surely than her memory. It was like following an instinct, though the feeling originated from outside her body. It was simpler with Harlow, who helped her focus and silenced the forest around them. The creatures of Chatuga held no fear of Nora Jo, and croaked and sang and skittered through the brush as she walked past.

What magic would Harlow teach her tonight? Could it truly help her find a future with Gloria? He had shown her so many secrets over the past months, but this seemed impossible. Still, she remembered Gloria wracked with sobs alone on her bed, and firmed her resolve.

It was a warm night, flush with the life of summer. By the time her rod led her to a solid rockface, her dress was dappled with sweat. She paced along the outside, but she couldn't find the small entrance they'd used before. Perhaps she had distractedly followed the tug of a different ley line and was somewhere new. Anxiety clawed at her stomach. Harlow had insisted that the spell must happen tonight, during the solstice. Surely, she wouldn't miss her chance to be with Gloria because she had gotten lost. Fate couldn't be so cruel.

Finally, she noticed the crevice at the base of the rock. She waved a hand and sent her fire to illuminate the gap. The opening was as narrow as she remembered, but the moss at the base had been scraped away recently by fingertips. The lines dragged to reveal streaks of dirt pointing like arrows. Harlow must already be inside.

Carefully, Nora Jo slipped her feet in first, and grabbed at the ground to lower herself down into the cave.

The flame lit the familiar cavern, glinting off the wet rock. She followed the path that Harlow had shown her toward the lake. Her dowsing rod added to her surety at each fork, tugging her forward. She walked carefully, mindful of the slick ground beneath her boots.

Finally, she climbed down a pile of rocks to the edge of the dark water. Her fire only illuminated a faint circle of the small shore in front of her, outlining the black water resting with utter stillness against the stone.

"Mr. Harlow?" she called. Her voice bounced off the soaring stone walls, carried by the water in the darkness.

There was a strangled shout from nearby, and Nora Jo whirled around.

The darkness was absolute beyond the glow of her flame.

"Hello?" she prompted, carefully making her way down the rock ledge around the lake.

"Please. Help." The woman's voice was ragged and desperate, but with the horrible echo Nora Jo couldn't track it.

She stopped, took a deep breath, then nodded at the flame. It burst apart, creating a dozen smaller fires that floated through the air around her like fireflies. She stretched out her arms, sending the flames outward.

A figure sat hunched on the shore to her left. Cautiously, Nora Jo approached. It was too small to be Harlow. The shape was strange, nearly inhuman.

She kept her hands up. She didn't know many defensive spells, especially any that could be flung at an opponent without preparation, but her flame companions held real heat. If anything, they could distract an attacker while she scrambled back toward the entrance.

The fire caught the sheen of wide, wild eyes. It drifted closer to reveal a tear-stained face, a girl with blue-black skin and a torn dress. Her wrists were bound, along with her ankles.

It took her a moment to recognize Kate Mayer.

Nora Jo fell to the shore beside her, narrowly avoiding a sharp, slender stalagmite that would have impaled her knee. Someone had bound Kate and propped her against one of the ridged pillars, but there was no one else in sight. How long had Kate been down here? Who had done this?

"Hold on," she said, and fumbled for the knot on the girl's wrists.

In the flickering firelight, it was difficult to grasp.

"Please," Kate repeated, voice thick with tears.

A sharp caw rang out over the cavern, followed by a man's voice: "Kate!"

Nora Jo jolted to her feet, standing between the bound girl and the newcomer with the dowsing rod held defensively in front of her. The man stumbled down the ledge by the entrance, a lantern swinging from his hand. He was panting so loudly she could hear it from yards away, as though he were breathing through a cloud of smoke.

She knew him. She had been thinking about him, silently cursing him, all day. Oliver Chadwick Jr.

What was *he* doing there?

Kate recognized him too. "*Oliver*," she croaked.

A bird soared over Nora Jo, so close that a wing brushed the top of her head. It veered suddenly, squawking, and darted back toward the exit. Further along the shore, another figure Nora Jo hadn't noticed slowly stood. Even as she sent her lights to illuminate him, she knew the silhouette of his trench coat.

She frowned and glanced back toward where the bird had fled. Harlow must have been possessing it, falling back into his own body once his goal had been completed. But why? What was his plan? If he hadn't wanted Gloria's fiancé to follow him, he could have left the bird before leading him all the way to the lake. He must know he was the *last* person Nora Jo wanted to see today.

"Kate, are you okay?" Oliver demanded, approaching them.

"I shouldn't have come," Kate gasped. "I didn't know, I didn't think. I just needed to help you. But you're here because of *me*."

"Shh, you'll be okay. What did she do to you?" He did a double take at Nora Jo. "You?"

She lowered her dowsing rod, holding up her other empty hand. "I didn't do this."

"Oliver, *go*," Kate demanded, tugging at her restraints. "Run now."

Oliver dove toward her, but part of the binding unfurled on its own and lashed forward. What Nora Jo had thought was rope was a living vine, which grew rapidly and wove itself around Oliver's wrists, tying them tight in front of him. He fell to his knees, still trying to reach Kate's side.

Nora Jo hesitated, feeling suddenly cold. She turned to Harlow as he approached in the darkness, the dancing flames illuminating his face. "What is this? Why are they here?" she asked. She gestured back toward Oliver. "I never said I wanted to hurt her fiancé. That's not how I want to do this."

Harlow sighed. "You were right," he said. "She was too weak."

"Who, Gloria? Or Kate?" Her alarm was growing, pounding with her heartbeat. "Kate works—worked—for my landlady. She has nothing to do with this."

"Of course I was right," Harlow continued. "It's better this way. Easier." He shrugged. "I know. But I hoped she might be like me."

Something was very wrong.

Slowly, Nora Jo reached for the protective jack in her pocket. She pulled it out and lifted it toward Harlow. It shook in her hand.

Harlow laughed. "Nora Jo," he said, in the brisk tone he used when she made a mistake during their lessons. "You don't really believe I'd give you something that would help you *against* me, do you?"

He snapped his fingers, and the twine binding the flannel pouch fell off. The jack opened in her palm. There were no feathers, no stones, no herbs. There was only a pile of dirt and dust that fell apart in her hand.

She lurched backward, but the vines from Oliver's wrists grew once again, snaring her. She fell hard as they wrapped around her ankles. Her knees scraped against the cave floor, and she felt the sharp sting of cut skin. She reached out, hoping to drag herself away, but the vines climbed up her body to bind her wrists.

She was held tight.

The fires she'd left dancing over the shore snuffed out, leaving them in utter darkness.

45

KATE

Kate screamed, fighting against her restraints. The blackness around them was complete and suffocating.

Suddenly, an eerie glow bathed them in a faint blue light. It came from everywhere and nowhere, casting dramatic shadows across the cave.

The stranger took off his leather satchel and began digging through it single-mindedly, as if he didn't have three captives sitting only feet away.

At her side, Oliver walked on his knees toward her. "Kate," he whispered. "Talk to me."

"How did you find me? You shouldn't have come."

After her horrible vision of Oliver, she had crept through the caves from their usual entrance, holding a lantern in front of her. It had been strange to be there without Oliver. Alone, the tunnels seemed ancient and endless, full of narrow gaps that fell into bottomless pits. They hadn't managed to find the lake before, but she knew in her bones she would find it that night. She had seen it.

She'd been on the edge of panic when the stranger emerged from a narrow gap in the cave wall. She'd barely had time to shout before his magic ensnared her.

Since then, she had been by the lake for an endless length of time, left alone in the darkness. After rubbing her wrists and ankles raw trying to break free, shouting fruitlessly into the dark, she'd slumped down on the rock, cursing herself, until Nora Jo Barker stumbled in. Nora Jo was undeniably the woman from her vision—not yet naked, not yet burned—but who was the stranger?

"He's going to hurt you," Kate said. "I saw it. I wanted to stop it."

"I'll get us out of this," he promised her. "I'll save you."

"What are you doing, Mr. Harlow?" Nora Jo demanded. She had fallen with vines wrapped around her legs, two yards away from Kate and Oliver. She'd twisted to sit up straight, dignified despite her bloodied knees and disheveled hair. "What's happening?"

The stranger, Harlow, placed a handful of long candles into cracks in the stone around him, wedging them into the ground. With a snap, flames crackled on their wicks. "I did tell you we would fix everything tonight," he said. "Tomorrow will be a new world. It's been a long wait. It needed to all be in place by the solstice." He looked up again, as if he could see the moon overhead through the layers of stone and earth. "This is the moment it will all finally come together. I told you it would. You did. I should have trusted you." He answered himself as smoothly as breathing, a full conversation in one voice.

He removed a leather folder from his bag and unrolled it to reveal a set of five knives. They glinted in the strange light. Each blade was pristine and viciously sharp, each handle as black as night. With a flick of his wrist, three of them rose into the air and hovered around him. The silver blades glittered.

Beside her, Oliver twisted his wrists over and over, fighting against the bonds that held them. The future was roaring toward them. Fear scalded Kate's blood.

"Mr. Harlow," Nora Jo pleaded. "I don't understand. Did… did a demon get to you? I can help you. You said we can fight them."

A demon. A shiver of terror flooded through Kate. *This* was what had been lurking in the shadows. This was what had killed the reverend, what Oliver's ghosts had warned him about.

But Kate didn't know this man. Why her? Why them?

"A demon did get to me," Harlow agreed. "We've been planning this a long time. Three young bodies with magic in their blood." He strode toward them, knives orbiting him. His dark trench coat was a monstrous shadow in the odd light.

The first blade lashed out toward Kate's back. Pain lanced white-hot through one of her bound arms, then washed over the rest of her. She swore at him ferociously, vitriolic blue phrases that spilled out nonsensically.

The knife rose back into the air, blood dripping from its edge. Ignoring her cursing, he said, "A stillborn girl brought back to life. The future and past are clear to her. But she couldn't see us."

The second knife jabbed down. Oliver hissed through gritted teeth. "A soldier touched by death, balanced between two worlds."

The third blade bit into Nora Jo's shoulder. She cried out in pain. "And you. The bud that hadn't bloomed, repressed for years. We had to draw it out of you, make you powerful enough for this to work. But now we have you here. And my brothers can return."

"Leave the girls alone, you monster," Oliver growled.

"Monster. Demon. Devil. Call us what you want, while you can. You'll be like us soon enough. Not *just* like us," he continued.

"I don't think these will be able to find our balance. No matter. Our brothers can take their bodies and swamp their minds. A partnership like ours is a rarity. Not everyone has the strength—or worth."

"This isn't you," Nora Jo insisted. "Mr. Harlow, are you still in there? We can stop this. You said we could fight them off."

"It's my body," Harlow said. "But it's also our body. This is the only me you've ever known, Nora Jo. I did tell you, once. Amans came to me on a dark night long ago. With no body, he was weak. With mine, we could both be strong. The partnership was the best choice I ever made."

Nora Jo stuttered, clearly searching for a response. "You… The… This whole time, you've been training me for *this*?"

"I showed you how easy it is to take over another body—especially one with a weak will," Harlow said. "I'd hoped you'd see things my way, in the end. Being bonded with a demon is the key to gaining more power than you can imagine. You want to change the world? You need power. By the time most witches gain enough, they die of old age. *We* don't grow old. We stay the same. With our brothers by our side, we'll bring our kingdom to this earth. You could be one of us."

"I don't want your *kingdom*," Nora Jo snarled. "I only wanted peace."

"You'll never find peace living under someone else's rule," Harlow said. "If you're not in control, you're in service to someone else." He stared up toward the ceiling again. "The Master chose to be a prince of hell instead of a servant of heaven. But what of the servants of heaven who became servants in hell? What about us?"

Nora Jo seemed stunned into silence. Kate couldn't blame her

—this man, this demon, was incomprehensible. Fear roiled in her chest like a flood, sweeping and drowning and inexorable.

"We have to get out of here," Oliver whispered to Kate, voice tight. His eyes were stunned, panicked, but his jaw was set. His fingers scrambled across the slick rock at their feet, searching for something. In the strange light, the blood flecking his pale hands seemed black. "Don't worry, Kate."

Kate screamed against her gag.

Harlow returned to the ring of candles and held up his hands. "It's time, my brothers. Our long wait is at an end."

"Harlow!" Nora Jo howled.

Kate watched the demon work, her panic so overwhelming it was almost like having a vision. She was present, but removed. Aware, but distant. The pain in her body couldn't be real. This couldn't be happening.

"Ultio," he called. One of the blades lifted and flicked its drops of blood into the center of the circle. The flames turned bright blue, a mockery of a summer day.

"Legatus." The flames grew two inches and burned blood red. Kate flinched back, blinking.

"Noct."

At first, Kate thought the candles had gone out. Then, they flickered, and she realized the flames had become black, barely visible in the darkness.

All three candles flickered again, turning bright white and stretching toward the cave ceiling. A wind whipped past Kate's ears and danced around the circle of candles.

"It's them," Oliver said, voice strained. He was staring away from the candles, away from her, toward the black lake in front of them.

"Help me. Please. *Grandpa Herman*. Tell me. What can I do?"

Kate tried to reach toward him, but he was just out of range. "Oliver," she cried.

The wind over the fire coalesced into three flickering forms— red, blue, and black. They circled the flames like hounds, then turned toward the three captives.

"All right," Oliver said. "I understand."

Oliver lunged toward Kate. She tilted her head, expecting one last desperate kiss. Instead, he jammed something sharp into her shoulder. It ripped through her skin, a bright shock of pain.

While she was still gasping, he turned the cracked stalagmite, stained dark and dripping, on himself. He twisted his bound wrists and shoved the makeshift blade down into his thigh. Blood welled around it, staining his torn pants.

"No! Don't let him mix the blood!" Harlow shouted, but his voice was lost as the wind picked up again.

The three demons shot toward them. The blue flames collided with Nora Jo like a wave, crashing over her and crackling along her skin. She screamed, the sound feral. The fire tore through the binding at her wrists and ankles as she thrashed against the cave floor. Her clothes smoked and blackened.

The other two advanced on Kate and Oliver, swirling around each other. Red, black, red, black, red, black. The flames barreled forward; Kate winced, hunching her bleeding shoulders and closing her eyes.

There was a rush overhead, and then a hoarse scream beside her.

She turned and gasped. Both demons had fallen on Oliver. He was lit from within by the flames. In one instant, he was subsumed by the red. In the next, there was only black. The two demons fought for space, roiling like a thundercloud. His back arched as the forces threatened to tear him apart from the inside. His shirt and bindings were eaten up instantly by the fire.

She fought to free herself, to help him, but the vines were still too tight. She could only watch as his body was buffeted back and forth like a ship in a storm.

Then, slowly, he lifted the stalagmite dagger again. He held it aloft over his chest, his movements slow and weak. He pulled the spike toward his heart as though fighting through a field of mud. His own body was resisting him.

Surely the makeshift blade was too small, too dull, to do fatal damage. Still, it was a horrifying sight as the stone moved inexorably toward his chest. Kate screamed again.

When he hit his skin, he slowly drew a line down. Blood followed the movement in a stream down his torso. Hands shaking, he lifted the spike and slashed a smaller mark through the first.

A cross.

With an inhuman shriek, the contrasting flames burst from him. The black fire flew through the air like a gunshot. Fast as a shadow, it was gone.

The red flame flashed past Kate, knocking her to the ground. The demon swept over the lake as if pushed away, though it seemed to be fighting to come back. Its bright flames flickered as it writhed in the air, hovering high over the eerily reflective water.

"Legatus!" Harlow shouted.

Power pulsed from Harlow in shockwaves. A shiver of energy spread over Kate's skin, invasive and unsettling. Ants marched along her bones, pressing through her veins and muscles and fat to burrow into the core of her. She screamed and fought her bindings.

Slowly, steadily, the red demon began to pull itself through the air back toward the shore. It approached like a storm cloud, roiling and relentless.

There was a heavy thud beside her. The slick shore scraped her bloodied arms and legs as Kate scrambled to look. Oliver had collapsed against the ground, his chest bloody and skin edged with soot. His face was chapped and reddened with heat. His breathing was the worst she'd ever heard, rattling through his lungs like dead leaves.

"Kate," he rasped. "I tried. I'm sorry."

He stared past her, and she turned to watch the demon inching inexorably toward them. It clawed through the air, inescapable as a tornado.

"Legatus," Harlow called, voice echoing over the lake. "You know the blood that's meant to be yours. Forget the false spill. The bond is still there. Fight. This is your last chance."

Oliver's voice was only a whisper. "I'm sorry for..." His voice trailed off. He coughed, and blood flecked his lips.

"Oliver, hush," Kate said. "No apologies, darling. Please, just breathe."

He frowned, concentrating on something she couldn't see. "Kate, they burned something... inside of me. My grandpa said no one could survive two, but it would weaken the demons. He wanted me to use you to save myself. He's so, so angry. But I needed..."

He tried to continue to speak, but the words were lost. His mouth opened and closed, breath shuddering. The sound hitched, and his eyes grew wide.

Her hands were bound, but Kate collapsed down to press her forehead against his. She closed her eyes and felt his skin against hers, hotter than any human should be. She wished she could tear off her bonds and comfort him. Wished she could turn back time and save them both. Wished she could apologize for wasting their final hours together being so uselessly mad at him.

His breath stuttered against her mouth, then stopped.

"Oliver." She pressed against him more tightly, chasing that last moment of connection as his body slumped.

He was gone. It was over.

She opened her eyes and screamed.

And the red demon descended, filling her eyes and mouth with crackling flames.

46

The candles snuffed out as Legatus poured into Kate Mayer, leaving only Harlow's conjured light behind. The brightness of the demons' flames was hidden by dull flesh, masked entirely. The cave fell silent and dark.

"Clever," Harlow panted. "It was always a risk to bring in Herman's grandson. The prophet bolstered him more than expected. You were sure he was broken."

Nora Jo twitched. She was nude, sprawled on the rocky shore. Every inch of her skin felt raw, but somehow numb. She was staring at her scraped skin through a dream. Her flesh looked pale and vulnerable, bloody and soot-stained. Fear and triumph and wonder and fury swept through her in an indistinguishable wave. She felt like she was going to be sick.

"He had help," Harlow continued to himself. To Amans. "That was too close. If Legatus were even slightly weaker, she would have been banished along with Noct."

"You're lucky I'm not," Kate said, rising to her feet.

Not Kate. Legatus.

"And Ultio?" Harlow called.

"I'm here," Nora Jo's mouth said.

Nora Jo's mind rebelled.

She thrashed like a fish on a hook, but her body was out of her reach. It felt asleep, but moved without her say. There was something *else* in here with her. Something electric and dark and ancient. Foreign emotions slipped in between her own thoughts like smoke.

Ultio swarmed through her from her mind to her feet. The demon was satisfied and relieved, though the feeling was being slowly doused by unease. As she fought, she felt the other presence trying to push her back down, like hands pressing a head below the surface of a deep pond. The abyss seemed to yawn below her.

Was this how it had felt for the rabbit, for the sparrow? Consumed by a being so large it was difficult to comprehend? It was no wonder they had died when she left them.

What could Nora Jo do to fight it?

The false jack from Harlow was emptied and useless on the shore—but her ma's ring on her finger burned with increasing fierceness.

It had been unnoticeable at first amid the possession, but it was growing so hot that it seemed to be welding itself to Nora Jo's skin. It was the only item that had survived the flames.

The numbness subsided. Pain came screeching through. It overwhelmed the weight in her mind, pushing through it.

"Amans…" Nora Jo's mouth said, slow and cautious.

Kate's head twisted suddenly to a painful angle, and she stumbled sideways.

"Legatus?" Harlow moved forward to hover his hands by Kate's shoulders. He didn't touch her, but searched her nude form for injury. "What's wrong?"

A loud, desperate wail burst from Kate's mouth, the sound deafening in the quiet before it cut off with eerie abruptness. Blood seeped through Kate's lips and down her chin.

Nora Jo flexed her hands.

Amans, the demon tried to say again, but she kept her mouth firmly closed.

The pain in her ring subsided to a dull throb. Her grasp on her body remained. It was hers once again—for the moment. How long would it last? She could feel the demon, prodding at her defenses, desperately searching for a path back into control. Her body was a town under siege, and any flaw in her walls would be her undoing.

"Legatus," Harlow snapped. "You have to focus."

Kate's body shuddered and then righted itself with serpentine grace. "Don't question me," she snarled. "I have her. She's mine."

Harlow stayed close to Kate's body by the water, concern on his face. Concern for the demon under the girl's skin.

It was all he had *ever* cared about. Nora Jo and the others were only vessels. That had been her only value to him. He had trained her for this. All this time, all their conversations, and Nora Jo had just been livestock for the slaughter.

She thought of the absurd puppet show the demons had done for her in this cave, playing at helplessness to encourage her complacency. She had believed them without hesitation. Harlow and Legatus must have laughed themselves silly after.

To survive the night, she needed to escape. If Harlow realized the demon wasn't in charge any longer, he would do whatever it took to erase her. He was stronger than her in every way, and had withheld the training that would have let her fight him.

A shout from the shore made her jump. Kate's body had found its footing, and her pretty face was twisted in a snarl. With vicious precision, the demon inside Kate kicked one of the larger stalagmites bursting from the ground. It crumpled under her foot as easily as if it were made of sand.

Ignoring Harlow's low words and the unsteadiness of its own body, the demon began to systematically destroy every stalagmite in sight with fierce single-mindedness. The sounds of crunching mineral and bright splashes filled the cave as the remains were hurled into the lake.

Nora Jo had to get away. Now.

Swallowing a sob of terror, she pushed to her feet, fighting to keep her balance. Unsteadily, she slipped back across the shore, using Harlow's floating lights to pick her way as quickly as she could. Carefully, she avoided the slick stone and deceptive ledges. Harlow's voice and the sounds of destruction still rang behind her, but she couldn't focus on them. She had to flee.

Her hip screamed with each step, injured in her collision with the ground. Warm blood dripped down her bare leg. Her breath shuddered in her lungs, and her hands were shaking.

She was sure Harlow's eyes were on her back, watching her escape and silently laughing. He would fall on her any moment with that same brutal speed he'd used to snare the rabbit by the pond. A hand would snatch from the dark to grab the scruff of her neck and strangle the life from her. Her body ached with tension, waiting for the blow. She'd fall as easily as the stones on the lakeside.

The demon Ultio clamored in her head, shoving and pushing

its way into her thoughts, trying to trip her. The ring held it at bay, but only barely.

By the time she reached the entrance to the next passageway, she felt she had been walking for hours. She risked a glance back at Harlow and Legatus. They were close together amid a pile of broken stone, seemingly unaware of Nora Jo's escape. Nearby, the sad, prone body of Oliver Chadwick Jr. had been abandoned.

Breath caught high in her throat, Nora Jo left the light behind and slipped toward the exit.

The tight scramble through the dark caves felt like being swallowed alive, though the air was as cold as death.

Nora Jo had been out in the forests of Chatuga in the middle of a moonless night, far from any of the lanterns from town. She had felt the utter isolation and disorientation. She'd thought she understood darkness.

Nothing could have prepared her for the absolute black of the caves. She didn't dare summon a flame, fearful it might attract the demons. She shouldn't have been able to take two steps without running into a wall—but somehow, even without sight, she could see the cave around her.

It was as unsettling as it was unnatural to navigate the darkness, surrounded by utter blackness and somehow also knowing the shapes around her. It shouldn't have been possible. *None* of tonight should have been possible.

And yet, it kept happening.

Harlow had shoved a *demon* under her skin. She could still feel it writhing inside her like a parasite.

Did it feel like her, trapped in a dark cave as it fought and squirmed to be free?

She shuddered and pressed forward.

Her own racing heart and the sound of her bare feet on the damp stones drowned out anything still happening behind her. Had they noticed she was gone yet?

What, even now, was stalking her through the cramped darkness?

Nora Jo had fallen into a nightmare, but there was no waking.

How had she not seen Harlow's inhumanity before? The eternally clean face. The unnatural speed. The way every animal nearby had the sense Nora Jo lacked and hid from his sight.

She'd been so desperate for someone to see her potential, for someone to care about her for even a moment. Harlow had offered her power and a place to belong. She was so foolish. So weak. He had taken her fears and used her. Oliver Chadwick Jr. was dead. Kate was worse than dead.

And Nora Jo...

Foolish. Weak.

Her thoughts were not alone in her head.

"No!" she breathed, terrified to make a sound louder than a whisper. Her voice was ragged, like she had been screaming for days. "Get out, get out!"

Don't prolong this, the demon murmured in her mind. *You'll only suffer. Let go, Nora Jo Barker. You've fought so long.*

"Leave me alone!" she whimpered, clutching her head. Her hair had fallen from its braid, tumbling over her shoulders. She stumbled into a jutting stone and crashed to the ground. Her hands and knees scraped against the small ridges of stalagmites and stone.

The scattered cuts from the night accumulated in bright, painful stars across her body.

You're mine now.

"I'm not," she snarled, squeezing her fist. The ring pulsed with heat each time the demon resurfaced in the depths of her mind.

Possession had never seemed to be one of her ma's worries. She'd thrown salt over her left shoulder with a casual assurance it would ward off evil spirits, but there had been no earnest warnings about demons. Had Ma even known what the ring could do? She'd only said it was a symbol of her love and protection, passed down from Granny Rhodes. Harlow had said it was too weak to do anything. Had he been hoping to convince her to throw it out, or was it a magic he didn't understand? She wished Granny Rhodes were still alive. She wished her ma were still alive.

Nora Jo had no knowledge that could help her now. "Get out," she demanded.

No. I've waited too long for this. There was a desperation to its clinging in her mind, as animal and violent as her desire to be free.

It *feared* her.

Suddenly, she could see its intentions as clearly as her own. The abyss of a foreign mind stretched before her in a dizzying vision.

The span of its past was incomprehensible. The eons were the breadth of the night sky, soaring endlessly in Ultio's memory, as old as the stones underground, the water in the lakes. Nora Jo had only lived for a single breath, and most of that was shrouded by the haze of childhood forgetfulness.

Most of the demon's existence had been spent in chaos, buffeted by wind and flame. It was a horrifying infinite maelstrom without hope or definition. The memories burned her.

The only calm came from brief times spent in a steady form, bound temporarily by flesh and blood to the earth. Those moments stood out like stars among the dark cacophony. A breeze cooling heated skin. The taste of rich wine. Sand shifting underfoot. Vast oceans as gray and jagged as the storm clouds overhead. The memories were sharp and sweet, but gone too soon. Over time, he'd lost his hold on all the bodies he had been given, becoming untethered again.

Nora Jo was an anchor he had been searching an eternity to find.

With that shared thought, Ultio surged forward.

Her thoughts were overwhelmed, sliced and shredded and forced into place like a stem in one of Gloria's flower crowns. She tumbled inside her own mind, lost.

Her body lurched to its feet and turned back toward the lake, its movements clumsy and forced. Each muscle and tendon was part of a complex system Ultio needed to relearn. The strangeness of being part of living flesh was disconcerting. And the scorching ache of the ring made it difficult for the demon to concentrate. It was no matter. He couldn't fail.

Nora Jo's hand reached up to press the agate ring against her cheek. It seared the skin with a hiss.

Ultio screamed. The sound echoed off the cave walls, grating and inhuman.

And Nora Jo fell to her knees, panting.

47

LEGATUS

Legatus broke apart another stalagmite, reveling in the visceral crack as she put an end to its millennia of growth. With a growl, she hurled it into the lake. The throw knocked her off balance, making her stumble. Amans caught her before she fell, steadying her new legs. There were so many pieces to a human body.

"Are you done?" asked Amans.

"Soft from your years here?" She leaned into his sturdy frame like a trembling new kudzu vine on a hillside. He was so solid inside his host. What must the insides of that body look like after so long in continuous motion, kept alive by Amans's flame? She wanted to slice off the skin and peer inside.

"Just tired of your tantrum."

Legatus scoffed and stepped away from him, but then jerked backward as a ghost swept across her path. His hands grasped for her throat, but he drifted through her without making contact. She swore, using an old tongue that felt unwieldy in her new mouth. "I thought we were done with this one," she said, waving a hand through the spirit as if trying to dissipate smoke. "You should have killed him after we were banished last time. He got so *old*."

"Herman's just a shadow," Amans said. "There's nothing he can do now."

Legatus resented spirits. Ghosts had once been of this world, and their spirits still called to the dirt. They were able to remain here so easily. Legatus had fought, every moment of her existence, to belong anywhere. And when the spirits let go, when they let themselves drift away, they would discover the worlds beyond this one. They had the potential to find peace there, an option Legatus had lost long ago.

"He told the soldier what to do."

"And look what he got for that," he said, gesturing to the body crumpled on the shore. Nude and broken against the rock, it seemed a small thing to have caused such problems.

The soul inside her thrashed against her hold like a drowning thing. The sight had given Georgia Kate Mayer a burst of new energy. A scream echoed in her mind.

Legatus looked away. There was no need to encourage rebellion. She dug her nails into her palms, letting the pain cement her hold on this body.

It was that boy's fault that Legatus was still struggling to keep hold of her host. If he hadn't corrupted the binding magic—if he hadn't weakened Legatus by bundling her in with Noct then expelling her, leaving her to crawl back toward this host—Legatus would not be fighting against her own eyes now. She hated him with a poisonous, roiling passion.

She stepped forward into Herman, inhaling as though to pull him in like oxygen. The ghost trembled around her with useless fury.

"You wanted so badly to succeed, Chadwick. You thought everyone would remember you. And what did you get? Your only grandchild, dead where no one will ever find him. Amans told me you locked up your daughter when she showed the first signs of power. Congratulations. She died without our help. Were you proud of yourself?"

Herman's expression was horrid. It was satisfying after a difficult night. He tried to say her name, mouthing the first syllable, but he flickered and lost the rest of the word.

"I'd burn down your little mill when I leave town, but I don't even need to do that. Your legacy is already over." She blew a cool stream of air through his wavering face. "You've lost."

In another juddering flicker, Herman Chadwick sighed and disappeared. Finally, the cave was quiet.

"He won't be gone for good," Amans pointed out. "Just back to where he died until he gathers his mind again."

Legatus laughed. "If he ever does."

Amans shook his head and looked around the cave. "Where's Ultio?"

She shrugged. "Covering his ears in some corner. He never adjusts well."

"No." He sniffed the air. "He's not here."

"Did the girl oust him already? Another excellent choice in hosts, Amans."

"We need to find her," he said. "She can't have gotten far. Even if she overthrew Ultio, he already had a grip. He won't let go. She shouldn't have managed to even disorient him, not with how unsettled her power is."

"Ultio was always the weakest of us."

"And *you're* still shaking, Legatus."

A furious growl ripped from her throat and echoed around the large chamber. Each ripple of the lake seemed to carry it forward.

"We need all four of us together," Amans said. "It's what we've been fighting for. Noct is back out there somewhere, lost. We need to redo the ritual *tonight* to tether him here, or he'll be stuck for another cycle. It could take decades. And you and Ultio will end up the same if you also fail. You were supposed to be stronger than this."

"I don't fail," Legatus snarled.

"Since none of you seem able to manage this on your own, we need to either begin our search together for Noct's replacement host and trust Ultio to reclaim his new body, or divide our energies to help them both."

"It seems easy for you to blame us and not the people you picked. You promised us they all had weak minds and a large pool of magic to sup on. What were you doing here all this time other than making me dance for that girl's entertainment? Curled up somewhere enjoying your body?"

"Nora Jo was unformed clay. Her magic needed guiding from the start. She could barely feel it. Ultio should have had an easy time with her."

"Well, he didn't," Legatus said, voice cracking like lightning. "You were too confident. You underestimated your opponents and lost our chance at this night. You've always thought you were cleverer than you are."

"You've just gotten your body and you want to start a fight?" Amans laughed. "I don't know why I missed your company."

"You and your host are too compatible. You've had no one to argue with in all that time."

The man scowled, the fire under the skin rippling. "It's what you should all dream of. Everett Harlow will be our salvation. You won't speak another word against him."

"Our salvation isn't won yet."

"But it's not lost either. Ultio's weak, but he's one of us. We need to find out if he can still win without our aid."

"For all our sakes, I hope he can."

48

The mirror of the lake's surface was broken by swirling, overlapping spirals of ripples. The jagged reflection of the ceiling blurred and shifted, as though it too might fall into chaos.

Small creatures wriggled through the water, sliding their slimy bodies into safe crevices. After decades, centuries, undisturbed, the jagged stones crashing into the lake were apocalyptic.

All that once seemed immutable was broken.

Blissfully unaware, blind, deaf spiders steadily wove the webs of their ancestors.

49

NORA JO

Time lost meaning until Nora Jo found the enchanting hint of fresh air coming through an exit. She pulled herself up through the hole in the ground. Dry leaves and mud scraped her naked skin, deep and painful, but she didn't slow. She fell to the forest floor when she was clear, pressing her cheek against the earth. The night air was warm and peaceful around her, free of the cold dampness of the cavern below.

Her panting was raucous in her ears. The forest around her was eerily silent.

She took a deep breath to steel herself, then pushed herself to her feet again. She couldn't rest yet. She had left her dowsing rod behind, and the dark woods were unfamiliar. She still stumbled forward. Her only destination was *away*.

The woods were a labyrinth. Every pine seemed a clone of the others. Branches lunged out to scratch Nora Jo's skin. Despite the darkness, she could see everything around her as clearly as if it were day. It was inhuman. How thoroughly was the demon woven into her body?

She lunged forward. Her movements were too fast, like a deer bounding from danger. She slowed again, spinning in a circle and looking up at the branches overhead. They were dark outlines against the night sky, but she could see every pine needle overlapping its brothers. Somewhere in that tree, tiny hearts beat quickly and muscles trembled. Every sensation was magnified by the demon's presence. The world felt new around her.

It was exhilarating. It was horrifying.

Why keep running? You know you can't win.

The voice was insidious, echoing the thoughts she'd had for so long. She didn't fit in this world. Her whole life, everyone around her had told her she needed to stop trying, to just hand the reins to someone else. No one trusted her with the power to shape her own days. She was too difficult for those around her. It was her obligation to make herself smaller, easier. Every day was a challenge against those skeptics, and against her own quiet voice whispering they were right.

There was another voice inside her now, agreeing.

She laughed. It had the shrill edge of a fiddle in the hands of an amateur, the sound too loud in the silent woods.

Rest. The struggle is over.

The struggle. Two whole months of training with Harlow. All those years of fighting to carve her own path in this world. All of it had been for nothing. She was just a pawn in a game she could hardly fathom. She was weak, too weak.

"Why me?" she asked, stumbling to a halt and rubbing her hands over her face. Mud from her palms smeared over her skin. "Why did he pick me?"

There is strength in your blood. I've seen it before.

One of the pinpricks of possession in the demon's past swept into her mind. The memory flooded her with as much clarity as the forest around her.

The solid body was as comfortable as a fresh tomato in summer, or the weight of a kind hand on their shoulder. It was the feeling of belonging. Wind whipped over the grass at their feet. The vast nearby mountains blocked chunks of the stars, but Ultio could still see the endless sprawl overhead. The heavens were close enough to touch.

He stood by a raging fire, grinning at the figures standing around him. He crowed their success to the sky. Ultio tested the range of motion, arms swinging as he prowled around the fire.

Lucy Rhodes protested quietly from the depths of their mind, stinging like a mosquito, but Ultio silenced her. She had agreed to this. During the long, difficult labor for her only child, she was cursed with a vision: her daughter dying as a young woman, wracked by an even fiercer agony in her womb. Lucy's midwifery skills weren't enough—she needed the strength only a demon could offer. It was too late for her to change her mind, even if Ultio wasn't the obedient power source she had expected.

It was nearing dawn by the time their celebration began to cool. After an age of waiting, they four were together again. Ultio would follow Amans and Legatus as he always had.

When the new human emerged from the tree line, the demons turned to him, still laughing. The fool did not know what he faced.

But the man did not blink at the carousing nude forms dancing around the bonfire. He wore a black suit, lined bright white at the collar and sleeves, and his eyes were as fierce as starlight. He raised a hand and began to speak.

Their laughter died. They lunged forward. It was too late.

Ultio screamed—and shattered.

Nora Jo looked up at the stars overhead, peeking through the heavy layers of branches. At some point during the flood of memory, she had fallen on her back.

"That was Granny Rhodes. My grandmother," she said.

Yes.

Nora Jo reached up and clasped the warm ring on her hand. An heirloom from that woman by the fire. She must have feared her line might face the demons again, to create such an object. Had she warned her daughter and taught her the ring's power, or spared her that knowledge, knowing she would die young? She would have despaired if she'd lived to see the way Nora Jo's dad had stifled her daughter's magic, pushing her to keep it secret. By the time Harlow came for Nora Jo, there was no memory left of the ring's power.

"Why show me that?" she asked.

My thoughts are yours now.

How much control did Ultio have over their connection? They seemed to both be drowning, lunging for the same fragile lifeline. She rubbed her fingers against her palms, grounding herself. This was her body. She wasn't Ultio, not Granny Rhodes, not the dozen others through history who now lurked in her memory.

"Harlow wanted me from the start," Nora Jo said, clamoring to her feet. "That's why he came to me. He had already tried this with Granny Rhodes and failed. I can't believe I was such a fool." She hesitated, glancing back toward the caves. Or was that the way to town? She had been disoriented by her fall. "Did he make them fire me?" she wondered.

I don't know. I wasn't here, Ultio told her. Amans can whisper ideas, but he cannot create thoughts. Did he need to sway anyone? Your memories show a town with no interest in you. You have always been an outsider.

She began walking forward, praying she wasn't strolling right back into Harlow's arms. "He could have pushed them to make that final decision. He needed me alone, desperate."

What did it matter? It had happened. The events of the past months had been carefully crafted by a man she hadn't even known was her enemy.

She stumbled over a branch in the eerie not-dark, but righted herself before falling. She needed a way to separate their mixing thoughts. "Where were you, if not here?"

There was a moment of hesitation, the catch of breath before a sigh. And then the image of the howling winds and crackling flames brushed through her mind. There was no up, no down, only chaos, fear, pain.

"Hell?" Nora Jo cautioned, the word dark and foreboding on the summer air.

There are things beyond words. Humans try to define everything. You are bound in many ways.

"You *want* to be bound," Nora Jo said. "I can see you. All you've wanted is to be in a body. It kept you going through all that. You want to be contained."

We lost our home; that place that is the beginning and end. Everyone is one there. To be a part of a whole—you cannot imagine it. And then we were torn apart.

The sensation of that place came back. Ultio had spent nearly an eternity there, utterly lost. The vastness of the demon's past threatened to swallow her, push her small mind into madness, but she clenched her fists to remember where she was. She wasn't in an infinite hell. This was *her* body—for now.

For a moment, they both found comfort in the movement of her legs walking steadily, her thighs brushing together, the summer heat on her skin. They were not in that place. After tearing at each other's minds for—minutes? Hours?—the moment of comradery was an unexpected relief.

There is no peace there. We are all searching for a way out. Only Legatus is powerful enough to lurk here without a body.

"And you get out by possessing people. By pushing them out of their minds and taking their bodies. Stealing peace by destroying your host," Nora Jo said. The words fell out more curious than accusatory. It was strange to talk to the demon lurking in her mind, but she could see the scope of its pain, and it could see hers. This wasn't Harlow, with his secret motivations and cruel plans. Ultio was terrifying and powerful and vast, but he was within her. They were bound like a fraying rope, loose and uneasy, but intertwined nonetheless.

That isn't what Harlow and Amans have.

No. She had seen that. The man and demon used the body interchangeably, speaking through the same mouth, sharing the same goals. The man Everett Harlow was still in there. Why had he allowed the demon to reside inside him? Was immortality worth whatever price Amans exacted?

They have been paired for a long time. Many cycles now. What Amans has found… It may be his own heaven.

"What cycles?"

Nora Jo stopped, hearing a murmuring nearby. In the eerily silent forest, the sudden sound made her heart pound. When she focused, it condensed into the sound of running water. The creek was close.

Amans can only attempt these bindings at the perfect confluence of events. They're sporadic—sometimes months, sometimes centuries between each one. It became simpler once he found Harlow and could remain on this side.

Chestnut Creek was a welcome sight. Nora Jo nearly fell to her knees beside it. She stumbled, pressing a hand to her heart. The relief of finding an end to the forest's endless labyrinth—and the assurance that she hadn't walked back to the caves—was overwhelming. She glanced over her shoulder at the still, still woods, and began to follow the creek east. It would lead her to familiar land soon enough, then she could break off toward the south.

"Amans has his body. He's been living on Old Blue for who knows how long. Why does he need you and the others here?"

Amans cares for Noct deeply. Theirs is a bond of brothers. And Legatus has been his lieutenant for a long time. They respect each other.

"And you?"

He needs more than himself and his host for what he plans. Amans has brought me many of my hosts. He has earned my loyalty.

The potential answers made her voice shake, but Nora Jo made herself ask, "What are his plans?"

It's been a long, long while since Amans and I were able to confer. His plans don't matter to me—he is offering me a host. A body for this world. I would be foolish not to accept.

"You don't get my body," Nora Jo snarled. "You don't get any of this. I'll find a way to stop him and all of you."

Perhaps, Ultio sighed. The wistfulness of a thousand lifetimes of loneliness filled Nora Jo, hollowing out her chest and strapping lead weights to her limbs. *We have failed again. Amans will need more than just Legatus to succeed. Noct is already gone. And I…*

She could feel the demon's attention sharpen on her. His presence in her mind rippled as he readied for another assault.

"You know how this ends," she warned. Ultio would sense her uncertainty as easily as she had sensed his plan to steal into her mind again. Her ring had worked to repel his full triumph so far, but it was magic she didn't understand—magic Harlow certainly hadn't taught her about. Would the ring work indefinitely, or could Ultio break through its defenses with enough patience? She would need to learn more to exorcise the demon entirely.

She stopped walking, staring blankly down at the flowing stream so she could focus on the swirling energies in her own mind. "You'll only hurt us both. We'll fight until we tear each other apart. I'm not giving up, Ultio." It was strange to speak his name for the first time, when its sibilance had woven itself into her mind. "This won't be easy for you."

It never is.

"I thought you wanted a partner," she pleaded. "Why not me? We don't need Harlow."

The demon pulsed with yearning, but held itself apart in her mind. *We can see each other's intentions. Your charm has given you a hold against me—it smells of your grandmother—but I can still see you. You can't fool me with offers of alliance. You're desperate to be rid of me. You've been thinking of ways to achieve it all this time.*

"And you've been watching me like a starving coyote," Nora Jo said. "Harlow needs you, but you don't need him—you only need me."

I need a body. Either an empty shell or a willing host. You're neither.

"I can become one," Nora Jo insisted, desperate. "I can."

There was a beat as the presence examined her. Nora Jo was surprised by her own honesty.

Ultio was as well. *You mean that.*

Nora Jo swallowed down a burst of hysteria. "I'm terrified you'll take over and throw my mind into a bottomless pit. You're terrified I'll banish you back to hell. Working together doesn't give either of us what we want—but it saves us from what we're afraid of. Can't that be enough?"

You believe this now, Ultio allowed. *But what about when someone gives you the key to expel me? We will only delay this fight until you feel sure you can win.*

"And what about when I'm sleeping or distracted? I've seen what you can do from your memories. You made my grandmother so quiet, it was like her body was yours. How do I know you won't get stronger over time?"

Then the fight is still only delayed.

"Maybe," Nora Jo said. "We might hurt each other later. But isn't it worth trying? You need me… and I need *help*. Let me keep my body, let me keep my mind, and I won't send you back."

There will be times you will want me to control your body, Ultio told her.

Nora Jo shivered, remembering the way her body had lurched back toward the caves against her will. "I won't."

You will. Now is one of them, Ultio said. *You haven't noticed the crow that follows us, getting closer with every sweep. It nears now. Even in your body, my senses are greater than yours.*

A jolt of fury and fear struck Nora Jo. "Harlow," she whispered.

Give me control. Let go.

"You'll give me back to him," she said, barely audible—but he didn't need to hear her to understand. She kept her eyes on the creek rambling past. Her spine tensed like a bowstring, shoulders hunched in fear of the scrape of talons and beak. She was sure Harlow's eyes were just behind her. From inside the crow, he would be mocking her escape attempt. She had only ever been laughable to him. A doll he placed however he wanted.

When they were safely back at the cave, Harlow would surely be able to remove her grandmother's ring and give Ultio the control he so desperately wanted. She would be lost.

You wanted help. Prove it.

What were her options? She could run. She could try to fight, using the limited magic Harlow had taught her while Ultio sabotaged her from within. She could see the aching expanse of the demon's power. Nora Jo could keep struggling alone the way she had her whole life.

Or she could take a chance on the monster inside her.

As soon as she made the decision to allow Ultio control, he swept over her like a wave. It was drowning, overwhelming. She was tossed in the currents of his emotions, strange but recognizable. At the roots of his tangled feelings were the familiar beacons that pushed everyone forward: hope, fear, anger.

She couldn't help but fight back, searching for a terrified foothold in the chaos. Her ring flashed, a searing burst alongside her panic.

A ripple of comfort brushed her mind. It was clumsy, but there— a hand outstretched.

She wasn't drowning, not disappearing, but floating just outside her own mind. She was still there. It was like a dream, watching Ultio take the reins of her body and directing her forward.

She—they—turned from the creek in a fluid motion. During his stay in her body, watching and feeling her move, Ultio had remembered how to operate the maze of muscle and bone. No, that wasn't quite right. She knew it as surely as if Ultio had told her; her cooperation gave him far greater power than her animosity.

Ultio spotted the dark flash of the crow behind them. He crouched, then pounced. Nora Jo's body launched into the air, quick as a snakebite. Clawed hands snatched the bird from the air and snapped its neck before she hit the ground. The crow fell limp, its glassy eyes staring blankly at the stars overhead.

Ultio followed its gaze and stood still for a breath to take in the night sky.

Then he retreated again, flooding her mind with his fierce satisfaction. Nora Jo sucked in a desperate, shaky breath. She dropped the crow's body and stared at her hands. "How did you do that?"

We're not limited by your body's boundaries.

She moved to nudge the crow with her foot, but stopped before her bare skin could touch the slick feathers. "But who was that? Harlow? Or Amans?"

That distinction is no longer relevant. If you or I left this body to possess another creature, we would lose our bond. Those two are so intertwined that they possess even other creatures as one. I doubt even they could trace the precise line between them anymore.

"So what happens now?"

They won't leave us alone. If they don't succeed tonight, they'll be waiting decades at least for another cycle. They'll send another set of eyes after us soon. Or come themselves.

Nora Jo nodded and began to follow the creek east again. "Then let's be far from here when they do."

50

LEGATUS

Amans woke with a gasp, eyes flying open, his hand pressing against a heart that had been beating steadily for more than a century. So long in such a fragile body. Fury overtook his face, hot and fierce.

Legatus leaned forward, elbows on her knees. She had been watching over the body of Everett Harlow as Amans and his host swept across the land after Ultio. The steady rise and fall of their chest showed the perfect functionality of their bond.

Legatus's new body had been battered in the taking, bruised and sliced and exhausted. It should have been subdued, but still it twitched and shuddered. It didn't want her. Legatus pushed her hands into the ground, feeling the rocks scrape the calloused skin on her palms. This body was *hers*.

Amans seemed content to seethe silently. Legatus raised her eyebrows. "The girl has expelled Ultio," she guessed.

"No," Amans spat, standing up and pacing. "He's still in there. But *she's* controlling *him*."

Legatus rolled her shoulders, hearing tendons crack and veins move. Harlow had given her a shapeless dress to protect her skin, but even the light fabric was an irritating sensory addition. "She's stronger than you thought."

"She's not," Amans spat. "I know the exact shape of her magic. I made it myself. She would have been useless if I hadn't helped kindle her power."

Legatus let her head loll to the side, testing the range of motion. When the muscles resisted, she pushed them further until her ear rested against her shoulder. "I did warn you. Ultio was always our weakest."

"That shouldn't have mattered. Nora Jo was never as strong as her grandmother, and even Lucy couldn't overwhelm Ultio. I gave him the easiest of them."

"You miscalculated." Legatus flicked her wrist dismissively, but the gesture caught partway as her arm began to shake.

The whispering grew louder in Legatus's head. The girl was trying to pull the limbs back under her control. Did she not know what she fought against? Legatus was the strongest of them all. She had roamed the plains of Mongolia. She had sacked Babylon. She had crawled through dark battlefields over the run of centuries, the wars only distinguishable in the colors of the bloodied uniforms and the fallen weapons. She had outlasted all.

Legatus wasn't Ultio. She would not be overrun by the death throes of the mortal inside her.

"What is it?" Amans asked.

Legatus looked up. Amans had moved while she was focusing on the fight inside her body, standing over her.

"You're distracted," Amans continued. "You'll tell me if something is wrong. I can't have you compromised as well. The entry was a difficult one."

"It's handled," Legatus snarled. "We knew her blood was strong when we picked her."

Harlow had summoned Legatus sometimes over the years, letting her catch glimpses of the life he lived without her. She had helped select this girl herself. They had watched and waited for a powerful heir to the preacher man who had thwarted them last cycle. A smile like the slice of a knife spread across Legatus's mouth. It was a late revenge, but a fitting one.

When Legatus had seen the girl in the woods, she'd been tempted to try to take her there. Her mouth had still been coated in the warm blood of the new preacher, and Kate's heartbeat was like a summoning bell. But outside the solstice, Legatus would have been at a disadvantage. Had the girl had a sense, even then, that her doom was in front of her?

In some possessions she could access the body's memories, but she was pressing Kate ruthlessly down into the depths to keep control. This prophet was too strong to be allowed any foothold. Worse, the hints Legatus could feel were a tangled mess, mixing past and present and future in a dizzying blend.

"You'd said you'd sculpt me a willing host," Legatus reminded him.

"Look how that worked last time. They all told us they wanted power, wanted partnerships, but they weren't dedicated. The bonds weren't true. Herman Chadwick was only tempted by the promise of more wealth to add to his piles. Lucy Rhodes thought she could change her daughter's future, but she fought Ultio from the start. And your host…"

Edward Russell. He had been eager for power. His mind had welcomed Legatus—at first. When the exorcism had started trying to drag Legatus from his new home, he had held on with all his power. As the holy words tore through Legatus, he tore through Edward's mind, seeking sanctuary deep inside the mortal's body, somewhere the reverend couldn't touch. Edward's mind had fought back. They'd had a bloody, dirty fight.

Legatus had felt the body dying around him, but he clung on until the exorcism ripped him away. Edward's soul had brushed past him, bitter and mournful, as they both lost their hold on the body.

"I think once you found your own perfect host, you just didn't feel you needed to waste your time securing them for us," Legatus said coldly. "I think that's why you didn't bother to look for anyone else. That's why you didn't bother to find a new town. That's why you only called me when you needed me. You don't remember the urgency."

"Don't I? It's time to make this world ours. No more scrounging for hosts. It won't matter if you don't have a perfect bond. All humanity will be yours to choose from. You can move from body to body as needed. If you're lucky, eventually you might find a bond like ours." Amans gripped one of his forearms, holding tight to his host. Like an embrace. "We're tired of being alone on this earth. We aren't willing to be limited by mortals any longer. We brought you here, didn't we? You don't know how long we've worked for this."

Legatus looked away from her leader and his body. Such intimacy between demon and host was difficult to watch. Amans had found what they all dreamed of—a connection of souls none of them had had since their earliest memories.

A heaven in this hell.

"We can't waste our time arguing. We have to find Nora Jo."

Legatus shook her head. "Ultio has the body. It is up to him to take it back. He can fight Nora Jo on his own. But Noct is lost to us until the next cycle if we don't find him a host tonight. He should be the priority."

"We told you; finding these three hosts took years of planning. Noct is already lost. Fixing Ultio is the only chance we have tonight to recover anything."

"Plans, plans," Legatus sneered. "That's all you can think about. Sometimes, the plans must be set aside... so the hunt can begin."

51

NORA JO

It was a long walk. The terror of Nora Jo's flight from the caves eventually gave way to a numb exhaustion. Her wounds throbbed with every step. When she stumbled to the edge of town, Ultio gave her part of his strength, helping her catch herself on a new wave of energy.

The collaboration felt strange, like sticking her hand in a roaring fire for warmth, but they were both relieved not to fight every moment for control. They were like two barn cats licking their wounds, watching each other with one eye while waiting for the next bout. But for the moment, there was quiet between them.

The farm was silent as she passed through the rows of green vines. She found an abandoned jacket hanging over a wooden post and pulled it on over her naked chest, buttoning it over her breasts.

A goat near the edge of the house startled when Nora Jo slipped past, choking on its breath and scurrying to huddle at the far edge of its pen. It stood still, quivering in fear.

The window was different through human eyes. Smaller, less

imposing. She climbed through it with more grace than she had ever possessed before—Ultio was wrapped in and around her body like a dye. She landed quietly on the wooden floor, hearing only her own heartbeat thudding in her ears.

Gloria was on the bed again, now tucked under her quilt, sleeping soundly. Nora Jo had seen her nap before on drowsy afternoons in the field, but there was an intimacy to watching it unseen in her bedroom.

In your time of need, this is your ally? Ultio's skepticism wove through her mind. *There's no magic here. We would be wiser to leave this place. Keep running. We'll be lucky to outpace Amans and Legatus even if we run our fastest.* She felt an experimental tug on her spine as the demon considered pulling her back out the window with or without her consent.

She ignored him and crept forward to put a hand on Gloria's shoulder. "Shh," she murmured when she awoke with a gasp. "It's me."

"Nora Jo?" Gloria asked, eyes wide but unfocused. Her mouth hung open as she panted high and fast. "What are you doing here?" She looked toward the door.

The household is asleep, Ultio informed her. Suddenly, it wasn't only her own heartbeat Nora Jo could hear. The tripping flutter of Gloria's breath and heart were loud in the small room. A pair of sleep-steady snores rumbled from nearby.

"No one else is awake," Nora Jo assured her. "I needed to see you. One more time."

"You can't *be* here." Gloria blinked and looked over her. "That's my brother's jacket. Are you *naked?*"

"Gloria," Nora Jo said, and her voice caught in her throat. "Tonight has been… very bad." She worked her jaw, trying to find more words. It had been instinct to come here, like a bird migrating home, but what could she do? The temptation to tell Gloria everything was overwhelming, but Harlow was too dangerous. The fact he believed they were no longer together may have been Gloria's only chance at safety.

"You're right. I should go. I only wanted to say goodbye," Nora Jo said.

Finally. Ultio nudged her toward the window again.

A cool hand caught her wrist. Nora Jo had no will to fight it. "You look like you've been through hell," Gloria whispered. Nora Jo choked on a laugh. "Who *did* this to you?"

"I can't tell you," Nora Jo said. "It's not safe."

"*This* is why," Gloria said. The moonlight caught on the tears welling in her eyes. "This is why we couldn't."

Nora Jo shook her head. "It had nothing to do with us." Though it had, hadn't it? Only not in the way Gloria thought. Gloria agreeing to marry Oliver Chadwick Jr. had led to Nora Jo handing herself over to Harlow. Nora Jo's fear had brought about something far worse than anything Gloria could have imagined. "Oliver's dead, Gloria."

"He's *what?*"

"I'm sorry. I know the two of you were going to…" Mentioning the engagement seemed cruel. "I'm glad you weren't there. It was… horrible."

"You saw it?" Gloria looked over Nora Jo's naked form, to the dark blood staining her knees. Her face paled. "You didn't…?"

"I didn't kill him," Nora Jo snapped. "I nearly died with him. But I'm leaving Chatuga. It's the only chance I have. They're still after me."

"Who? What *happened* tonight, Nora Jo? I don't understand. You're scaring me."

Nora Jo sighed shakily. "It was a mistake to come here."

When she shook off the grip on her wrist and turned for the window again, Gloria stood up. She was wearing a long white night-gown, its edges frayed at the collar and sleeves. The hem brushed her bare calves.

"You can't go back out like that," she said. "Let me find you better clothes and clean your cuts, at least. Please."

Gloria held out her hands to tell her to wait, then crept out of the room. Ultio urged her to leave while Gloria was distracted, but she couldn't pull herself away. *Give me this*, she told him. *Just for a minute*. She sat in the small bedroom, listening to the quiet sounds of Gloria slipping through the house to help her.

"I found the tincture we always use when one of us gets cut. I think there's St. John's wort in it," Gloria murmured when she came back in and pulled Nora Jo over to sit on the old iron bed. "Damn, I wish I could see better. The moon only shines in here until midnight."

With Ultio's help, Nora Jo could see clearly. "Sorry," she said. She itched to summon a flame to illuminate the room for Gloria, but it would only cause more alarm. "I'm sorry about all of this."

We have to leave, Ultio warned her. With me here, it would take far, far more than some cuts to kill you. This is a waste of our time.

Gloria put a hand on Nora Jo's knee as she began to dab at the dark spots of blood. Those shadows were visible even in the night. Her palm was warm and rough.

Nora Jo and Ultio fell still.

Carefully, gently, Gloria worked the tincture into Nora Jo's injuries. It burned like a string of insect bites, but Gloria's hands were tender. There was nowhere safe left on Earth, but Nora Jo felt protected in the dark with Gloria's skin on hers.

As the terror of the night faded in the quiet stillness of the small room, Nora Jo's limbs began to tremble. She gritted her teeth, trying to slow the shuddering that started behind her tongue and spread through her body.

"Are you all right?" Gloria asked, pausing with the cloth just over a cut on Nora Jo's thigh.

She nodded jerkily.

Gloria reached forward to cup Nora Jo's chin in her palm, searching her face. "You truly have had a horrible night. I wish you could tell me what happened."

Nora Jo's jaw clenched, and the muscle pressed against Gloria's fingers. She felt surrounded and secure, despite the demons lurking inside and out. "I wish I could too."

"Let me finish cleaning these cuts. Take off the jacket."

Hesitantly, every movement clumsy, Nora Jo unbuttoned the coarse jacket. Gloria hissed when she saw the full extent of her injuries. Nora Jo had writhed on the broken spikes of the underground shore when Ultio poured into her body, raking the skin on her arms and back. Her run through the woods had only made it worse.

Nora Jo's trembling worsened. She was flayed open in every sense in front of the girl who hadn't chosen her.

Gloria gestured for her to turn. Nora Jo twisted toward the wall, face falling now Gloria couldn't see her expression. It *hurt* to be touched so carefully, so lovingly, after the horrors of the night. Gloria's bed was soft and warm. How could this be the same world where she'd seen a girl bound and tormented, a boy slumped dead, her mentor laughing about it all?

Once Nora Jo's entire back was stinging from a layer of medicine, Gloria hesitated. Nora Jo hunched over her knees, staring down at the aged quilt.

Now, Nora Jo would leave. Find a horse or a train and run as far as she could. She had thrown away enough time already. It was time to leave everything behind.

Delicate hands pushed Nora Jo's hair over one shoulder. Chapped lips brushed against her neck. "When I first saw you... I was terrified. I've spent months scared for you, and then you turn up in my room bloody and wild-eyed."

"I'm sorry." Nora Jo stayed still, every ounce of her attention on her neck. Gloria's mouth felt like a butterfly landing on her skin, gentle and impossible.

Gloria rewarded her stillness by dragging her lips up to her ear. "I thought I'd agreed to marry someone else for nothing. I thought you'd been hurt because of me, and I wasn't there for you." She pressed her forehead against the back of Nora Jo's hair. "I'm so afraid this will be something I regret, but I'd rather regret having you than giving you up."

Nora Jo turned clumsily to face her. "I'm afraid for you too," she said. "I was so sure I was invincible. I thought I could handle anything. I was an idiot. I shouldn't even be here."

"But you are," Gloria murmured. "Please, Nora Jo. This can't be it. Not after everything."

In the dark, their lips came together.

Gloria's hands traced again over Nora Jo's bare skin. The slick tincture had been rubbed off her palms, but the touch still felt healing.

Nora Jo reached out blindly, one hand on Gloria's cheek, the other tracing desperately down the side of her nightgown. The fabric was soft and worn with age. How many nights had Gloria slept in its embrace? Beneath it, her skin was warm. Nora Jo wanted to touch every inch.

She had never known someone else's body. She wanted to climb inside Gloria, learn every beat of her heart. To know the bend of her fingers and the dip of her belly and the curve of her thighs.

Inside her, Ultio unfurled, stretching out to move with her fingertips as she pulled Gloria's nightgown off over her head.

"You're still trembling," Gloria said as they lay down on the narrow mattress.

"So are you," Nora Jo said, pulling her into another kiss.

52

Time no longer existed.

Before, actions had moved endlessly forward, trapped in a steady river. Every man, creature, animal, and stone was caught in its trudge. There was no fighting the current, no swimming back to the moments that came before. Birth to decay, unerring and constant. The water would never stop flowing. For some, the journey was brief, only a splash before being flung from its depths onto the shore. For others, like vast mountains or great fields of glacial ice, the millennia marched onward. But eventually, decay came for them as well.

This place was beyond the river. A soft, unreliable shore, full of vanishing pits of loose sand and sticky marsh. A place of transition. A place that shouldn't exist.

Beyond the shore was a shrouded land.

It would not do to look too closely at that land.

The monsters called Legatus and Amans were running together, quiet hunters on a dark night. The full moon painted the landscape in stripes of silver, but their bodies moved through the dappled shadows with ease. The fire wreathing their bodies left the world around them untouched. Fragile leaves and pine needles remained unbroken underfoot. In the surrounding trees, predator and prey cowered.

The animals were safe. They were not the ones being hunted.

Legatus was not the only one in that body.

The woman had her own name. The name had meaning. It was important.

It was the reason he couldn't stop following them.

This place, these events, they meant something. The burning woman was...

She was...

53

LEGATUS

The forest smelled of sap and decay. Hot blood and flush green and rot. It was vivid in a way Legatus had forgotten. Life and death thrived in a pulsing beat.

The trail from the bleeding schoolteacher was far behind them. Amans had stopped at a scrape in the dirt, inhaling the scent of his wayward pupil like a promise. Legatus had won the argument to find Noct's replacement host first, but she understood Amans's fire. Legatus ached to rend the impudent woman to shreds for threatening their goals, but there would be time for that later. The sky was clear. There would be no rain to wash away her trail.

She could be tracked down at their leisure.

Instead, Amans led them toward the local town.

She wanted to enjoy the thrill of the forest, but having a body was irritating. The dress scraped against Legatus's new skin, and the boots Amans had given her weighed her down. Meanwhile, Amans moved with the ease of familiarity, ducking around trees and soaring over logs. His body responded to his every whim.

How many times had he taken this route? Did he still notice his surroundings, or had he grown complacent in this world?

What had he done to deserve the loyalty of his host, Everett Harlow? Why had *he* been given the chance to stroll in peace, only occasionally thinking about his allies he'd left trapped in endless isolation and torment?

If Legatus had been the first of them to find a host, perhaps she would have done the same.

No, that wasn't true. If Legatus had been the first to find a permanent host, it would not have taken her centuries to find suitable matches for her allies. And when she had, she would not have been so inept at completing the bondings.

Amans had earned her loyalty over their long existence. Before Everett Harlow, it was Legatus who had shared a gravitational bond with Amans. Not one of love, but of alignment. With Amans as the visionary and Legatus as the ruthless lieutenant, they had swept through Constantinople and Baghdad and Heidelberg, the forests of northern Europe and the plains of central Asia. Mortals had wept to behold their approach.

They had taken on countless bodies, as short-lived as sparks from a fire. It was more than a millennium since they had first quietly discussed a search for permanent hosts. There were rumors of partnerships strong enough that they could live on infinitely together. The endless cycles of destruction, of draining every scrap of life they could from this world, had changed into a desperate hunt for an end, for stability.

Amans had found it. His allies had not.

Legatus felt her new face morph into a scowl. She smoothed it as she prowled forward.

The ghost continued to trail them. He was unimpeded by the forest, passing through the trunks without notice.

This one, unlike Herman, was faint and erratic. Her host was blind, pressed down far away from the world, but her mind was stirring like a fish below the surface of a lake. There was still a fight to be had here if Legatus wasn't careful.

From her host's reaction to seeing the soldier's corpse, she could only imagine what the sight of his ghost would cause.

The soldier had already damaged Legatus's bond. Now, he risked destroying it by lingering. She imagined finding a way to grasp the threads of his soul and tearing them apart. The question was whether she could succeed before his proximity gave Georgia Kate Mayer a foothold.

"Legatus," Amans scolded. "Keep up."

"I just need to get rid of these horrible shoes," she said, hopping to kick them off as she ran. She flung them with enough force to snap the laces as they flew into the woods. One went through the ghost's body. He flickered and vanished. Good. He'd be back at the cave, reliving his death, until Legatus could find a way to deal with him permanently.

Amans slowed suddenly, holding up a fist as his attention focused somewhere to the west. Stopping alongside him was instinct.

Ahead of them, leaves crunched under a heavy tread. In the otherwise silent forest, the noise was sharp and clumsy. The wind caught and carried a quiet muttering.

A human.

Amans gestured again.

They slipped forward silently, following the noise until they could peer through the leaves at the girl stomping through the woods. Her lantern cast dramatic shadows against the black forest. The young woman wore a long red dress and a fierce scowl.

Georgia Kate Mayer lurched forward with the sudden ferocity of a startled rattlesnake. Legatus's mouth opened as Kate tried to scream.

For a moment, there was a blind, frantic wrestling as demon and woman battled for control. Legatus snarled and pressed her host down again, quashing her ruthlessly. She stomped on the previous owner of the body until she was alone again.

Beside her, Amans was focused on the lost girl. He seemed not to have noticed the near slip.

"Perhaps this night ain't so unlucky after all," he breathed.

54

NORA JO

Nora Jo held Gloria tightly, staring up at the ceiling. She needed to keep running, but didn't want to be anywhere but here, sweaty and tangled together. It was like a dream.

She had sparked tonight's horror with the force of this desire, walking straight into Harlow's trap. Somehow, she had ended the terrible night with Gloria in her arms. With her newfound calm, she knew one thing. Nora Jo didn't deserve this reward for what she had done.

She shouldn't have walked away from that cave.

She loved Gloria, but there was a demon under her skin, a man dead underground, and Kate Mayer overtaken by the worst of Harlow's allies.

"I have to go," she murmured against Gloria's hair. "I shouldn't have come here."

"I'm glad you did."

"So am I," Nora Jo admitted. "But now I have to make things right."

Gloria propped herself up on an elbow, peering at Nora Jo in the darkness. "I don't like the sound of that."

"Everything that happened tonight was because of me. And I'm glad I got this time with you, but this can't be who I am."

"You want this too," Gloria said. "You were right. This is who we could be. Don't take that away from me."

"I want you with all my heart. But I can't take and take and leave other people to suffer. That's what started this. I wanted power, no matter the cost. I thought I deserved it. I thought I deserved happiness, however I could find it."

"You *do* deserve happiness," Gloria said, her jaw set tight.

"Maybe I do," Nora Jo said carefully. "But so do other people. Taking happiness by destroying other people is what my enemy is doing. Miss Ethel died alone this week. She never told me how sick she was. She didn't expect me to take one *minute* away from my own goals to be by her side. I need to be different. I need to be better."

"I just want you to be mine," Gloria said.

"Me too," Nora Jo said. She squeezed Gloria's hands. "But first I need to be the kind of person I can live with."

Nora Jo gave Gloria a final kiss, hard and fierce with the knowledge it might be their last.

And once again, she left her, crying and alone.

"Are you going to try to stop me from going back?" Nora Jo asked the demon in her body, voice ragged, as she strode through the dark streets of Chatuga. She had pulled on the clothes Gloria gave her from her brother's laundry—the pants were too long and the chest too loose, but they covered her.

No, Ultio responded.

She hesitated on the dirt path, peering into her own mind.

It still felt clumsy to share that intimate space. Ultio had settled in at some point during her time with Gloria. He had carved himself deep into her bones like a river through a canyon. That ache that defined him, that yearning for connection, had been soothed by what they had experienced with her.

Nora Jo bristled. Why had she brought a demon into Gloria's bedroom? "She's mine," she warned, hands clenching into fists.

She is, Ultio said, sounding satisfied. *And so am I.*

Nora Jo didn't know how to feel about that. It wouldn't matter for long either way. "We have to go back to help Kate," she said.

Legatus has her. She's lost.

"This was my fault. My grandmother helped give Harlow a foothold to this town in the first place, and I fell into the same trap. I *want* to run away. Of course I do. What can I do against the man— the *thing*—that taught me everything I know? But this was my fault. It's on me to fix it."

You didn't know what he planned.

"I knew I was playing with power I didn't understand. I just wanted it too bad to look more closely." She shook her head. The guilt would only slow her down. She cut from the path into the forest again. "How were y'all expelled last time? That man in your memory did something, and my grandma was fine after."

Kate's grandfather. He performed an exorcism. You don't know how to do it.

"I'm not a preacher," Nora Jo agreed.

It's not that. You don't need the title—only knowledge and conviction. There are many rituals that can expel us. Every culture has developed one over time. If your teacher had been a true witch, you might have learned one of the methods.

"Then what can I do?"

I don't know, Ultio admitted.

"What will Harlow do if he sees us?"

He'll assume you've suppressed me entirely, Ultio said. *Killing you is the fastest way to free me again.*

She nodded to herself. She had expected no less. She'd known when she left Gloria's room that she was likely walking toward her death. Harlow was ancient and powerful. He had been leagues ahead of her since before they met, anticipating—shaping—her every move.

It was foolish to fight him. She would die. If she left Chatuga now, before Harlow found her, she could discover some other way to free Kate. There could be secrets even Ultio didn't know. There were other witches in the world. Someone might know a way to fix Nora Jo's mistakes. Even Miss Ethel had known secrets Nora Jo didn't. She could find someone else to help.

And while she searched for an answer, Kate would suffer.

She stared up at the stars through the boughs overhead. She had been so grateful to see them again when she stumbled out of that horrible cave. Was she truly willing to go back down there? "If I go, if I put our life in danger, will you really not try to stop me?"

Ultio was unresponsive for a long moment. She felt him swirling in her head, tasting the waves of her mind. He was like an old man walking through a meadow in spring, examining each flower, relearning their petals and discovering new facets. Shadowed by the awareness that it would be his last time.

"What are you doing?" she asked.

Human emotion. The complexities. It's more intriguing than I remembered. Everything is so vivid. The feelings with your Gloria were like the rays of a summer sun. This pain, this guilt—they're the yawning depths of a cold abyss. They all dance around so quickly.

"Focus," she said.

That's my answer. I wouldn't stop you, Ultio told her. You've given me more tonight than Amans has in centuries.

"All right. Let's go."

55

LEGATUS

Unlike before, when they had needed to lure three headstrong youths into the same place at the same time without arousing suspicion or damaging their bodies, it wasn't difficult for Legatus and Amans to bundle one girl back to the caves. Eileen Mayer was a cacophony, wailing and crying and screeching. Though she wasn't strong, she was relentless. Legatus preferred humans small and quiet.

The girl squirmed in their grip until she finally caught a glimpse of Legatus in the moonlight.

"*Kate?*" she whimpered. "Why are you doing this?"

"Silence," Legatus said. The name threatened to stir her host from the depths again. Legatus freed a hand to strike Eileen, but Amans snarled at her.

"She can't lose consciousness," he snapped. "Surely my lieutenant can hold onto one little girl."

Legatus bit down her growl.

Quickly, aware of the oncoming dawn, they slipped back through the opening into the cave and set Eileen down on the shore. Legatus twisted one hand in her thick hair and used the other to hold her still while Amans conjured ropes to bind her.

"You're sure this body will work?" Legatus asked. She wanted to kill this one and move on, find an option who didn't rile her host so badly.

"Of course I'm not. There's a reason I didn't pick her in the first place," Amans growled, dodging a clumsy kick. He bound her feet first, jerking her ankles together with the dark vines. "She has the preacher man's blood, but any magic she has is mild and latent. Even if we can activate it, she won't be as powerful as the others."

"Then we're wasting our time," Legatus said. "There must be others."

"Noct should feel lucky to have a host at all after he let the soldier expel him so easily. This will have to be enough," Amans said. Quickly, angrily, he bound Eileen's hands in front of her torso. She flinched and whined.

Legatus let go of her hair and stood up, rubbing her hands together as if it would rid her of the scent. It was too familiar, invading her senses. She wasn't like Ultio. She wouldn't allow her host to resurface, no matter the provocation.

"This one will do." Harlow stared toward the ceiling, where the moon called to their blood. "The night is almost gone, and we still have to find Nora Jo."

"No, you don't."

A ball of flame arced over the shore, aimed at Harlow.

Nora Jo Barker clambered through the cave, dressed in oversized clothes. Her hair was loose around her shoulders, her expression fierce.

"Foolish girl," Harlow said. "I always appreciated that about you."

"You underestimated me." Nora Jo strode over the sharp rocks without wincing, summoning another ball of fire to orbit her.

It was a flashy show, but useless. Maybe she was confident after beating Ultio, but he was the least of them. Against Amans and Legatus, who had faced a million foes both together and apart, this small human stood no chance. They were fortunate she was stupid enough to make a stand anyway. Humans were always so eager for death.

Legatus stepped forward. She would enjoy feeling something other than stalagmite break under her hands.

"Keep her alive," Amans instructed. "We still need that body. We'll find out how she beat Ultio and try again."

"You don't know?" Nora Jo lifted her hand. "My grandmother's ring. You didn't think she'd search for a way to stop you, after what you did last time? You never understood me, or her."

Ultio's spirit must still be locked inside her if she could access those memories. Perhaps that was what Legatus could become if she lost her own battle of wills—a pitiful store of empty memories inside a human vessel. She had never been attached to Ultio, but his wasn't an enviable fate.

Nora Jo suddenly spread her hands. A volley of rock erupted from the floor at their feet and sliced upward. Amans laughed and snapped his fingers. The rock turned to dust, falling harmlessly back to the ground.

Legatus didn't flinch. There was nothing this little witch could do to her. "This saves time," she commented. "We couldn't have planned it better ourselves."

As one, Legatus and Amans darted forward. There was a thrill in their easy silent communication. How long had it been since they fought together? All those years of complacency in Harlow's body hadn't slowed Amans.

The spirit of the soldier interrupted her path, but he was insubstantial as fog. Legatus slammed through him and pressed forward. The night was growing old. It was time to end this.

She rolled under another fiery blast and landed directly in front of Nora Jo. She slammed a fist into the girl's chest. If she wanted, she could punch through those thin bones to her heart, but they needed this body alive. Still, the blow would crack some ribs, and certainly incapacitate her. Legatus grinned in gleeful triumph.

Nora Jo flew backward, but righted in midair like a cat, landing on her feet.

There was too much power in her. There was only one explanation. Legatus stood, her fists clenched at her sides. "*Ultio?*"

"I gave you that body," Amans snarled, skidding to a halt beside Legatus.

"It wasn't yours to give," Nora Jo and Ultio answered.

There was a clattering across the shore. They turned as one. Eileen Mayer had slipped free of her leg ties and was stumbling away from them in the dark, sobbing weakly.

"Get her," Amans said.

Nora Jo lashed out, aiming another rock at Amans's head. He swore and summoned another burst of magic.

Legatus didn't hesitate. Harlow had brought Ultio and Nora Jo into this. He could handle his own problems. Legatus would tackle hers. These Mayer girls were untenable.

She sprinted across the shore. Her soles scraped and bled against the jagged edges of the decimated stalagmites, but mortal pain was nothing more than an irritation. It was the work of moments to catch up to the hobbling girl. She would be blind in the dark cave now that the lights from Amans and Nora Jo Barker's battle were behind them, and human limbs were weak. She screamed when Legatus grabbed her by the shoulder and jerked her around. Her wrists were still bound in front of her, leaving her defenseless. Her crying grew even louder and more grating.

"Shut up," Legatus snarled.

The soldier hovered beside them, watching the scene unfold with a devastated expression. He stretched out his hand toward Legatus's face, and she snapped her teeth at his fingers. Immediately, she knew she should not have acknowledged him. His glow brightened, and his expression hardened.

"Let me go. Kate, please," Eileen whimpered. Somehow, this fool thought her sister was still in control. "I don't understand."

"Shut *up.*"

Legatus wrapped her hands around the girl's throat and squeezed with inexorable pressure. She could have simply twisted her wrist, snapped her neck, but that was too simple. She wanted this to be *slow.*

There would be no more resistance.

56

Kate.

That was *Kate*.

And she needed him.

57

LEGATUS

Eileen Mayer writhed in her grip, bound hands thrashing against Legatus's stomach, clawing at her shirt in frantic desperation. Legatus leaned down to look into her eyes. "This is my body," she told the girl, tightening her hands. "There will be no more resistance. *Mine*."

The girl's face was growing dark, a vein in her temple pulsing against the skin. Human bodies. They were so fragile, for all the power they carried. They were better off in the hands of those who could appreciate them.

The ghost of the soldier reached between them, its hand passing through Legatus's body in an icy wave. It took effort for a spirit to manifest on the physical plane. Some, like Herman, had the knowledge to ease their way, but even then it was difficult. The soldier had been untrained. Only luck had rid him of Noct.

But in that moment, he pulled his essence forward into the tepid air of the cave. He was trying to manifest, trying to break through.

Legatus ignored him. He couldn't hurt her. She was too powerful. No freshly killed spirit could do anything to her. No one could.

There was a ripping sound as fabric tore.

Something clattered from Eileen's nightgown onto the ground below.

Keeping her hands tight on Eileen's throat, Legatus glanced down to see the final act of the boy's spirit.

A pale fang rested against the ground, barely visible in the darkness.

But everything I've done, it's been for this family. It's been for you.

58

KATE

Kate surged forward.

She had been smothered for an eternity, pressed into nothingness by the dark shadow covering her mind. It had been a nightmare, a slow death deep inside her own body. The flashes of reality she had glimpsed flayed her soul: her bloody hands rending stone apart, bright bursts of sourceless light, the wind on bare skin that was no longer hers. The terrified face of her sister.

The fire inside her lashed out at her reappearance, but she would not be cowed. She scrambled and shoved and clawed her way to control. There was a mad, desperate fight, a swirling battle like thrashing against the current of a river, but Kate broke through the surface.

Everything I've done, it's been for this family. It's been for you.

She was cold and sore, cuts across her skin standing out as bright as stars. Her body felt massive and unfamiliar around her.

There was fluttering warmth clasped between her hands.

Eileen had lost consciousness, slumping entirely into Kate's hold.

Frantic, she lowered Eileen to the floor, barely cushioning her head from the controlled fall. Without the demon aiding her muscles, she had no strength left.

"Eileen," she rasped. The journey of the air from her lungs to her mouth seemed insurmountable. How had she never noticed the vast expanse her brain had to control? There were so many muscles and tendons and organs all demanding her attention.

And there, still lurking in her mind like an eel in a drying pond, was the demon.

Kate ignored it, tracing shaking fingers against Eileen's arm in the dark until she could clasp her wrist. "Eileen, *please*." Did a heartbeat still flutter there, or was that only Kate's imagination? She held her breath, focusing with all her might.

There it was—the quiet pulse of life.

Kate gasped with relief.

Around her, the darkness was nearly impenetrable apart from the bursts of light coming from two fighting figures. Under the demon's control, Kate had only gotten brief flashes of what her body was doing. Something had also gone wrong with their attempt to control Nora Jo Barker—she was fighting Harlow with inhuman speed, conjuring vines and flames and clouds around her with flicks of her wrist. Gone was the hollow-eyed woman who told her Miss Ethel had passed; gone was the confused figure who had tried and failed to cut Kate free from her bindings. This Nora Jo was alight with power as she met Harlow head-on.

Kate had her own battle to win. She turned her gaze inward, a general surveying an enemy force.

The demon lashed out at her, attempting to subdue her again. It was stronger than she could have imagined, even in her worries after the reverend's death. This very creature had once been banished by her granddaddy, and here it was in Chatuga again. Perhaps there was no way to destroy it—only to stop its spread for one more moment.

Kate looked down at Eileen, then pressed back against the demon. This monster had nearly killed her sister. Kate had spent the past months dreading whatever horror could force her hands to attack her own blood. And it was a horror, but it wasn't born of Kate.

She fervently wished Reverend Castor was still alive. As much as she'd hated him, she knew now why he'd been killed. He was the only person in Chatuga with the knowledge to exorcise a demon. Kate had seen it herself firsthand, trembling in the church basement as he'd shouted at her.

Kate had heard the words often enough during that horrible week. She'd been sure she would never forget them, but they were like a song she had once known and forgotten. The patter still haunted her, but the flow of the words sat just beyond her reach. Surely there was *something* she could remember to give her the power to do the same.

I will kill you for this, whispered the voice in her head. *I will wipe the Mayers from this earth with your own hands before I turn them on this miserable body.*

Kate shuddered and looked away from Eileen, unwilling to let the demon use her eyes to mark her sister as prey.

A burst of light from the ongoing fight between Nora Jo and Harlow illuminated a pale form crumpled on the shore.

Oliver.

Grief washed over her in a black wave, and a sob burst unbidden from her mouth.

Her hands ached to rush over and hold him.

After everything that had happened between them, he had come to find her. He had taken two demons into his body to try to save her. He had died to help her, and she had nearly fallen to the demon's hold anyway. The thing inside her had killed Oliver and left him behind without another thought.

Kate's head twitched as Legatus tried to jerk her gaze away from the body.

Why was the demon afraid of her looking at Oliver?

He had managed to expel them earlier. Could Kate do the same, even without knowing the reverend's exorcism?

Pain lanced through her skull, sharp as lightning. She crumbled to the ground, clutching her head. She had never felt such agony. Poison pulsed through her mind, searing and unbearable. She squeezed her eyes closed and keened.

I'll destroy you, Legatus told her, cold and furious.

But Kate could destroy her too.

Squinting against the pain, agonized whimpers cluttering her throat, Kate scrambled on the uneven ground, the slick stone littered with chunks of broken stalagmites. The light from the fight behind her was erratic as lightning, disorienting her despite the demon's ease in darkness. Finally, though, another flash lit the ground. The fallen wolf fang was pale, illuminated like a star in the sky against the pale stone.

She lunged forward, wrapping her fingers around the bone, so familiar she could have traced its shape in her dreams.

Something warm and wet slid over her lips and clogged her mouth. She coughed in startled alarm before she realized her nose was bleeding. The taste of blood was thick on her tongue.

You are nothing compared to me. Nothing.

Kate was in an unfamiliar dress and barefoot, but the neckline was loose enough to pull aside from her chest. She lifted her hand to her heart, the same place she had seen Oliver do this. She winced against a fresh throb of pain, then dragged the fang down her skin.

Compared to the forest fire of agony burning in her mind, this gash was like the burn of a candle. Finally, there was a spot of light, of hope.

I have all the time in the world, the demon warned. I will make you suffer.

Was this not already suffering? The lancing pain, Eileen unconscious with bruises on her neck, Oliver dead and abandoned?

You don't know suffering.

Kate was suddenly buffeted with memories, a whirling infinity of chaos and pain. They drowned her, washing over her mind with their sheer immensity. Kate and her body were so small. In the face of this ancient force, Kate was nothing.

Nothing.

No. Not nothing. The demon couldn't erase her. She was here, and she would not be cowed.

Oliver had shown her the way. She wouldn't fail now.

She lifted a shaking hand and found the slice in her chest. Her muscles were weak and trembling, but she swallowed the blood in her mouth and slashed another line across the first.

The volume in her head increased. She was blind and deaf to the world around her, living in an endless moment of fury and agony.

Then, her vision was overtaken by bright red as Legatus poured out of her body.

Kate collapsed onto her hands and knees. The roaring in her head was gone, leaving only a dull ache.

The demon pulsed in front of her, still fighting toward her even as it flickered out. A stray flame licked across Kate's face, lancing her with a fresh burn, and then Legatus was gone.

Kate had seen enough memories in those last moments to know the demon hadn't been destroyed. Legatus would be returned to that endless hell she had shown Kate, and from there would fight with all her power to break free once more.

Let her. Kate would not lose her body again.

She climbed to her feet. She swayed, but found her footing. She wanted to rest, to curl up beside her sister until they both woke in a different world, but this wasn't over yet.

She turned to Nora Jo and Harlow. Kate's fight against Legatus had seemed to last its own eternity, but Nora Jo and Harlow were still locked together as though it had only been moments.

Kate limped forward, clutching the fang tightly in her palm.

The fight didn't seem to be going in Nora Jo's favor. "You're weak. Ultio is weak," Harlow said, easily dodging another magical burst from Nora Jo. "You were a fool to come back, Nora Jo."

Kate stumbled over the shore. They both turned to her. She nodded to Nora Jo. "It's me," she rasped.

Harlow shrieked, an inhuman noise that cracked through the air and raised hairs across Kate's body.

A roiling white cloud burst from him, pulsing with its own light. It roared out toward Nora Jo and Kate, sizzling and popping like it was scorching the air. It was a morning fog come to life, clawed together and poisoned to the core.

Nora Jo stepped forward and met it. The burst swirled around her like an aura, expanding wider and wider. Then, with a whoosh, it rushed into her skin. She glowed faintly with the magic, a beacon in the sudden darkness.

She fell to her knees, heaving for air. In the quiet cave, the noise felt too loud, and it had a desperate edge, growing more ragged as the seconds ticked by.

It reminded Kate of Oliver and his constant struggle to breathe. Oliver, who would never breathe again.

Nora Jo lifted a hand toward Harlow—then collapsed.

Harlow laughed, triumphant and cold. He strode toward his fallen opponent, hands alight with a pale flame. He would kill her, just as he'd killed Oliver, just as he'd tried to kill them all.

Gritting her teeth against the tapestry of pain across her body, Kate lunged toward Harlow.

59

NORA JO

G et up, *Nora Jo Barker.*

Nora Jo reached out and found Ultio's strength waiting for her. She had been vulnerable, but he hadn't used the opportunity to take over her body. He waited for her, patient, as she shuddered her way through the vicious curse Harlow had flung at her. She took the support he offered and climbed to her feet.

When she had arrived in the cave, she hadn't known what to expect. Certainly not for Kate to save herself. She had seen the red flame shoot like an arrow from the cross carved into Kate's chest, the demon propelled by the force of Kate's faith out of this plane entirely. It was a horrifying sight. Ultio's eyes allowed her to do more than see in the dark. She could see the surreal shape in the flames, the massive, immortal spirit of Legatus as it was thrust out.

With Ultio's eyes, she was also able to see the ghost in their midst. He hovered behind Kate, expression glazed with confusion but achingly sad.

Kate had thrown herself at Harlow. She was bloodied from the rest of the night, and there was a fresh, shining burn across her face. She wielded a small bone like a weapon, but he treated her like a pup nipping at his heels. As Nora Jo found her balance, Harlow swatted Kate aside. She went tumbling through the air, bouncing and skidding across the sharp stones of the shore. She landed in a heap near the water's edge.

She twitched, then twitched again.

Had Harlow broken her spine? Her movements were unusual, distressingly weak. Nora Jo watched in horror as the twitching became a full-body convulsion.

If she hadn't seen Legatus expelled, she would have thought the demon was still inside Kate, twisting her limbs like a doll. Harlow must have broken something inside the girl. Was there no end to the torment he would inflict tonight?

Nora Jo took a step toward her, but Harlow was suddenly in front of her. "You traitor," he snarled. Only Ultio's reflexes allowed her to dodge the black whip that appeared in his hand and lanced through the air toward her. Long white thorns slammed into the ground. "Why won't you just die, Ultio? I've given you everything."

Nora Jo let Ultio use her tongue. "Except the only thing I wanted." Nora Jo took control again. "You used me. This ends tonight." She cracked a long piece of rock from the ground and let it hover beside her. "I'm sending Amans back to hell."

"The soldier's little trick won't hurt us," Harlow said. With a snap of the whip, he sent the rock spiraling away out of their control. "That only worked because their bonds were unsteady. We have been bonded for years. I was a fur trader, an amateur witch, destined for an early grave in some frozen Canadian winter.

Instead, I found fire. We made a pact and haven't been parted since. And we won't be ever again."

He lashed out with the thorned whip. Nora Jo was too weak to get out of the way. It wrapped around her ankle, stabbing deep. She screamed, and Ultio screamed with her. He had the benefits—and limitations—of a mortal body now, and the pain threatened to overwhelm them both.

Blindly, she lashed down at the whip with a flame. It broke the line between her and Harlow. She sliced her palm on a thorn as she tugged it free from her leg.

"I taught you—both of you—everything you know. You owe me," Harlow said.

Across the cave, there was a rustle as Kate climbed to her feet. As though no time had elapsed at all, as though she hadn't just been twisting out of her skin, she walked toward them.

60

KATE

Kate stumbled over the dark cave floor, but didn't hesitate. Her back ached with new cuts, souvenirs of her latest vision, but they were a small price for what she now had.

She had learned the fiddle from her daddy, who had learned it from his daddy. She had never known him, the reverend who had once exiled Legatus and her allies, but she had his blood in her veins and his legacy in her mind.

She had been the victim of the next reverend, a child overwhelmed by her own power and by the hatred of men.

She knew the words. She had already heard herself say them.

61

NORA JO

Nora Jo staggered to put herself between Kate and Harlow, limping and panting. "Are you all right?" she asked Kate, keeping her eyes on Harlow.

"I know what we have to do. I saw what comes next," Kate said, voice calm. "Trust me."

What was it Harlow had said about choosing Kate? A *stillborn girl brought back to life. The future and past are both clear to her.*

"What do you need?" Nora Jo asked.

"Hold him down for me," Kate instructed.

Nora Jo let Ultio take full control of their body. Without her hesitations, he was able to move unimpeded.

Harlow spun to meet them—but jerked to a halt as the ghost of Oliver Chadwick Jr. grabbed his neck with spectral fingers.

Oliver had eyes only for Kate.

Taking advantage of the help, Ultio grabbed Harlow around the waist, pinning his hands to his sides with one arm. With a quick motion, he tore the ring from Nora Jo's finger, and slammed it against Harlow's chest.

Nora Jo felt a pulse as its magic left her and she lost her grandmother's protection against Ultio. When she'd fought against his hold before, the ring had burned her flesh and seared his spirit. Now, with her trust, he could take it without harm.

The ring in their hand pulsed with bright heat, protecting Nora Jo not from the demon inside her, but from the one who had tried to steal her life.

Harlow screamed and twisted in their hold. Oliver and Ultio held tight.

"Do it," Nora Jo instructed Kate. "I don't know how long this will last."

Kate nodded and began speaking. "O Lord in Heaven, I pray to thee to rid us of this servant of the serpent of old. I ask that you sever each and every connection between the cursed demon and its host. Let the demon perish before the presence of those who sign themselves with the cross. You who defied death gave us your venerable cross for driving away all enemies…" She spoke the prayer with the confidence of an established preacher on his pulpit, or a musician on a stage, the formal language of the church easy on her tongue.

"Stop. Just kill me," Harlow rasped, thrashing against Nora Jo's hold. "Stop being so weak. *Kill me*, you cowards." His voice broke. "I can't go back to being alone."

"It hurts when someone else has control over your life, doesn't it?" Nora Jo snarled in his ear.

Kate stepped closer, still chanting her prayer. Harlow had once told her that faith powered magic. What belief could be more powerful than a future you had already lived?

Kate put a hand on the center of Harlow's chest and shouted the final words. "To the Son and to the eternal Father and to the life-giving Spirit, we send up glory and honor, now and always and forever and ever. Amen."

Harlow writhed in Nora Jo's grip, pulled to and fro by an unseen force. If she'd thought Kate's fit was bad, it was nothing compared to this. It seemed the exorcism might tear Harlow to pieces, like a tree splintering in a storm.

Blinding white flames burst from his skin and scattered into the night. The light left a stain on the darkness, gone as quickly as it had come. Even with Ultio's power to aid her eyes, Nora Jo had to blink.

Kate pulled her hand back, head bowed. "It's done."

As if Kate's will had been his only tether, Oliver's hands fell through Harlow's neck insubstantially. His expression faded like mist, replaced by a confused mournfulness.

Nora Jo panted, still holding Harlow tight, but in her mind, Ultio pulled back. *She's right. Amans is gone. There is only Harlow now.*

"What *was* that?" Nora Jo asked. "It didn't look like that for Kate."

Legatus did not have complete control of the body. She was expelled, pushed on to the other place, the one you call hell. Amans had lived within Harlow for more than a century. After so long, he was water spilled from a vase. Without the form to hold him together, he fell to pieces.

"He's gone? For good?"

Yes.

Harlow sagged in their arms. They let him drop, and he curled like a pillbug on the jagged shore, weeping.

Slowly, the black hair turned white, spreading like snow from his temples to overtake the rest of his scalp. A beard sprawled over his face, first scraggly, then tumbling to the ground. His skin withered and shrunk, pulling tight against his bones.

Kate squinted down, keeping her distance. "What's happening to him?"

Nora Jo knew the answer. Had she deduced it from Harlow's story, or was she pulling the knowledge from Ultio? Their minds were becoming too intertwined to tell the difference. "Amans was the only thing keeping him alive. He's stayed young and whole with magic. His body can't stay in stasis without the demon."

"Good," Kate snarled. She turned without waiting for the inevitable end, stumbling across the dark shore toward her sister, who had woken and was weeping quietly by the water. On the shore, Oliver Chadwick Jr.'s ghost had reappeared back where he had died, staring at the spot where Kate had been bound.

Nora Jo sent a flame to accompany Kate through the dark, but stayed where she was.

Nora Jo and Ultio stood still—an execution and a vigil—to watch as Harlow drew his last breath and crumpled into the dirt.

62

KATE

The true heat of a Tennessee summer always arrived after the solstice.

The week after the longest day was sweltering, made worse by the sticky salves Mama smeared over all Kate's cuts and bruises. The burn on her cheek was carefully bandaged, but old Miss Devon from next door said she was sure it would scar. She shook her head, apologizing while delivering the news, but it felt fitting to Kate. That night had left many scars, after all.

Kate and Eileen told their parents what had happened. Daddy trembled to hear of the return of his daddy's worst fear, and held them close. In the morning light, the story already seemed impossible. If not for the injuries the girls had brought home, it could have been a shared nightmare.

They all swore never to tell the story again, to keep it in that room. There was too much danger in telling anyone else what they'd seen.

The only part Kate left out was how she had known Oliver. To her parents, the gathering of Oliver, Kate, and Nora Jo had been random. How could she explain all Oliver had been to her, and would now never be? Kate thought Eileen knew more than she let on, but she said nothing.

The next morning, Kate woke to Eileen sitting beside her bed. She had a book open on her lap. From the light, it was late—their other sisters must have been long awake.

"Eileen," Kate said, relieved.

When Eileen tilted her head, the dark bruising on her throat was clear as a flag. "Still you in there?" Her voice was cool. She propped the book up on her knee, grip firm. It had a worn cover and creased pages from its years on their granddaddy's pulpit. The Bible.

"Yeah, it's me," Kate said, surprised and uneasy. "Just me. They're gone. They're not coming back."

"They have before." Eileen rapped the Bible against her knee and then stood up. "Next time, we'll know."

As Eileen left the room, Kate scrunched her eyes closed and buried her hands under her pillow.

It took a week for Kate's parents to let her out of their sight again. Finally, she got dressed and walked out the front door, promising them she would be back soon. Daddy offered to come with her, but she told him there was something she needed to do alone. Their eyes lingered on the bandage on her face, but they let her go.

Kate picked her way through the forest, limping slightly, then stood at the entrance to the caves. The forest smelled flush and alive around her. It could have been any other summer day.

The world moved on without a care for the past.

She had planned to slip through the opening to sit in the small room where she'd gotten to know Oliver Chadwick Jr., but the sight of the cold stone made her shiver. She wasn't sure she would ever be able to go underground again without vomiting. Instead, she leaned against the rock face and stared up at the clouds.

"I'm going to Nashville," she said. "I don't want to stay in Chatuga anymore. I'm going to try fiddling there. It's a musical city, you know, and I'm sure I could find a good teacher. My granddaddy would have liked that. Following in his footsteps again. He always wanted to play for money, but preaching drew him in.

"Besides, I'm not ready to say goodbye to my family. Eileen and I… I don't know if she's mad at me, scared, or what. Hell, it's not like I can blame her. I almost killed her, Oliver, even if I wasn't in control of my hands."

She closed her eyes, imagining a dark room, a flickering lantern, and a smiling boy. He had always listened to her so intently. He had cared what she thought.

"I guess it's a good thing we never did figure out how to get rid of our sight. It saved me, in the end. The visions have started back again like before. Maybe that night was still unsettled until it happened. Maybe those monsters fogged the future too much. I don't know. It's still not easy, but I've got the past and the future to guide me. That's something, isn't it?

"It's a miracle no one saw me, Eileen, and Nora Jo hobbling home that night. If Nora Jo hadn't been there, we might not have made it back. She came by the house earlier this week to check in on me. I didn't think I'd see her again, but she said she wanted to make sure we were both okay. Miss Ethel told me she was acting strange, but none of us could have guessed what she was doing.

"She told me that her own monster left the morning after the solstice. It got its revenge and didn't need this world anymore." Kate reached up to absently pat the bandage sitting over her heart, where she had carved a cross into her skin. "I worry it was a mistake to just let it go. Nora Jo's monster and mine could come back some day. Yours too. Mine said she would, and I don't doubt she can hold a grudge. The things I saw in her mind… I used to think I was angry, but there was rage in her like I've never imagined. Eileen's scared of it too. But we've got each other, even if she doesn't believe it right now."

A breeze rustled through the forest. Kate turned her face into it. Maybe there would be a storm tonight to break the building heat, if only for a day.

"Lord, I miss you, Oliver," she said, closing her eyes. "I had to leave a note with the sheriff tipping them off where to find you." Her voice broke, and tears burned in her eyes. "They would never have believed me. Your funeral was in the white church. I didn't go. I'm sorry. I'm so sorry. I couldn't think how to." She let her head fall back against the rock. "No one knows about us. But I know it was real."

She swallowed with difficulty and blinked up at the clouds. "The things I saw in the demon's mind… Are you still here in this world? Or are you in that other place? Are there other endings? I was never jealous of your sight before, but if I could just see you again…"

The leaves rustled again. The world was still moving around her. Time was still rolling on. She put a hand to her forehead, trying to rub away the tide of emotion. "No," she decided. "That's not what I want. I don't want you to be one of the haints you told me about, stuck on the same paths for eternity. After everything you went through, you deserve to move on. You deserve peace, Oliver."

She straightened up. She couldn't look back at the hole in the ground. Instead, she kept her eyes on the sky. "I hope you find it. I love you."

She felt there should be more to say. There was still so much more inside her, a riot of anger and despair and devotion. But no more words came to her. Oliver had seen her, truly seen her. They had fought, but he found her, and saved her. He was gone. It was over.

And she would keep on living.

She had a future because of him. She wouldn't squander it.

"Goodbye, Oliver," she said, and began the hike back home.

63

The river continued to flow.

It would never end.

It was possible to spend an eternity on the shore. To pace its edges and pretend there was a way to step back in. To haunt the places and people within.

He could see others like him. The ones still unable to let go of the ebb and flow of life. They swirled around him, their eyes unmoving from the river.

But there was an infinity waiting beyond the shore, in the new, uncharted lands that stretched unseen in the mist. The river held the allure of the known. Beyond was the unknown, and it was beginning to call to him.

Kate Mayer was walking away, blinding with life. She didn't need him anymore. The river would continue to flow with her, and she would thrive in its currents. He didn't have her gift for seeing its oncoming twists and bends, but he knew her. There was nothing she couldn't do.

He hadn't been brave for a long time. He had seen the price of bravery, paid by the one who died, carried by the one who lived. It hadn't seemed worth it when the life that had been saved was his own. But with Kate... He finally understood. Bravery was the only choice.

It was bravery again to turn his back on the river and step from the shore into the shrouded lands.

He didn't look back, but he knew the river would be gone if he turned. The decision had been made.

Quiet.

Light.

A boy stood before him. He had never smiled like this in life, had never been so completely unguarded. He was as fresh-faced as they had been before the war, young and bright. Beyond the riverbank, the stains of death had vanished from his skin.

Tucker Lee Selecky nodded to Oliver.

Gone were the months in the blood and the mud. Gone were the freezing nights and damp wool. Gone were the creased letters from home shared like cigarettes between lonely hands and mouths.

Oliver had practiced his apology a hundred ways, but there were no words here.

Tucker Lee held out his hand, and Oliver took it.

64

NORA JO

"How is the packing going?" Beau asked.

Nora Jo had finally accepted her brother's invitation to supper. Ruth cooked skillfully, laying out a spread of catfish, green beans, mashed potatoes, fried okra, and cornbread. Nora Jo ate so much that her dress felt uncomfortable around her stomach, and still found room for the peach cobbler that came after the meal.

For the first weeks after Miss Ethel's death, neighbors had brought dishes of food to her house. Nora Jo wasn't Miss Ethel's kin, but people in Chatuga were unable to cope with a death without turning to their stoves. Since then, though, her diet had become lean. She'd sold Miss Ethel's house and belongings, but she had plans for that money.

She had also found a bag of money in the Lyes' guest room, which they were happy for her to take along with the rest of Harlow's possessions when Nora Jo told them their tormentor would not be returning. Since his arrival, the Lyes—spelled into silence—had provided blood for Harlow's spells and an outlet for his temper.

"I'm all done," Nora Jo said. "I don't own much, other than my books. They take up more crates than the rest combined."

"You're taking all of them with you? Haven't you already read them all?"

"Yes, Beau," Nora Jo said patiently. "They're too expensive to scrap. Besides, I like to reread them."

He nodded, though he clearly didn't understand.

She'd once thought that Beau had the life she wanted. A job, a wife, a house. And those were all things Nora Jo craved, but she wanted her *own* version. She couldn't be slotted into his place. She couldn't put on a pair of trousers, slide her arm around Ruth's waist, and take his life. Her future would look different from his present, and she no longer resented him for that.

When the meal was over, Ruth said goodbye and stayed to clean the kitchen while Beau walked Nora Jo to the door. Ruth still didn't like Nora Jo, but it wasn't worth pointing out to Beau. After everything, she could withstand some dislike.

"Will you ever come back to Chatuga?" Beau asked, staring out over his small plot of land. There was a furrow between his brows as he avoided her gaze.

"I will," she said. "I want to see how my students grow, even if they're not mine anymore. And I want to meet my new niece or nephew."

Beau turned to her. "How did you know? She's barely showing."

"I have my ways." Nora Jo smiled. She pulled on her hat, tying the ribbons under her chin. "It will take me some time to settle into my new home. I'm going to find out what happens to a woman alone in the world. But I'll be back."

"Tell me if you ever need help up there."

"Honestly, I don't expect I will."

"Need help, or tell me?" He shook his head. "The invitation is open either way. But... I have faith in you. You've done a lot, Nora Jo. You should be proud of yourself."

After submitting to a brusque hug, Nora Jo left the porch and walked toward the road. August was coming fast, and with it the dog days of summer. The sun was red and low on the horizon, the air still thick with heat and humidity. The road seemed quiet and lonely after the warmth of Beau's house.

You aren't alone. Not with me here.

"I know that," she said, taking the turn back toward Miss Ethel's house. "But it's safer if no one else does."

The adjustment to the second spirit in her body had been easier than Nora Jo could have anticipated. Ultio breathed with her, ate with her, woke with her, slept with her. Nora Jo, who had always valued her independence above all else, found a quiet comfort in Ultio's contentment with their life. The smallest normalcies were magical through his eyes—the rolling shadows of thunderclouds, the thrumming buzz of cicadas, the sweet taste of honeysuckle, the warm splash of summer rain. She understood, in a way, Harlow's bond with Amans, despite their differences. Amans and Harlow were ambitious. Amans didn't want to find a place to call home in this world, but to dominate it.

Ultio, like Nora Jo, was searching for peace.

Together, maybe they could find it.

"There," Gloria said, arranging the violets in a vase. "That's the welcoming final touch."

They had finally finished unpacking their belongings and decorating. In a luxury not often found in log cabins, there were individual rooms sectioned off by walls, which would help them keep warm during the winter.

Nora Jo had found Harlow's cabin sitting abandoned on the side of Old Blue, the only residence on the mountain. From what Ultio had sensed in the woods, there was no inherent evil that kept other people away—it was Harlow who had run off anyone who dared set a foot on the path.

Ultio and Nora Jo had searched the cabin thoroughly, using Ultio's senses to look for any nasty surprises he'd left behind. They found a bottle under one of the unpainted pine floorboards near the back entrance. Inside were strands of hair and rusted nails in a mysterious dark liquid. It was grotesque in an indescribable way. Drawing near it felt like being flayed alive. Ultio had carefully walked Nora Jo through its safe disposal.

The cabin had been cluttered with furniture and decorations, abandoned when Harlow trekked down to find his prey in Chatuga. She burned his stranger curios, but kept some that spoke to her. She found an ornate woven basket, sturdy and intricate. She left it in the kitchen alongside Miss Ethel's favorite pitcher. On the windowsill was a line of colorful broken bottles; at the right time of the afternoon, the light stained the floor blue and purple and red.

By the time the cabin was fully cleansed, Nora Jo's shoulders and hands ached, but the small space felt larger. The grunge of Harlow's misdeeds wasn't a permanent stain. This place could move on from him—and so could Nora Jo.

Gloria came up with a mule and cart a month after Nora Jo settled in. After Oliver Chadwick Jr.'s tragic death, Gloria's father agreed to Nora Jo's offer to hire Gloria for her new venture in the mountains. Everyone knew Nora Jo had inherited Miss Ethel's money, and that stability seemed enough to assuage his concerns. Gloria would have to take the mule back down at least once a month for Sunday dinner to assure them she was okay, but at least there had been no mention of another betrothal.

"Are we plumb crazy for doing this?" Gloria asked, stroking one of the violets' petals. The splash of purple and green brought a new life to the cabin, though it couldn't compare to Gloria's smile.

Nora Jo wrapped her hands about her waist and set her chin on Gloria's shoulder. "Could be. But we won't know unless we try." She swallowed, grateful Gloria couldn't see her. "If you change your mind, Chatuga is only an hour away."

"Don't write me an escape so quickly," Gloria said. She twisted to return Nora Jo's embrace. "I chose this. Everyone else wanted another life for me, but this is the one I picked. We'll visit Chatuga. But this is a space for us."

Nora Jo flicked her hand. An apple lifted from a bowl on the table and drifted to her.

Nora Jo had shown Gloria her magic before inviting her to the cabin. She didn't want to start a life under false pretenses. Gloria accepted the witchery easily—Nora Jo hadn't been as subtle as she'd thought—but had taken more time to understand Ultio. In the end, Nora Jo let Ultio take her tongue to explain. It was strange to have a conversation with three people between two bodies, but Gloria still agreed to come with her.

"Summer'll end," Nora Jo said, handing the apple to Gloria. "We won't always have fresh fruit and the thrill of a new start. There will be hard times."

Gloria ran a thumb over the apple's green skin. "There are always hard times. I'd rather have them with you than without you."

"Me too," Nora Jo confessed, pressing her nose to Gloria's hair.

With the money left behind by Miss Ethel and Harlow, they had enough to survive until next spring when they could begin sustaining themselves in the garden. Until then, Nora Jo had a project to start.

Soon, Nora Jo would introduce herself in the small towns that dotted the mountains and valleys around Old Blue's ominous peak. She was ready to learn to craft spells for health and luck, the way Granny Rhodes once had. She could take care of the people who were isolated here in the mountains. Women like her mother, suffering alone through recurring illness, needed her help. Ultio would help navigate the thorny misinformation Harlow had taught her, pulling the truth out from the lies. And once she learned enough, she would find her own apprentices to teach.

With her granny's agate ring to inspire and guide her, she would also craft her own charms to protect people from Legatus and Noct, if either managed to crawl their way out of hell and back to Chatuga.

They will, Ultio warned. *They have an eternity to plot their revenge. Sooner or later, it will come.* His voice was wistful. *I will mourn you, when I lose you.*

"I don't plan on being lost," Nora Jo said briskly. "We stopped them before. We can do it again. We have the advantage. They don't have hosts. You have me."

I do, Ultio agreed.

"I'm making my home here. I won't let go of that so easily."

Harlow, despite his dark motivations, had helped Nora Jo uncover the magic in her bones. She would carry on without him, and reclaim her legacy.

There was a new witch in the mountains.

ACKNOWLEDGEMENTS

From my earliest years, I learned the story of my ancestors from *Dorie: Woman of the Mountains* by Florence C. Bush—a moving biography of my great-grandmother and her life in early twentieth-century rural Tennessee. As I grew older, I started to wonder what stories I didn't have on my shelf—the stories left unwritten, or kept secret from even friends and family. And so this story was born.

Thank you to the team who helped get this book into the world. My agent Michael Carr. My insightful and brilliant editor Katie Dent. My ever-impressive cover designer Julia Lloyd. My dedicated copyeditor Louise Pearce. My talented marketing and publicity team: Katharine Carroll, Isabelle Sinnott, Charlotte Kelly, and Kate Greally. From the teams at Titan and Penguin Random House to every librarian and bookseller, it takes a village to bring a book to readers.

I want to thank my family—Mom, Dad, Clint, Jenna, Paul, and Emily—for your unwavering support of my happiness and creativity. I'm grateful every day to have you in my life.

To my steadfast friends: from online fandom buddies to my beloved FYA ladies, your enthusiasm for my life, writing, and character headcanons brings me endless joy. In the droughts during the slow process of traditional publishing, your support keeps me flourishing. Special thanks to Anna and Shae for being with me every step of the way.

I owe a special acknowledgement to my dear partner, Katherine. Thank you for always believing in me and encouraging me to be my truest self. You've shown me a love I could never have imagined. I treasure every day we have together.

And lastly, thank you to my readers. This book would not be here if not for you.

ABOUT THE AUTHOR

Nicole Jarvis writes speculative history novels. A graduate of Emory University with degrees in English and Italian, she lives in Georgia with her partner and their many cats and dogs. She is the author of *The Lights of Prague*, *A Portrait in Shadow*, and *A Spell for Change*. Nicole loves musicals, pottery, and learning about strange histories. Instagram/X/Bluesky: @nicolejarvis.

For more fantastic fiction, author events,
exclusive excerpts, competitions, limited editions and more

VISIT OUR WEBSITE
titanbooks.com

LIKE US ON FACEBOOK
facebook.com/titanbooks

FOLLOW US ON TWITTER AND INSTAGRAM
@TitanBooks

EMAIL US
readerfeedback@titanemail.com